BLUE EYED DEVIL

PARANORMAL POLITICAL THRILLER

MJ McDUFFIE

BLUE EYED DEVIL
Copyright © 2013, 2023 MJ McDuffie

Design & Formatting by Palmetto Publishing
Editing by Michelle Krueger

www.mjmcduffie.com

Magic Moonlight & Madness LLC

Hardcover ISBN: 979-8-8229-1758-3
Paperback ISBN: 979-8-8229-1759-0
eBook ISBN: 979-8-8229-1760-6

Charleston, SC
www.PalmettoPublishing.com

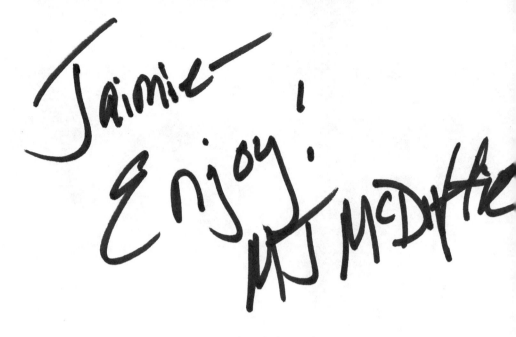

This novel is dedicated to

Dale Robert McMannis

Cursed with cancer far too young in life.
A misfortune many are tormented with every day.
This book is my promise of remembrance.

www.livestrong.org

Table of Contents

Prologue

May 1944

As each spray of the sea washed over the crew, a twenty-two-year-old Reid MacAlister stood looking wistfully at the coastline, impatient to step foot upon the mother country once more. It had been a long while since the weary Scot had walked the High and Lowlands of his home. Now that it was within sight, his heart swelled with something close to pride. The splendor before him seemed to help quell his anger, which had been raging for many years. He had barely become a man when this damn war had sent him to the far corners of the Earth, forcing him to watch too many good men die. This horrendous experience would alter Reid forever.

The rain from the darkened sky had plastered his No. 5 dress uniform to his skin. Although drenched, he was unconcerned with the discomfort and continued to stare out over the open water. Reid found himself enthralled by the magical spell of his homeland but was weary down to his core. Unfortunately, the captivating view could not hold him long as the exhaustion had turned his thoughts to the real storm approaching.

The allies were betting the outcome of the entire war on a last stand invasion, planned along a strategic stretch of French sand. To stop the Nazis, the United States and Europe were gambling everything on the upcoming campaign. This would be their final chance of stopping the evil that had swept the globe because the good guys were losing. As the training grounds for Operation Neptune, the Orkney Islands of Scotland were hosting thousands of men from both continents for this final coordinated attack. The landing at Normandy Beach was just four weeks away but Reid understood D-Day would be here before he knew it.

He became lost in his thoughts and when again noticed his surroundings; the Northern Isles were roaring their ire. The crossing had been difficult, and the sea had constantly warned the crew to show respect. Its power had forced most on board to stand topside, holding on for dear life while praising the Lord at the sight of land. "Skipper, we be ashore here, right soon." Shouted one man on the front line. "Expectin' we'll be liftin' a real pint before a few hours are up." The slight quiver of the sailor's voice revealed his underlying fear of the upcoming event. "Aye?"

Drawn in by the picturesque countryside, the second in command had to drag his mind away, acknowledging the midshipman with a sharp nod. "Right you are, old chap." After a slap on the sailor's back, Reid walked the rest of the inspection line admiring his troops while dodging the wind and increasing waves. Although the jokester's statement might be a strange one for most officers, it was not for him. Unlike others who held a rank, Reid drank with his men regularly to garner their loyalty. A trick he had learned from his father, the duke, and employed all during his stretch in the Royal Navy. This unique trait had served him well.

After hours of much activity to secure the boat, the newly promoted commander and his motley crew headed off to find a tavern for some much-needed libation. The boys promptly chose the Blackthorn Inn and disappeared inside to begin their short-term leave. Instead of joining his men, he decided to walk the cobblestone streets relishing the familiar sights and sounds of home. Despite the overcast weather, Reid strolled through the lively town of Kirkwall, delighted to be back on his native soil. Even caught himself smiling at the town's infectious atmosphere and was pleased to find his own mood improving.

Reid had not felt this good in months and decided on a whim to head up a small side street to see where it might lead. For years, he had dreamed about this day which had helped during the many battles the tormented sailor had fought. Doubt was always lurking in the dark corners of his mind. *Would I live long enough to see home again?* After the things he had witnessed these last three years, even his doubts had experienced doubts.

Still, he was ecstatic to be home in his beloved Scotland but this walk reminded him of everything he had left behind. The thoughts turned Reid sentimental, but he quickly shook off the oncoming melancholy. These reflections made him realize the war had not diminished his animosity and the anxiety crept in again when contemplating seeing his family this weekend. They were due to visit on Saturday because even the powerful MacAlister clan had to wait on gas rations. In a note from his mother, learned his father would also be in attendance. For several blocks, the duke's second son deliberated this unexpected and shocking development. After much internal debate, concluded the old goat most likely was doing so to brag about his brother's war triumphs and find fault with his own.

Now was not the time, so he shook off the gathering dark thoughts. For midweek, the quaint town bustled with activity and the large crowds of people surprised him, considering the persistent threat of rain. It helped to be among Scots and with each step, his disposition improved. Then, as soon as Reid rounded a corner, he stopped dead in his tracks because could not believe his eyes. A glimpse of heaven itself shined over by a vegetable stall. To draw a breath seemed out of the question because beauty radiated before Reid, the likes of which he had never seen.

Mounds of honey colored hair flowed past shoulders that accented a flawless profile. Reid watched while her perfect silhouette examined an herb. *A face touched by angels.* Spellbound, stood as she scrutinized a piece of spice, yet took no notice of him. The enchanting lass appeared to be unaccompanied but found himself unable to move because of the magnificence before him.

At last, snapped out of the trance and took a moment to gather his composure. Then made his way over to the little pretty. The fifty steps seemed to take forever but when arriving by her side, he discovered she barely came up to his shoulder. "Good afternoon." Addressing the top of her tiny head while silently admiring that luxurious mane.

For the first time since joining the navy, he found himself nervous and it took form in a cracked voice. "I'm Lieutenant Commander Reid MacAlister of His Majesty's Royal Navy, assigned to the HMS Nottingham." To appear more like himself and gather some nerve, the young man cleared his throat. "May I inquire as to your name?" Closer to the girl, surprised to discover she appeared even prettier than he first thought. *What a wee little thing.* She reminded him of a tiny fairy and could be no more than sixteen, therefore, he needed to proceed with caution. Yet, possessed everything Reid had ever dreamed of in a woman. Beauty, innocence, even a little mysterious, and the dumbfounded officer found her dazzling.

Ashamed by his growing desire but still enchanted, the newly promoted lieutenant turned his most charming smile towards the vision. It would be impossible for him to return to war without attaining more information about this fascinating girl.

The pretty lass, stared through long eyelashes, at the fine-looking officer but immediately stepped back to a respectable distance. Reluctant to give someone one more reason to report his outrageous behavior to her father, although, a shy smile formed on her face at someone else making him mad. What astonished her the most was the audacity of the handsome sailor. *The nerve of him.* The rake had just come up and spoke, without obtaining permission from her parents. His boldness frightened Morna but it excited her more.

Sheltered for most of her life, the rare young woman was unfamiliar with what to say or even how to act around a man. This wicked behavior would cause problems, but she could not help herself. The sailor was very dashing and was desperate for him to go on speaking. Yet, could not escape the strict rules dictated by her father and it showed on her face. Eventually, she remembered his stern warnings. "Good sir, me father has not given permission to be speakin' to me." But not before sneaking one last peek at the handsome officer, then, quickly, casting violet eyes to the ground. "Therefore, it would be improper to do so.

Especially here on this public avenue for all of town to see." *And me father to hear about before me even gets home.*

"Forgive my bad manners, miss, I've long been at sea and have forgotten my place." Found himself shocked by her statement and quickly regained his composure. The high-born lord then delivered his best nobility bow. "If you please, I would be happy to discuss permission with your parents." Turned his head back and forth, searching the busy thoroughfare. "Perhaps you'd be so kind to point them out." The war had jaded Reid but found himself at a loss in this situation. With each minute spent in her company, his yearnings grew but the experience was unnerving.

Surprised by the antiquated statement, Reid was shocked society still observed such ancient rituals. Lord MacAlister was quite familiar with how to play the social game having walked its passages his entire life. Even after all this time, his tutor's nasal toned voice echoed through his head. After snapping out of his unpleasant childhood memories, he turned his attention back to the lovely girl and leaned down to hear her better.

"Me parents are not currently in town, sir. They be at me family's estate in Sinclair." A giggle burst from a ruby red mouth that quietly apologized. "Please forgive, normally me don't be speakin' with complete strangers." Slightly turning, while pointing behind her. "Me be here with Wilson to purchase some supplies but we be heading home soon."

The tiny pixie seemed to have magic swirling around her, as she twirled back and forth. Caramel colored hair sparkled like yellow diamonds in the sunlight, which picked that moment to shine through the clouds. Enchanted by the vision, Reid did not see the large man come around the far stall and spot his proximity to the young lass. Stunned because he mistakenly had assumed it was impossible for anyone so large to move so fast.

Within moments, the giant swooped in, grabbed the girl, and placed her up on a nearby wagon. Before Reid knew what happened, the silent mountain took off, whisking her away. Fraught with panic, his feet moved without his consent because he could not let this woman go without finding out more. Convinced he would die in the upcoming battle if unable to at least gain her name. As the cart pulled away, shouted up to her and appeared like the biggest fool but he did not care. "Please tell me who you are." All the while running alongside the moving cart. "Where might I find your family's estate? In order to pay a visit to your father and gain permission to call upon you."

The infatuated girl grabbed his outstretched hand, smiling brightly. "Me name is Morna, Morna Bruce, kind sir. Me lives in Sinclair about three miles west, right outside of town. It's where ye' may be callin' on me father, he's the Earl of Sinclair."

As her palm slipped away, the young sailor stood mesmerized staring after his dream. Thrilled with his good fortune because not only had Reid found the perfect woman but his father just might approve, if she really was an earl's daughter.

For the longest time, he stood rooted to the spot and watched until the wagon disappeared, carrying away his future. Being the second in line to a title was a difficult life and the ambitious young man had spent countless hours fantasizing about forging his own path. Reid dreamed of doing so in America, away from his controlling family, but that was most likely nothing more than a fleeting fantasy. It would be almost impossible to achieve, thanks to Randall's continued reckless antics in this bloody war. Although, the resourceful sailor was determined to do so, on his own terms. His brother and father be damned. Those dreams might be possible, with this incredible creature by his side.

After a few inquiries in town, the young officer found Sinclair Castle and then secured an appointment with the earl. Groomed his entire life to meet people such as Rutherford Bruce, Reid found himself astonished by his sweaty, shaking hands, when entering the estate's large library. After the customary exchange of pleasantries and hours spent reviewing his clan's history, her father finally granted permission for a lord of Lothian Castle to court Lady Morna Bruce, the Earl of Sinclair's beloved which was the English translation of her Celtic name.

On cloud nine and walking into the crisp spring night the elated young man stopped to catch his breath and wondered about the Spear's reaction to the young girl. To his astonishment, Reid promised the earl he would always treasure his future bride. In part because It had silently spoken of the incredible opportunities that awaited him, as soon as he acquired her. A bright future had been an impossibility that morning and those unexpected but amazing visions had blinded him to the Spear's sudden influence.

Those were the happiest four weeks of Lord MacAlister's life.

CHAPTER 1

Seeing Colors

March 2012

hile descending in the elevator, Remy glared at his reflection and cursed his bad luck. *First, last night the plane was three hours late.* Balled his fists at his sides in frustration. *Second, no wake-up call this morning.* Naturally, it caused him to oversleep. The mirror threw his unhappy likeness back at him, along with the deepening lines the rotten hand life had dealt him. *Sweet Jesus, I really am cursed.*

The lighted numbers above had almost reached the lobby when he looked down and shook his head in self-disgust. Even two years later, it seemed he could not forget the lovely Mrs. Randall. *This was definitely not going to be a good day.*

As the doors opened, he exhaled slowly and stepped off the elevator. Silently blessing the coffee gods, as he spotted a small shop at the exit, relieved he would soon be enjoying his morning fix. Remy waited his turn to order but he noticed something seemed off about the bright-eyed girl working inside the kiosk.

Eventually, he stumbled to the counter and requested his standard order. "I'll have a Grande with double cream and two sugars, please." *Huh, that's odd. Coffee chick should be a bright turquoise because the little thing is certainly a bundle of energy.* Instead, bombarding Remy was the tiny woman's churning gray tone, which probably meant she was just experiencing boyfriend problems.

He stood there staring after the little sprite while pretending to ignore the loud, angry colors swirling around her. *When would his stupid self ever learn?* Every time he acted as if they did not exist, the auras only became brighter until blinding him into paying attention. While she poured his only real addiction, Remy flashed his customary Prince Charming smile. "Are you okay?"

She responded with a smile that was as fake, as his was charming. "Of course. Why do you ask?"

As she placed his drink on the glass countertop, the glaring colors reminded him that help would be possible if he would only make the time. After her painful response, he shined his wicked smile while mustering up some charisma. "Because I'm trained to notice these things." Teasing her with another of his talents. Remy had used his smooth seductive voice, to put her at ease. Although he did not show his badge, the gesture was unnecessary because another of his unique gifts was the ability to make people instantly comfortable with him. In his line of work, it was a handy skill but as a loner, rarely shared his talents with others.

Bone tired, he leaned over and grabbed her clenched fist. "He's not worth the effort." Gave the cutie a wink, then headed to the exit with his cup of joe. As Remy savored that first sip, he looked back one final time, taking notice of her smiling face before walking out the hotel door. *At least something has gone right on this trip.* Happy to see the girl's aura was returning to its natural turquoise color.

Once outside, the brilliant sun in the bright azure sky blinded him. Its dazzle had added to his mounting problems, including shaking off the full-body-sweat three a.m. nightmare, which had bolted him out of bed. *Damn, it's really bright.* Cursing again because hated to be out of sync and Remy was definitely out of line with the universe today. *I should have set the phone.* Overpowered by the sunshine, he stopped to put on designer shades then clicked open the automatic locks on his rented SUV and climbed into the truck.

Maybe that's why the colors are so loud today. Almost always, the auras were just there, completely encircling people. Once checked, Remington

Nicholas Montgomery could then move on without becoming involved. It was a rare moment when he felt compelled to get entangled with people and their problems – especially perfect strangers because their troubles were normally everyday things, like boyfriends and bosses. Rarely did it involve the illegal kind. Although during the last three years, a few cases had transpired that made Remy's secret weapon invaluable.

Today's episode bordered on the extraordinary, with its unusual brightness and intensity. Something strange seemed to be happening but he brushed it aside for now. Yet, in the back of his mind, knew it was only a matter of time before having to see Dr. Elliott again.

"Stop it!" His large hands clamped on the steering wheel, as Remy's many demons battled internally. His fingers braced the circle tightly, while his knuckles turned bone white. It took almost five minutes of deep, cleansing breaths to bring himself back under control. Slowly, unwrapping his ten digits, flexing them in a familiar rhythm.

After a few reps, found himself back inside the rental car. *First the coffee girl, now this. What in the world has come over me?* The lack of sleep must have made the colors more prominent, but Remy was too tired to process it right now. As he started the engine, his left hand brushed his face, in an attempt to ignore his weariness. As soon as he pulled out of the parking lot, started reviewing in his head the few scarce facts available on his former foe's illicit activities.

Later, while driving south on Interstate 95, Remy discovered his emotions were returning to normal. Traffic here was nothing like the slow crawl of the nation's capital and the easy drive permitted his mind to somewhat wander. Allowing his thoughts to drift to more pleasant ones and wondered if Sam's girl was as beautiful as he recalled. A clear picture of her formed in Remy's mind just as details from the case slipped back into his memory and shook his head to help rid it of the images regarding the lovely doctor. This nonsense needed to stop, because the FBI agent's job was to focus on the case and not the gorgeous woman he remembered.

Turned his attention back to driving, while recalling his adversary's weakness for overindulgence, therefore, Remy was not surprised when the GPS led the Suburban over a series of bridges to the island of Palm Beach.

The third day after the fanfare of Sam's funeral, Belle awoke before dawn and contemplated what constituted a new chapter in one's life. "Does it occur every year on your birthday? How about on New Year's Eve? Does it start at midnight?" Slowly, she climbed out of bed while brushing the sleep from her puffy red eyes.

Next, spent a few moments checking messages on her cellphone, surprised to discover it was already March eleventh. Too many items still needed attending, but waved the lost days away because there was little time to dwell on them. The daunting list prompted her to head straight for the shower, grabbing a robe along the way.

Slowly, she stepped inside the bathroom, stopping to adjust to the bright light. Shocked by the swollen, red-eyed reflection that stared back, pleading for an answer. "How about when you get married, have a child, or get that big promotion?" Looking like death warmed over, Belle raked fingers through her tangled hair, unhappy with the likeness standing before her. Angry at the turn in her life but she could only shake her head at the haggard image. When no answers appeared magically in the mirror, she stepped into the shower.

Ten minutes later, even the rainwater massage could not help her mood this morning. Again, stared at her reflection, while contemplating the same conversation in her head but there was only one question Belle wanted answered. The one which would not go away or stop circling inside her brain. "How did I get here?" Challenging the person in the oval mirror to answer. After several more minutes, found only disappointment because no reply came into focus and hung her head in frustration, as additional unanswered questions swirled inside.

The stress of this nightmare had become overwhelming, but her husband's estate needed to be settled. The smartest thing to do was to get dressed and start packing Sam's belongings but instead, stood there feeling sorry for herself. Brazen in her self-pity, Belle glared at her wretched image and pondered life's chapters. Since she had never been a widow, Campbell Brooks Randall thought a little pondering might be in order.

At long last, looked deeply into the mirror and drew in a cleansing breath. Unfortunately, Belle only found disappointment with what life had thrown at the woman who stared back. This time, instead of a pity party, practiced Granny's breathing exercises which gained her the strength to withstand the pressures of the difficult day ahead.

Her trembling hand opened the medicine cabinet, found the toothpaste, and applied it to her electric brush. "And no." Mumbling to herself, as she cleaned her teeth. "In my opinion, none of those things formed a new chapter." After rinsing out her mouth, dropped her head for another moment. The act was necessary when remembering the difficult decision, she had recently made about not having a child. Positive it had been the right one.

Unfortunately, the other achievements Campbell Brooks had experienced had felt nothing like this. *It's too early to be this defeated.* When glancing into the mirror, she was met with the sight of a complete stranger. Belle had been unaware of the crippling loneliness, bumpy ruts, and cavernous pits that grief caused until the paralyzing pain and sorrow had come calling at the tender age of sixteen. Tragically, she had faced each of those awful feelings, when her father had died in a senseless car accident, forcing Granny Brooks to help her finish high school. It was during this period of darkness that grief had almost killed her. Against all odds, her grandmother somehow was able to break through to the broken teenager, gently guiding her from succumbing completely to the heartache.

A sad smile formed on her lips, as Belle's thoughts turned to Daddy, who she still missed every day. That spring had been the only time she ever remembered her grandmother coming off the mountain, smiling when thinking. *I'm alive today because of that determined old woman.*

The unwavering matriarch was all the family she had left, so Belle had been caught off guard, eighteen months ago, when Granny refused to attend her wedding. She had begged and pleaded for weeks to no avail. Mavis Brooks was a force to be reckoned with and the old healer did not approve of her new husband. Nothing on Earth could change her grandmother's mind and no amount of 'spit and polish' as Granny would say could convince the willful mountain recluse, he was good enough for her little lass.

Even though Belle had tried numerous times, Granny never wavered in her dislike of Sam and the elder Dr. Brooks had always declined to give a reason. The only answer available from her grandmother was one of those famous sideward glances, meaning Belle should know better. The conversation always ended the same, with Granny walking away, shaking her head while muttering to herself.

Gathering clothes for the day, she stopped and spoke aloud. "I wonder if she'll tell me now." Sounded a touch crazy because like Granny, Belle talked to herself too, but she had not answered back. *Well, at least not out loud yet.* Which meant she might still be sane but after the last ten days, was not so sure about anything, anymore.

After a glance at the clock, it reminded her how quickly time passes and all those circling unanswered questions. Surprised to discover that according to her own calculations, this chapter would be the third one in her life and Belle was clueless on how to manage it.

The last one was after her father's death and the honor student had struggled to finish high school, followed by spending the summer dealing with her enhanced powers. Afterwards, Granny shipped her off to college, then Belle obtained her doctorate at James Aurelius University in Baltimore Maryland. School had kept her busy for eight long years, finally returning to her much-loved Washington, DC childhood home. The time had helped heal most of the pain which allowed her to embark on a new life along with a promising career without the past raising its ugly head.

Shortly after finishing her residency, this mess began when Samuel Lloyd Randall erupted into her life. From the start of their whirlwind romance, her husband was determined they should marry. With a rock-hard athletic build and chiseled good looks, Sam was every woman's dream come true. *Until you saw his true colors.*

As she stared into the mirror, thought about his obsession with her because it had always been confusing. Although pretty, she did not consider herself anything special and Belle had never understood Sam's relentless pursuit. Her mind floated back to the first days of their romance. A few of the crazy things the man had done to wear down her defenses popped into her head and a rare chuckle escaped her lips, in recognition to Mr. Randall's creativity.

With all her might, wished it had turned out differently but alas, they were doomed from the start. In the beginning, her husband had been so carefree and charming. He had even mentioned marriage on their first date. Two months later, Sam popped the question, surprising Belle with a whirlwind evening that included a dozen roses and a too-large diamond ring. She had grown up in a home, with only a single dad so was not too keen on getting married, plus they had only gone out for a brief period of time. Besides being flattered and a bit scared by his unexpected proposal, she thought him sweet, along with a tad insane.

As time passed, the ladies' man became more smitten with the new doctor and it made Sam determined to win her over. The world's press became obsessed, hounding them wherever they went. Something Belle had never become accustomed to. The international playboy wined and dined her across several continents, each outing more outlandish than the last. Until one night at a black-tie charity affair, honoring the heroes of the 9/11 tragedy, Sam orchestrated the perfect moment. He proposed in front of twelve hundred of Washington's most elite power players, which included a spotlight, an even bigger ring, and champagne flown in from France. Six weeks later, they walked down the aisle.

Now looking back on that spotlight, she could hardly remember either one of those people. "How did I get here?" The hairbrush was poised in midair as a foreign image stared back from the mirror. That woman's reflection shined the perfect mask, Belle continued to show the world but truthfully, she was simply sad and lonely.

Furious at Sam for the ridiculous things he constantly pulled off, but this one took the cake. "Thanks to my darling husband I'm the laughingstock of almost everyone in the country." As soon as the anger began, it transformed, forcing her emotions to take another plunging dive. They were constantly changing course, like the *Rebel Yell* roller coaster she loved to ride as a child. It was guilt this time, not anger that entered her psyche because she had been unaware of Sam's drug use. As a medical doctor, Belle should have seen the signs. *So many what ifs to contemplate.*

Another question suddenly erupted onto that imaginary screen inside her brain. It was the one which desperately needed to be asked but she did not want answered. *Did I even know the man who had been my husband?* Ashamed because after surviving the last ten days, Belle did not think so.

For thirty-two years, Sam Randall had spent his entire existence in the public eye while his private one had followed the hard and fast road. Living life, the way he wanted and always his own way. "Oh, no!" Incapable of maintaining a low-key lifestyle or dying by normal means. "Not Sam!!" True to form, dying with flair on a luxurious yacht in swanky Palm Beach Harbor with not one but two naked women. "Well, that was just like Sam." Graphic photos had spent days splashed across every newspaper and television station in the country, as well as around the world. "Lots and lots of pictures along with a perfectly focused video!!! No grainy shots for Sam!"

In anger, she threw her brush at the face in the mirror. "There will probably be a disgusting audio tape before this is over." Belle fumed as a nonstop onslaught of images flipped through her mind. The embarrassment continued, her elbows slamming onto the table as long hair cascaded around her dropped head. The sad widow just wanted to get control of herself and her life, but doubted either would occur anytime soon.

Up down, up down; her life had become pure torture. The bad dream would not come to a stop and Belle had no clue when it would end. The feelings were a relentless journey of vastly different emotions, like an endless demented carnival ride. She sensed nothing except a black hole surrounding her and felt isolated from everyone.

Right when self-indulgence came close to consuming her, Belle's brain took another sharp turn as another distasteful memory flooded it. This time, anger grabbed her emotions back because they had moved to South Florida in order to fix their crumbling marriage. Just like everything else, Sam demanded it occur on his terms and expected it to happen without question.

An impossible task.

Suddenly, she collapsed on the table because defeat came calling as the worst of the anger passed. But Belle was not getting off that easy this morning, as more devastating emotions flooded her mind. Ashamed of her stupidity because had believed her selfish husband would have at least tried. Instead, Sam pretended nothing was wrong and everything was perfect between them. Truth be told, the shy doctor had been miserable after only a few months of marriage and had spent much of her time in DC, to be close to Granny but mostly to hide. Belle had known Sam was not capable of being faithful, but she had been a fool to believe his many lies.

This morning, she did not want to dwell on her mistakes but was curious if Sam suspected that given more time, she would have run and that was the reason he insisted they marry so soon. Her broken heart recognized how clever her husband had been because Sam had rushed Belle to the altar, with no chance of getting to know him. *But why?* Her head rattled at that absurdity. *Why insist I marry him, then run out and sleep with someone else the very next day?*

Bitterly remembering it was this infidelity that led to their move to Palm Beach. *Yep, that's my beloved late husband.* Loudly sighing. *Oh well, I've been such a fool by turning a blind eye for so long.* Her major mistake was now over but she still would have to learn how to live in this new chapter. Sad to discover, this one might prove more difficult than the other two combined.

After glancing at the clock, she needed to get moving because had been staring at mirrors all morning while accomplishing nothing.

Jumped up when remembering the movers were taking everything back to Washington in only two days because Belle was determined to tackle the most challenging task next, Sam's private office along with his personal space. Off in search of more boxes to complete this unpleasant task, she rushed down the hall, towards the guest house located at the far back end of the property.

Until today, it was a place Belle had avoided for almost two years.

CHAPTER 2

Perfect Spotlight

There were multiple issues buzzing around in his brain, while finding himself stopped on Worth Avenue, but Remy was unaware he had entered the swanky town of Palm Beach. The tired agent was too engrossed with what had happened that fateful night to appreciate the charming island. Replaying in his mind, over and over, was the first time he glimpsed Mrs. Sam Randall because the lonely guy could not get it out of his head.

But it was especially bad to fantasize about the good doctor regarding his career because she could end up a potential suspect. Not to mention the trouble those vivid pictures were causing other parts of his body, while driving down the highway. He tried thinking about a cold shower but apparently it was not going to work this time.

Finally, smacking his longings into remission, Remy recalled what he should do which was forget the beauty floating around in his brain and focus on work. *Damn, damn, damn.* A feat which seemed impossible to achieve. *This is not how I thought this day would go.*

He envisioned flying down here, snooping around, maybe lucking out by finding a few clues to what was really going on. *Anything that would lead to whatever Sam was mixed up in.* Because, as sure as they were childhood rivals, the very grown-up Agent Montgomery could definitely link Sam with some very nefarious folk. Yet, stumped by the reason his longtime adversary would have gotten involved with such shady connections. Those findings had shocked him at the overall extent of those dealings. Remy had plenty of proof but lacked specifics and more importantly, the why behind it.

The ace profiler knew Randall's vast net worth and was mindful the billionaire playboy rarely let these lowlifes in the back door. Confident Sam ran in a much different circle, meaning none of this nonsense was making any sense. Until he worked it out, Remy would not be satisfied with a simple drug overdose and needed better answers because he did not like the easy conclusions being drawn by law enforcement.

Blessed with a close relationship to the director of the FBI, his decision to join the Bureau, after his wife's tragic death, had been an easy one. It also had come in handy, when approaching the director with his suspicions surrounding Sam's shady dealings. Parker Anderson agreed to give him some leeway and keep his investigation off the books, but he was not a happy man. His star protégé had connected the wealthy, high-profile rogue to people who appeared on the FBI's Most Wanted List.

The potential political fallout from Randall's influential family could be astronomical, to say nothing of career ending. There were others, both foreign and domestic, elected and appointed professionals, who were somehow connected to this complex plot. *But what exactly was it?* These unknown factors made the two of them extremely nervous. *And who all did it involve?* That was the million-dollar question but the answer to this simple sentence had eluded him for months.

Remy flew down here, eager to figure out any part of it and desperate for Sam's widow to shed light on a few items. From what he pieced together, it involved the recent Irish election and possibly the upcoming 2012 United States presidential election. What scared him and his boss were the number of important people that could be involved and how high up this nightmare went on the political ladder. With every step, he needed to take care.

Despite the warm day, shivers from those ugly thoughts caused goosebumps to break out. Once again, Remy cursed his rotten luck and rolled his head to rid it of those nasty notions, at least until he obtained further proof. The break, allowing for his reflections to wander back to more pleasant ones and the honey-haired beauty.

Unwilling to admit it, even to himself, over the years he experienced interesting thoughts of Campbell Brooks. A smile broke out on his face, recalling her in that spotlight. To this day, unable to get over how much she affected him but reflecting on that period of his life was always hard. The pleasant memories of her also dredged up how unhappy his parents had been with their only child. Disappointment did not begin to describe their emotional state regarding his career decision to leave the law firm founded by his grandfather.

Especially his incredibly unhappy father.

In his dad's opinion, after almost two years with the Bureau's Behavioral Analysis Unit, Remy had spent enough time getting this nonsense out of his system. By this point, his only son should have come to his senses. *Act like a Montgomery.* Painfully, that statement still echoed through his head. Although his parents were sympathetic regarding Amanda's death, never understood or supported his burning need to find the person responsible. That necessity was always his main motivation for joining the FBI.

Unexpectedly, Remy was jerked out of his distressing memories by flashing red lights and ringing bells of the railroad crossing ahead. A freight train must be passing through town, and he would be stuck at the intersection for the next few minutes. A smile appeared on his face while studying the unforeseen inconvenience. The exhausted guy closed his eyes to take advantage of the delay.

The pause allowed his mind to drift back to that significant night and the incredible Dr. Brooks.

September 2009

The three Montgomery's were attending some sort of charity benefit, with the usual Washington power players in attendance. In line, he shook hands with the vice president, several members of Congress, along with a few governors. The extra VIPs made the entrance security insane, as it always tends to be at those things nowadays.

He fought his way through, only to be greeted with the usual family lecture. Remy wanted nothing more than to tune out his father's highly focused, teal-toned aura and enjoy the evening but no such luck. Quentin Montgomery's famous duty to the law firm speech began immediately after his warm greeting.

Abruptly, the lights dimmed in the large ballroom; even for Washington, this stunt was rather unusual. Almost at once, everyone stopped whatever they were doing and dropped their voices to a mere whisper. To Remy's delight, this halted his dad's sermon because his parents were part of the 'in' crowd and their table gave him a front-row seat to the show about to begin.

A single spotlight illuminated the area directly in front of him. Thrilled because inside the brightness stood the most stunning woman but it was also the exact moment when Remy lost his ability to breathe.

Tha thu bréagha! The lady in the limelight was even more beautiful than Amanda. *Okay, why did I just think in Gaelic when I looked at her?* With soft, luscious curves and a cute turned-up nose, this gorgeous girl ignited something deep inside of him he thought long dead. *Holy shit! Why do I want to blurt out 'you're beautiful!' to a perfect stranger?* Certain he looked a fool but unable to alter his reaction. *What the hell is wrong with me?*

Shocked by his unusual response, Remy's brain could not comprehend what was occurring. *Good lord, I need to get myself under control.* Unfortunately, somewhere deep inside, it registered that catching his breath seemed out of the question for a long, long while.

Vivid emerald-green eyes turned toward him, as another powerful sensation plowed into his core. The entire room disappeared, and time stood stock still.

Even his dad found interest in what was causing such a fuss and stopped nagging, but nothing registered with Remy except the girl before him. Captivated by her presence, he only noticed the lovely was bathed in the iridescent radiance, which twinkled in the spotlight's glow. The beauty seemed to sparkle in the brilliance, resembling magic come to life.

Only once before had he seen an aura like hers. It surrounded a woman he spotted during the spring of his sophomore year of college. No words existed to describe the stunning sight of that aura. Although Remy had tried to reach the older woman, locating her in the crowd had been impossible. Now, here stood another person with a similar aura and this time he found himself powerless to move. All the multiple blinding colors, along with her incredible beauty mesmerized him. Ensnared by the swirling sensations, he stood helpless to describe this experience which was flooding his senses.

After his dad eyed him strangely, he realized his emotions were overwhelming him. *Damn.* His suspicions were confirmed when the pretty lady smiled and found himself rather off balance. Quickly sitting to gather his composure.

Grief hits each person differently and four years had passed since Amanda's unexpected death. Four long years that Remy continued to struggle through. Those first two years, he could recall little, except the pain. Unable to experience passion for any woman, he rarely dated since losing his wife. *So why this one?*

Once more, battled to get himself under control. *What in the world is going on?* After several moments, a touch of his composure returned. "Who is she?" Asking, while leaning towards his mom, whose aura always shined a bright yellow glow.

Joy constantly radiated from Sarah Montgomery, who brightly smiled at her son. "Why sweetheart, that's Campbell Brooks. You might remember William Brooks, the *Washington News* editor who died a while back. Well, that's his darlin' daughter." His mother's eyes never wavered from the vision in the light. He grabbed her hand, eager to ask another question because his mom knew everything related to DC society, when karma rudely interrupted their conversation.

Rotten luck continued to haunt him because joining Beauty in the spotlight was none other than – Beast.

Located before him was the one person in the world, Remy would have given good money to never lay eyes on again because pretty boy Sam Randall stood next to the enchanting girl. *Are you kidding me?* A familiar dark gray aura swirled angrily around his childhood arch-rival, but its chaos did not surprise Remy. The dismal color correlated with menacing and depressing thoughts, exactly how he always envisioned his adversary whenever forced to think of the jackass.

To make matters worse, Sam got down on one knee and proposed to the only woman, who had finally sparked something deep inside of Remy. *Can you believe this?* He actually wanted to ask her out on a date. A first for him.

When the captivated agent lost his breath this time, it felt more like a punch in the stomach because the past was rearing its ugly head again. Just like years before, the lying bastard swooped in and won the girl because of course, she said yes. *Don't they all say yes and go running off with Sam?*

Infuriated, he watched as she slipped on Randall's ring, while painful childhood memories flooded Remy's mind. Flashbacks of their countless competitions with any and everything, roared through his thoughts.

It had always been that way, between the two of them growing up. Either playing sports, racing cars, or chasing girls; if one of them did something, they forced the other to do it better. Rivals first, then good friends, Sam and Remy were practically inseparable for most of their young lives.

Until that momentous summer night when Jennifer Randolph drove a wedge between them, forever. One impossible to repair.

As the caboose went flying past the windshield, he blinked, shaking the recollections away. The crossing guards lifted into place and forced Remy's attention back to the busy seasonal traffic. Sadly, it seemed he had nothing left but old memories.

After taking another deep breath, focused his concentration on this complicated case. The cover story he and Parker had put together was one which stayed close to the facts but far from political attention. What he told his boss at the FBI had been the truth. As an adult, Remy had no contact with his old enemy and in no way would their childhood relationship compromise him. With legitimate leads but information a struggle to obtain, the expert profiler lied to his supervisor about everything else. This case was a powder keg and the director decided to keep Bob Tolbert in the dark.

Sam had been doing business with known arms dealers, which kept Remy quiet to Bob about those crimes too. Also, the wealthy mogul was laundering the cartel's dirty money, but he only needed a few key elements like the shell companies to trace the cash directly back to Randall. Once he gained those facts, the pieces of this complicated puzzle would come together, and he could fill Tolbert in on the particulars.

Until he possessed hard evidence, it was simply too dangerous to discuss, due to Randall's influential name. Instead, using that same family name as cover, Remy appeared to merely be wrapping up the details on Sam's very public death. Nothing unusual or out of the ordinary, then on to another assignment or so Bob believed. *Let's hope he buys it.*

Trying to prove what he understood Randall to be up to, could shake the foundation of the country. His gut told him those shady dealings involved more than drugs and weapons. Scared by Sam's possible twisted plans, Agent Montgomery did not want to imagine how much more would turn up. He remembered some of his enemy's childhood plots and those thoughts coiled to terror, imagining the diabolical opportunities Randall could achieve.

Everyone in the country should be afraid but Remy shook off the evil possibilities because he needed to concentrate on the job. His attention found him back in the front seat, once again irritated by the slow pace of the case. *Crap.* Slammed his fist into the steering wheel and tried to refocus his energy on driving instead of his distressed emotions.

What the hell is wrong with me today? Secretly knowing the reason, yet afraid to admit it. Remy's feelings were off the charts because he would be in her presence again. Merely thinking of Campbell Brooks made his blood warm up and the loner wondered what state he would find her. *Was she devastated by Sam's death and a mess or simply numb towards life? How about being angry or sad by the awful incident?* He had experienced all those places of grief and more. Aware of the many pitfalls it can create for the one left behind.

Apparently, just like her unconventional mountain grandmother, the younger Dr. Brooks practiced medicine the unorthodox way too. By doing so, she had helped hundreds of difficult to reach patients. People, who many others had failed. With all his soul, Remy hoped to find the person in the FBI files. The strong, independent woman who only worked with people who seemed to have nowhere else to turn. It was another quality of Campbell Brooks he admired.

The weary agent refused to call Belle by anything but her maiden name and bristled when thinking about her with Sam. Remy could not bring himself to consider her a Randall. Silently, he sent up a prayer asking that she not be damaged by the experience. Another woman destroyed by Sam, especially one he could not forget, would be impossible to survive this time.

Since that spotlight night, Remy dated a few women here and there but none he could even remember. Every one of them, either a set up by close friends or worse by his mom, because he did not see the need to date. Blondes and brunettes, pixies and amazons, attorneys and doctors; Remy had dated every type. Once and only once.

Boy, did this make his mother steaming mad. A wide grin broke out on his Hollywood handsome face when thinking about his matchmaker mother. Although, the sparkling smile immediately disappeared, when remembering their most recent conversation. Frankly, there was no talking with her regarding anything else because Sarah Montgomery wanted grandchildren. Period.

When his momma decided something needed to happen, then by gosh, it got done. One determined woman, she knew how to work every southern charm on a person. Miss Sarah Kathleen Davis always got what she wanted, every single time and had been a highly sought-after Richmond Virginia debutante before attaining her political achievements. For the past thirty-five years, Sarah Montgomery had shined as an A-lister's wife, while excelling in the shark-infested waters of Washington, DC. Plus, by golly, there was not a person alive who did not adore her.

However, these last few years his mother just did not understand him. Even after begging her not to, Mrs. Montgomery continued to put what she considered the proper women in his path. Remy felt for his momma because there was only him to give her those desired grandbabies which were not in the cards right now.

Chuckling when remembering the *'when hell freezes over'* comment his mother recently mumbled under her breath but he had to agree. It was a perfectly accurate one. What Remy could not grasp was why everybody kept making a big deal about it because there was still plenty of time to have kids. They were all pressuring him to move on and start producing them soon, especially his parents. *How am I supposed to do that, when the person responsible for Amanda's death continues to roam the streets?* Justifying to himself, the years needed to try and find the bad guy. *Why didn't everyone understand that?* Irritation and aggravation oozed from the tired agent as the large iron gates of the sprawling Randall estate came into view. "I'm in for a very long day."

The comforting finger exercises were not working and jadedly, Remy proceeded towards the call box.

CHAPTER 3

Little Miss List Maker

"Where...is...that...key?" She had no trouble locating his keychain inside the police envelope but was frustrated to not find the key to Sam's office on it. Convinced, he would have carried it on there, however that ring only held the keys to his car, the annex house, and the yacht. *Ah yes, the stupid boat where all this fun began.* Back to the one thing Belle did not want to think about, or disgust would slip into her thoughts, triggering a Granny scolding in her head about not having such malicious feelings for the dead.

After searching high and low, found no sign of the key. Frustrated and sad from rummaging through the house, this hunt reminded Belle, she had only technically shared it with her husband. Their marriage had been a joke. Although, she was grateful for the monotonous task because it allowed her reflections to drift to more mindless things.

The first deliberation concerned the large crowds of media crews, which had her wondering if they had thinned out around the compound. The cameras with their constant flashbulbs had been everywhere — before, during, and after the funeral. They still blocked the entrance when Belle arrived two days ago, but she was unsure of their numbers now. Too scared of their nonstop pursuit and afraid to step outside, it was also too soon for the shy doctor to face people. *Okay, I'm a chicken.* She snickered at herself for being such a coward.

Even though avoiding the cameras forever was not an option, she still was not ready to venture out into the world. Belle braced for the momentous occasion, dreading the catastrophe it would set off. The grieving widow was convinced that as soon as she did, the swarming paparazzi would descend because finding peace from those vultures was impossible. In all likelihood, they would never leave her alone and hung her head in frustration. *But there is no need to worry about them currently.* Quickly, she adopted a Scarlett O'Hara attitude, while screaming at no one. "Cause such considerations are for another day. Right now, I'm just looking for a damn key!"

Irritated after an hour of intense searching, she had found nothing but mindless thoughts with mountain accents. Ready to contact a locksmith, when she stumbled across the blasted office key in a room Sam rarely occupied. He had concealed it within a well-hidden compartment of his bedside valet box. Stopped and thanked the Lord for reminding her to touch all his possessions, otherwise it might never have been found.

With the key in hand, Belle started toward the office to begin the unpleasant task of going through her husband's things. The weary widow dreaded the upcoming feelings she would need to endure from handling his belongings.

Walked outside, while studying the curious set of keys but continued to push the mounting apprehension away. While strolling toward the romantic guest house, Belle spotted the key for the cottage right away. The chain also held what appeared to be a safe deposit box key, but it looked different from the one they opened shortly after their marriage. *Why would Sam have another box?* This struck her as odd.

Unable to dwell on the question because the third item on the chain called to her and was something not to be ignored. The extraordinary object was like nothing Belle had ever seen.

It appeared to be a cross between a Triskelion and a Celtic knot but not quite. Vivid green in color, the circled object was approximately three inches round and resembled a challenge coin. The captivating piece encompassed the most unusual elements, in addition to being strikingly beautiful. Fascinated, she intently studied the deeply disturbing item while continuing toward the back of the property.

Both their families were of Scottish descent with heritage being an important part of her everyday life. The most attractive factor about her husband had been his extensive knowledge of these values. No one except Sam had possessed such a widespread understanding of her customs and culture. As a small girl, grew up learning from Granny the many traditions and symbols of the Scottish and Irish nations. Every summer and winter break, Celtic, Wiccan, and all forms of Christian beliefs were Belle's daily childhood lessons. She prided herself on being an expert in all of them but had seen nothing quite like this piece.

The woman stood riveted, running her fingers over the remarkable craftsmanship, while admiring the intricate details. Its beauty was enthralling but touching the face of the piece sent a sense of evil shooting through her. A loud bang echoed throughout the outdoor patio, as the keys dropped to the concrete pavement. *Bless my heart.* The noise they made on the pool deck caused Belle to practically jump out of her skin.

Her eyes darted around, checking the area to confirm no other person was present. *I'm just being silly.* After a pause, her heartbeat slowed down but the wicked impression would not leave. With a strained smile, stared intently at the piece. *There is something vile about you. You beautiful key.* Taken aback by the strange statement. *How do I know it's a key? Because it didn't look like any key I've ever seen. More like one of those specialty coins they hand out to folks in law enforcement and the military.* It was a key; she knew it was one, just like she knew her name was Campbell.

Gingerly, picked the chain off the ground and attempted to shake off the bad vibes, while careful not to come in contact with the evil beauty. With a worried brow, Belle continued toward the cottage while shaking off the fear, but she still dreaded having to pack up Sam's possessions.

Upon arriving at the dwelling, reached for the handle, careful to avoid touching the unusual key. For the first few minutes, just gazed around the large guest house because before today, Belle had never stepped foot into Sam's personal man cave.

Besides the traditional office suite, it was no surprise to find a fully stocked bar, a theatre-sized media room, and two large bedrooms. Although, she was shocked to discover one was filled with state-of-the-art toys for fulfilling Sam's sex shenanigans. It was a small comfort he had kept those antics from under her roof. Belle made a mental note to have Huntley make arrangements to clear it out. With one final look, quietly shut the door on that part of his life forever.

Drew a breath having nearly been holding hers since entering the house but was still tense. Belle tried to shake off the engulfing dread, eager for this chapter of her life to be over. Before losing her nerve, she hurried down the cottage hall and turned the handle to Sam's inner domain. Right away, noticed the laptop was not on the desk or anywhere in the area. *Where is it?* There was no sign of Sam's computer in the room. *How odd, it's got to be here somewhere!* The strange disappearance frustrated her. Several days after Sam's death, the police had released her husband's effects, but the laptop had not been among them because Belle had specifically inquired about it. *Where else could it be?*

She was baffled after searching the main house, the smaller house where she resided when in Palm Beach, along with this place. After looking everywhere – in, under and around everything she owned – it had simply vanished because there was no other explanation. *This is so bizarre.*

Even in the rare instances when they slept together, Sam had never let it out of his sight. He had kept the computer on the nightstand, right beside him, to always be accessible for work but the memory triggered another problem, which was being married to Mr. Sam Randall. *What would he put before her?*

In the middle of the room, stopped her search to mull over the question. *Not before work. Or his parents. Or his women. Or his adventures or even his precious laptop.* Depression edged its way back into her mood. *It seems not much of anything.*

She stood in the middle of his realm shrieking at the top of her lungs. "Oh, I was sooooooooooo stupid!!!"

At the drop of a hat, her lying husband would run out of town or out of the country. "On quote, unquote, business." She stated aloud, while using her fingers to make the invisible quotation marks. "He expected me to stand by and say nothing like a good little wife. Happily waiting for his return, with open arms and no questions asked but Sam was probably returning from one of his numerous flings around the world."

An argument they had many times, yet he was incapable of understanding why Belle would not act more like his mother. "Josephine Buchanan Randall was a ruthless corporate executive but to the world, presented herself as the model Washington wife." Sarcastically, describing her almost royalty mother-in-law who could do it all. "Ha, what a joke thinking I could be anything like that woman." Resentment mixed with bitterness slipped back into her reflection.

Found herself on the brink of tears but refused to allow it. Belle had become too strong to let Sam control her any longer. After counting to ten to regain her composure, went back to the task at hand by resuming her search.

The decision helped her to stand straighter and gather more internal strength. *A stiff upper lip.* A smile formed, as Granny's old-fashioned saying lightly brushed across her thoughts because thinking of her grandmother made Belle feel better. Although eager to finish boxing up her dead husband's stuff, it still distressed her at having to touch all his things before the next chapter could begin.

Again, with the chapters. Her mind wandered back to the reoccurring topic but should not be surprised, with how the last one had ended in public death and humiliation. Hands clenched by her side. "Oh, dear Lord, I will not cry!" The scream helped to let out her frustrations.

To get back on track she grabbed a pen, along with a pad of paper and began a list.

Lists were a calming exercise, really a comfort which she had practiced her entire life and Belle would compile lists for just about anything. Like daily items that needed to be completed, along with the goals she wanted to accomplish, and one for the supplies Granny Brooks needed from the general store. *Oh, which reminds me.* As she stared down at the blank sheet of paper. *I need to call Granny and let her know I'm doing fine.* Fondly, Belle's thoughts turned toward her beautiful grandmother. *Otherwise, she will be worried sick about me.*

It surprised her how much her mind continued to wander all over today. Something that rarely happened, and she hoped it would settle down soon. It was highly unusual for her not to be clear headed because there was not a more level-headed person. At the first sign of trouble, her reporter father had run headfirst, into war or conflict. For sixty plus years, her eccentric grandmother had been healing mountain people with herbs and other unusual remedies. With that kind of family tree, someone in this unconventional trio needed to be responsible. A burden, which seemed to always fall on her.

Finished with throwing another pity party for herself, Belle stood dreaming about Granny and her beautiful homestead. Even thought about calling, but this was her grandmother's usual outdoor time. A broad smile broke out again at the memory. Granny did not own a cell phone, so Belle's call would go unanswered until later in the day. In fact, no technology had really interested Mavis Brooks since the invention of the rotary telephone.

Belle glanced at the new smart phone in her hand. If she told it to, it could probably write the lists for her, but the organizer had always drawn comfort from putting pen to paper. The type of contentment that soothes your soul. Still thinking about her grandmother, wrote *Call Granny* followed by *Find Sam's laptop.* After marking both down, stood for a second with a silly grin on her face. Her mood improved tremendously simply by putting it down on a piece of paper.

Setting the list aside for the time being, Belle decided to move on to more important things. Distressed when contemplating the large task ahead, remembered there was no one to blame except herself. Her in-laws had offered to fly down and help with the packing. Sam's father had strongly insisted, which she found odd, but had firmly declined their kind suggestion. She was reluctant to have them hovering while suffering the difficulty of going through her husband's things. "They mean well but I couldn't do it." Whispering to the empty room as a lone tear trickled down her cheek. "I will not cry!"

Upset to find herself back on the cruel roller coaster ride. First hot, then cold. Quiet and just as sudden, screaming at the top of her lungs.

This seemed to be her life these days. No rhyme or reason but Belle should have expected that from Sam. Truthfully, she had no idea what to expect or how to behave, certain there was no handbook for when your husband is found dead like hers.

To stop the fury building internally, came to a complete stop, and recited the familiar calming words from her grandmother's teachings. Paused while drawing a deep breath, then letting it out slowly. She became still as a statue to calm her being because this simple exercise helped to release the pressure forming inside. *Let's see if I can do anything today.* Worried the engulfing sensation would consume her. *Accomplish anything, otherwise I'll be forced to call for help. Something I refuse to do.* Upon completing Granny's exercises, she was relieved to find some of the heaviness had escaped. To take her mind off the sensations churning inside but determined to finish packing her husband's belongings, she reached for a roll of tape and began assembling the boxes she had dragged from the main house because Belle had delayed for too long.

After working over two hours, she stood in the center of the room and took pride in her progress. Strolled over to the desk and dialed the kitchen, softly asking for coffee to be sent over. Cook replied she would also send warm scones along with honey butter and homemade preserves because the culinary chef had been attempting to fatten her up ever since their wedding. Just like her husband, she doted on Belle because the family chef had been pampering Sam since he was a small child. Acting as his second mom, Cook had cared for him, one way or another, every day since he had been born.

Unfortunately, she was also one of the reasons Sam had ended up in an early grave. The legendary Buchanan family, along with Cook, all had a hand in his untimely demise. All guilty because of their complacent behavior were his world-famous clan and prominent parents. Forever enabling or allowing him to do whatever he wanted, whenever he wanted, to whomever he wanted, and then bailing him out whenever he got in too deep. Sam had never faced consequences.

A spoiled little rich boy described him to a tee. Again, Belle caught herself thinking ill of the dead and remembered how she had been raised. It triggered a Granny scolding echoing inside her head. *"Mind ye' manners lassie."* The internal reprimand made her chuckle out loud.

Back in the present, Belle could not turn a heartbroken person away and there was no one more brokenhearted over Sam than Cook. Therefore, Belle did the right thing and spent a few extra minutes consoling her. Afterwards, hung up the telephone with a more relaxed smile and delighted in the surrounding tenderness triggered by another memory of her grandmother. Most of Belle's good qualities, like a soft kind heart, were due to Mavis and it warmed her to rejoice in Granny Brooks's many pieces of wisdom, along with her eternal strength.

A few moments later, the house maid quietly brought in the tray. True to form, the magazine-perfect display boasted fresh squeezed orange juice, along with a bowl of crisp juicy strawberries topped with real whipping cream. Coffee carafe in hand, she stood appreciating the spread. Belle grinned at Cook's kind gesture. Popped a ruby red berry into her mouth and glanced up at the clock. Shocked to discover it was already after nine o'clock, and now found her progress disappointing. Having been awake before dawn, had hoped to be further along on Sam's office. Upset with her husband for all his ridiculous antics and mad her morning had not gone as planned.

Belle recognized it was exceedingly difficult to get anything done when your mind wanders all over the place. Not to mention the current uproar her mystical talents were in, because she was forced to touch all of Sam's things. Frustration was seeping back in but pushed that distasteful emotion aside.

It was hard not to admire this feast before her and poured herself a cup of coffee, adding her own special mixture of cream and sugar. Stopped to savor that first sip to just enjoy the java because that initial taste was always the best. Quickly, drinking the cup of liquid energy while reviewing the to-do list in her head. After eating a few bites of Cook's morning masterpiece, she went back to boxing up the last of Sam's things.

Following another hour of non-stop work, it surprised Belle to find there was not much more to pack; sad to discover Sam had left little behind. To be sure, the perfectionist went through each of the drawers again. If an important paper or file went missing, she would never hear the end of it from her barracuda mother-in-law. An employee of his mother's company, Sam had worked for a subsidiary of Buchanan Industries, the largest privately owned company in the world. It was started shortly after WWII and owned exclusively by the members of the Buchanan family and their close friends, of which Sam's mom was the majority stockholder.

Thoughts regarding Sam's famous family caused Belle to remember something important. *Crap, I totally forgot about the will.* While moving another box to the floor, cursed to herself. *I'm sure the prenup is all that's needed to complete everything.* The appointment with the Buchanan family attorney was on March thirteenth, only two days away. She hated to be rushed and reached for her pad of paper. Belle pulled out her list and made note of the significant item, writing the reminder on the line marked number three. *Attorney Meeting on Monday — Pull out paperwork.* As soon as she wrote it, Belle also made a note on her online calendar to avoid any scheduling conflicts. Being in this agitated state, she was relieved to have remembered the meeting.

Worried, she opted to go through Sam's desk again because something was bothering her about it. It was impossible to let go of her instincts without touching the piece of furniture a second time.

Frustration surged through her as she yanked out each drawer but this repeat exercise netted nothing, until touching the last one on the left. This time when she pulled on the handle, a familiar impression struck her and produced a sensation similar to a door opening deep inside. Instantly, Belle flung her hand away because it felt like touching a *'hot potato'*. Unfortunately, this was a well-known sensation she had experienced in many forms but liked to pretend that it did not exist. It usually meant what Granny Brooks called one of her *'feelers'* had come calling.

At first touch, she wanted to dismiss it as a bunch of nonsense, because something this intense could not be on the property and she not be mindful of it. Deep down, Belle knew her non-scientific gift was desperately shouting out something important. Those screaming feelings were the same ones that helped her breakthrough to her many difficult patients.

The ambiance resonating from the drawer made her uneasy, which prompted her to search around some more. After finding nothing, she relaxed a bit and blew a few strands of loose hair out of her eyes but still could not shake her apprehension. In the far corners of her mind, alarms were going off. Loudly.

None of these feelings were familiar but the level-headed doctor knew she needed to get a grip. *Don't be silly. There is nothing in there that will hurt you.* Belle had never experienced a *'feeler'* this intense which was a big cause for concern.

Unable to shake the awful sensation, when first touching the drawer, practical Campbell Brooks decided to take over and pull it together. *This is all just my imagination.* If paranormal activities were occurring in this cottage, she would know about them but none of those triggers had gone off. Still, Belle could not shake the lingering evil impression.

The doctor dragged herself together, struggling to push her fears to the far corners of her mind. I'm just tired to the bone. Shifted her method of dealing with the strange sensation, while plotting another course of action. *I better get it over with.* Anger would be more efficient because it always worked when dealing with Sam. She adopted the highly effective get-mad-at-something tactic. *If I know my darling husband, it's probably pictures of his girls or his all-important little black book.* Belle was certain her cheating spouse had never gotten rid of his, accidentally finding it shortly after they wed. That loud, monumental argument began playing inside her head. The unhappy memory made her even angrier, but it also succeeded in building up her nerve.

With false courage driving her, Belle took another deep breath and snatched open the drawer. "Empty, huh?" She mumbled at the odd find. "Well, that's very weird." Puzzled by the psychic stimulation that continued to bombard her. "Why would I get such strange feelings from an empty drawer?" That was impossible and knew it. "So, where is it?" Asked while frantically searching because was convinced Sam had stashed his stupid bimbo booklet in here somewhere. No longer in denial of her special talents, an angry flushed-faced Belle knew there was something hidden inside. She fiddled with the bottom of the drawer, until a board popped out into her hand, but no book was underneath, only a large manila folder, filled with a bunch of old newspaper articles.

"Funny, hiding this…below you." She wiggled the wooden panel in the air at nothing. "Wonder why Sam would use a fake bottom drawer to stick old newspapers under?" Perplexed by her unusual find, sat at the desk with her head in her hands confused by what was going on.

For now, left the drawer and the folder where they lay because with all the magic swirling inside, she was too bewildered to do anything else. The malevolent feeling overwhelming her was not going away, nor was it getting any better. In fact, it was becoming much worse and seemed to be getting closer.

After a while, grasped sitting there doing nothing would definitely not solve the problem. Just as she reached for the strange file again, the desk phone rang. The sound spooked her so badly; she jumped up, knocking the handset onto the ground. The act sent the instrument flying across the polished hardwood floor, forcing Belle to chase it on her hands and knees.

After reeling in the long cord, placed the receiver to her ear. Out of breath after fumbling with the escaping handset, she gasped into the telephone. "Hello."

"Mrs. Randall, I hate to be disturbin' ye' but the FBI be calling at the front gate." Spoke the voice over the line.

Too surprised to say anything else, a shaken Belle croaked. "WHAT?"

"The FBI be here, me lady. There be a man, he be at the front gate. Showed me hims badge on ye' monitor Mrs. Randall. He be wantin' to see ye' but don't be hav'en no warrant."

She sat slumped against the desk, unaware of the young woman's words. The maid rambled on, but Belle was too shocked to listen, desperately trying to remember the girl's name. At last, came up with Millie but then decided it might be Molly. Stunned by the appearance of a federal agent, she was not handling this call very well.

"I be askin' that right away." The girl continued to babble. "Learned that from them telly shows, I did." Pride came through in her voice. "Seems real nice. He's a big bloke and handsome, too." The young Scottish girl gushed. "Should I be lettin' him on the property madam?"

Astonishment spread through her. *What could they want to talk with me about?* Perplexed by why the government stood outside her door, Belle could not believe the FBI was in front of the house. She had done nothing wrong. Sam's death was public humiliation and just a stupid, accidental overdose, nothing more. *Right? Oh God, please don't let it be anything more.*

"Mrs. Randall?" A soft kind voice asked Belle once more.

Flustered and confused, finally found the ability to speak. "Of course. Show him into the morning parlor and I'll be there shortly." As the shock of the government visit set in, it surprised Belle to have answered in her proper wife voice.

Hung up the phone but she sat for a moment. *The FBI.* Just staring blankly into space. *Oh, sweet baby Jesus.*

Quickly she bowed her head. "Dear Lord, please watch over me." After finishing her prayer with a respectful amen, she felt more at peace. Remembering she had survived far worse over the last ten days. Nervous to face the Feds, pushed herself off the ground and stood upright. Next, Belle bent down, picked the phone off the floor, and placed it back on the desk. Kicking the drawer closed with her foot, as best she could because refused to put her hands on it again.

Soon after, the worn-out woman made her way to investigate what unpleasant surprises the Federal Bureau was bringing to her door on this beautiful morning.

CHAPTER 4

Lennox House

"Come in sir, and please follow me." Cheerfully, an impeccable but overdressed butler greeted Agent Montgomery at the door. "Mrs. Randall will see you in the morning parlor." Even the hot tropical climate did not affect the calm ocean blue aura, radiating from deep within the man's core. It was an unusual characteristic and one the gifted agent rarely saw. The exceptional treat was unexpected, and Remy happily followed the interesting fellow through the mansion.

They traveled down several two-story high hallways until reaching a set of mahogany double doors. Much to his surprise, the hand-carved pieces of art opened into a room straight out of the Scottish Highlands. Featured inside was a six-foot-tall fireplace, along with a series of what appeared to be family portraits on the walls. He stood taking in the setting, while enjoying the man's rare chakra. The butler silently indicated for him to take a seat, then quickly began departing. After Remy declined, shutting the door on his way out and leaving the agent alone to admire the stunning furnishings.

The world traveler acknowledged this room rivaled most of the great castles of Scotland, although this was not what Remy expected from the beauty who had shined in that spotlight. Now that he was in her home, his nerves were in shambles. The centuries-old grandfather clock, keeping time in the corner, added to his stress as it loudly counted each waiting moment. Confused by his feelings, he spent a few minutes trying to match this house with that woman. His only conclusion was the various morning incidents had affected him more than he suspected.

The tired man then pulled himself together, enabling his mind to settle down to concentrate and diligently review old memories, along with the FBI files he studied before this trip. As soon as he closed his eyes, Remy remembered Sam's mother was a member of the famous Buchanan clan. This was her family's remarkable Palm Beach mansion with its own murder mystery attached to it.

Much had been written about the legendary Lennox House built for Morgan Buchanan in 1919 by the famous architect, Addison Mizner. The barrel tiled, chateau-style compound featured thirteen bedrooms in the main house, six in the annex house, and three in the guest house. It was a distinctive one-of-a-kind Scottish stone seaside estate, which boasted two stunning swimming pools, along with four premier tennis courts. All of which sat on over eight acres of prime Palm Beach real estate stretching from the intra-coastal to the Atlantic Ocean.

Yes, that explains the paintings on the wall. Remy ignored the many stunning antiques and turned his attention toward the featured works of art hanging above the magnificent mantle. *These all must be Josephine Randall's ancestors.* He walked over to the portrait of the old man himself. "Some FBI agent I am, huh, Morgan? Today, I'm off my game because I didn't remember you or the house you built." Even dead, Sam seemed to have the upper hand and kicked himself for letting Randall get the better of him. Angry at the rookie mistake and he vowed to not let it happen again but knew it would.

Internal turmoil drew him toward the windows, where turquoise water glistened in the sunlight, although, this unusual case made it impossible to appreciate the stunning scenery. Instead, closed his eyes again, focusing only on the details about the beautiful girl who had died here long ago. A death which occurred under mysterious and suspicious circumstances.

With ruby red lips and legs that went on forever, Mary Montclair was probably the most popular movie star of the 1940s. Her many motion pictures made millions for the studio. Most of the fighting men of World War II carried her pin up onto the battlefields and Hollywood loved the little spitfire beauty. The title of 'America's Sweetheart' described her perfectly, and she lived up to it in every way. Right after the war, Morgan's grandson, William Buchanan hosted a large house party at his family's Palm Beach mansion. Seventy-five of the most elite Americans including Marvelous Mary were on the invite list. Sadly, by the end of the long weekend, the beautiful actress would be dead, her neck broken by a fall down the grand staircase Remy had just passed.

After the coroner conducted an autopsy, definite signs of a struggle were found and had ruled the starlet's death a homicide. Although the staged incident appeared to look like an accident, someone had actually strangled the star. The tumble down the stairs had been an elaborate setup.

Unfortunately, after months of intense inquiries, no viable suspect could be discovered. Everyone at the party could account for their whereabouts at the time of the actress's death. However, the police along with many others, believed Will, Sam's grandfather killed her. Rumors during that period had them a hot item. The handsome war hero had a solid alibi for the time of Mary's death and could never be formally charged. The case continues to be the only unsolved murder on the island of Palm Beach to this day.

Intrigued by the family mystery, Remy looked towards Morgan Buchanan's portrait. "I wonder why so much death follows you and your clan?" Quickly brushing away those thoughts because he understood it was time to get back to the present. The weary guy ran his hand down his face while glancing toward the water and the magnificent English gardens.

Suddenly, with the bluest ocean backdrop Remy had ever seen, a vision in yellow came walking toward the house. Just like last time, his heart stopped dead in its tracks.

Midway up the path, she stopped and considered what awaited her at the main house. On the go for hours at Sam's cottage and drained to the core, she needed to collect her thoughts. Angry about facing more questions, she veered toward her house, wanting to be presentable before confronting whatever unpleasantness the FBI was bringing to the door. If Belle knew Sam as she believed she did, this meeting would not be enjoyable. Absolutely nothing during their marriage had turned out favorable for her. *So why on Earth should his death be any different?* The question made her angry at her very dead husband. Again.

She was relieved the authorities had been kind enough to wait until after the funeral before darkening her doorstep. The media coverage since his death had been an around-the-clock fiasco and it took little to recall the intense scrutiny of the press. A federal investigation at the same time would have been a breaking point. Not something the emotionally fragile lady could have handled and continue to uphold her carefully constructed facade.

If truth be told, Belle was not devastated over Sam's passing. Heartbroken and without a doubt, sorry her husband was dead, but she was not destroyed by the tragedy. Their marriage had been a sham, not the perfect love story the press reported. With the spectacle of his death over, she would no longer pretend Sam was the love of her life or that theirs had been a make-believe fairy tale partnership. Finished with the farce, she had decided to no longer live a lie.

During the days leading up to and including the funeral, she had put on a false face to fool everyone. When combined with the difficult acting and the hovering media, the misfortune had turned into a living nightmare. At times, it had been frightening trying to fight off the cameras. Every step had been a struggle, getting to and from the police station, morgue, and funeral home. Vividly recalling the two-day horror, it had been to get Sam's body out of Florida and on to DC, but nothing could compare to the enormous commotion awaiting her in Washington.

After tending to the details in Palm Beach, Belle fulfilled her duties during the three-ring circus that was Sam's memorial service. She had kept her widow mask firmly in place for the over a thousand guests that had packed the pews and balconies of the Washington National Cathedral.

By far, the longest most agonizing day of her life.

As she reflected on it now, it had seemed like a dream, but a smile formed on her face when remembering her difficult but perfect widow performance. With the obligations to her marriage complete, she would continue to perform her public responsibilities as the wife of the late Sam Randall. But Belle would no longer pretend to be racked with angst and heartache over a miserable relationship built on lies.

Her plan involved a face that would not draw too much attention but one where her true feelings were shown, when gazing at her reflection. Hopefully, one that looked like her genuine self and not a fraud. *I wonder if people will think I'm horrible. I sure hope not because I can't keep doing this much longer.* Her face searched for answers in the large entrance mirror but like this morning, no magic appeared. With a quick nod to the image, Belle seemed satisfied with her life's direction from now on. She quietly turned and walked toward the powder room.

To complement her creamy complexion, freshened her makeup with pale pink blush, then applied a quick swipe of clear gloss to moisten her rosy lips. *There, that's better.* Last, ran a wide comb through her hair and scooped most of the long, caramel-colored tresses into a twist, attaching the clip firmly back in its usual place. *Now I'm ready to face anything Sam has thrown my way.*

Happy with her reflection, opened the bathroom door and made her way out. As she passed by the large mirror again, felt compelled to stop for one final inspection: turning right, then left, while running her hands down the front of the sunshine-colored dress. When she had smoothed it back into place, Belle noticed it hung looser than it did only two weeks ago. With the troubling scrutiny complete, glanced one last time before hurrying to the main house.

Deep trouble in bright yellow had arrived and all at once, there was no air in the room. *Good Lord, please help me.* It felt like Remy had been struck by lightning.

The patio door swung outward, and the nervous woman made her way into the room. She barely took a step inside before a freight train hit Belle or at least, it sure seemed like one. Unaware of what was going on, when something rocked deep within her, another sensation she had never experienced. It seemed today would be one of those kinds of days. *Yip...pee!*

The phenomenon *scared her something awful* and she surveyed the room for clues but found nothing out of the ordinary. Funny, Granny's odd but comforting sayings like *there's nothin' to fear...if your haystacks are tied down,* always crossed Belle's mind when the unusual like this happened.

The bizarre impressions continued to bombard her, but she brushed them off and attempted to recover gracefully. Blinked to make sure she was seeing correctly but Belle was observing him all right because standing before her was the most gorgeous guy. The Adonis stretched to well over six feet, two inches tall, with broad shoulders that narrowed into a rock-hard middle. Even though she could not help it when finding herself staring into sparkling, turquoise-colored eyes that were framed by almost blue-black hair. After a closer look, she realized the silky strands were badly in need of a trim. The oppressive Florida humidity had curled them around his starched polo collar.

So, this was the FBI agent the maid had been gushing over. A silly grin appeared on her face because the helpless fellow seemed just as thunderstruck. This discovery aided in snapping Belle out of the trance she seemed to be under. *Goodness gracious.* Unable to stop a low giggle from slipping out. *It's not proper to be thinking such thoughts, especially so soon after my husband's funeral.* Proper or not, it did not stop her from considering them all the same. It also did not stop the blush from reddening her cheeks.

After a moment or two, remembered who she was and what needed to be done. "Hello, I'm Belle." Her performance was underway and the face she had so skillfully worn for the last ten days was back in place.

Arm held out; she walked tentatively toward the good-looking guy. "How can I help you today?" Her alabaster hand shook, and Belle prayed he would not notice.

Caught in her spell, the innocent question broke Remy's dazed state. His mind stumbled to cover up his open-mouth stare, with a fake cough but gathered from her facial expression it was of no use. Remy was a goner and knew it but needed to start acting like a professional.

Finally, he found the strength to snap out of whatever had overcome them both and put his tough guy face into place.

Remembering he was here for work, Remy pulled out his FBI badge from the left-hand pocket of his dark khaki pants. After flashing it for her review, quietly slipped it away. "Mrs. Randall, or should I call you Dr. Randall?" Stepped forward, tenderly capturing her small hand in his. "I'm Special Agent Remington Montgomery with the FBI."

After shaking it, he held onto her soft skin, a little longer than suitable. "I'd like to ask you a few questions about your late husband. That is, if you don't mind." Not offering any condolences or apologies for her loss because Remy refused to lie to this woman. It staggered him just touching her because doing so brought that night back with such color and clarity. Once more, reminding Remy of the impact she continued to wield over him. This seemed to be the only woman he could not get out of his head.

Regrettably, now was not the time or place for such speculation and reluctantly, he let go of her hand. His head buzzed with different sensations, forcing Remy to focus his mind and to concentrate on the job.

"Of course, Mr. Montgomery, please have a seat. Would you like coffee?" Belle made her way over to the desk, because wanted to put distance between herself and the government guy. "I will have some sent over, if you would like to join me."

It took significant effort to make it to the rolltop. After he touched her, walking across the room felt like each step Belle took was on big, white fluffy clouds. She found herself surprised by the powerful pull just being in his company. Her fingers gripped the desk's edge to steady herself, because she had never run into anyone who had this kind of effect on her before. Certainly, no one had ever done so, in such a positive way.

Unfortunately, there had been a few folks who had an adverse effect on her. They were a common occurrence as Belle's patients were special, having been through horrendous experiences. When violent incidents 'bled' through in a session, it was at those times the trauma psychiatrist would suffer the full brutal effect of their tragedies.

This unusual man was projecting pure and positive sensations at her inner essence. It was a glorious feeling, and she took a minute to just enjoy this amazing feeling.

While appreciating his overwhelming presence and awaiting his response to coffee, the perceptive doctor pulled herself together and studied this person. *Who was this man? More importantly, why does he affect me so?* Maybe the strange reaction was due to the insanity she had experienced lately and was just run down. Subconsciously, Belle knew these white lies were what she always whispered to herself and normally they calmed her scientific mind. But not today

Stunned to find the unusual spell his emotions were casting, sent her talents into overdrive. Only Mother Nature would calm her in this state, Belle turned toward the windows to draw strength from the ocean. Eager to convince herself there were no unusual things going on between them, shaking her head to clear it. *More like worn out, that's what this must be.* Still not buying any of her clever conclusions.

Over her shoulder came the blue-eyed devil's reply because this impish description was the only way Belle could picture him. "I'd love coffee, if it's not too much trouble, Dr. Randall and please call me Remy."

His response interrupted her X-rated thoughts, forcing Belle back into her grieving widow role. *An incredibly desirable devil.* Because with him in the room, no rational thoughts were coming to mind. Plus, those deliberations were taking a mighty naughty turn and stunned her in their intensity. After taking the phone in hand, she figured out a way to dial the kitchen and requested a tray. Then, hung up the receiver and fussed with several items on the desk until the coffee arrived. The girl, who had phoned her earlier, slipped into the room, set up the service and exited quietly. Once more, they found themselves alone.

The quiet time gave Belle the opportunity to wonder if he too felt this thing bouncing between them. At last, she left the safety of the desk. "How would you like your coffee, Mr. Montgomery?" Walking back to the sofa, she carefully sat and poured them both a cup. "It's Dr. Brooks, not Randall but please just call me Belle." All the while trying to contain her nerves.

"Double cream with two sugars would be fine. Thank you, Belle." Flashed his standard nice guy smile as Remy studied her. "I assume it's short for Campbell?" Silently, thanked his lucky stars that his heart had finally slowed, even his breathing had returned to normal. He watched as across from him the lovely lady perfectly added cream and sugar to his coffee. An art, he greatly admired, as a cup made of the finest bone china was passed to him.

"Yes, it's from my mother's family name Campbell-Bannerman. My great-grandfather was the first Scottish prime minister of Great Britain in nineteen oh five." Unsure why, within three minutes of meeting this man, Belle was babbling her family history.

"Do you add the E onto your nickname?" Casually inquiring to keep it light but it had been the first item Remy discovered about her.

Unable to hear his question, because while he spoke, the following statement kept repeating itself inside her head. *What in the world has gotten into me today?* Looked up from her drink and was surprised to find the agent awaiting a response. "I'm so sorry. It's been a difficult couple of days." Caught talking to herself, instead of listening to him, as embarrassment spread across her beautiful face. "Could you please repeat the question?" Powerless to focus properly, Belle was unsure of what was taking place. Something strange seemed to be occurring between the two of them because she had never felt like this in her life. The interesting experience made her eager to talk with Granny.

"Of course, please let me add, how sorry I am for all you've endured since Sam's passing." Remy was not sorry about Randall dying, only unhappy about the public humiliation she suffered and Belle's constant hounding by the press. "I'm not sure, if you knew I grew up with Sam." Uncertain about her awareness of their shared past, yet, unable to stop himself from reflecting internally about her. *She still glowed those beautiful multi-colors.* They appeared to be touched by something like sadness but not quite. *Huh, I wonder what that's all about.* For right now Remy continued to ignore his humming intuitions, as she calmly sat across from him.

"No, I didn't. He never mentioned you." She confessed softly while trying to understand this thing between her and this umm…umm, dirty dancing slash sexy George Clooney kinda man. "How did you know one another?" While internally she screamed. *Lord…please forgive me. What is wrong with me and does this man think I'm an idiot?* Closed her eyes to bring inner calm and mentally sinking deep within herself. *'Clear everything out of ye' mind's path.'* In her head, the sound of Granny's peaceful voice filled Belle with some much-needed tranquility. Her breathing slowed within seconds.

Those gemlike green eyes snapped open in time to hear. "For most of our lives, Sam and I went to prep school together. We were good pals, well really more like competitive archrivals until almost the end of high school. Then, um, well, um, you know how it is."

Belle watched as he fiddled with his delicate coffee cup.

"Things just kinda happened and we ended up going in different directions. Well, we, um graduated and that was that."

The FBI guy looked incredibly uncomfortable with his fabricated childhood statement. The pings rebounding inside Belle signaled there was lots more to this interesting tale. Clearly, Sam's good-looking friend did not intend to go into details. Unfortunately, his fictitious story would have to wait because she just wanted this interrogation to be over quickly. *This man does things to me he shouldn't.*

Her doctor *'feelers'* as Granny would call them, were going straight through the roof, while her gift kept prodding her to pursue Remy's tale. Positive, that was something she had no intention of doing. Although, the strange intuition made her wonder what had put such a look on his perfect face. The subject was almost too irresistible to drop but it surprised Belle to discover she also would love the opportunity to explore this further. *Huh, funny how she hoped he would need more time.* It seemed her wicked brain would enjoy getting closer to this sinful man. *Now, where did that thought come from?* Sneaked a peek to see if the blue-eyed devil knew what she was thinking. Blushing even though he could not possibly hear her thoughts.

To get his sensible self under control again, Remy slowly sipped his coffee. Perplexed by his burning desire to tell this woman about Jennifer, he was certain it would be a terrible idea to allow Dr. Brooks into his life.

When Belle was not looking, he stole one last glance, then, reluctantly pulled his notebook out of his pocket and went to work. Back on track and determined to complete his job, Agent Montgomery took his time asking her a list of questions of both people and places that involved Randall, carefully covering every item he had collected on Sam.

All the while, unable to simmer his raging emotions.

CHAPTER 5

Hidden Beneath

Approximately forty-five minutes later, Remy stood up, stretched his large frame and stuck out his hand. "Belle, I appreciate you answering my questions. I believe I've covered everything on my list, so thank you for your patience." The big man looked rather shy, which was a situation he rarely found himself in. "There is one last request."

To give her some space and to settle down his turbulent feelings towards this extraordinary woman, the nervous agent walked to the other side of the room. "If you wouldn't mind, I'd like to look around Sam's office." Not wanting his gifts to bully her into granting him access. "I promise not to remove anything without your permission. There's a possibility I might uncover information, which could help with my investigation."

Desperate for her to agree, as he paced the floor, waiting for her to answer because Remy did not have a warrant and knew one would be impossible to obtain. "No item is too small. It's possible you might not know its importance. I just want to take a peek where he spent most of his time. To get a feel for a guy, I haven't seen or heard from in a long time." Practically holding his breath, impatient for her reply.

It was an unusual demand but after their talk, found herself remarkably comfortable with him. "I've packed most of Sam's things." Deciding it could not hurt if Remy looked around even though it would mean extending this upsetting interview. "I suppose." Softly replying, while never giving away her delight at spending extra time with this intriguing man. "I see no harm granting you access."

Suddenly, the impact of the FBI visit hit her. "Exactly what are you looking for?" Timid about the question, but convinced Sam must have been in the wrong place at the wrong time. "If you don't mind my asking?" The agent's forthcoming answer made her a little anxious. Uncertain if Belle really wanted to know what her husband had been up to in the last days of his life. Whatever the reason, it could not have been good. Sam had been avoiding her since the holidays, which meant he was screwing something up one side and down another.

On the other hand, an actual federal investigation put a whole new spin on his outrageous escapades. Embarrassed by her husband's outlandish exploits because Belle knew it involved something stupid or childish. When it came to her famous spouse, the more adventurous or dangerous the stunt, the better. *If it was fast and an adrenaline rush, then first to try it? Mr. Big Shot Sam Randall. If you wanted to sky dive out of an airplane or drive a prototype car at the speed of sound. Well then, by gosh, Sam was your man.* It should not surprise her the FBI had come calling.

After a few minutes thinking about his antics, it occurred to her it should not have taken them this long. Although, Belle had a hard time wrapping her head around the fact he could have done anything unlawful. *Jumping from a helicopter to snow ski down a strictly off-limits mountain top. Absolutely. But not something really illegal.* Sam had been too busy getting laid, to be bothered by much else.

Off to the side, Remy stood admiring this unique individual who was once bathed in that brilliant limelight. Now, covered in sadness and shrouded with shame, Dr. Belle Brooks still radiated elegance. Something about this woman literally glowed and it was not just her brilliant aura. He opted to be honest without putting her in danger, along with unwillingly causing her more pain.

Once again, Remy found himself drawn to the wall of windows. "This is some view you have here." Nodded his head toward the picture postcard outside. After pulling in a deep cleansing breath, began the unpleasant task of explaining Sam's illegal activities. "I'm sorry to be the one to tell you but I believe your husband was involved with some very bad folks."

His statement was dripping with venom, toward his childhood rival but it was the truth, even if he had omitted most of the details. "These people are among the worst on the planet. I'm here today to look for any evidence to back up what I've already uncovered regarding the late great Sam Randall." Hopefully she would draw her own conclusions because Remy did not want to hurt Belle.

Unprepared for his scandalous announcement or his obvious hatred of Sam, she sank back down onto the couch in slow motion. "What?" His accusations left Belle speechless. The good wife in her did not want to believe him. Try as she might to contradict Remy's words but several bad memories stormed through her mind. Understood, he was telling the truth about Sam's dirty deeds and decided that her husband was not someone she had known at all.

Fascinated with her reserves, Remy studied her as she took in his accusations and struggled with his allegations. Belle's aura still shined brilliant iridescent colors but now it glowed cloudier and gray. That was not unusual after his startling statement, especially factoring in the recent loss of her husband. Wished he could help but she needed to work this through by herself, something he understood firsthand. He wanted to spare her the ugly details of Sam's crimes, and hoped no more heartache would visit Belle Brooks' door. Again, reprimanding himself because refused to think of her as Randall's.

Out of the corner of his eye, Remy spotted her collecting that proud confidence, marveling at this remarkable woman. He enjoyed watching, as Belle rose off the sofa and gathered herself together with a cool reserved passion, then stood as tall as her small frame allowed. The surprised agent continued staring, as she pulled her poise into line and straightened her back erect. The sight was something beyond extraordinary, watching as she turned toward the ocean, with her head held high and her dignity firmly in place.

After making her way to the French doors, opening them wide to the crystal blue ocean waters. Appearing to be in a trance, Belle still displayed proper manners but seemed completely unaffected by the stunning surroundings. After a brief pause, to pull herself together internally, the perfect hostess politely led the way to Sam's private territory. All the while those aura colors swirled around her, spinning faster than before but she seemed oblivious to the surrounding chaos.

The two of them walked past a spectacular infinity pool, then continued around another gorgeous house with its own large walled outdoor area. Four tennis courts came next. Until finally, among the lush tropical landscape, a perfect match to both the main and smaller home appeared. The bungalow backed up to the adjacent property near the far west wall of the estate. Ever cautious, Remy took a few minutes to scan the perimeter before joining Belle inside.

Still in disbelief by what she heard at the main house; the dazed woman stood to the far side of the room, attempting to come to terms with Remy's revelations.

Sam was only capable of thinking of himself. Her husband seemed too self-absorbed to be mixed up with anything as far-fetched as this wild tale but her *'feelers'* confirmed, the government guy spoke sincerely. Also, those same instincts signaled there was much more to this story. Her only choice was to get to the bottom of it because Belle wanted to learn the whole truth about her famous late husband.

With countless boxes stacked along most of the walls, the intense investigator spent the first few moments going from one to the next. He was absorbing Sam's personal space because as Remy understood it, this was where pretty boy Randall had spent much of his time. Strange, he had not spent it in the Washington, DC house Belle Brooks had lived in since birth. *But why?* The century's old brownstone was where she did her unusual work and still lived much of the time.

His biggest enemy had lived most of his marriage here, in this quaint guest cottage and not in the nation's capital. Not even in the large matching second house they had just walked past, which made no sense to Remy. *Why would he sleep with hookers and bimbos when he had this exquisite individual right next door?* Stole another glance at the woman across the room. *According to every account, she had loved him and been faithful during their entire relationship.*

For the time being, Remy needed to push Belle aside, concentrate only on Sam, along with whatever evidence he'd collected. The job was all that mattered, and he quietly reminded his libido of that fact. Soon, he prayed both of his heads would be back on track and under control. *Another impossible feat.*

The tense man focused and although he had not seen his enemy for a long time, Remy had known him well. Maybe too well, as things were not adding up in this bizarre case. None of the information he had uncovered was even remotely like the man who shared most of his childhood memories. Or the Tony Stark, whiz-kid, slash entrepreneur who the jerk had presented to the world for the last ten years.

Frustrated to be beaten by Sam again, he vowed to find out what the hell was going on. Also, desperate to discover how Belle Brooks fit into this whole mess because Remy hoped for his own sake, she did not. He badly wanted to go back to that minute in the spotlight and ask her out on a date, long before Randall ever became involved.

After waiting patiently for over ten minutes, the quiet doctor's politeness had come to an end. The FBI guy had forgotten all about her because from the look in his eyes, he seemed to be a million miles away. Hoping to get some answers, Belle cleared her throat. "Hum um." Then shot him one of her grandmother's famous stares, determined to understand Sam's crimes.

Remy caught her deadly glare. "I'm sorry, please forgive me. I was just remembering old times with Sam." A hint of blush touched his cheeks.

Unable to find his center Remy continued to take in the room, moving around in a slow methodical grid. He picked items out of the many boxes, then set them in the same place as before. This exercise of tuning everything out but the suspect helped the detective get a good sense of someone. The thorough investigator enjoyed spending quality time with people's personal things, while drawing solid helpful deductions from the suspect's possessions.

After a few minutes of perusing, it seemed Sam had not really changed in all these years. This conclusion made Remy sad because it meant the fool had never grown up. It did not surprise him, Randall appeared to still be the spoiled rich kid. *Forever doing, whatever he damn well pleased.* "Dr. Brooks, when you packed up the boxes, did you find anything out of place? Anything unusual?" Casually, he inquired over his shoulder to pull himself together and hide his erupting emotions.

"Well, I realized this morning Sam's laptop is missing. It's not among his things the police returned from the boat." Her voice sounded tiny, and Remy looked up in time to see her cheeks turn a bright red, confused by her obvious embarrassment. "It's not here in his office so I have no idea where else it might be." Belle nervously stared toward the mortifying access door, which led to Sam's kinky extracurricular activities. "I suppose it might be at the house in DC, but I doubt it."

Anxious about the lost computer, but she was really worried the agent would ask to see the rest of the house and discover Sam's humiliating collection. The nice guy seem to presume her shame stemmed from his embarrassing death. Remy appeared clueless regarding her husband's secret fetish and Belle would like to keep it that way. Finally, breathing a sigh of relief when the government man moved away at long last.

Unaware of the real reason for her discomfort, Remy gave her some space, quite familiar with death's shameful feelings. She watched in fascination, as he continued poking through Sam's things, checking each box thoroughly.

Once finished, the agent was convinced he had missed something important. Making Remy adopt a laser-type focus to find it. He wandered back over to the desk, spotting something near the floor. Instantly, the discovery switched him into cop mode.

He reached down and yanked open the bottom drawer. After finding the secret folder Remy waved it in the air, with his left eyebrow arched toward the heavens. "What's this???"

His harsh tone confused Belle. "I honestly don't know." But was delighted because they were talking about something that was not Sam's secret bedroom activities. "I found it right before you arrived."

Tentatively, she moved around to the back of the desk and discovered herself standing right next to him. Nervous about being so close to Remy, in such a small space, as a shiver of something wonderfully strange went through Belle.

Quickly, remembering her responsibilities and proceeding with her explanation but still upset about touching the troubling piece of furniture. "The folder was hidden in here." Whipping out the bottom drawer a little too fast, it landed hard onto her foot, making Belle see stars. "Jiminy Crickets!" The lady-like curse slipped out, but quickly composed herself. The solid wood drawer was heavy, and she stumbled when sitting it on top of the desk. He tried to help but Belle would have none of it.

Next, she showed Remy how the bottom slid out if you worked it a certain way.

Fascinated, he leaned closer to study the delicate workmanship. "How did you figure this out?" Very interested in the answer because he was astounded she had found the file. After careful review, deduced a highly trained professional would have had a difficult time finding something so painstakingly hidden.

"I don't know." Crossed both arms over her chest, taking a step back. "Sometimes I have a way with things." Her voice, becoming even quieter. "With things and sometimes with people." It was a tough admission, Belle stole a glance to gauge his reaction, yet none came.

To her surprise, the unusual guy continued to basically ignore her. He was too busy to be bothered with anything other than the hidden compartment. Slightly relieved, Belle continued. "When I ran my hand over the drawer, I realized there was something underneath and moved my fingers around until I found the latch to unlock it."

Finished with her difficult confession, the shy lady looked up at Remy, eager to hear his response to her unusual declaration. Shocked, she continued to share so much of her life with this stranger. Uncomfortable with the sharing, Belle moved back over to the other side of the desk, far away from the too-gorgeous-for-his-own-good guy.

As for him, Remy did not understand this complex woman because she had turned out to be an interesting mystery and not at all what he expected. Without the ability to read her colors, the pretty lady seemed next to impossible to figure out.

To concentrate, he turned his back and for the thousandth time that day, attempted to collect himself. Ultimately, decided to ignore his humming instincts, even though they screamed at him there was a lot more to this alluring specimen. Instead, Remy focused on the work. *Coward.* Chastising himself because of his fears.

Watching his internal struggle made her appreciate him even more. It was strange because she understood how Remy felt but hoped it was not written all over her face like it was on his. Instead, it would be better to stand over here to try to figure out whatever mischief her late husband had gotten himself into.

Back to concentrating on Sam, Remy opened the previously hidden folder and discovered articles in every major newspaper from around the world. The articles appear to give detailed reports on significant events over the last sixty years. Everything from the landing on the moon to the JFK assassination. The US embassy bombing in Beirut and Margaret Thatcher's landslide election win. Even the famous American Legion convention, which had killed attendees with the unusual Legionnaires' disease, was among the many clippings. Close to two hundred articles were in the folder. Some positive, some negative. Mixed in, were a few minor items, such as a new patent awaiting approval that fights Alzheimer's. Financial, manufacturing and even media articles were also part of the folder.

Over the next ten minutes, Remy's attention on Belle vanished, as he sat creating piles of the different articles. But for the life of him, could not figure out their mutual significance. "This makes little sense." His habit of talking to himself went on. "They have nothing in common." He disregarded everything but the work; meticulously sorting the clippings as best he could, all the while combing his hands through his hair repeatedly.

The stacks grew as Belle scrutinized his unusual lifeforce. She did not want to disturb him but could not stop the squeak that burst out. "What?" By the looks of things, the intense guy had no idea the strange clippings continued to distress her and chuckled because he seemed unaware of her outburst. To Remy, nothing else existed except the newspaper articles in front of him.

What an interesting man. Amazed at his powerful energy, she sat down to enjoy the view of him. Just then, the awful sensation she had experienced earlier when handling the cursed folder came roaring back, causing goose bumps to break out on her skin. It was the same evil impression that had happened after touching the folder, just before the FBI showed up and ruined breakfast. *Huh, I have to admit.* A short snicker escaped Belle's pink lips. *When I woke up this morning, I didn't see that one coming.*

Desperate to find anything to make light of the seriousness of the situation, she struggled to keep calm. Unwilling to help with the odd folder, much less, touch any of those pieces of newsprint or explain it to the Federal Bureau of Investigation. This would require Belle to explain why she did not want to handle the clippings and she did not want to do that. It was something the scientist had a hard time believing herself and knew the government official would not either.

Closed her eyes, while wrestling to get her feelings under restraint. This man unnerved her, and she was experiencing several unfamiliar emotions. Plus, there was a terrible something going on deep inside. To gather her wits, stood still. Instantly thought to herself, how surprised she was to have been running off at the mouth to this unusual man. Stunned to have shared family things and all kinds of personal stuff Belle told no one. Ever.

Snuck a glance at Remy. *What makes him so special?* Boy oh boy, this was without a doubt not your typical day. *Why was he causing her to act so irrationally?*

The doctor never told Sam about her *'gift'* as Granny called it. Her *'curse'* as Belle thought of it most of the time, unless it helped with her patients, then it was a gift from God. Her grandmother had taught her since birth about her special talents, which enabled the caring MD to help her clients with their unique type of pain. *'Right as rain.'*

Another of Granny's uplifting sayings popped into her head. The positive feelings washed over her when her spirit most needed the inspiration.

Belle's instincts screamed at her to stay away from the desk. The folder held nothing but corrupt impressions and personal heartache. Those wicked sensations were building inside again, and they scared her something terrible.

Another item she did not want to explain to the agent.

CHAPTER 6

Election Connection

The agent's muffled voice suddenly came from somewhere behind the desk. "What were you doing hiding under here?" It was impossible to see the good-looking guy, but she sure could feel him. Even from the other side of the office, Belle sensed his irritation because oozing from every part of him was his frustration. Although difficult to hear, Remy's strong internal impressions were loudly traveling throughout the room.

It was unnecessary for him to speak, in order to comprehend how much turmoil he was experiencing. What an opportunity she was getting to explore his hidden talents, especially while the unusual man was in this strange state of chaos. The curious doctor would love the opportunity to investigate the extraordinary sensations pulsating from him. Unfortunately, Remy only seemed to amplify her own unique skills causing her much mayhem. For that reason, unraveling his remarkable ones were out of the question currently.

His head darted back up without warning, but the preoccupied man continued to ignore Belle. "These articles are important but how?" His concentration was focused exclusively on the stacks of newspaper clippings. "How are you connected?" Now and then, Remy stopped to examine one in particular. "Because you sure as hell are all related somehow."

It was adorable when he talked aloud to no one. Watched fascinated, as he acted uncaring toward her because to him, Belle was not even alive. "Sam wouldn't put these all together for no reason." Nothing else mattered to Remy. Nothing except the evidence. After observing him for some time, it dawned on Belle she was drawing closer to this strange man. A smile appeared on her face at the sudden kinship when he spoke aloud to only himself. Lately, she had plenty of experience with that peculiar trait.

Unfortunately, while he had been studying the data, the strange vibrations inside had gotten stronger, causing her alarm. This was something that rarely happened to the cool as a cucumber physician and these building sensations troubled her. The *'feelers'* were indicating there was little time before her insides literally exploded.

Remy continued to stare at the clippings while moving his fingers in a constant, repetitive motion. "What are these for?"

The engrossed guy did not expect a reply, although Belle gave one anyway. A small voice, which did not want attention, called out from the other side of the room. "I, um…do not know what they are." Fear of the pending eruption was the only reason Belle had disturbed his sleuthing.

Once again was startled to hear someone answer one of his thinkin' questions, because Remy had forgotten she was even present. While he was reviewing the hidden articles, Belle had moved to the opposite side of the office, as far from him as possible. Now those lovely green eyes looked mighty fearful, and Remy could not figure out why.

Nothing seemed to be as it should today and took a few minutes to discover what was going on. Positive his biggest problem was the beauty queen on the opposite side of the room. She was a major distraction, with a capital D. *Sweet Lord, I'm totally clueless about what's happening here.* The closeness to her must be causing him to lose focus.

Frustrated by the turmoil brewing inside and unable to get a firm grip on his instincts, Remy slowly sunk down in the chair. The confused man struggled to get his bearings and center himself. He took a deep breath and gathered some much-needed calm before staring directly at Belle. With a wave of his hand toward the black leather chair, Remy encouraged the anxious lady to take a seat.

When she did not move, gently approached the subject that they needed to discuss. Using his smoothest voice, Remy pointed to the thick piles of clippings. "Can you come over here for a few minutes please? Let's see, if the two of us, can figure these out." The different expressions that crossed over her face were fascinating, but sad to watch.

"Together." This last word, he spoke with the hopes she would not bolt out the door because it appeared she intended to do exactly that. A few long minutes later, Remy was relieved when she took a step forward. *I wonder what has her so spooked.* Puzzled by her obvious fear, he did not understand why Belle looked terrified.

When she found her voice, it came out barely above a whisper. "I will peek at them but I'm not sure how I can help." Belle agreed to do just that; take a quick glance, then move back to the other side of the room. Far, far away from those articles.

Gingerly, took another step, treading closer to the desk. With that step, the sensation inside her became an actual sound. A humming noise that resonated deep within. With each stride, the uproar became increasingly prominent inside her head.

She stopped and remembered her grandmother's golden rule of perceiving phenomena with all six senses, then slowed her breathing, pulling herself together. The strange reverberations were indescribable, and the peculiar stirrings rocked her soul.

Frantic to find the culprit and desperate to learn what might have caused such a commotion, Belle focused on the frequency. Once done, its location was impossible to miss. It was resonating from an article on the desk, just sitting there, close to the top of one of the piles.

The haunting sound called to something deep in her core. Its lure forced her forward. With the offense now discovered, peeked at the federal investigator but he was unaware of the unusual activity. In fact, the man was so preoccupied with the folder, Remy did not even know she was in the room.

Meanwhile, the curious fellow continued to ignore everything around him except for the evidence and plucked a recent article from one of the many piles. Dated February twenty-seventh, 2011, it described the overwhelming defeat of the popular conservative party of Ireland. "What do you know about the Irish political machine called Dochloite Laoch?" At last, Remy paid attention to her but only because he needed something. The strange sound continued to resonate in her head, as she took another step closer to the desk.

It seemed impossible to take her eyes off the piles of articles that she found both frightening and compelling. When she looked up again, Belle discovered the big brooding man awaiting an answer. His question required her to think an extra moment because the strange vibration continued to fog her memory. "Not very much." The noise forced her to concentrate, making her voice come out strained. "Other than they recently delivered the worst election rout of a sitting government in the history of Ireland." With a shiver, recalling Sam's violent reaction to the change in party power.

Her soft voice brought him back from deep contemplation. Lifted his gaze to meet hers, but with a guilty look, because once again, forgetting about Belle. A bad habit of his when concentrating on evidence but perceived his question had been unexpected. Noticed that by asking it, the terror seemed to have faded from her face, making Remy feel better. The sensation was swift, because found himself staring into her penetrating eyes again. The amazing pull he experienced from them was shockingly strong.

Unsure about the spellbound feelings coming from his gaze, she took a few minutes before answering his question. "I believe their name derives from the famous Invincible Celtic Warriors of Legend." Desperate to remember Sam's rantings about them. "I understand they beat the ruling party that had run the country for much of current history but that's roughly all I recall. Why do you ask?" The buried article creating the unusual noise continued to make her afraid. If she wanted answers regarding her criminal husband, along with these strange occurrences, Belle needed to put the fear aside and get herself grounded. If not, she would never figure out what was transpiring in her life.

Earlier, when they first entered the cottage, she had studied Sam's childhood friend. The psychiatrist in her figured out the handsome devil had not been completely honest. Without a doubt he was withholding something from Belle, and it was big.

Amusement spread through her because she also understood Remy suspected her of hiding something too. *I wonder what he thinks I'm holding back.* Aware of her secret but she was quite sure it was not what Remy assumed. *Not at all.* Belle doubted the government guy was ready for her special kind of surprise, as a chuckle slipped out at that thought.

"Have you or Sam visited Ireland recently?" Remy asked with an innocence in his voice, still trying to do his job; too preoccupied with the case and his jumbled-up emotions to pay much attention to her.

Without warning, her humor disappeared and whatever had been building inside her came rushing out as fury, erupting toward this man and his simple question. Unable to prevent it, Belle was powerless from it exploding into the conversation. Forgotten were the humming article, and her building fear, as she stormed the desk. "I'm sick and tired of these games." Her face flaming red, while slamming her fists onto the top of it. "Exactly what is going on, Mr. FBI Agent???" A furious Dr. Brooks growled, not knowing how to stop this rage from gushing out of her.

"Just what do you want and what was Sam involved in? We were in Ireland in November! He was there again in January and February!!" The bright flush continued down her neck, as she pointed a perfect fingernail toward Remy's nose. "For that matter, he spent many days and weeks in Europe on business!"

Angrier than Belle had ever been, she was unable to keep from bellowing. "You work for the F.B.I.! You're aware of our every move!! Where we are and where we've been!! Don't deny it!!!" Inches from his face, Belle used her index finger to make every point. "Quit playing games and start talking. NOW!!!"

Caught completely off-guard, Remy sat back in the chair, stunned by her sudden frenzy. Because of the sheer intensity of her emotions, he required a few extra minutes to pull himself together. To lighten up the mood, the agent put on his best wickedly fetching smile, drawing deep on his charming talents. "Okay, okay, I'm sorry. Please forgive me.

Yes, I have documentation you went to Ireland in the fall, but I wanted to see if you would tell me. Since you flew by private jet."

Perplexed by his statement, Belle was still tentative regarding his motives. "Well naturally I'd tell you. Why wouldn't I?"

"You wouldn't, if you had something to hide." This was the only response the almost guilty looking man could give.

"But of course!" Sarcastically sassing back at him because that answer had never occurred to her. Raised properly, Belle was not capable of thinking such thoughts, although suspected Remy needed to do so in his line of work.

By this point, her consuming rage had subsided and was being replaced by disbelief and deep sadness. "What does the election in Ireland have to do with Sam's death?" Still not backing down, Belle continued to chase the perplexing issue.

How could he blame her for not giving up? Carefully, he studied the lovely's face to determine which way to proceed, because if anyone understood about not letting go, it was Remy. This woman had earned his respect and warranted the honest facts. "I didn't come here today to bring more misery to your doorstep." Paced the floor, trying to decide what to tell her and what not. "Because you've had enough to last a lifetime."

Inhaling the deepest breath, Remy decided to speak from his heart. "Truthfully, I think you deserve to know what your husband has been up to for the last two years." Spun around to gauge her reaction. "There is evidence which links Sam to a group of people. Who among other things, are known international drug and arms dealers."

As he glanced over, found Belle sinking into one of the wingback chairs, facing the big mahogany desk. It surprised him the little pixie was not hysterical, a state most people become when told such a declaration about a loved one. They either defended them or not but were usually adamant about their opinions. *But not Belle.*

At any moment, Dr. Campbell Brooks looked like she would shatter into a million pieces.

"This is just a nightmare. So much has happened." She just sat there, unable to move. "This must all be a bad dream because it can't be real." Belle imagined she might even faint.

"I'm sorry to have to tell you, but this is definitely happening, sugah." Out of the fog came a compassionate response to her thoughts. "Unfortunately, everything I've told you today is very real." Blinking to focus her eyes, the sound of a man's gentle voice was the first clue, this was not some bad dream. At last, Belle picked her head up and stared directly into those almost turquoise blue ones.

That was when reality hit.

Her vision cleared and found herself in Sam's office being questioned by the FBI. *Bless my heart.* This time the words brushed like butterfly wings across her mind, and she needed several minutes to pull herself together.

Confused by his staggering emotions toward this woman, Remy turned to what worked best for him. Instantly resorting to FBI mode, he pronounced every word clearly and with authority. "Unfortunately, I understand your shock Dr. Brooks, but it seems Sam was involved in multiple criminal activities. Drugs, weapons, money laundering and several illegal acts in Ireland involving government corruption and possible election tampering are some of the crimes your late husband appears to have committed."

Continued speaking in his official voice because he needed to get through to the dazed woman. "It's only a matter of time before indictments are issued. I'm here today because the FBI is trying to determine if Sam acted alone or if others were involved." He hoped to bring her back into the conversation by using Belle's formal title but so far, it had failed. Unfortunately, with one look, Remy understood the panic building within the tiny lady was coming to a boil.

This simply could not be happening. Whirled through the shocked widow's mind, unable to fathom how much more she could handle. "So, you're saying when we went to Ireland last year, Sam conducted illicit business?" Worried because her stress level had escalated beyond anything she had ever experienced before.

To defuse the situation, he returned to the desk chair because it brought him down to her eye level, but Remy dreaded giving his answer. He hated himself but especially Sam, for putting him in this position. With eyes cast downward, the kind agent delivered his conclusion gently, although, he still felt guilty when confirming Sam's criminal activities. Reluctantly, Remy provided her with the only honest response. "Yes, in all likelihood."

His touching answer was the last straw. Unable to hold back any longer, the tears silently flowed down Belle's pale rose-colored cheeks.

Fascinated with this woman who took everything he said and just sat there, softly crying, while barely making a sound. Astonished, someone could be so strong, yet so incredibly tender and soft. Belle Brooks was an amazing woman and Sam Randall, sure as hell, had not deserved this incredible human being.

The gentleman in him rebelled but if anyone merited the truth it was this extraordinary person, although, he had never felt more like a heel. Also, pissed about having to be the one to share the horrible things her jerk of a husband had done during their marriage. He would set those feelings aside because she expected honesty, so he would give her that courtesy. Though, for now he would just let Belle cry without interruption.

Eventually, Remy walked around the desk to join her on the arm of the chair, softly stating his theory. "I don't know every crime he's committed or when Sam did his illegal business. We've connected him with three major arms associates, along with two officials in the national election office in Ireland."

"He's in deep but I not sure how deep or how far up the political chain it goes." Obligated to report the transgressions of the great Sam Randall, his hands rubbed her shoulders to provide soothing gentleness and sending much needed relief through his special touch. "Given his family's business and influence makes catching who's involved even more dangerous." Just speaking about Sam's crimes out loud made Remy nervous. "As of today, I could not determine any involvement by Buchanan Industries. None of any kind or of their subsidiaries but I need to be sure." Out of habit, he looked around to check the perimeter.

The edginess pouring from Remy pulled Belle out of her misery, bringing her back to the present. Gone was the hopelessness of Sam's capers, replacing it was the internal fear from before. "Why is the FBI involved with Irish elections?" Once more, the menacing clamor loudly radiated from a pile on the desk. "Aren't you only responsible for domestic incidents?"

The pretty doctor had asked the question he had been waiting for the entire meeting. "Yes, Dr. Brooks, the majority of the cases the FBI work on originate in the United States." Got up from the chair and he paced the floor. "The drugs and possible money laundering could make it part of our jurisdiction." The pause Remy took was quite lengthy, debating whether to tell Belle the whole story.

At last, decided she deserved to know about Sam's illicit activities and continued with his account. "I went to school with a huge Irish chap that's now a bigshot at Interpol. He's collected some interesting information over the last few months. Information that seems to point toward a real threat to the United States election system."

Hesitated but he quickly pushed forward. "There's a possibility, someone has tampered with the recent Irish election. I also have reason to believe, there are plans to fix the upcoming US presidential election too." Chills ran up Remy's long spine because had only uttered those words to two individuals in the world. The director of the FBI and now, Dr. Belle Brooks.

He hoped like hell it was not true and he was wrong, but his gut kept telling him he was not. Also, his instincts screamed Sam only played a small part in this grand scheme. A much larger plot with multiple high-level participants was in play here, hidden from everything and everyone.

Which left no one else except Remy to stop them before it was too late.

CHAPTER 7

Two of a Kind

The shaken woman sat stock still, her face struck ashen by his shocking statement. For a long time, she did not move while contemplating his scandalous confession. Eventually, lifted her eyes to meet Remy's and sensed this man had told her something few were privy to.

This thought scared Belle to death.

After staring into those penetrating blue eyes, found herself filled with an unexpected boost of nerves from their intensity. Prompting Belle to do something she rarely does.

Trust someone but unfortunately Sam's treachery still lingered.

To soothe her soul, began her calming exercises because desperately needed the inner peace of Granny's lessons to properly perform her bizarre demonstration. Her upcoming magical display filled Belle with concern about Remy's reaction to her strange display of talent.

The insightful part of her brain screamed how important it was for Belle to divulge herself today, but the practical portion told her to run like hell. Strange because she felt almost compelled to help with this investigation. Another troublesome new experience.

Determined to discover what Sam had been within this secret group, and what outlandish conspiracies they had planned because fair elections were the United States' founding principle. Without honest elections, America was not the land of the free. It disturbed her to find a loved one might be mixed up in something which would shake the foundation of this country.

Unable to allow this to happen, she refused to just sit by and do nothing. Instead, Belle took a leap of faith. "Hand me the article and no matter what, do not touch me until I come back."

Balanced upon the arm of her chair, Remy stared down with a bizarre gaze at the tiny thing who appeared to be on the verge of passing out. Belle just sat there, with a hand flicked out, while the other one barely held her upright. Confused by what she wanted but when glancing down, he discovered her desire. Clutched in his left fist was the Irish election clipping and she appeared to be waiting for him to obey.

With his insides in knots, Remy shook his head and twisted toward the window. The view was stunning, but he noticed it was not as spectacular as the one from the main house. He needed a moment to gather his thoughts because this woman turned him inside out. Disappointed to find no solace in the nature before him, he raked his big hand down his face and stared straight ahead. Then, blew his breath out with a sigh. "Okay but if I may ask, where exactly are you going?"

From his perch atop the chair, he studied her while struggling to muster his most dazzling smile. Currently the fine-looking field agent was not feeling very charming, simply very confused.

All morning, Remy had been experiencing an unusual reaction to Belle's presence. Another commotion he had never faced and been denying since shaking her hand. Unsure how or why he was becoming magically in-tune with this unbelievable individual, but his normally sensible brain seemed to have trouble accepting this fact. Something which seldom happened to him and never with such force.

His instincts and her body language all pointed to one certainty. This remarkable lady was about to reveal a rare part of herself. The curious man understood something extraordinary was coming and did not want to miss this valuable gift. Gently picking up Belle's hand, Remy waited for her reply.

Flustered because she was unsure how to describe her talent and not sound insane. "I'm sure you'll think I'm crazy, and maybe I am." Nervous to put into words what Belle herself denied numerous times each day. "But sometimes I can get you know, um…I guess you would call them feelings from, um." Softly whispering, while internally admitting her gift to a complete stranger was the hardest thing she had ever done. "Oh jeez, I don't really know how to say this other than…" Due to her uneasiness, she stated the next sentence with more force than necessary. "Well, I get feelings from touching things."

Terrified of his reaction, Belle sat motionless with her head bent. Refused to even look at him, afraid of the rejection she expected to see in his eyes, along with the thoughts of madness at her statement. Oddly, instead felt herself drawing comfort from Remy, who still held her hand. The uplifting sensation was an unexpected pleasure rather than her anticipated reaction.

At first, Remy was unable to move a muscle and he merely sat there. *Did I hear her right?* Slowly releasing Belle's fingers, certain he had heard her correctly.

Abruptly stood up and walked over to the middle of the room, as all sorts of information raced through his brain. *Good God, I've read about such people.* Excitement crept in as he recalled the years of research he had uncovered. *Since I wanted to find out if there were others out there, like me.* He had discovered an enormous amount of material on the supernatural and had even run across several real people in books, but never in person. Although, there were tales of such folks. Persistent rumors had circulated for years about a group of people who existed and worked together on clandestine missions for the government, but even after extensive searching, the methodical sleuth had found no such unit.

Now, here before him, sat the real deal. Stunned to find himself face to face with an actual magical person. *Could it be possible this woman is like me?* Her revelation shocked him to the core.

Ultimately, he kneeled beside her, grabbing the chair on both sides. "Do you mean to tell me you can touch something and identify all who have handled it??" With an intensity bordering on obsessive, Remy crouched over the startled woman. "Where an item's been???" Zealously, he used the intimidating position to lock Belle into place.

Shocked by his outburst, she pulled back from the wild-eyed man, frightened by the passion which flashed in those incredible irises. Hastily, Belle dragged herself together while brushing off his questions. *Why would he be asking such things?* Becoming suspicious of his odd behavior. *His reaction is not normal because Remy should be running away or calling me crazy.*

Mistrust flashed across her mind. He was taking her announcement way too well, although a bit too intensely and this thinking switched her thoughts into words. "Why aren't you laughing at me?"

As a specialty medical doctor who treated extremely traumatized patients, her stare could stop anyone in their tracks, and she was directing her best one at him. As she glared into Remy's stunning eyes, Belle realized now was definitely not the time to admire them. Back on point, a stern toned Dr. Brooks proceeded. "Or hauling me off to a padded room?"

There was always the standard FBI line about only collecting the facts Remy could quote her but that would be far from the truth. An impulse within him, insisted he be honest with this woman. Her questions allowed him the opportunity to capture his composure.

Gradually, he rose from his knees.

Slowly, he turned away and walked back toward the windows. At long last, Remy solemnly spoke. "Because I think I know what you mean."

His response caught her off guard and she gasped. "How???" Unprepared for that reaction and shocked he had admitted such a thing, but Belle believed him. Again, somewhere deep inside, sensed Remy spoke the truth.

With his back still turned toward her and staring out over the grass tennis courts, went on with his confession. "I see colors. Everyone's auras."

Totally captivated, Belle nudged him to continue. "Go on."

"Auras are natural circles of light which encompass every human being. I see them swirling around everyone and every color tells a different story for each individual person." Tentatively, he turned towards Belle but did not look at her.

"I can tell if they're happy at the moment or sad. Can tell if people are in love or depressed, based on what shade surrounds them. The worst is when they're sick or in pain." He cringed at the memory of a recent encounter with an old friend.

Deeply worried, because it was Remy's turn to be nervous about her reaction to his odd revelation. Cautiously, went on with his description, when sensing this unusual woman might not be repulsed by his burden. "Auras are a part of every person. It's just how I see them, so I don't know. I don't really think about it too much." Since he had been a child, had told no one of his affliction and found himself surprised by the easiness of telling her.

Relief filled his face as he sensed her acceptance. It seemed to wash over him, and Belle's approval staggered him. Her respect helped Remy find the nerve to turn around and actually face her. Surprised, because the little thing was still sitting in the chair, although no longer looking pale and fragile. Pure astonishment shined on her face.

After getting over her initial shock, she gushed. "That's absolutely amazing! Oh, my gosh. What a beautiful way to go through life." In wonderment, she declared. "To see colors everywhere, around every person. Why it must be spectacular." Belle smiled from ear to ear while gazing at him with amazement and if he was not mistaken, admiration too.

The embarrassed man grumbled under his breath. "Leave it to Belle, to liken my jinx to a colorful kaleidoscope." A difficult subject, Remy had always had trouble discussing his condition. "You still haven't answered my question." Quickly countering, to get off the subject of himself. "Where are you going?"

In her heart, Belle understood she could trust this man with her secret because the charming devil had trusted her with his. As a smile formed on her pretty face, she realized Mr. Remington Montgomery had not confessed all his talents. Also, willing to gamble he was a damaged man who had told no one in a long time about the colors he witnessed daily.

These conclusions helped the supernatural doctor share more of her secrets but first, drew in the deepest breath. "I just don't know who touches something. I, um…can actually um…you know." Murmuring delicately. "Um…go back to where an item has been. Or if it's an article or photograph, I can actually go to the event as it's occurring."

Literally struck dumbfounded, Remy spent the next few minutes just trying to absorb her disclosure. *If what she had just admitted were true, well then Dr. Campbell Brooks had one amazing gift.*

After a while, the shock of her statement wore off and his mind spun with all the potential opportunities. *If this were really possible.* The nervous habit of wiping his hand down his face returned. *I could solve hundreds of cold cases. Think about how many things could be discovered.* A million ideas swirled through Remy's head, particularly all the tough cases on his desk.

When he turned all the way around, before him sat a ghost white person frozen in the chair. As he stared at her strained facial features it suddenly dawned on Remy. Her incredible declaration came with a catch. "There's a big but, to your gift. Isn't there?"

Only able to nod her head, Belle eventually found the nerve to go on. "Yes, there is. An enormous one." Quietly, the bewitching woman added. "It's why I rarely use it and only with my most difficult patients. Those poor souls need it to achieve a breakthrough."

Crouched back down by the chair but Remy no longer confined her. "You don't have to do this. It's unnecessary Belle. I'll find another way to figure out what's going on."

Clearly, her mind was still not focusing properly, because at that moment, all that came to mind was foolish. *Turquoise is exactly what color his eyes are.* As she continued staring into those gem-like orbs, Belle discovered those ocean sapphires were not the reason she would help him. Different like her, she also sensed this man had suffered the pain of losing a loved one. Also like her, Remy had experienced endless shame, along with debilitating humiliation too. There was no hiding suffering like that, and it showed in those Caribbean blues of his.

Not knowing who he had lost or how, but abruptly, Belle desperately wanted to help him. For the first time in forever, convinced she was doing the right thing, and stared directly into that serene gaze. "Please put the column down in front of me."

Still somewhat confused, Remy did what she asked. After placing it on the desk, sat down in the other chair and remained quiet while waiting for her to proceed.

Scared because for the first time she would be divulging her gift to a perfect stranger. This terrifying thought put Belle back on the fence, because telling someone and showing someone were two vastly different things.

Glanced over at the clippings because the noisy article was still making a racket. The haunting sound humming away seemed only to be getting louder, while the unknown evil continued to linger nearby. A quick peek to the side confirmed the FBI agent appeared unaware of anything out of the ordinary. He still stared at her and not the paper making the loud noise, so she took a deep breath and called upon her grandmother's lessons. The words to the calming ritual immediately spilled from her lips. It was unwise to 'travel' under these unusual conditions, but Belle needed to find out what Sam had been up to in Ireland.

All the while, her brain screamed loudly. 'No, no, no!' Ignoring every instinct, she picked up the article, disregarding the excellent internal advice and turned toward Remy. "Just remember, do not touch me."

As soon as her eyes closed, Belle slipped back into time.

CHAPTER 8

Back in Time

February 2011

he engines of Buchanan Industries' newest plane were still spinning when Sam Randall stepped through the jet's doorway into the cold Irish night. There was much riding on this, and he counted on nothing going wrong with the elaborate plan. Icy air blew through his bones, while he stood reviewing the society's directive. *Lose the election but not by too much, Sammie old boy. Oh, and let's not forget the biggest factor. The political party which needed to lose had won every time for much of the last century. Every bloody election.*

Panic crept into his psyche. *Not too difficult a task, huh?* The hardest part was the society liked and supported this political party. *But they needed me to get them out of the way to secure their precious prize.* The Seachd Righrean would fix it all down the line but today, whiz-kid Sam had to accomplish the impossible.

Do they have any idea what they were asking? Of course, they did not nor do the members even care. They required everything to be followed precisely and adopted a no questions asked, no problems expected kind of attitude. *Just do the job Boy and keep your mouth shut.* The thought reminded Sam of how much he hated the Boy nickname.

Real terror started to set in but shook it off because that feeling always made him nervous. Nerves made Sam feel weak and he hated any form of weakness. Elevated blood pressure should not be a problem at his age, but it was no wonder he might have it when implementing a scenario this elaborate. Although, the society was not interested in his health problems, only in his results.

The trapped man would not allow himself to fail. He had never failed in his life and Sam would not start now. *Never.*

He looked over at the old man who had hammered that no failure statement into him since birth. After a deep cleansing breath. *There, that's better. Never!* He was still on edge but more relaxed. *Come on Sam, you have everything under control, you just need to stay on track.* Decided to go back to reflecting about the society and their decree. *Do they have any idea how good I am? Because they will never believe what I'm really up to.*

The pressure was so incredible, a cackle burst from Sam, which forced him to dig deep, drawing on his over-inflated but fragile ego. *If they will not grant it after all I've done, then by God, I'll just take it.* At this last thought, a sly smile formed on his sinister face.

He grasped the railing and descended the slippery steps, onto the snow-covered tarmac below. Upon reaching the bottom, Sam turned to his right, searching frantically in the dark night. "Great, no one is around to meet us and where the hell is the car?"

Slowly, Belle opened her eyes.

It took a moment to get her bearings but right away, recognized this was not Sam's office. Unique as it was, her gift worked differently, each time when using it. But the one thing that always remained the same was this place. Her *'landing ground'* as Belle liked to call it. Sometimes, she would visit this space during difficult sessions with patients because it allowed her a tranquil state to gather her thoughts, wits, or just some much needed strength. It was a sacred location to her and a most peaceful spot. The space had become a true blessing because it did not require her to return all the way back to the present.

The mystical looking place was comprised of swirling dark clouds and sparkling mist but did not appear ominous. For Belle, it always gave her much needed solace. Now that she could catch her breath, found herself confused by what was happening with her gifts. They seemed to be on maximum overload. Usually, only bits and pieces of the actual event came through but this time Belle had apparently just witnessed Sam arriving in Ireland. That made it several days before the election in late February, which was impossible, and bewilderment ran rampant throughout her mind.

As the tension built again, she heard her grandmother's calm voice whispering in her ear. *'Find ye' center and clear all the other gibberish away.'* Warm breezes blew, reminding her of Granny, instantly settling her nerves. Although, Belle could chalk up another strange incident she'd never experienced before.

For now, she needed to focus, while pulling herself together and concentrating yet again on the election article. Determination fueled Belle to find out what Sam had been up to, despite being worried about the changes taking place with her talent. Not willing to let fear stop her but becoming more aware with each passing minute, she had not known her husband at all.

Fixing her attention on the task at hand, Belle dropped back into the article's next scene.

"We need all the players in place, by midnight tomorrow night." The old coot grumbled but Sam had heard this speech before. Instead of listening, he indulged in a little fantasy and imagination. The Irish beauty, who would be waiting for him in the hotel suite sprung to life in his mind. A dream come true, Shannon O'Malley was every man's desire in living color, and he became hard just thinking about the beautiful vice president of *Electronic Voting of Eire*.

The resourceful man had always mixed business and pleasure. *Why else would they allow women in the workplace, right?* While riding in the back of the limousine, a smirk slipped onto Sam's face. *Look at my pleasing wife. A perfect situation which merged both quite well.* A full smile appeared before he could stop it.

Hastily collected himself together and remembered his duty before another lecture could occur. The old windbag's reprimands were legendary, and Sam was not in the mood for one tonight. To occupy his time, reached inside his briefcase with the *E.V.E.* folder to stimulate his brain but not before allowing himself one last thought of the raven-haired temptress awaiting him later.

"Yes Uncle, everything is in place, and we will meet the deadline." Once again, reassuring the ancient relic sitting beside him of the success they would achieve within the next few days. Irritated, because it was necessary to answer to this fool. Then pulled himself together because too much was riding on this to take any unnecessary risks.

Besides, Sam would not have to put up with the old man for much longer because everything seemed to be falling into place. For two long years, he had been waiting and planning. Now, it was only a matter of time. His intricate plot would sweep away the old guard of the society and a new regime would come to power, thanks to his brilliant sleight of hand. A smile appeared again because Sam could almost taste the supremacy of it all.

Before his companion noticed anything was amiss, he buried himself behind the file folder. Sam prayed this ploy would keep the irritating old man beside him happy until they reached the hotel.

When using her special gift, it felt similar to her safe landing space, the shimmering sanctuary Belle visited to get her bearings. Similar but not the same. Not a giant sparkly otherworld level but more like a large corridor. One she travels, zooming down both horizontal and vertical — at the same time.

One minute Belle had been comparing her different gifts, the next she was slamming back to the present.

At first, she faltered when opening her eyes.

After hearing Sam's true affections, believed his confession had flung her back from the past but was surprised to find Remy shaking her out of the chair and screaming. "MOVE!!!"

Barely coherent, she was only able to blink.

"What in the world is going on?" Still not sure what was happening, Belle could not process much of anything.

Random thoughts broke through to the dazed doctor. *Gun shots. Rapid-fire gun shots. Shots hitting the house and shattering the windows of the cottage.* What was happening outside had begun to sink in. *Gun shots like the kind bad guys shoot in the movies.*

Not knowing how but when Belle's consciousness cleared, she found herself on the floor scrunched underneath Remy. After checking to see if she was all right, the special agent sprang into action and quickly drew his gun. She must have blacked out because when looking around next, he stood over by the front door.

So far, Remy could see no one, moving a single slat on the plantation shutters, attempting to locate the shooter but he could not find a clear view of the area where the agent surmised the gunfire had originated. Turned his head to check on the lovely lady and noted even in a daze, Belle appeared exquisite. That look had assured Remy, his heart would not survive if anything happened to this unique woman. *Then don't let anything happen.*

At the sound of a twig snapping, instantly, he went back on full alert. His razor-sharp focus returned to the danger outside while lifting a finger to his lips, indicating for her to be quiet and to stay down low.

Impressive but who's shooting? This was a different side to the man Belle had met earlier. The poised FBI agent was prepared for an all-out attack and welcomed his protection but needed answers more. "Remy what is going on?"

Slinking around to the far corner of the room, relieved to find the neighboring compound through a small break in the estate wall. "Get down, Belle and keep quiet." After mouthing the command, he returned back to his attack mode, and assumed his calm tactical stance.

Sometimes she did not understand men and muttered. "Good lord, what did he think? I was going out there to take on the troublemakers?"

Looking madder than a trapped hornet under glass, Remy brought his finger to his lips again, because she had not obeyed his orders. Sternly indicating with a wild hand gesture for Belle to get down.

Suddenly, his powerful senses plowed into her, and those sensations persuaded her to promptly kneel. Belle marveled at his magical strengths even amid her dazed state. Although, she did not like people who were bossy. It was at that moment her brain caught up and she recalled they were being shot at. This thought moved Belle swiftly along the floor and away from where the bullets had been flying minutes before. As ordered, she slipped behind the desk and slid under it to hide. Finally coherent enough to be concerned about the mayhem outside.

After another round of gunshots, which sounded further away than before, Remy came over and whispered in her ear. "It looks like there are two suspects next door. Over by the far wall. SWAT is moving in, and it should be over with shortly."

For another ten minutes, she stayed huddled under the desk as Remy vigilantly stood guard with his back toward her. Shocked by everything she had learned over the last two hours about Sam and the additional stress of the shooting taking place. Plus, she was unable to shake the feeling there was an evil presence lurking just beyond the chaos outside. Something which could not be explained but Belle soon forgot about it because of the loud approaching commotion. Footsteps pounded on the pavement out front, sending Remy into an even higher combat mode.

All at once, turmoil erupted inside the small cottage, as local law enforcement entered, checked both of them completely, while others secured the perimeter. A while later, a whirlwind blew into the crime scene, as the prissy dressed butler followed by a huge woman, barged into the room in search of their mistress. Shortly thereafter, Remy learned the butler's name was Huntley and even with all this excitement his aura still glowed a calm ocean blue. The cook's aura sported a strange mixture of brown, tinted with pink. Although, he had no time to scrutinize that peculiar combination because questions were coming from dozens of people.

With pandemonium taking place, the guest house had become part of a much larger crime scene but throughout it all, the pale widow seemed to hold up well under pressure. Belle had little to contribute but cooperated in the investigation as best she could.

Lone Ghost, Remy's nickname around the Bureau, needed to sort this whole ugly mess out. Immediately, the federal agent identified himself to the folks in charge and resorted back to that stealth mode. He handed her over to the help, then spent hours taking part in the complicated investigation, First, he answered questions, then reviewed tons of evidence, along with filling out endless government forms. So many agencies were involved with the shooting next door he could not keep all the acronyms straight. What authorities here were writing off as a large drug deal gone wrong, Remy knew to be much more. This development appeared to be too convenient and felt sure Parker would agree but followed their lead for official purposes and wrote his answers to match the task force conclusions. Closely sticking to their official scenario to arouse no suspicions.

During much of the investigation, Belle just sat in the chair spending a long time gathering her strength. Using her gift took an enormous amount of energy and it drained her. Sometimes it would take days to recover, depending on the intensity of the event.

This one, well, she did not know where to begin.

After a while, she decided not to think about any of it because this had pushed her nerves to the edge. Plus, someone had shot at her today. *Bless my heart.* Another first for her. *I'll probably be on the national news again.* After what had occurred over the last ten days, Belle was at the end of her rope. Not sure she could deal with whatever Sam was mixed up in, if it meant people would be pointing guns at her. *Dear lord, does it ever end?*

The police had said drugs played a role, but she could not accept their explanation, although Belle did not know why. Somehow, this shooting was tied to something much more significant than discovering her marriage had only been a business deal for Sam. She sensed something far more important was taking place. *But what? And what did Remy know?*

Unfortunately, Belle could not wrap her head around anything because of her exhaustion. *No, I'm not thinking about Sam or the shooting or anything else right now. I want to go home. Home to Granny because I know she can help me figure this out.* Decided to head for the mountains soon. *That old woman knows something about all this. I just know she does.* Once and for all, she was determined to get answers out of her grandmother about her husband. First, Belle needed to return to Washington to settle Sam's will.

Mind made up, the exhausted lady politely asked Huntley to call for the jet.

CHAPTER 9

No Place Like Home

By late afternoon, Remy felt inundated with anger and confusion over this unforeseen fiasco. What made him even madder was he never found time for another private moment with the badly shaken Belle. Shortly after the shooting, had spoken with her, but she could only briefly fill him in on her experience. Too embarrassed by Sam's hurtful words, she had kept much of his callous feelings to herself. Clearly, it had cut deep while also keeping her silent but the changes in her aura gave her distress away.

Remy ignored his training because of the tremendous shock both had suffered that day and he did not push Belle about her unusual talents because it looked like she was going to faint. What little she had to say confirmed what the crack investigator already suspected. Sam had been in bed, literally with Shannon O'Malley from the voting booth company. Unaware of how deep the Irish executive's involvement had been, deducing this pair manipulated the election using her machines which caused the Dochloite Laoch to lose.

Until this point, no one had been able to establish any connection between the two of them. The redheaded beauty had slipped through the initial investigation virtually squeaky clean. This latest information was another piece to this complicated puzzle. A riddle, that was giving him a headache because Remy could not use his normal FBI resources. Eager to verify Shannon had been in Sam's hotel suite but would need to do so through his numerous dubious channels.

Stepping outside, he connected with a trusted contact. A guy he had known for years, who spent his career on the fringe of the official investigative community. Quickly, he instructed his associate to run extensive searches on activities Sam and Shannon might have conducted during earlier rendezvouses. "Man, think for yourself. What would you be doing with all of this info?" Rattled off on his fingers everything he could think of, giving his connection the go ahead and finished by asking. "What kind of mayhem would you be causing? Give me a head's up as quick as you can, and I'll pay you well." Laughing at his buddy's last bit of smack talk. "Come on man, you know I'm good for it."

After hanging up, something continued to bother him about all of this and he still lacked actual proof of their actions, along with the why. Therefore, he would also make the long-distance call to Dooley, to fill him in on this new development and see what he could find out from his Interpol ties.

Once finished with his business, the agitated agent returned inside to complete this Florida farce. Remy knew how the judicial system worked and played along. Whenever he needed a boost to push him through his exhaustion, he just sneaked a peek at the pale widow and his heart perked right up.

It was evening before either of them could return to DC, but each went by separate means. Earlier, she was the lone passenger on a Buchanan private plane. Later, he lucked out and snagged a first-class seat on a commercial airliner.

On his flight home, when reviewing what little he collected, becoming frustrated because Belle had no inkling why Sam fixed the Irish election. Also, she could not identify the second person in the limo. Adamant the man was no male blood relative of Sam's because she had been subjected to all of them.

Once arriving back in Washington, Remy spent the next three days studying every piece of evidence in a desperate effort to forget all about the gorgeous Campbell Brooks. Grudgingly, he admitted putting a great distance between himself and Sam's widow was the only way to deal with his unusual fascination with the beauty. That separation ended late last night and left only the shootout to be reviewed.

The information regarding the so-called drug deal came up on his screen, which forced him to think of her. Lonely, he let his guard slip, allowing a rare indulgence into racy daydreams about Dr. Belle Brooks.

After almost two years, amazed to find the woman from that spotlight was still stunning. Maybe, even more gorgeous than before. Her inner loveliness had come shining through after surviving another tragedy. A second in less than two weeks. Throughout this whole ordeal, had kept her dignity from beginning to end. Remy doubted there was anyone else who could have carried themselves better than Belle.

The next astonishing fact was something the magical man could not believe. The lovely lady was like him. Different. Gifted.

This totally freaked him out because Remy had met no one with special talents like his. All the incredible possibilities raced around in his head. *This would be so cool.* Then remembering why that was impossible. *Well, if she didn't belong to Sam. Or Sam's very recent widow to boot.* Mentally kicking himself. *Which just puts a frigging damper on everything.* Surprised by his thoughts because none of this made any sense. *I shouldn't be thinking about her like that.* Shaking his head to rid it of such thoughts.

He was not supposed to be interested in anyone or anything, except catching Amanda's killer. *What the hell am I doing?* With the bad guy still out there, it was Remy's sworn duty to uphold. *I have a case to work and it's much more important than my dick.*

After deciding to take the coward's way out, he dragged himself together. Instead of going to her, Remy planned to visit Belle's eccentric grandmother because the research on the good doctor and her family still did not add up. Like the shadow he was, got up from the desk, grabbed his car keys and headed out, all without making a sound. *The Lone Ghost strikes again.*

As he walked to his car, Remy remembered the trick had been a huge hit in college and recalled the crazy antics his fraternity had pulled off due to his silent talent. A smile crossed his lips at the happy memories, as the car exited the parking lot and pulled onto Pennsylvania Avenue.

Once out of the city, he went over in his head what little information was available on the subject Remy was on his way to see. He could not find many facts on the famous Granny Brooks, which was the name most people called Belle's grandmother. As best he could tell, Mavis Brooks has been practicing medicine since landing in America approximately seventy years ago. It looked as if Dr. Brooks possessed no medical or other type of degree from any accredited college. Rarely did she charge money for her services, although, many loyal patients paid with homemade food and livestock, along with credit at the local general store.

It seems the elder Dr. Brooks was the most popular physician in McErin County and in at least three of the surrounding ones, of the Commonwealth of Virginia. Almost all the people of those same counties, under the age of sixty, had Granny Brooks to thank for bringing them into this world.

Once again, the agent found his insides twisted into knots at this remarkable woman and the unusual people surrounding her. The case in point was how little additional information he could uncover about the older Dr. Brooks's remarkable medical practice, along with the interesting Appalachian Mountain people she assisted. Also, Remy could find nothing regarding her former life in Scotland. It appeared she sprang directly from the ship that carried her as a young woman across the Atlantic.

The biggest shocker – the diligent investigator could not locate one photo of her anywhere. Not in any of the files in the FBI database or on any legal or illegal Internet website.

None.

In his entire career, Remy had never come across this and made some discreet inquiries. Although finding it rare, he discovered a few older people who had managed to stay off the grid.

Apparently, Mavis had been a teenager when arriving in the United States and all alone. Another surprise he had uncovered about the popular Dr. Brooks was she did not appear to have a legal husband. To date, Remy had found no trace of one. *I wonder if Belle Brooks knows this about her grandmother.*

But the biggest mystery of all pertained to her farm.

Since the year she landed, the property has been owned by a European shell corporation. One with so many layers, even he with all his connections, was unable to uncover the actual owner. "Now, why would a false company with no proprietor or listed titleholders own an old woman's mountain land? What exactly are you hiding Dr. Brooks?" His habit of talking to himself was back and was hopeful the answer to that exact question was at the end of this five-and-a-half-hour drive.

In addition, there was little information surrounding Belle's mother's death, making Remy curious about the particulars. More important, why had Katie's name been omitted from all the news accounts. He had pored over the large FBI file for days, but it contained little regarding the late Kathleen Brooks. Remy hoped the senior Dr. Brooks could provide a few missing but key details.

Thankful for the long drive because it allowed him to review the evidence in peace. The weary agent just prayed his mind would stay on the case and not the woman he had some rather stimulating dreams about lately. His fingers flexed in a familiar rhythm on the steering wheel, but the habit only magnified his exasperations.

Remy turned on the radio and settled down for a long frustrating ride.

With dusk almost three hours away, she glanced first at the GPS, then at the dashboard clock, attempting to determine how much further it would be to the cabin. Belle wanted nothing more than to make it to Granny's with plenty of sunlight left, unhappy about having to travel the winding mountain roads this close to nightfall. They were dangerous, especially after dark. Unfortunately, it looked like the delay at the lawyer's office would mean Belle would not be arriving until almost sunset. Though none of that mattered because at last, she was heading toward home. That was how she always thought of Granny's place.

Home.

Too large to be considered a cabin but since it was the name her grandmother used for the unique structure, she did too. Built into the side of the mountain, the three-story stone house boasted seven bedrooms and nine baths. The beautiful building featured a wide wraparound porch which welcomed visitors at all hours of the day and night.

Ahead of its time, the homestead even generated its own electricity powered by the water mill attached to the main structure and fueled by the roaring Sinclair River. The large sprawling complex also included two huge gardens. Closest to the back door was a rather exotic herb patch and the second plot was bursting with just about every kind of vegetable. Both gardens covered much of the cleared area around the main house.

The spread also contained a smokehouse with a fully stocked pig pen and a dairy barn with milking cows. Granny also owned a large herd of beef cattle which spent various times of the year on the many parts of the mountain. The greenhouse for growing winter herbs was larger than most folk's regular barns. Also on the property was a henhouse which contained hundreds of chickens, both for eating and egg laying. Plus, her grandmother kept a herd of goats, along with the usual cats and dogs.

The ancient healer even tended a flock of sheep to bring a piece of the old country to the farm. Dozens of work sheds, some of which still housed old fashion ice boxes, were located across the property, and completed the unusual estate. All this eclectic hodgepodge was situated across one thousand nine hundred and forty-seven acres of Sinclair Mountain. The times she spent at Spring Sage Farm were her fondest memories. Technically, she had grown up in the house on Capitol Hill, but the cabin here in Kirkwall, Virginia was the one Belle considered home. *Thank goodness, I'll be there soon, and Granny will make everything better.*

While driving down Route 81, smiled at her good fortune. A song by one of the greatest guitarists to ever live started playing over the airwaves and she turned up the volume of the stereo. The wailing guitar helped to relieve the stress and anxiety of the last seventy-two hours. Belle relaxed, allowing the Stevie Ray Vaughan song to do exactly what the late great musician intended. To take all her troubles away. It was a welcome break in the craziness of her life, and she enjoyed the penetrating music. The next few minutes were spent singing every word at the top of her lungs and doing nothing more than reveling in some kick-ass Texas blues. Because tomorrow was soon enough to deal with the pending problems still facing her.

When the song finished, reality came crashing back as Belle's mind wandered to the noisy article from Sam's hidden folder. The copy was safe inside an envelope Remy had given her but even the replica would not shut up. The paper continued to hum but not as loud as before. Probably because it was secure inside her briefcase and locked in the back of the truck. She had placed it there after the shooting, to get it as far from her as possible.

The article was from December 1983 and detailed the infamous IRA bombing at London's Harrods Department Store. It had scared her. Belle was unsure why and desperate to know the reason for the unpleasant sensation resonating from the printed piece. Its continued allure prompted an increased desire for Granny Brook's company because somehow, the old healer could help.

Although, Belle knew whatever the outcome, the article held nothing for her except great personal sorrow. *But why? What about the article I touched back in Sam's office? How did I see something that happened several days before the actual event?* Another experience which had never occurred before and scared her even more. These unusual incidents were frightening because it seemed her gift was changing again.

Closed her eyes, recalling the details when it transformed the last time after Daddy died. The *'feelers'* prior to her father's passing had been there but she could not draw magic from much of anything. At his funeral, surprised when she started *'reading'* people, something Belle could not do before. Discovered, she could also extract significantly more information when touching items, especially after spending the summer training with her grandmother.

I'm hoping Granny will know what is going on or at least will know what to do. Silently praying her grandmother did because these things scared Belle. Now that the shock of everything else had worn off once again, remembering Sam's conversation with himself. Because her husband had indeed manipulated the Irish election with the beautiful Ms. O'Malley and had also talked about orchestrating something else. *Ushering in a new regime. But what? Or who?* Convinced, there was much more going on. Not knowing why but she got the feeling Granny knew more about all this craziness, than the old woman was letting on. Before the day ended, she intended to get to the bottom of it.

In the meantime, Eric Clapton's "Tears in Heaven" came on the radio. *The cosmic music gods are lining them up for me today.* It dredged up bittersweet feelings, but she reached for the volume knob anyway. The profoundly appropriate song came blaring out of the speakers as a picture of rose-colored glasses popped into her mind.

Surprised by the image, she stopped singing and reflected on her life. Reluctantly admitting her marriage had never been the beautiful fantasy everyone, including Belle, had pretended. Sam's comments while riding in the back of the limousine came to mind, only confirming what her heart knew all along. The last two years were all a made-up invention and nothing more than a business deal for him.

Listening to the words, grief's path had led another remarkable guitarist down was helping to heal her. The poignant tune had allowed her a much-needed core cleansing cry. To wash away all the painful lies in her life because just like Sam, the marriage was now dead too.

When the final note finished, she sat straighter. *This next chapter has started rough, but it will get better. I have to keep going because I'm a glass is always half-full kind of girl.*

Finally at the turnoff to the cabin, smiled at the beautiful picture of the sun dipping behind the mountain's peak. The sight made her feel as if a huge weight had lifted off her exhausted shoulders and her spirits soared for the first time in a long while. The soul purifying ride had healed her heart a little. In only mere minutes, Belle would be reunited with her favorite person in the world — Granny Brooks.

As she drew closer to home, drove up the well-traveled dirt road admiring every creature and plant living on this mountain. Belle slowed down to appreciate all the multi-colored buds and newly sprung leaves which were her grandmother's pride and joy. This part of the country was so unlike exotic South Florida but breathtaking in its own beauty.

As she drove along the ascending road, Belle marveled at Granny's amazing ability to put everything to clever use for the local mountain folks. Never throwing away anything because someone could always use it for something. *Ashes to ashes, dust to dust.* Even if it just ended up as compost. Her grandmother was right. *Why should something go to waste only to sit in a landfill? Doing no one any good.* Grinning when remembering Granny's constant conversations in her head. *No one else is quite like the one-of-a-kind Mavis Brooks.*

Outsiders to these hills, would consider her breaking the law for practicing medicine. *'Without a piece of government paper.'* She chuckled at the many famous Granny sayings, but Belle did not care what other people thought. Considered an angel by all in these parts, the elder Dr. Brooks was a miracle worker to everyone she encountered.

All at once, the evil presence from Lennox House seemed to burst back into her mind. Strange, she sensed the menacing spirit again but was surprised to feel it here in the mountains of Virginia. Its continued presence made Belle even more eager to see her grandmother. Thankful she would soon sit at the large kitchen table surrounded by endless love and sipping Granny's famous ginger root tea.

Warmth enveloped her by just thinking about the unusual woman who was her beautiful grandmother. Although, Granny had to be well into her eighties, Mavis Brooks was still quite a looker. Her long luxurious honey brown hair was a bit darker than Belle's and she also carried a couple more wrinkles but only a few. The two of them could easily pass as mother and daughter.

According to Granny, she attributed her secret to two things. *'Good clean livin' and eatin' the right fruits and vegetables.'* She was always sending Belle home with jars of something or another to be added to dishes or boiled in a tea. The old woman constantly instructed her on this herb or that remedy to prolong her life. A custom Belle practiced regularly. She approved of the treatments because her grandmother appeared to be at least twenty years younger than her actual age.

The thought caused her to laugh because no one could get her to reveal that exact number, not even Belle. An amusing memory of a patient trying to get Granny to reveal how old she was, made her chuckle again. "Boy, he sure will not ask such a silly question anytime soon."

Up ahead was the final curve of the drive.

With the last of the sunlight slowly descending, Belle strained to peer through the trees at her beloved home.

First thing out of the ordinary was the foreign car parked out front. There were always cars or trucks in the driveway because the popular country doctor tended to ailments twenty-four-seven. Granny set the house up to function as a temporary hospital and numerous times it had been used by people unable to get to the one in Bristol.

Many of the vehicles that graced Granny's place tended to be work oriented. However, this one was too impractical to belong to anyone from the Appalachians. In fact, it was a brand new shiny red Porsche nine-eleven coupe. A luxury few folks in the surrounding counties could afford.

Who would visit with such great taste? Belle reconsidered because truthfully, she did not care who had come calling. After everything the weary widow had been through recently, she had only one thought. Her eyes looked longingly at the far-off stone cabin.

Dorothy had been absolutely right...there is no place like home.

CHAPTER 10

Seachd Righrean

As the champagne-colored Mercedes Benz made the final climb, she hoped the unexpected guest would not delay her reunion with Granny. Belle appreciated the precision automobile sitting out front and could not help being puzzled over the owner. *It sure is awful pretty.* Her secret passion for fine lines and tremendous speed was undeniable. The gorgeous machine especially piqued her interest, and she pulled up to the final curve of the long drive, then slowed down to get a better look.

While admiring the fine car, the last person she expected strolled out of the doorway. Belle should have known because when the screen door swung open, none other than the good-looking G man, Remington Montgomery came waltzing out of the house.

It took a moment to gather her wits because finding him here had sent a jolt to her system. Thankful he could not see her but good golly, Belle sure was getting an excellent view of him. *Damn, he's as handsome as I remember.* Aware her wickedness was wrong, when considering Remy in such a way but unable to help herself.

It seemed like she was back in Florida again, holding the dreaded newspaper article. *Great, the roller coaster ride starts anew.* Revelations about Sam and their marriage had complicated everything in her life, but his admission did not mean she was a free woman. In fact, the meeting at the lawyer's office today only confirmed that statement and confused Belle more. She was convinced the ancient charmer who lived on this mountain could fill in some important pieces to this complex mystery.

Unsure why but Belle's *'feelers'* hummed in sync with this theory. Certain, beyond a shadow of any doubt, her Granny Brooks had been withholding information.

Belle allowed the car to roll to a stop and sat back to just observe him, enjoying the pretty picture he made in front of her home. He appeared to be looking around at nothing, but Remy was always an FBI agent: constantly cunning and on-duty continuously. Shocked to find the heartthrob guy here, she was even more surprised he had not called on her since their return to DC.

Another unexpected twist to her crazy mixed-up life.

Shaken by his unforeseen appearance, Belle collected her inner self in preparation for their upcoming confrontation, convinced an explosive altercation of sorts would take place with the blue-eyed devil. Uncertain if it would be a positive or negative clash but knowing it would certainly transpire.

To prepare for the reunion, she closed her eyes and focused on their first meeting. Mentally reviewing all the details of the events, along with the information Belle had obtained over the last few days.

This allowed her mind to drift back to the last time she had seen the fiendishly handsome gentleman currently standing on her front porch.

Three Nights Ago

After the pandemonium of the shooting, followed by hours of questions, she was relieved when Huntley called for the plane. The jet swiftly flew her back to Washington and away from Agent Montgomery. The gentleman had Belle experiencing things she should not be feeling.

After running away from today's unnerving situation, she was thankful to be returning to her residence on Capitol Hill because it remained a place of comfort and a welcome refuge. Once back in town, Belle pledged to ignore her strange feelings for the FBI guy. Instead, decided to deal with all the information Remy had revealed regarding her late husband. *And it sure is a lot.*

Confused by what she had learned about Sam's dealings, Belle needed to focus only on the facts. Slowly, counting them off to understand each inexplicable act.

"One. He married me for business, making our entire marriage a lie." If she had not heard him herself, Belle would not have believed it. The ridiculous statement was impossible for her to understand. "What kind of business could I have possibly been for Sam?" Perplexed by his odd announcement but unwilling to delve into it right now because his other actions seemed far worse.

"Two. Did business with international drug and arms dealers." This act was the one that made the least amount of sense. "Why would he conduct business with known criminals?" Sam possessed all the money in the world and certainly did not need more. "So why?" Shaking her head at the absurdity. "Why would he risk everything for such nonsense?"

Unable to grasp the reasoning for these illegal dealings she moved on. "Number three's insane act was Sam fixed the election in Ireland for a secret society. He might also be planning to rig the presidential election here in the States." She was not capable of understanding this insanity. "Pure craziness! Why would my dead husband do such a thing?" None of the items Remy had disclosed made sense.

After some time, felt confident enough to deal with the ultimate fact Sam had shared on that snowy airfield. "A society, which is my number four issue. A group of people, who apparently, my husband was an important member of."

Suddenly remembering another one of Sam's diabolical actions. "Oh, let's not forget this one." Her finger pointed toward the sky. "Also, he was actively plotting to take over that same secret society."

From the intense concentration her features became drawn when focusing on her husband's far away conversation, as she struggled to remember his exact words. "I also believe he might have stolen something very sacred of theirs but I'm not sure what it was. Good Lord, this is like one of those blockbuster Hollywood movies." After reviewing the lengthy list of Sam's dirty deeds, laughed at her sarcastic reflection because reluctantly, Belle seemed to be starring as its troubled leading lady. *That's not so bad right?* Snorting first at her twisted humor; then, just woefully shaking her head. *Feeling sorry for oneself rarely accomplishes anything.* Her constant inner voice chimed in, making her smile.

All this fretting about Sam and his deceptions confused her but the more Belle dwelled on his lies, the angrier she became. To have married her, as part of a business deal, was completely insane, utterly senseless, and she screamed her frustration at no one. "What type of damn deal???"

Despite being rattled by the day's frantic events, she was determined to recall all the information Remy had shared. This insanity made her head hurt because too many factors kept flying around. There was no point in concentrating on the sham of their marriage because fixing elections equaled big conspiracy plots. A broken heart and her damaged ego would have to wait, especially if all what the interesting agent had said were true.

Apparently, her billionaire rebel husband had also been scheming to rig the upcoming national election. No doubt, a feat Sam's brilliant mind could easily achieve. "If this society pulled off such a thing in Ireland, why couldn't they do it here, as well?" Shivers took over Belle's body after deliberating those implications.

Not even bothering to unpack, Belle sat cross-legged in the middle of her living room and drew strength during the quietest part of the night. After spending time with Granny's teachings, went straight to figuring out what was happening in her life.

It seemed critical to completely understand this society, which prompted the determined woman to grab her laptop and log on. She searched several websites until finding one, which translated Gaelic. After numerous attempts with misspelled words, she entered. *'Seachd Righrean.'* The translator typed out. *'Seven Kings.'* As soon as the translation appeared on the screen, Belle's *'feelers'* told her this was the correct name of the society Sam had spoken about in Ireland.

"What does it mean?" The interpretation only made Belle more frustrated and confused.

"Seven Kings, Seven Kings, Seven Kings. Why would you name your super-secret club Seven Kings?" By this point it was late, well past three in the morning, but sleep would not be taking place for her that night.

Found herself pacing the full length of her first floor, having always discovered comfort walking the old tongue-and-groove floorboards, with the round trip running through the living and dining rooms, then around the parlor and den. It had always been a soothing solace but tonight, the circle seemed to only be a frustrating loop. "Why would they call their group such a name?" The answers were right there if she could move past the fog clouding her brain.

"Come on Belle." At the top of her lungs bellowed. "THINK!!!"

The walk was not working and stopped to sit again. Belle hoped this would clear her mind of the hectic day and the mob scene at the airport. "Kings are leaders of their lands."

Insight eluded her and paced once more, seeking clarity to figure this dilemma out. "Seachd Righrean is Gaelic. Who would have been a king of Ireland?" At once, Belle recognized this was an important detail to discovering their identities.

Sat back down on the floor and once again used Granny's teachings to meditate for a while. "An Irish king would have been a champion, a leader. A leader, wait a minute…who would have been a leader in Ireland?" Belle noticed for the first time the enhanced psychometric powers were helping to focus her energies on the riddle.

"Aha, I got it!" They were guiding her to the correct answer. "Chieftains of clans would have been the highest leaders in the country." In the past only the king of England held more power than the clan chieftains. "The clan system is still in existence today but back then; powerful clans would have ruled over all the Isles. Therefore, certain clan leaders would virtually be revered like kings."

Conscious she was on to something; Belle reached for a pad of paper and wrote. *'Seven Kings = Seven Clans.'*

"Now I have to discover which ones are a part of this." Without having more information, she knew it would be difficult to figure out the ones involved. "There are fifty original clans of Ireland alone. That doesn't include the clans from Scotland and Wales." Yet, felt she was making progress. She set the notebook aside, it was late, plus all that had happened over the last ten days had not sunk in. The stress had taken its toll, especially after today's unexpected commotion.

Distastefully, the last twelve hours of upheaval at Lennox House came roaring back to life, making her cringe at the memory of the shootout, which led to the press having a field day. The horde waiting for Belle's arrival at the airport had pounced as soon as she emerged from the plane. All the extra security the family hired was most welcome, but it still took almost an hour to make it through the ruckus. Mostly, Belle ignored the media because they would print whatever they wanted, regardless of what she said or did.

What really had her on edge were these unusual feelings for the special agent and the unsettling sensations were still unclear to her. They bewildered Belle, along with her mixed-up emotions about Sam and she was having a tough time understanding any of it. Therefore, she spent a couple of extra minutes finding balance and cleared a path. Drew a mental garden hoe in her mind, like the one Granny had taught her to conjure and went to work.

Soon, Belle was sitting cross-legged on the floor of her cherished house with a clear conscience again. *I still don't understand what kind of business deal I could've been for Sam.* After ample pondering, left that one alone for another day because none of this was making sense and frustration continued to pour out of her.

Irritated by his confusing statement, she gravitated back to this secret society. "If Sam is involved, then his family is as well. With this influential of a group, you can bet the ultra-successful Buchanan clan played a key part in it." Would put good money down on that statement, but the Buchanan's were Scottish not Irish. Therefore, discovering the other six would be quite a challenge because of the impossible number of clans involved.

Then, a small spark flamed deep inside as the clairvoyant realized it could be accomplished with a bit of special assistance. The thought triggered a twinkle to sparkle in her eyes. Instinct informed Belle that

Granny's help would indeed be necessary to figure out this dilemma because the Appalachian sorcerer was an expert on anything involving magic and the Celts.

Another wicked shiver ran through her. The persistent evil sensation Belle had felt since this morning's shootout was something else, she needed to discuss with her grandmother.

"Hooooot hooooot." Came the owl's nocturnal call, snapping her back into the car as another shudder occurred because of those continuing evil perceptions. With the beautiful cabin back in focus, she smiled, relieved to have made it. At long last, she could kick back and spend time with the one person in this world who understood her. Granny.

After everything that had happened it was a wonder she had not already collapsed from the immense pressure. The funeral, the media frenzy and even people shooting at her would not break Belle. She let out a much-needed heavy sigh. Just thinking of her steadfast grandmother lit up her face with joy, while the peaceful feelings of home filled her soul.

Movement in Remy's peripheral vision caused the agent's head to turn, glimpsing a car in the distance. The vehicle was too difficult to make out because it lay slightly beyond the dense trees.

He stepped outside to get a better look and closed the screen door behind him. Remy inched his way past the car, while heading in the motion's direction. Like a magnet, he was being drawn toward something out there in the distance. Somewhere down in his core, his essence knew exactly what drew him out there.

Her.

Spellbound by whatever lay beyond the curve, Remy was also curious to know if lightning would strike him, when he laid eyes on the lovely Campbell Brooks again. *Did she have the same earth-shattering experience when encountering me?* To get the answer to that question, he would give up everything he owned.

Nervous about finding the unexpected man standing in front of her home, Belle started the car moving toward the house. She breathed in the *'winds of change'* as Granny liked to call times like these. *'Blowin' gentle now but ye know it's gonna be a changin' on a dime.'*

Funny. The spine-chilling sensation continued, as she feasted her eyes on this incredible guy. *It's sooo not a good feeling I'm having right now.* Surprised, because with her interesting feelings for the agent, Belle was positive they should have been. She spent another minute ignoring the lingering creepy feelings and just savored the sight of him. *Sweet Jesus, he stirs some kind of awful good feelings deep inside me though.* A wide grin appeared on her face, at the way how Granny's sayings became more conspicuous in Belle's speech the closer in proximity she got to her.

Those lingering, suspicious impressions made her head twist from the delicious specimen and back toward the house. *Where is Granny?* Astounded because her grandmother had not come out to greet her. Positive, Granny Brooks had heard the car's approach, which Belle found strange since the old woman possessed the heighten senses of a werewolf. *What could be keeping her?*

The beginnings of worry edged into Belle's mind as almost six weeks had passed since she had laid eyes on the elder Dr. Brooks. It seemed a lifetime and Granny should be out here by now, greeting her with open arms.

Panic crept in, that something might be wrong, but Belle dismissed it. *Stop right now.* Shaking off her apprehension. "I'm just being a silly goose." Another of Granny's famous sayings fell from her lips, as a shiver of evil ran through her soul again. It seemed to be the same malevolent sensation she had been feeling since the incident in Palm Beach. Nervous about the vile impression but quickly switched her misgivings to anger. It was her most successful method of dealing with the challenges in her life, instantly she became madder than a swarm of stirred-up fire ants.

"And why the hell is Remy here?" She slammed the car into park and turned toward the unpleasant interruption. Furious, he was interfering with her homecoming, but Belle was glad to have something to target her uneasiness on. The anger was a welcome distraction as she bent over to unbuckle her seatbelt.

At first, the sound roared like she was standing right next to a fast-moving freight train. Beneath her, the ground moved as the explosion from the back of the house rocked her big vehicle. A second sound wave exploded from the right side of the cabin over by the water mill. Neither blast registered with Belle before the truck tumbled up into the air. The last thing she remembered was screaming Granny's name, as everything turned black.

When opening her eyes next, Belle did not know where she was or how long she had been unconscious. After the fog lifted from her brain, she found herself upside down and covered in glass. It took some time to understand what happened because Belle had been knocked out cold.

Once regaining her senses, scanned the area and found from the looks of things, the blast had flipped the truck several times. Her large SUV had landed down the hill from the front door.

After taking stock of her injuries, aside from some cuts and bruises, found the big Mercedes had done its job. She was fortunate that there had not been enough time for her to remove the seat belt and it had protected her well. In her dazed state, she struggled with the still fastened safety harness. Eventually remembering her father-in-law's Christmas gift of a car protection device and fumbled around in the door compartment for the tool as confusion continued to cloud Belle's judgement. Ultimately, she became coherent enough to cut the belt off. The upside-down drop to the ground was excruciating and pain screamed from her head, but it was better than continuing to dangle.

After crawling out of what remained of the truck, Belle ran up toward the house in search of her grandmother. Upon reaching the top of the hill, she stood amazed at the destruction before her.

Her adored family homestead was ablaze with flames and not much remained of the house. Primarily, only the stone parts of the cabin along with the partial water wheel were still standing. Numerous pieces of flaming debris were scattered across several acres of land.

Shocked at first by all the structural damage, Belle stood and tried to decide how long she had been out. Suddenly, remembering her grandmother was still inside. "Granny, Granny, where are you?" She sprinted up the long rock-covered drive toward the front of the cabin. "Oh, my God!" Blinded by her tears and an all-consuming need to get to her grandmother. "Please Granny, answer me!!"

A pair of strong arms grabbed her around the waist only moments before she dashed into the fiery blaze. "Hush now, sugah. Everything's going to be okay, I promise." The injured agent pulled the hysterical woman back from the burning porch and tackled her onto the dew-soaked ground. "Here, let me look at you."

Belle continued to struggle but wasn't lucid enough to recognize the probing fingers frantically searching for any injuries.

"Are you all right sweetheart? Is anything broken?" Someone whispered in her ear, but the shocked woman did not understand who held her or what they said. In her pain filled traumatized mind, Belle acknowledged it was comforting all the same.

While her senses attempted to come back to life, her logical mind punched through. Belle knew Granny was gone, which made the world meaningless now. Her beloved grandmother had been inside when the house exploded, perishing right in front of her. That horrible image was now burned into her closed eyelids. *Right now, all I want to do is lie down on this cool, damp grass. I think I'll stay here and sleep, wrapped up in these big strong arms. I wonder who they belong to.*

Obscurity started edging in and the pain vanished, which was a miracle because Belle knew this had to be Sam's handiwork.

As tears poured down her face, the grief-stricken woman recalled one of her favorite memories of Granny, as she softly whistled in the kitchen, while baking her delicious homemade cinnamon rolls. The vision helped Belle pretend this was all a bad dream. *Because, surely, this cannot be real.*

The familiar memory was her last thought as blackness slipped into her mind.

CHAPTER 11

Stirring Patience

"Beep, Beep, Beep." Late the next afternoon Belle clawed out of infinite darkness. "Beep, Beep, Beep." The annoying noise was the first thing she heard when regaining consciousness. Clueless to her surroundings but deep down, she knew for certain waking up was not a good thing. A little voice whispered inside her head. *Do not open your eyes.* Somehow through the fog in her brain, it tried to warn her that life would never be the same if she did.

While napping, Remy missed the first flicker of Belle returning to life, yet it stirred within his subconscious. Asleep in the chair next to her hospital bed, he certainly recognized the unusual sensation the second time when it burst through to his brain. The odd impression prompted him to sit up, open his eyes and wait for her to awaken.

Worried because of the traumatic ordeal she'd endured during the last twenty-four hours, Remy was also curious about the strange turmoil swirling around them. Something was definitely going on, although he could not quite figure out what or why it was happening. For now, he ignored all the internal commotion taking place and prayed she woke soon.

Stood and stretched his long frame in the hopes it would help with the all over hurt, but the movement only aroused additional aches and pains. It was a miracle they survived the blasts. Other than Belle's coma, both had come away with only a few minor injuries. Tenderly, Remy looked over at her. *I could care less about myself; however, I'm terrified about, um...you.* His only concern was for the unconscious pale pixie, who had shown no signs of waking up. Her vitals all registered normal, meaning Campbell Brooks should be awake, but was not.

To make matters worse, when she regained consciousness, this would be the most difficult day she had ever faced. According to all available intelligence, this poor woman's last blood relative had been her grandmother and was now alone in the world. Remy was at a loss for how to help with her devastating grief.

At two, her mother died and for the most part, her Granny Brooks had raised Belle. At an early age, also had lost her dad and Remy was concerned this heartache would break her. Life had been rather unfair to this beautiful person and her horrible sense of loss consumed him.

The badly bruised agent got up and walked around to clear his head. Frustrated by recent events, Remy wanted to accomplish something, so decided to focus on the job. He had made no real progress with the investigation, but the final crime scene reports should be here soon. Certain Mavis Brooks did not survive because when the two blasts exploded, she had still been inside.

All day, Remy tried to piece together the limited clues, while continuing to monitor a slumbering Belle. But, so far, he had been unsuccessful in discovering much of anything. *Why blow up her house?* Muttering to himself about the slim details available on the mysterious Mavis Brooks, while turning his attention back to a stack of preliminary reports. *What is really occurring with this unfortunate woman and her grandmother?* Because none of this added up.

Something unfamiliar awakened inside him again, forcing him to turn his head towards Belle. The practical part of his brain was still unwilling to acknowledge any connection between them, even though Remy felt it stir deep within his spirit.

Suddenly, a raspy whisper cut through the silence. "Where...am I?" Belle blinked back at the brightness of the room.

Remy found himself stumped by what was transpiring, speechless by all these unusual sensations. Furthermore, clueless as to what to say to this poor, grief-stricken person. Once again, he took the coward's approach and reached for the water pitcher to avoid answering the question. Poured Belle a glass and gently brought the cup to her lips. "How ya feeling, sugah?"

She struggled to swallow the cool refreshing drink, but answers were more important than her parched throat. "Why are you not telling me where I am?"

Ignored the warning voice inside her head and opened her eyes. From the surroundings, she gathered this was a hospital. "What's going on?"

Eyelashes fluttered rapidly from the brightness, and Belle took a moment to adjust to the light, unable to recall exactly what misfortune had placed her here.

Big emerald eyes looked up at him, pleading while the misery of her plight engulfed him. Remy could not believe he was being forced to hurt this incredible person once more. "What do you remember?" From the confused look on her face, yesterday's events did not exist for Belle, and he hung his head in defeat. Unfortunately, that meant it would be up to him to explain the war zone that had transpired at her grandmother's place. This put Remy back in the hot seat requiring him to divulge all the ugly details to this poor soul.

The bleary lady watched him through partially closed eyes, as the fog continued to clear. She recognized this man from some place but could not recall where. With bandages on his arms and above his right eye, it appeared the good-looking guy was also injured. Except for some distant familiarity she could remember nothing else besides a bad sense of something residing deep inside. The strange impression resembled a menacing figure or maybe more than one figure, somewhere in the far back corner of her mind. She couldn't quite grasp the trouble that appeared to be brewing in the distance.

Otherwise, Belle's mind was a scrambled blank.

Then, the gorgeous guy spoke three simple words. "It's your grandmother."

And just like that, a notion similar to fingers snapping, triggered an avalanche of images in her mind. Last night's horrible memories flooded her brain as soon as the words left his mouth.

It was agony, seeing those tragic events flash across Belle's face. Remy watched, as first recognition, then deep pain set in on her lovely expression. The poor girl cried silently which hurt him far worse than hysterical weeping.

Baffled because had expected such behavior from a woman but this one did nothing at all like he anticipated. Nothing. Her resolve prompted him to do something he had never done, even with Amanda.

After standing vigil over her all night, he got up from the chair and crawled into bed beside her. Remy snuggled up, wrapped his arms around Belle and pulled her, as close as possible. Desperate to make her feel safe and protected because through no fault of her own, so many terrible things had gone wrong in her life. The tiny thing had absorbed everything thrown at her, all with a silent dignity which she maintained throughout each heartache.

Gently placed his arms around her, patting Belle on the back, while sending her his special soothing relief. For quite some time they lay with their arms wrapped around one another in silent comfort.

At last, he whispered to the poor soul. "It'll be all right. I'm right here sugah. You'll see. Everything is gonna be just fine." The caresses carried his special relaxation, but his own words still surprised him. Shocked by the things he had said to Belle because had never said them to any woman and meant them. Ever. Even with his beautiful wife, Remy had never promised to take care of or be there for her. A grin formed on his face when remembering Amanda, who would not appreciate being thought of as that kind of woman. *I would never dare say anything like this to Mandy Edwards.* It always made Remy chuckle whenever he thought about how much his wife hated her childhood nickname.

Finally understanding, this one lying by his side needed him more than the other beauty ever did. Sharply shaking his head to forget that woman now gone, Remy turned back toward the other one who was still here.

Right then, the nurse burst into the room to check on the awakening patient. Reluctantly releasing Belle, he was sorry to be leaving her side. The nurse's bright green aura made Remy smile, because it meant she possessed natural healing abilities. Smartly stepping out of her way, which allowed the nurse to take Belle's stats. "How's she doing?" Remy was still worried about her almost 24 hours of unconsciousness. He was thankful her tears had mostly stopped but noticed, Belle looked pale and withdrawn.

"You're doing just great Mrs. Randall." The sweet, energetic thing loudly pronounced, so Belle could hear. "She's doing real good." While writing her statistical report inside the old fashion flip chart, her perkiness continued. "All them tests, they came back just fine, and her readings are all in them ranges they supposed to be in." In order for the next words to reach only his ears, she leaned over. "I'm thinkin' she had a spell." Quietly giving Remy her opinion. "Heard her Granny Brooks' place went up last night with her Granny in it. Also heard she was there and all, which is a darn shame." Nodded her head toward Belle. "Don't expectin' many folks could take somethin' like that and not keel over."

Tears glistened in her eyes. "This little girl's grandmother was one of the finest women to ever grace the Commonwealth of Virginia. Good lord, this here county and all the surrounding ones, are sure gonna miss her." With that, the nurse scurried out of the room.

Unsure how much of the conversation Belle had overheard, he turned to find her facing toward the window. Her pale reflection looked so small and weak, making his voice break. "I'm so sorry Belle." Cautiously approaching the delicate subject. "So…so sorry about your Granny."

She was still staring out the window, unable to look at him. "I know but please, let's not talk about it right now. Okay?" Belle turned back towards him. "Right this minute, I can't think about any of it. Can you talk about something else?" Practically pleading with him.

Her skin appeared translucent in the afternoon's dying light, almost what he would call a faerie-like color. It was mesmerizing and Remy just stood staring while trying to figure out a way to make everything better for her.

"Please, talk about anything else. The weather, serial killers, anything…just not last night, okay?"

Something shifted inside of him, which allowed the ghost white woman to penetrate deeper into his essence. An almost impossible feat because of his solid steel emotional barrier but Remy knew from now on, he would do anything to help this beautiful person. Now, there was a burning deep inside him to find who killed her treasured grandmother, erase all the pain her despicable husband had inflicted, and remove that haunting look in her eyes.

Although, Remy remained confused by this consuming desire.

After drawing in a deep breath, understood the time had come to tell Belle his sorry story. On some level, the heartbroken man knew exactly what she was going through. Remy had not lost everyone like she had, but it sure seemed like it. The heartache, guilt, anger, and shame of it all were huge burdens and he carried the weight of them too. Not nearly as well as Belle but with as much dignity as he could rally. Although ashamed to admit it, even Remy had limits but needed to do this for her.

In all these years, he had never really talked to anyone — about Amanda's death.

Not about everything.

Oh, I've answered plenty of questions. Collected stacks of files on it, hundreds of useless photos, along with a few pieces of actual evidence. Gathered tons of data from the many private investigators Remy hired. He talked with anyone who would listen but in all these years, he had never found a credible suspect. Also had pestered local and state investigators, even involved some of his federal friends in the case but so far had found nothing to change the cause of death on her certificate.

Never once though, had Remy sat down and told one person the entire story of Amanda's death. Most people liked to call it otherwise, but he refused to call it anything other than murder.

It was about time he told someone the whole sorted affair.

CHAPTER 12

Open and Shut Case

The luscious landscape outside the hospital window was beautiful but Remy stared at it with such sadness. Hoped and prayed the scenery would give him strength as he breathed in to gather some much-needed courage. Not thrilled about sharing this part of his life, the weary man wanted to be talking about anything but his dead wife.

The setting sun drew his attention. "Dusk sure starts early in the mountains." Nodded, while gazing out the window at the spectacular array of colors. "I met Amanda during my junior year of college, but we didn't hit it off right away." As he snickered, the windowpane reflected the sad smile on his hardened face. "In fact, I kind of grew on her." The fond memory was one he had not thought about in years.

"Amanda was first in everything. She graduated first in our class and attended Jamestown on a full scholarship for volleyball." Remy recalled her achievements lovingly. "The Hoyas won the Big East Tournament both years Amanda was the team's captain. Miracle Mandy was also a member of the two thousand USA Olympic Women's volleyball team in Sydney, Australia." Remembering the oncoming pain was the reason he did not share memories of his amazing wife. "There's nothing Amanda Edwards could not accomplish."

Regretfully, turned from the window to regard Belle. "I was crazy about her from the start but so were all the other guys on campus." Love was written all over his face.

Surprised by the pull Remy possessed over her, it was becoming increasingly more difficult to deny how much better she felt whenever he was near. Even though smothered by grief, Belle wanted to make this confession easier for him and offered him a kind smile along with a pat on the side of the bed to come sit beside her.

Incapable of joining the thoughtful lady just yet, Remy's feelings were currently out of control. If she were too close, he could not continue with his tale. "We dated on and off but didn't get really serious until grad school at Jamestown Law. The two of us had a goal and it needed to be achieved before anything else."

The longer he spoke, Belle noticed a real smile forming on Remy's face and tapped the covers again to show the place would be there whenever he wanted.

"Also, something we both understood." Staggered by the strong internal compulsion to join her, but ignored the offer and went on with his story while fighting his impulses. "Typical lawyers in love type of stuff. We married in June oh four, right after we both passed the bar. Of course, we went straight to work for my dad's law firm." No more could the tormented man withstand the compelling inner force. Intense sensations coerced him to her bedside and surprise caught both when Remy lay beside Belle again.

Stared straight at the ceiling because he was desperate to keep his emotions under control. With a distant gaze, tried pretending he was not beside her. Eventually, Remy continued with his sad story. "It wasn't perfect, but I swear to you, it wasn't bad either."

Adopting his stance, Belle stared up at the ceiling too. "What color was your wife?" Not interested in her own aura but desperately wanting the answer about the woman he loved.

"Red." The widower promptly responded. "Amanda knew exactly what she wanted, and nothing ever stood in her way. Passionate about everything, there was never any question, which color Amanda would be at all times." Remy was suddenly overcome with melancholy. "Successful and driven, Amanda always shined red."

After answering her question, it took a while but eventually pulled himself together. "We were good for one another, fit well together. Right before she died, we purchased a beautiful condo off Dupont Circle in an old mansion from the eighteen hundreds." Something close to excitement entered Remy's tone, while his speech was coming in rapid stretches. "The woodworking and craftsmanship in it were remarkable." Belle noted, a happier person talked about the old house he had shared with his wife.

Though nervous about revealing such a private part of his being, Remy wanted her to understand the joy his previous hobby had brought him. "Sorry, I love fixing up old houses. It was kind of a passion of mine." Embarrassment spread across his face. "Anyway, I just wanted you to understand."

Not quite getting it but Belle thought he looked adorable and understood she was glimpsing a piece of the man he once was.

Emotions back under wraps, Remy continued to describe what his existence had been like. "Amanda and I worked together but saw little of each other during the day. We worked in different divisions, on separate floors. Other than occasionally going out to lunch, we rarely ran into one another. But outside of work, we hardly ever were apart."

Abruptly, he stopped talking for a long time.

Staying silent during his lengthy pause, Belle recognized he was building up his courage to say the next sentence.

"So, to accuse her of doing drugs." He continued to stare blankly at the ceiling. "Well, I didn't believe it and that was only the first part." His words came out in a tortured whisper. "But it wasn't the worst."

Not knowing how to respond to such a raw statement, because tonight, the woman in her was struggling with the psychiatrist inside. After several seconds of getting both under control, encouraged him to go on. "What happened?"

When Remy spoke, could barely hear him. "It started the week before Christmas in two thousand five."

Right then, it did not seem like he was even in the room, and to reassure herself, grabbed hold of his arm. Although Belle could physically see Remy lying next to her, his existence seemed to have vanished.

"They found her at a hotel in Annapolis." Another long silent pause occurred. When he spoke, his voice was not as steady as before. "I was in Scotland on MM Law business working at the partner's family estate."

Another extended break followed before Remy began again with a quiet vengeance. "The police wrote it off as a drug overdose. An intentional suicide because Amanda's lover didn't meet her, but I refused to accept it."

"What else?" Gently pushing him, when she normally would not, because Belle understood there was more. Much more.

"They had doctor files, with appointments Amanda supposedly attended." The poor man was struggling but Belle left him be. "Allegedly getting prescriptions of those oxycodone pills." She stayed quiet to allow him to get this out in his own way. "It's ridiculous." Lightly taking his hand, so Remy would realize she understood and was there if he needed her.

After receiving another unusual bolt of magic from her touch, the brokenhearted guy went on. "I also found among her things, little notes of appointments made to look...well, to look like she, um, you know." Hardly able to speak, finally he finished the uncomfortable sentence. "It listed dates when supposedly Amanda was having an affair."

Now, turned toward Belle because Remy wanted to witness her response. "When I checked the appointment dates against my revised calendar, I found discrepancies."

Curious, Belle tenderly rolled over onto her side to face him. "What do you mean?"

Fueled by a burst of energy from her kind expression, Remy began talking fast. "On some of those dates I should have been out of town, but my plans changed all the time." It was almost like he could not get the information out quick enough. "In one instance, only a few weeks before her death, Amanda and I were together at the very restaurant the note refers to. Ah…regarding her, um, affair." By this time, Remy's eyes were practically pleading with Belle to believe him.

Then, he stopped talking for a long while.

Belle understood there was still more to this, so she waited patiently. Out of the blue, Remy grabbed both of her arms and jerked her toward him. "I can prove I was there, because I paid the bill that night." Beseeching her to have faith in him. "Whoever set this all up was smart enough to give Amanda a bill for that night but didn't check to see if I had one too. They assumed my calendar hadn't changed and I'd gone out of town." With anxiety building all around him, the tension was noticeable in Remy's tone and throughout the room.

Though her heart was already broken, Belle's cracked a little more. "People presume you were there that night, with someone else in the restaurant, and you can't prove that you weren't." Unable to bring herself to look at the wronged man, she was only able to whisper her conclusion. "Can you, Remy?"

How had she known? Once again, it seemed like he had been punched in the stomach. *How had she reached deep inside and pulled such a secret out of him?*

His own parents did not understand. Even now so many assumed exactly that about the two of them. Amanda's closest friends. The police. His parents. Her parents. Everyone assumed the worst. They all presumed his wife had seen him that evening with his new lover and concluded both had been cheating. When Amanda's new guy deserted her so close to Christmas, the lovesick lawyer checked into a hotel and killed herself.

Up to this point, he had told his standard version of the story, but Remy had always left out the ultimate secret. He would never stop thinking about it because it had seared every moment of that magical evening into his brain. He would never forget it for as long as he lived because the night was so special having spent it with his charming wife.

After all these years, whispering the truth aloud. "It was the best night of my life."

Unsure what made the evening so special, but her internal crystal ball, said Remington Montgomery was telling the truth. He had been with the Mrs. that night, not having an affair. Belle was also aware, there was still more he needed to disclose. Therefore, she lay silent.

It occurred to him when he glanced over at her again, this woman understood him like no other person ever had. Gently placing his hands on either side of Belle's face and looking directly into her bright green eyes. Finally revealing his darkest most private skeleton. "You see, that was the night."

Remy struggled to swallow with great difficulty and took another long pause.

Then continued in a distressed choked whisper. "It was the night she told me we were going to be parents, so I know she would never kill herself."

By this point, the tears were streaming down his face, but he did not care. "Not the excited person who told me I would be a dad and who carried our child within her."

Shocked to find out how good it felt to tell someone his darkest secret because the sting of losing not just his wife but child as well, still affected Remy deeply.

The decision to bury the information and not share it with anyone had been a hard one. Even his parents had not known about the baby because it would have caused them more heartache.

After confessing to the lovely beside him about the child, a dam inside Remy had broken free, allowing him to continue. "The difference between my story and the dates included in the notes, is what enabled me to generate some interest in the case. As ridiculous as it seems, it's the only reason I got anyone to listen to what little evidence is available."

Keeping that last secret had endless pain attached to it he had been unaware of, but it had subsided quickly, after acknowledging his secret. Remy found himself overjoyed by this amazing reaction. However, an ache still burned deep inside. "There are two firms still investigating the possibility she might not have killed herself. I've had them on retainer for over two years."

For a moment, he allowed the anger to again enter his manner. "Most people think I'm crazy and in denial because the evidence is overwhelming, but I don't care. Mandy wouldn't use drugs or kill herself!" The caring man had experienced all the stages of grief and Remy learned the hard way; you could permit none of them to reign over you. "Not Amanda Edwards."

After his declaration, even the sorrow bottled up inside him seemed significantly lighter, but it still took time to get himself back under control. The next sentence, Remy delivered quietly but laced in a dreadfully chilling tone. "It's what police refer to as an open and shut case."

Back to glancing at the ceiling, Belle's feelings overwhelmed her as she lay next to a man, who no one believed but who still had faith in his deceased wife. She continued to shed tears for his loss, while huge emotional blocks crumbled inside her chest. Grateful, he was somewhere far away while the walls around Belle's heart collapsed. To her disapproval, the more she became familiar with this dark-haired Legolas look-alike, the more Belle was falling for him. Now was not the time to be thinking about the sexy guy beside her and she attempted to push those mixed-up emotions away.

She wanted to deny her growing affections for Remy but after everything the weary woman had been through, she did not want to lose any more precious time. Yet, knew she needed to tuck those weaknesses away for the time being, although not before stealing one last glance at the grief-stricken man. *Lord, this man just complicates everything but he's sure easy on the eyes.* Afterwards, Belle resumed staring at the ceiling, patiently waiting for him to return to the present.

Unfortunately, Remy was unaware of anything except the pain. *How could someone be so good?* The deliberation made him feel deflated inside, but that was how he still thought of the murderer: good, clever, and sneaky because the person had left few traceable clues. The butcher had made mistakes because he found several of them and would go on looking until discovering who killed Amanda. It was the least Remy could do for her.

Somewhere deep inside, a persistent little voice kept telling him to notice who lay stretched out beside him. This was the one woman who stirred something, no other on earth had ever done, including his beautiful Mandy. Gradually, Remy pulled himself together, while silently acknowledging something magical was definitely happening between them.

As he laid beside her, gathered the pretty lady back in his arms and allowed his inner being to appreciate this exquisite creature. However, both instantly ignored those defiant feelings and for now, merely drew comfort from one another. After a long while, they drifted off to sleep, wrapped in each other's arms.

When opening his eyes hours later, found it pitch dark outside while the woman beside him lay watching. "Hi." Quietly mouthing to Belle because for the first time in his life, Remy was at a loss for words. Darkness made it seem like the two of them were caught in a spell. The only lighting came from the various pieces of medical equipment, adding a mystical ambiance to the room.

With a soft, slow touch, pressed her fingers against the side of his face, gently tracing his chiseled jawline down to those inviting lips. The provocative move caused something to literally 'shift' inside her. With a bolstered confidence due to the blackness surrounding them the shy doctor leaned in closer until their two noses touched. Their reactions to one another bordered on magical and was something that could not be ignored for much longer, but it also left her confused.

Her pink lips whispered against Remy's enticing ones. "Hi...back at ya." But Belle decided that instead of using logic and reasoning, she would only go on instinct.

For once in her life, deciding to throw caution to the wind and allow her swirling emotions to take over. By kissing those luscious lips, she was hopeful of forgetting all about the trouble that had hounded them over the last few days.

Just once, she would like to do what was not right.

Unfortunately, etiquette dictates there are several acts strictly forbidden for a new widow. Right when she was contemplating committing one, reality swiftly slipped back into her reasoning. *Sweet Mother Earth, save me from myself.*

Belle pulled herself together, remembering who she was, but more importantly, who she had just lost. Instead of kissing the gorgeous god, cast aside her smoldering yearnings and began crying softly.

Not wanting to admit it, but Remy was just as confused by his churning emotions too. Out of options on what to do for tonight, gathered her back into his arms and continued to hold her tight until sleep eventually returned. Each slumbered uninterrupted and peacefully throughout the rest of the evening.

When the sun came up at daybreak, both of them awoke refreshed and ready to take on their mounting problems.

CHAPTER 13

Southern Gentleman

After speaking with the local sheriff's department, the next morning Belle checked out of the county hospital. Although reluctant to allow Remy to drive her back to the city she had declined her in-laws' kind offer to send the Buchanan helicopter. By the end of their conversation, Belle had reassured the Randalls she was doing fine and promised to visit soon.

This was a crucial step for her self-worth because this journey of grief was one, she needed to travel alone. Belle intended to spend the drive time discussing the events of the last few weeks with Remy. Too much had occurred, in such a brief period, for all of it to be just a coincidence. They needed to compare notes because several things were just not adding up.

Now that Belle decided to pursue those needed answers, found herself hesitant. The more time spent with Remy, the less she trusted her reasoning. Yesterday's heart-wrenching testimony regarding his wife and unborn child had only reinforced that point. This terrified her because the damaged federal agent was making her experience things she should not. Even scarier were these emotions that she had never felt before. In addition, this was occurring during the worst time in her life following the loss of her beloved grandmother.

To cast out those mischievous impulses, Belle shook her head. *My wicked mind should not be fantasizing about getting up close and personal with a man.* The sinful thoughts were wrong, and she knew it. But those naughty notions continued to intrude into her grief. They kept slipping back in and reddening her lovely pale cheeks. With a quick glance, checked to see if he could read her mind, and she was relieved to notice Remy could not.

The best decision would be to put those wayward ideas aside and go back to what Belle did best, which were lists. She lovingly caressed her favorite notebook. *Lists are comforting, like an old friend or a warm blanket.* Vibrant eyes glanced upward, as she said a thankful prayer her journal had survived the blast. Once more, she peeked sideways to make sure Remy did not notice her increasing discomfort.

At last, settled down in the front seat, and opened the first blank page in her much-loved pad of paper. To calm her nerves, Belle began a record of everything she remembered Sam had said along with a list of things making her *'feelers'* tingle. Also, decided to compile a list of the information she had uncovered while doing her own research shortly after the shooting. It was time to put their cards on the table. *Did we really trust one another yet?* Shyly, stole another peek from the passenger seat and studied Remy's rugged profile. Embarrassed when he caught her looking but Belle returned to the list on her lap because was not ready to talk yet.

The Appalachian Trail ran outside his window, but its splendor did not help lessen the lump in Remy's throat. The desire to talk with her was burning his insides but the coward in him would not allow his mouth to move.

If he had not been so miserable, the outdoorsman would have enjoyed the ride with the beauty beside him because spring colors splashed across everything and in all directions around their car. The passing scenery was some of the most magnificent he had ever witnessed. Vivid shades of color exploded in the fields and flowers seemed to burst from every kind of tree, shrub, and plant. Remarkable vegetation was present for as far as he could see, and Remy appreciated Belle's Granny was somehow responsible for this parade of color. He stole another quick glance at his lovely passenger, while acknowledging Mavis also had a hand in shaping her too.

There was much more to this situation than he could have imagined, plus, still had no idea how her interesting grandmother fit into the whole ugly affair. Remy spent the next few miles deliberating that scenario with himself. *If she knows, will she confide that information to me?* Determined to discover what prior knowledge Belle had of Mavis Brooks' death and how it might fit into his investigation of Sam.

To break the ice, he started with something easy. "How are you feeling?" Turned his head to see her reaction but got nothing. Apparently, this would not be as simple as he imagined and began again. "Are you comfortable?" When she did not answer, became nervous but kept pushing. "Do you need anything?"

At long last, a squeak came from the front seat. "No." With her head bowed, Belle ignored him, concentrating on the notebook in her lap. This was difficult because old scars now stood wide open on one of them, while new ones were still fresh on the other.

For the first ten miles, those festering wounds forced the two of them to ride in dead silence. Neither was willing to take the essential steps toward the crucial conversation that needed to occur.

The miles continued to pass but she would not lift her head. Remy's patience was wearing thin, and he ran out of excuses to stay silent. Convinced it was time to figure this whole outrageous mess out, he first cleared his throat to get Belle's attention. "Umm."

The unexpected disruption made her head snap toward him.

"I'm so sorry." Those were the only words Remy could manage to say before his feelings interfered with the sound of his voice. Grief is always difficult, especially when losing everything. It was something he understood firsthand, having had a similar experience. There were no words to comfort her, but he desperately wished to supply any that might.

It startled him out of his thoughts when Belle spoke.

"Remy please, I know you're sorry and I appreciate it, but I can't talk about this. Not right now." Her soft voice floated from the other side of the car. "If we're going to figure out what's going on, I can't think about Granny. If I talk about her, I'll fall apart." Big teardrops dripped onto Belle's lap. "So please, let's not do it, okay? Let's figure out who killed her. When this is over, I'll have time to grieve for Granny but not right now."

"Not right now." Noting the longer she spoke, her southern accent became thicker and in the worst way, Remy wanted to fix everything but that was not possible.

By this point, the tears streaming down the lovely lady's face trickled onto her handwritten notes; the ink smearing with each tear. Slowly, she raised her head and those vivid gemstone eyes pleaded with Remy to please move on.

The shaken man changed the subject because this conversation was not going the way he planned. "What did you see when you touched the election article?"

The gentle question made Belle's head snap around again. For a few minutes, sat there contemplating his question because he had used a sympathetic tone to draw her in. Its soothing manner made the cynical woman want to confide everything to the blue-eyed devil.

But she would not fall for it this time.

To combat the enchanting sound, focused her famous stare on him. Tried to gauge without his magic interfering if she could truly trust this man. Even after everything they had been through, the skeptic in her was still not positive. To settle her churning innards down, she drew a deep breath and asked a question of her own. One, which she desperately needed answered. "Why were you at Granny's house?"

Not ready to answer the question yet, Remy stared straight ahead because he needed time to think. His rotten luck had caught up with him again, forcing the first thought stumbling around in his head to just slip out of his mouth. "Okay well, that seems like a fair question."

Sounding like an idiot and trying to stall, he was hesitant about how to word it because his intuition shouted to proceed with care. "I um, went there, to um, talk with her." His eyes peered out the front windshield, and Remy did not dare look at Belle, for fear she would see his distress.

From the strange expression on his face, the experienced shrink thought this hottie was hiding something. *But what?* The anger became loud and clear in Belle's voice because of the suspected secret. "Exactly what kind of discussion did you need to have with my grandmother?" Also annoyed because of her growing weakness toward Remy and his many superior attributes.

Crap. He hit the steering wheel with his palm, uncertain how to handle this circumstance. *She requested a copy, so obviously there had to be a reason. Right?* While Remy's instincts screamed, Belle's legendary stare continued to bore into his skull. His magic shouted to remember how fragile she was. The injured little dove was apparently ignorant of the details regarding what happened on that street in London almost thirty years ago.

"I went there to ask your grandmother, um...ah well, to ask questions about your mother's death." Briefly twisting his head to see her reaction. Unfortunately, she was displaying a shocked expression on a much too pale face.

"Why drive over five hours?" The white-faced beauty stared out the windshield. "To ask Granny Brooks such a simple thing?" With each passing mile Belle looked like she should be back in a hospital bed.

"I'm so sorry but I needed to get more information." His words muddled as Remy tried to explain. "The FBI file didn't..."

A look of pure shock broke out on Belle's face. "The FBI file?" Twirled around to confront him. "WHAT FBI FILE???" Gone was the timid patient. "Remy what the hell is going on?" In its place sat a rattled and frightened person, as panic slowly built inside her.

Belle spun around further to reach the car handle in the back. Frantic to grasp anything to get out of this small car. She flung her leg up on the seat because was only interested in exiting the vehicle.

Suddenly, a glimmer of reason surged through her because it was imperative, she get a grip. The panicked woman needed to gain control of this unusual anxiety. Although, somewhere deep in her brain, concern rose about the number of odd incidents that continued to occur. After a few minutes of Granny's relaxation therapy, Belle determined the strategy was not working today. Gracefully, she attempted to get out of the awkward position and pleaded with her brain to make sense, but nothing seemed to be helping.

Although, even in full blown panic mode, Remy thought her stare was piercingly scary.

"What are you talking about?" Something had always seemed off about her mother's death, but Belle had ignored the lingering doubts. Positive Granny or Daddy would have told her anything important. *They would never lie.* After several awkward moments, her newly enhanced *'feelers'* kicked in, right when she comprehended what his astonishing revelation meant. Belle found herself stunned in silence and slipped back into the passenger seat.

This man sitting beside her had just disclosed there was a file somewhere inside the FBI. A file with details about her mother's death and Belle did not imagine it involved cancer. *This is unbelievable.*

The volcano once again bubbled deep inside.

Still scorched from her glare, Remy was uncertain how to handle his passenger's outburst, which made concentrating on driving very difficult. She looked ready to either pass out or scramble from the car. Undecided, he debated whether to turn around and take the frantic woman back to the hospital or keep going. If driving was his decision, he needed to concentrate on these dangerous mountain roads and not the pretty beside him.

It's too hot in this car. Didn't Remy understand I have to get out right NOW? Multiple subjects were rushing through Belle's traumatized mind, not allowing her to think straight. "Oh my God, there's a rest station up ahead." She pleaded, as claustrophobia started setting in. Unable to halt the frenzy churning inside, shouted because she did not know what else to do. "Please stop the car."

"Belle I'm sorry." Remy quickly countered. "I didn't know." His head searched right and left, then glanced over to see how she was faring but from the look of things, not well at all. She looked close to keeling over. *Dear God, maybe I should turn around and go back to the ER.* The decision was a difficult one, because he did not know her well enough to judge. Although, from what he could tell, she seemed to hold up remarkably well.

"Remy just stop the car." Quietly whispered, a ghost white Dr. Brooks. "Please, just pull off and stop the car." The next thing he heard was the awful sound of her forehead crashing against the dashboard. With the upcoming highway ahead, frantic for anywhere to pull over, worried she had fainted.

Relieved when he spotted a place up ahead. "Thank God." Picked up speed after exiting the ramp and he sped past the blue rest-stop sign as the entrance came into view. The pale woman sprang to life and tumbled out of the moving automobile as he pulled into the almost deserted area. At a loss for what to do, Remy threw open the door and rushed around the car.

Almost at once, he was bombarded by the most powerful magic he had ever experienced. It washed over him briefly and Remy had to catch his breath, from the might of its force. Once recovered, discovered Belle flung onto her knees and vomiting atop the frozen landscape. Unable to do anything for her, other than to hold her hair out of the way, the gentleman gallantly did just that until she was finished.

"I'm so sorry Belle." Handed her a bottled water from his pocket and went to grab a towel from the back of the car while dissecting this newest phenomenon.

Upon returning with the cloth, continuing in his most charming southern voice. "You feelin' better now sugah?" Watched, as she wiped that enchanting face but felt horrible because she looked pitiful, so put the unusual magical occurrence on hold for now. As he turned the charm up to an eleven, Remy was hopeful his special type of 'talents' would give some much-needed assistance. He was doing everything he could think of to aid this poor creature. The pain written all over her face affected him more than he cared to admit, and wished there was something he could do to take it away.

"Yes, thank you." Meekly replying from her position on the ground, while clinging to the empty water bottle. "Could we just sit over there for a bit?" Pointed a shaky finger at the nearest bench, as she ignored his supernatural help.

Her ability to compose herself, under the most strenuous occurrences, intrigued the anxious guy as he helped Belle to her feet.

"Goodness gracious, thank you." The color somewhat returned to her face as she brushed herself off. At which point, her manners kicked in. "I must look a sight."

Remy offered Belle his right arm and escorted her to the park bench. The act performed naturally, like any decent southern gentleman. *My momma would be mighty proud of my conduct today.* "Dr. Brooks, it seems every conversation I have with you starts with the words I'm sorry." The comment was his attempt to infuse some much-needed humor into the horrible situation while being humbled by her unbelievable strength and dignity. His admiration continued to grow while trying to keep her respectfully warm, as he assisted her to the *Virginia is for Lovers* bench.

"It appears that's exactly the way all our conversations begin, Mr. Montgomery." Belle responded slightly above a whisper, not looking up at him but not letting go of his arm either.

Remy sat next to her for a while but soon realized staying here much longer was not an option due to the possibility of a large spring snowstorm moving in that afternoon.

It was time to get the unpleasantness over. "Belle, what do you think happened to your mother?" From her earlier reaction, the distraught woman appeared ignorant concerning the details regarding her mother's death. Which meant, Remy would bring heartache to Belle Brooks' doorstep once more. He had had nothing but this kind of luck since their meeting in Florida. Why, just this morning, he was thinking his luck could not get any worse, but Remy had been wrong. Again.

Belle surprised him when she answered right away. "My mom died when I was two years old." She stared straight ahead at nothing. "I don't remember her. Just pictures but she was so beautiful." Calmly, she recited the information with little emotion. "My dad loved her very much. Occasionally, he would go out with women, but Daddy never remarried." She spoke like a robot. "Mom had breast cancer and died right before Christmas in nineteen eighty-three." It was almost like she had memorized a script of the details as a child.

Not understanding how this fit in with Sam Randall or what was going on, bells rang loudly inside Remy's head. Too much occurred in such a brief period, making it impossible for the special agent to process all the unusual instances. What he needed was time alone to think and assemble the different pieces.

Finding himself perplexed because instead of getting answers, he had ended up with even more questions. *Why would William Brooks hide his wife's cause of death from his only child?* Frustration set in and he found his fingers tightening up again. Without thinking, Remy began his exercises, then added the much-needed deep cleansing breaths to his relaxation routine.

In the meantime, sitting here on this cold bench a ferocious storm brewed inside Belle. The last two weeks had finally caught up to her. At the moment, she was having difficulty keeping it under control and seemed to be losing the battle. Those emerald eyes stared straight ahead, afraid to glance at Remy but not sure how much longer she could hold it together.

After a long pause, Belle asked the dreaded question. It was the one she desperately wanted answered since hearing about the government folder. "What does the FBI file say about my mom?"

Another question the pretty widow seemed unwilling to back down from, and unfortunately, it looked like stalling time had come to an end. But it still did not make it any easier to tell her.

Those big, beautiful eyes turned toward the caring gentleman, expecting him to tell her the truth. The burden was killing him because in a few minutes, those jewel-like orbs would hurt once more. He was furious at his continued bad luck. *Because it will be me, yet again.* Cursed at his misfortune of causing Belle's upcoming pitiful, heartbreaking look.

To ground himself, he drew a deep breath and assumed the role of delivering the unpleasant news. "Your mother did have breast cancer, but it was in remission." Positive, this tangled mess fits together in some way but unsure how or why. Confident this theory rang true by his pulsating reflexes. Finally, Remy went ahead with the horrendous details.

"There was a bomb that exploded at Harrods."

CHAPTER 14

Hum's the Word

"Oh my God, that's the reason!" Suddenly, Belle leapt up from the bench and started pacing.

Confusion spread across Remy's black and blue face. "What reason?"

By now, Belle had a look of delight, not despair upon hers. "It's the one that keeps making all the noise." The poor guy was both concerned and confused but she just ignored his question, certain he would not like her explanation.

While she paced, contemplated how best to inform him, eventually decided on the truth. "Okay, I didn't tell you the article has been humming at me."

Shocked silly, Remy shot off the bench. "WHAT???" Forced to bite his tongue, could not believe he'd heard her correctly while trying with all his might not to get angry. Confident, he did not want to scare her, but this was some serious shit. He stopped walking back and forth, then took another deep breath, through very clenched teeth. "Please explain, what does humming at you mean?"

The calm was not holding, and walked away because not all his gifts were positive. Some required Remy to keep a tight rein on his anger lest it strike out and actually harm someone. Things were talking to her, and Belle had blatantly ignored them. *Good God, she really didn't get how all of this worked.*

From firsthand experience, Remy understood how dangerous paranormal activities were if snubbed, as numerous, unpleasant childhood memories ran rampant through his consciousness. The types of phenomenon Belle was referring to only got worse, not better, when being slighted and even contemplating doing such a thing, made his apprehension level go through the roof.

First, thinking her clueless. *Does she have any idea what the hell is going on?* Then, sharply repeating the question aloud. Unable to contain his anger about the article's uproar and Belle's ability to hear it. He was especially mad because of her naivety in disregarding it.

She hated it when he became bossy, but irritation was unlikely to get her answers and Belle desperately needed those. "I don't know what's going on and I'm sorry for causing such a fuss. Maybe we should, you know..." She sweetly suggested. "Could we maybe, both of us start over again?" She was determined to learn what the FBI file had to say, which would not happen if they continued to argue and fight with one another.

"Let's sit back down." Always a gentleman, Remy indicated with his hand for her to go first. "Please?"

After a few awkward moments, sat down reluctantly because sitting this close to him made Belle uncomfortable. Fretted at her repeated weakness for him but also laughed at herself because those same emotions were making her feel alive. Those weak sentiments were the biggest clue she was still among the living.

Back in the present, pulled her straying emotions under wraps. "Okay when I first touched the folder, I got a terrible impression way down deep." A bone white finger, pointed toward her chest area. "I also sensed dreadful corruption and profound sorrow but as I started to examine it, the desk phone rang." Looked up into Remy's eyes but so far, appeared to accept her story. Belle still did not want to talk about handling the file, therefore, proceeded tentatively. "The folder scared me, so I didn't touch it again. You did, when you came back to the office with me."

Quickly sneaked another glance at Remy to build up her nerve. "When you put the articles into the piles." Suddenly finding it hard to swallow. "One made a humming-like sound." Being uncomfortable with her gift started showing on Belle's lovely face. "That's when I first heard it from across the room." Lowering her head, she waited patiently with hands clasped together in her lap, expecting Remy's irate response because his disappointment coursed throughout the air.

Astonishment covered his face because she calmly discussed a talking article like it was an everyday occurrence. An abnormality himself, Remy knew the confession had been a difficult one because he would have had a tough time telling it too. To put her at ease, he did not doubt the validity of her statement but did gently question her. "Has this ever happened to you before?" Brilliant blue eyes searched Belle's for an answer. Although gifted like him, he was discovering the remarkable woman could accomplish things Remy did not think possible.

What else is she not telling me? He wondered to himself, while considering what other magic she had up her sleeve. Unsure how, Remy sensed the anxiety gathering steam inside her. Instead of dwelling on the impossible, opted to help her by adding his own magic into the mix. Tenderly taking her hand in his, he looked into Belle's eyes. "Has this ever happened to you before sugah?"

She wanted to just sit there and forget everything while staring into those Caribbean blue eyes, but Remy deserved an answer. "No…Never. It scared me something awful." Softly, she confided. "I was afraid to touch it without Granny near me."

While he had been talking, a revelation had occurred to Belle. As soon as Remy touched her, the volcano trying to erupt inside her soul had just disappeared. Now, in its place flowed a calm gentle stream. The experience made her think of happier times like those spent at Granny's playing in the beautiful crystal-clear waters of the Sinclair River. Thankful that peace had returned to her psyche, and she was able to think again.

Now clearheaded, Belle remembered the article's current whereabouts. "I locked it in my briefcase after Florida." She jumped up from the bench. "I want to touch it and see what I can get from it." Heading toward the rental car, a picture of Remy's beautiful but destroyed automobile flashed on her internal brain screen.

Remy grabbed her hand, pulling her back from the fast car daydream but she was not giving in so easily. Twirling toward him, Belle stomped her foot. "My briefcase made it. It's in the car. Let me get it and I can touch it now." Tugging the much larger man along towards the rental and the secrets about her mom.

"NO!" Surprised by Remy's intensity, Belle jumped. "I'm sorry." Again, found himself staring down into those gorgeous green eyes. "See, I'm saying it again."

"Remy, I have a right to know about my mother." Almost daring him to stop her, while demanding he set her free. "You cannot keep me from finding out."

He spoke in his calming voice because clearly, the semi-hysterical woman was not thinking straight. "Belle, I'm not trying to stop you from finding out about your mom." Spun around, with his hands spread wide for her to take notice of the surroundings. "But I'm suggesting we do so in a place that's a little more private." The two of them were no longer alone, as he pointed out the cars and trucks that had pulled into the almost full parking lot.

Although embarrassed by her ill-mannered behavior, Belle could not seem to help herself but managed to drag her remaining ego back under control. She needed to apologize. "You're right Remy, this time it's my turn to be sorry. Let's go back to Washington and put our heads together." Resignation dripped from every word, but she knew the captivating rascal was correct.

They walked back to the car, arm in arm as Remy kept sending his soothing magic toward Belle to help steady her footing. The events let him relax a bit because for now, had avoided the question of her mother's death. Although, accepted it was only a matter of time before he would have to tell her about the violent details. A conversation the worn-out agent did not want to have but he acknowledged, she did deserve to know the truth but dreaded having to be the one to deliver the shocking news personally.

The volcano churned even deeper inside but she continued to receive some welcome relief; it seemed touching Remy's arm kept it at bay. Another experience which had never happened before, and Belle appreciated his help. The loud humming noise echoing from the trunk of the car was overwhelming her senses and she desperately clung to him for support.

Certain she was not strong enough to withstand the long ride back to town, her obvious pain had Remy torn to pieces. He urged Belle to contact Sam's parents to ask them to send the company helicopter and breathed a sigh of relief when she agreed to the plan. They rode back to the hospital, primarily in silence.

Once they were secured into the transport, the two of them spent the forty-five-minute trip just observing the scenery because it was unwise to discuss sensitive information inside a Buchanan Industries vehicle. Remy had spent the flight pointing out photographic features below, with witty descriptions thrown in for her enjoyment and had even gotten a smile or two out of the reserved woman on a few.

When flying past the Capitol dome, he marveled at how gorgeous their hometown was at this height and was relieved to see she was almost her normal self by the time they touched down. The chopper was the lap of luxury and they had little difficulty when landing at Reagan National. A chauffeured limo waited for them on the tarmac, with surprising little media.

They headed to Belle's house on the Hill, but it was well into the afternoon by the time they arrived. Exhausted from the hectic last twenty-four hours, plus each needed to freshen up, the gracious host offered Remy use of her third-floor guest suite. An invitation, he accepted gladly.

Happy to be back on familiar ground, immediately jumping into her big relaxing shower. The spray of warm water washed over all the aches and pains, which quickly made themselves known. While the all-glass enclosure fogged up, she mulled over how it had been only a few days since meeting the FBI guy, but it seemed more like centuries. Something the practical part of her mind had difficulty accepting.

She struggled to overlook those facts, but the tough thing was ignoring these feelings that were stronger than her wounds. Feelings for the intriguing gentleman that would not go away, and also seemed to be growing. Too much had happened too fast, and she still could not comprehend it all. Allowing herself another long cry, she eventually gathered whatever muster she had left. Afterwards, vowed this weeping episode would be her last for a long while. Many items still needed to be taken care of and there was no time for Belle to be wallowing in self-pity.

After drying off, she got ready to confront Remy. To combat those erupting emotions, Belle picked out a set of comfortable clothes for their showdown. Deduced that working herself up into a good mad was just what the doctor ordered, and she wanted to be comfy for their confrontation. The anger allowed her to concentrate on something besides the good-looking agent.

Instead of focusing on her want, Belle needed to find these guys and stop the bastards who wanted her dead. Not ready to lie down just yet, she stood tall at the top of the stairs after collecting her inner strength. It was critical to hunt down the horrible people who had killed her beloved grandmother, acknowledging Remy's help would be necessary to track down these creeps.

Belle sauntered down the beautiful winding staircase caressing the familiar carved banister, which helped build up her nerve. Momentarily, she stopped on the creaky sixth step, to draw reassurance from her familiar surroundings. Like the mahogany carved credenza, which had always sat by the front door since before she was born. Or the detailed handmade Oriental rug. The one Daddy had brought back from an early trip to Asia. Last year, it had been the signature piece of her *Vanity Essence* featured living room. The work of art had always been her favorite.

All these cherished belongings filled her with a sense of contentment and bolstered Belle's emotional sentiment. A sensation not everyone was as fortunate to experience, and she felt blessed. Being in this house, surrounded by these things, reminded her of the values she had been raised on, along with who she was and what was expected of her. Took solace from what her eccentric family had provided, along with all the important beliefs they had instilled.

Unfortunately, it was impossible to avoid the crazy predicament that was the rest of her life. Still unsteady from her ordeal at Granny's, Belle slowly entered the downstairs level in search of Remy.

Smiled when finding him of all places, in the kitchen. The cutie was cooking breakfast but from the looks of it, preparing a meal for ten, not two. For his concocted masterpiece, it looked like he had pulled everything out of the refrigerator, piling it onto the center island. The only thing currently visible at the Sub-Zero was his gorgeous butt, because Remy's head was still buried inside.

At the doorway, she stopped to admire him a little longer. She was sure no good would come from this fascination but for the time being, Belle did not care. At this angle could tell he wore a pair of dark blue, baggy FBI sweatpants along with a plain white T-shirt. She was certain there was not a man alive who had ever looked so incredibly sexy. *OK, where did that come from?* She meant every word of the impish idea but had no clue where it originated.

A rare wide smile broke out on her face while thinking back to a favorite childhood book. *Wow, this must be what Alice felt like, after she fell through the looking glass.*

Just as quickly, reality came crashing back into her life, reminding Belle to keep the focus on the killers, and what was important. Hopefully, that worthy thought would help take her mind off such a beautiful backside because his ass looked like one of those mythical gods. *Absolutely perfect.*

Damn, time to get back to reality. "Are you looking for something or are you cleaning that out to be nice?" A brief giggle slipped out before Belle could stop it.

Her approach made Remy's head seem to spring out of the appliance. "Hey…you." He whirled around and flashed her the brightest, whitest smile Belle had ever seen. "How are you doing?" Marveling at her ability to look so healthy and composed when she had been in a coma only the day before.

"Better, thank you." Waved her hand over the heap of assembled ingredients. "What are you doing with all of this?"

"Since there isn't that much in this huge fridge, I decided to whip up my Marvelous Montgomery Omelet for dinner." He shined that captivating smile towards her, warming Belle's heart. His infectious laughter rang off the kitchen walls and it echoed through her soul. "Not something that is made for just anyone, mind you." Playfully pointing a utensil at her. "Only for the most V I P of people."

Charm and charisma oozed from every one of Remy's pores. He just stood there with a tempting but innocent grin on his face and a wooden spoon in his hand. Looking extraordinarily gorgeous and terribly comfortable in her kitchen. Belle giggled again at his silly declaration and if she did not know better, could have sworn Remy had been living here for years.

Dear Lord, this man does something to me insides. One of Granny's heartening sayings sprung into her head.

The warm laughter of her enchanting guest continued to echo throughout her house, and it soothed her aching heart. Another act her husband had never accomplished because he had always been a visitor here. Home, sweet home was not a phrase Sam would have ever used for this old brownstone and Belle was glad he never had. This critical detail made Remy's laughter that much sweeter to her ears. She decided to just stand there for the time being and let it roll over her. The tinkling sound comforted the distressed woman like nothing else had in a long time.

Weary, she simply was looking forward to spending the evening with this incredible man. Because Belle had a sneaking suspicion there were more surprises up this gorgeous gentleman's sleeve.

Contentment settled in and finally, she permitted herself some much-needed relaxation. Teasingly, she smiled back at the strapping, blue-eyed devil and grabbed one of her kitchen bar stools. "If you'll pass me a knife, I'll help with the dicing." Held her hand out while a surprised but pleased cook placed one of her cutting knives in it. After playfully kidding with her, he handed over a yellow pepper as well. A wide grin broke out on his face, as Remy grabbed another knife and started in on the red one.

For a few minutes they chopped in silence, and he stole one last peek at this amazing individual. Reluctantly, turning back toward the stove to begin his cooking magic. Grateful for the distraction of the preparations to pull himself together because again, this woman was having a most unusual effect on him.

The pile of colorful minced vegetables grew but his comfortable presence continued to perplex her. With his back still turned, she took the opportunity to look over the dashing Agent Montgomery. His raven black hair was wet and still in need of a haircut, a cute fault which caused her to break out in another wide smile but had no earthly idea why. Belle found this was occurring more often in the scoundrel's company.

The man seemed so comfortable and looked so right, while standing in front of her big kitchen stove, almost like he owned the place but in a non-threatening way. Remy's company made her feel rather strange, both good and weird.

Unable to stop the broad grin affixing itself to her face, Belle inquired sincerely, when considering the specimen before her. "What else do you need cut?" Popping a piece of raw pepper into her mouth.

"Nothing. I've got everything under control." Remy sweetly remarked over his shoulder. With the beginnings of relaxation setting in, she was amazed at how incredibly familiar Remy looked in her kitchen. Again, another feat Sam could never pull off. The thought made Belle smile even wider, and it helped to push her criminal husband out of her head.

While staring, could not help appreciating the agent's terrific physique and that gorgeous ass. She sat speculating, whether he had to work hard to maintain it or did it come naturally. Her conclusion, his fine form and good looks were another of his extraordinary gifts and she wondered how folks responded to this straight-out-of-a-magazine man because of his magical form. Belle thought they might because the view in front of her was definitely one fine man as she continued to take special note of his backside. *Boy, did it look yummy.*

Turned toward the stove while cooking, Remy was oblivious to the way the appreciative woman was scrutinizing him longingly. Because her current situation filled his mind, making him determined that Belle be comfortable and for lack of a better word, safe.

In addition, he was attempting to force his libido to calm down and it seemed to only partially be cooperating. Something he would never let her know, pretending nothing was amiss. Affectionately asking while continuing to cook. "How about a cup of coffee?"

Belle noticed he handily worked many containers all at once.

"A fresh pot is almost done brewing."

She chuckled, as both his hands flew about and much of what he did was a blur.

"I hope you don't mind but I found your extensive collection." That bright grin of Remy's slipped over his shoulder; then he went right back to work. "I'm very envious."

A few minutes later toast popped up and he caught both pieces with one hand. The other sautéed an abundance of veggies as delicious aromas emerged from the extensive pans assembled on the stove. The worn-out woman appreciated what little relief could be attained and sat back to enjoy the simple act of cooking a meal with someone you find pleasurable. Grateful to him for creating this small reprieve from the madness which had been haunting her for weeks.

After some time, Belle found herself relaxing. To help prolong this wonderful feeling, took several deep cleansing breaths, releasing each one slowly and thoroughly. This let some of the last couple of days *'run out of her,'* as Granny would say. Smiled again when Remy turned toward her with that Prince Charming grin.

"I didn't think anyone could have a greater passion for the coffee bean than me." He teased Belle, as soothing, genuine happiness came through in Remy's voice. "Dr Brooks, I must say you put me to shame." A serene, relaxing smile broke out on her face. The first one in weeks. It spilled into her aura which glowed brighter than Remy had ever seen before.

So, he found my caffeine stash. Belle was enjoying herself. Out of the blue, her stomach rumbled just as another giggle slid out. Both hands flew to her midsection in embarrassment at the noises coming from her body, but she could not recall the last time she had eaten anything.

Still facing away from her and unaware because he had not heard her hunger growl. "Not to mention your rather exotic tea collection." As soon as the words left his mouth, Remy stopped dead in his tracks because the teas had probably come from her grandmother. He had become so content cooking in her home, the embarrassed man had temporarily forgotten the rest of the world and the last few days.

Quickly, he turned around to see how to fix the damage that had been done. It surprised him to find a woman, more like the one from the years ago spotlight than the one from yesterday's hospital bed.

The mention of the teas had shocked her, and Belle gasped for air because had momentarily overlooked the tragic death of her treasured Granny. Her many famous sayings cropped up throughout the day and were always an important part of Belle's internal conversations. She was just starting to realize how difficult life would be without her loving grandmother.

At the same time Belle found herself feeling stronger than ever and she knew Granny would always be a part of her everyday life. Just like the saying, which had popped out of her mouth a few minutes ago. One of the many phrases that constantly rattled around inside her head. The melancholy reflection brought a sad smile to her face, an image Remy was glad to see instead of the tears. "I'm sorry again." Tired of always apologizing to her but he was not sure of what else to say.

"No need but thank you." The words tried to get stuck in her throat. "And yes, most of the teas are from my grandmother." She stared at this magnificent man, thinking Granny sure would have appreciated him as well. Went on with her back straighter and head higher than before. "But I was taught at an early age how to make every one of those teas. Know how to grow every leaf too." Pointed out the window at the large backyard garden, something that was now obsolete for most DC households. "My collection will live on." Softly adding. "Just like Granny."

To help lighten up the mood, plus to move away from losing her grandmother, hopped off the stool and headed over to the large pantry. Grabbed a jar of Granny's famous ginger root tea because she needed the enjoyment of the blend's relaxing and calming properties.

For a moment, stopped just to watch her walk across the tiled floor. She was stunning in her black workout pants and too big *Harrington College* sweatshirt. Not to mention her incredible hair which flowed like smooth liquid silk down her back. The cascading curls fell well below her shoulders, a dazzling feature which had been hidden during their meeting in Florida.

Without warning, he fantasized about running his hands through Belle's caramel-colored tresses. Remy stood with his arms crossed, admiring the spectacular view from across the room. *All of five feet, three inches tall in her bare feet.* Shaking his head approvingly at the sight before him. *Campbell Brooks is sure one hell of a woman and handling this a lot better than most.* With an unquenched hunger, enjoyed every step as she made her way to the pantry. Remy loved looking at the fetching lady even if she was just walking across the kitchen floor. Here in this house Belle seemed to have blossomed and was nothing like the woman he had met in Palm Beach.

Although somewhere deep inside, something would not allow him to trust the pretty little thing or her incredible abilities. His internal intuitions kept indicating there were just too many unanswered questions and his talents seemed to fail him when it came to Belle. *Could he trust her?* Unfortunately, trust was difficult to keep in mind when inspecting her backside as he smiled that gifted grin at her walking voluptuous form.

Remy decided to settle his internal conflict with a compromise, by making an agreement with himself to just chill out and appreciate the much needed down time. He spent a few extra minutes gathering his composure while completing his culinary craftsmanship.

Once he allowed himself to do so, Remy found he had not been this relaxed in a long, long time. Gone was the burning need to find Amanda's killer; replacing it was just the desire to cook this amazing woman an omelet. Staggered by his good mood, he just wanted to enjoy this evening for what it was, a break from insanity.

There were still too many missing pieces to this mysterious puzzle but tonight, he would not let his obsession get in the way. For now, Remy was just going to let his imagination run wild and pretend he might get a shot at that date.

After they finished eating, the two of them cleaned up and both walked away with the impression they had been sharing meals together for years. Neither wanted to deal with those explosive feelings and quickly disregarded them as figments of their imagination. They went to their separate rooms and gathered their collected materials for an overdue consultation of their accumulated data.

Agreeing to meet back downstairs in thirty minutes to go over everything each had found.

CHAPTER 15

Boy Scout Honor

Belle smiled when grabbing her beat-up briefcase, happy it had survived the bombs at Granny's. Inside it were the many lists she had been assembling over the last several days. As soon as she touched the case, the unusual charm inside came roaring back to life. In all the confusion, Belle had forgotten about the talisman from Sam's other key chain and was still torn about what to do with it.

Opening the attaché, she studied the key closely, after pulling the remarkable piece out of the bag she had stored it in. Just like last time, the same evil surfaced as soon as she touched the mystic-like key. Although she was prepared for the malevolent impression, Belle still experienced a horrible sensation.

At first touch, a second awareness overwhelmed her and the uneasy psychic sensation made her hesitate. Confident, this was like the malicious consciousness she experienced in Palm Beach and knew it was a warning. Although, she was not positive about what to do, certain her *'feelers' were gonna come callin'*. The familiar sensation made Belle pay close attention.

Although she was bone weary, Granny's saying still brought a smile but instead of dealing with it, Belle decided to delay her intuitions. Gently removing the nightmarish key from the ring and placing it back into the designer bag for safekeeping, until she could figure out what to do. There was plenty to discuss with Remy tonight without bringing evil objects into the conversation.

For now, she would follow these new enhanced and demanding instincts while showing Remy only the safe deposit key. She would find out what they could and see where that would lead them. By leaving the other one in the locked case, Belle prayed it was the right decision. Turning out the light, she stopped and collected herself, along with the rest of her things; then headed downstairs.

Before retrieving her materials, she suggested the two of them meet in the dining room and Remy had helped insert the leaves into the table. The antique was now expanded to its maximum sixteen-person capacity. By the time Belle arrived, his computer and stacks of papers covered three quarters of it. She smiled at how comfortable he seemed in her home, then found an open space for her briefcase. For the first few minutes, pulled out and organized her lists, pads of paper, felt-tip pens and various printouts, along with her own laptop. Avoided him while nervously moving things around and she anxiously waited for Remy to begin.

Apprehensive, the FBI guy paced. He had been dreading this since their conversation on that cold bench, earlier today. *I get she deserves to know what happened but I sure as shit didn't want to be the one to do so.* When the silence grew too much, he took the first step. "Okay where would you like to begin?" Remy looked at her timidly and hoped like hell, Belle did not say her mother's death but knew he was doomed.

Calmly, she sat down across from him while pulling a pad of paper from the pile in front of her. Desperate for answers, Belle was certain none would come quickly if she did not share with him.

Pointed at a line on her notepad and she surprised him by going first. "Seachd Righrean is who we are looking for. I don't know their actual identities but that's the name of their society." Glared at him, ready to confront his reaction and daring Remy to challenge her statement.

"What???" Again, he was surprised because her mother's death had not been the opening item. "What society?" Astonishment covered Remy's face.

"How do you even know this?" The keen investigator watched, as those beautiful shoulders dropped. He noticed the fatigue had caught up to her and realized barking at her would help neither of them.

"I guess you would call it my gift. Its correct name is psychometric, and their name just came to me after I touched the article." Stress overwhelmed her softly spoken voice. "Please Remy, if we're going to accomplish anything, you'll have to trust me on a few things." She sat staring, and waited for his response, eager to see if he had somewhat entrusted her. "There are things you will just have to take on faith and let it go, okay?"

Sweet Baby Jesus. She has got to be kidding me. He quietly challenged her. "Well, that's one hell of a leap." Yet, his instincts were zinging every which way, meaning Belle was on to something. *Damn.*

"Yes, it is." The only whispered response she could utter because both of them would need to decide tonight, whether to trust one another. Maybe not completely, because Belle did not plan to share the malevolent second key with him yet. She knew the dutiful civil servant had not shared everything with her either but needed to find out if there was enough trust to work together. It was necessary they catch the people who killed Granny and tried to kill them — twice. *If Remington Montgomery will not help me, then by God, I will find someone else who will.*

She sat nervously across from him and held her breath awaiting his answer.

Her words were mulling around in his mind. *Sure, the astonishing statement she had just professed was another puzzle. No, it's some kind of test.* He got up from his seat to contemplate her declaration. *That's what this is, a test. She wants me to pass but how?* Remy would need to consider his answer carefully.

The pressure mounted and he paced around the impressive furniture. Took his time for it to sink in because deep in his core, this sang out as a test. *To see if I have faith in her. Confide in her.* The confused guy stood there next to her huge table and stole a glance at her. The added time had allowed him to figure out something important. A particularly important something.

There was no one in the world he trusted more than Belle. Although, he had no idea why.

Remy started his finger exercises because he would need all his relaxation tools to get through this troublesome night.

At last, with his emotions back under control he came to a halt on the opposite side across from her. "Let's say I believe you." Looking Belle straight in the eyes. "What does it mean and how does it fit in with Sam and the Irish election?" This woman seemed to be talking rationally, so she must be going somewhere with this unusual train of thought. While his nerves pushed him to pace the length of the room, Remy was curious to see where Belle was heading. Trust was only one of the many things Remy felt for her. Although, he was not ready to admit such a thing, even to himself just yet.

Prepared to talk at last, Belle lifted her head and stared straight into his paradise-colored eyes. "I'll share what I have Remy but only, if you share too." She challenged him to defy her.

Sweet Jesus, she would not let this go. Brushed his hand down his face. *No way am I getting off that easy.* His pacing increased. *We're back to her mother's death, even if she hasn't asked about it yet.* The finger exercises were intensifying with each step.

Unfortunately, from the look of determination on the doctor's face, backing down was not an option and Remy could not blame her. It still puzzled him why William Brooks had told his daughter a lie. It would kill him to bring her more heartache, but Belle deserved the truth.

Stumbled when he realized his time was up. This made him turn around, slow down, and walk back over beside her.

Taking a minute, he tenderly stood overtop this extraordinary person, who continued to delve deeper into his soul. Sat down and gently gripped her small hand in his large rough one. "I'll tell you."

"I expect everything. Even if it hurts me." An unwavering Belle demanded. "You promise not to keep something from me to protect me?" She insisted, while tugging her clenched fist away.

He raised his hand in the three fingers, Boy Scout honor pose. "Promise." The impression Remy gave of taking a solemn vow could not have been cuter and the look on his face showed the man truly meant it.

Inside, Remy hoped like hell he could sustain such a pledge. As he grabbed her soft hand again, knew in his heart he would do anything in the world to keep her safe. Anything.

Even if it meant breaking his sworn oath to her; something Belle would not take kindly.

Unfortunately, his charming gifts currently seemed to be failing him, which made Remy think about making light of this somehow, but he was at a loss. So, waited for the uncomfortable subject that was inevitable.

Belle sat staring into space, until quietly asking. "Tell me about my mom."

Even when he recognized it was coming, the look on her face made his heart break in half. Which surprised him, considering Remy no longer imagined he owned a heart. Certain it had died a long time ago with Amanda. He stood up to catch his breath and found swallowing was also difficult. Ducking into the kitchen to regroup, he refreshed their coffees before having to continue with the ghastly truth.

After pulling himself together, reemerged and moved directly to her side. Suggested they both move to the living room and Belle decided that was a superb idea.

At last, their cups were refilled, and both were seated in the living room. After a deep breath, finally, he told her what little he had discovered about the death of Mrs. Kathleen Brooks. "Your mom was in London right outside Harrods Department Store on December seventeenth nineteen eighty-three."

Remy took another sip of his coffee to delay hurting her and to help bolster his nerves, but the time had come to tell her the violent truth. "On that morning, the IRA packed approximately thirty pounds of explosives into a car. The rebels then parked the automobile outside the side door of the popular department store during the height of the Christmas shopping season."

He looked up and found she was taking it better than expected, so went on. "The official report published in all the world's newspapers stated the bomb killed six people that day. Three police officers and three civilians."

After a long silence, she waited for him to continue, but instead, Remy's tortured eyes just stared blankly. His vacant stare forced Belle to nudge him. "And?"

It appeared he needed permission to continue, finally doing so after drawing in a big breath. "What those same reports don't contain is your mother was the seventh victim."

Without warning, Remy jumped up and dashed back into the dining area. She heard him shout beyond the archway. "For some reason, Kathleen Campbell-Bannerman Brooks isn't listed among any of the reports." The crumpled sounds were piles of papers being scattered and tossed across the table. "Anywhere except on one."

The noise made Belle smile as he relentlessly dug wildly through all the mounds of files. Silently, she sat grinning at his tenaciousness, patiently waiting for Remy to return from the next room to clarify his surprising but mistaken statement. Still convinced her mother had died from cancer and not in some foreign country.

"This one here." He came running back into the room, waving a piece of paper in the air.

He tried handing it to Belle, but she could only stare down at her mother's name, afraid of touching the report. The whole incident had sent her back into a state of shock and she waited for him to explain.

Too excited about finding the buried report to notice her discomfort, Remy pointed at the paper. "This one lists your mother as victim number seven, but she's nowhere on any of the others."

Shaken by his account, Belle could only mouth the words, instead of speaking them aloud. "But that makes little sense. Why would she be left off all the other reports?"

The kind man had been dreading just that question, pausing, because even in her current disarray Dr. Belle Campbell still directed her formidable stare at him.

Glaringly.

Unable to put it off any longer, Remy went on. "There is only one reason for something such as that to occur, but I can't believe it's true."

"What do you mean?" Bewildered, Belle's glance snapped up at him.

This entire time, he had been stumbling around because had been scrambling for a way to explain the sordid details. Meanwhile, she just sat there, eyeing him more harshly.

So far, Belle had been listening patiently but knew Remy's answer would be a doozy. Her anxiety was building but she wanted to keep herself from interrupting with lots of questions or hysterics.

Every time he turned around, she surprised him, but his grace period had come to an end. Gone was the woman from this morning, who had tried to climb out of his moving car, which troubled him. Instead, a calm person sat in front of him, and he was still having difficulty figuring this woman out because her recovery rate was remarkable. Remy wondered if that was another one of her gifts but knew the thought was just a way to distract his growing discomfort.

Stuck between a rock and a hard place, the special agent would have to tell her his gut opinion. Afraid of what her reaction would be, Remy knew the only conclusion he could come to was too over the top to believe. This theory was even more outlandish than all the other outrageous events and there had been some crazy things that had happened in those four days.

OK. Here it goes. He drew a huge cleansing breath and began. "The only time I have seen anything like this is when an operative is killed on a mission and the CIA wanted to keep it quiet." Uttering the words with his head bowed down.

After sharing his ridiculous deduction, looked up because he needed to see her belief in him. This was the only logical explanation for the oddities surrounding her mother's death. When glancing over, Remy found astonishment awash over her face.

Suddenly, Belle burst out laughing. The kind which comes from the belly and once it gets started it's almost impossible to stop. She gasped through the laughter. "Let me get this straight." Tried to speak but her giggles would not cease. "What you're saying is my mom was some kind of spy?" Tears were once again streaming down her lovely face. "Come on Remy, you must be joking."

Sat down next to her and grabbed her small shaking hand, sending his calming magic deep into her psyche because Belle looked on the verge of hysterics. Although, he could not blame her and waited patiently until she regained some control over herself. "It's no joke. The only other time I've seen something of this magnitude covered up, it was for the Agency." He continued to send serene feelings. "The Company can do something like this if your mother was working on something important. I don't know, maybe something the administration didn't want to get out." Remy leaned back tensely after he finished delivering his opinion.

Disbelief was stamped across Belle's face. *My mother, a spy.* Giggling oddly. *Maybe this really was some made up motion picture.* Panic was trying to push back in, but Remy was doing something to keep it off to the side. A gift she was grateful for because confusion clouded her judgment even with his supernatural help.

Her wits and special talents were critical to figuring this out but were a bit jumbled up at the moment. *Surely, my father would have told me.* Belle needed her brain to stop and reason. *But would he have really?* Barely sixteen when her dad had died in a car crash, her mind was struggling to be rational. A trick that was impossible to accomplish, due to the absurdity of it all. *Truly, when would he have had the time to tell me?*

Fascinated, he watched as the different emotions marched across her stunning features because she needed to work this out for herself. One, Belle would need to come to terms with, before they moved on to more pressing matters. Like, who killed her grandmother because those blasts were no accident. For right now, holding her hand was enough and Remy sent her as much magic as possible. Hopefully, his gift was helping her deal with this grueling revelation.

Numb. The only word Belle could use to describe how she felt right then because no other would do. Although she would love to pretend Remy was insane and her mother did not work for the CIA but somewhere deep inside, she grasped he spoke the truth. *How can I experience such a thing?* Wondering to herself but needed to understand more and raised her head, latching that glaring but lovely stare onto him. "Do you think she was a spy?"

Dropped his head because he could not bear to look at her. "Yeah, I do." *Jesus, it hurts too much to inflict any pain on her.* Rolled his eyes and blew out a big breath of frustration. *Remy old boy, you've got it bad.*

"Then I need to know for sure." Belle jumped up and headed straight for the dining room.

Remy followed not knowing what she was talking about. "What do you mean?"

As soon as the words left his mouth, remembered the newspaper article and his instincts took over. "NO!!!" He shouted much louder than expected, startling both of them with his passion. After a brief hesitancy, Remy continued with his rant. "No, you will not touch that article and go back there." Pointed his finger at her, coming around to her side of the table and placing himself only a few feet away.

Annoyed, Belle was already reaching for the briefcase, her hands poised on the latches. She was all set to open it in an instant. "You cannot keep me from this, Remy."

His irrational behavior was unexpected, but his only worry was her getting hurt or worse. Neither were matters he would allow.

It was then the fasteners on the attaché echoed throughout the downstairs. The locks clicked open, and Remy stood watching, as a defiant Belle pulled out the envelope, he had given her at Lennox House. He paced again, knowing she would do what she pleased. The agent in him appreciated this was a bad idea but the stubborn woman did not appear to be in any mood to listen. There was no talking her out of this.

Accepting his fate, he shook his head and followed her back into the living room. Remy was not happy about how any of this evening had gone but he still joined her on the couch to see how this would play out.

Nerves coursed through her as she sat cross-legged with a throw pillow in her lap, shifting back and forth to get comfortable for the '*trip.*' On the one hand, Belle would capture a glimpse of the woman who had given birth to her. On the other, she realized she was in for an unpleasant experience.

From time to time, the talented mystic had considered using her gift to visit her mom but had never done so. When it came time to sit down and touch a photo of her magnificent mother, Belle had always found an excuse not to complete the process and suspected her senses had been sheltering her from the painful truth.

In the meantime, Remy was a nervous wreck. Begging and pleading with her. "Please wait until you're stronger or at least until tomorrow." The determined woman would have none of it.

After many minutes of arguing, concluded she would do this, with or without his help. Eventually, Remy accepted her decision but registered his displeasure. Tucked an Afghan around her shoulders to make her comfortable and then he moved to the opposite chair to wait for any unforeseeable trouble.

"Thank you for being here. It's nice to know someone will be waiting." She spoke in a soft, child-like voice. "No one has ever helped me except Granny or Daddy." Sadly, smiling at her next sentence. "I usually go through this with a client. Their loved ones help them home, but I'm left here afterward by myself. Those sessions always leave me bone tired while he was unaware of my gifts, I hadn't realized Sam never once bothered to even ask me about those difficult times. Forget about helping me in the challenging days that followed each one."

Tenderly looking at him. "Funny, how you find the little things in life, end up meaning the most." Ignoring the distress pulsating from the paper, Belle reached down and picked up the article.

Suddenly, it was snowing again.

CHAPTER 16

Christmas at Harrods

December 1983

With a young child at home, along with a demanding career Katie Brooks found little time to shop. Enthusiastic about the mission because she planned to also purchase most of her holiday presents during this trip.

Back in her native London made Katie happy even if she had to be here for work. Clueless as to which contact would show up or how it would all work out, giving this assignment an extra kick which she loved. The Russians were threatening to pull out of the summer Olympics in Los Angeles, scheduled for next July. It was a growing embarrassment, which did not sit well with the president. Tensions were escalating between the two superpowers over the USSR's continuing war in Afghanistan.

Katie was here to produce a final solution on stopping those mounting conflicts. They were close to generating a resolution to those discrepancies, but the conclusion hung in the balance. The mission was to make sure the scales tipped in America's favor, and it was imperative she succeed. Katie needed to divert the impending international incident and secure the top-secret file.

While she walked along the streets of her hometown, the first snow of the season fell. Large white flakes floated softly down, lifting her spirits, and making it feel like the holidays. The new mommy was excited to see her baby Belle's face when she woke up on Christmas morning. Yule was Katie's favorite time of the year, and she could not wait for the celebrations to begin. Her little lass would be two this holiday and old enough to tear into her presents.

Last Christmas Eve, she and Bill sipped champagne under the gorgeous tree, enjoying each other's company, along with all the beautiful twinkling lights. They got little sleep while waiting for their sweetheart to wake up. Of course, their little one had been way too young to know about anything going on but what fun they all had giving Belle her gifts. Even Granny stayed for a few days and planned to join them again this year.

For now, the covert operative needed to focus on completing her mission and she had the perfect cover. A rich reporter's wife doing last-minute holiday shopping, which was Katie Brooks's real life, too. Because of the retailer's huge holiday crowds, she had decided the famous Harrods Department Store provided the perfect place for a clandestine meeting. It would allow her to make a quick getaway in case something went wrong. A good solid plan but something about today did not sit right. Hovering on the edge of her magic, lurked a nudge of worry.

Her special talents did not specify what trouble approached and since they were not helping, the experienced spy was being extra careful. She strolled along, enjoying the snow as it continued to fall and tried to push aside her growing fear. To help, she forced her mind back to Christmas again. Yesterday, Katie had purchased a Celtic charm for Belle, delighted it would shield and protect her always. It had been worth all the extra hours the proud parent had spent searching for just the right one.

Unexpectedly, her holiday daydreaming instantly ceased.

Her years of training and highly tuned instincts came immediately back online because someone was following her. *But who?* Not taking the chance and alerting the culprit, Katie continued with her clever charade of harmless holiday window shopping. She stopped to peruse different storefronts, attempting to identify who followed her in the reflective glass but to no prevail.

Then she rounded a corner and coming into view stood Harrods, decked to the rafters with holiday decorations. Time had run out, so a decision needed to be reached. Katie wondered if she should keep the meeting at the building up ahead or stay the course on the street and figure out who had her under surveillance.

She was fully aware of the stakes and the significance of this meeting with her Russian contact. Achieving peace with the Soviet Union was of the utmost importance. It was even more important than her own beautiful family. Thousands of lives were at risk, along with hundreds of undercover intelligence officers who could be exposed if she failed.

Instead of waiting for her stalker to make a move, decided to gamble. The seasoned agent dropped a package on the ground. An innocent action but a useful ploy to get a peek at her pursuer. Even after several skirmishes with presents, Katie still could not identify her follower.

Left with no alternative, made her decision, and continued toward the big department store as it played well with her cover.

Determined to lose the tail quickly, Katie hoped there would be enough time to meet her contact inside.

When the bomb exploded in 1983, Belle jumped in the present.

The sudden movement brought Remy out of his seat but quickly remembered his previous promise not to touch her. He determined keeping such a pledge was the hardest thing he had ever done.

Slowly, he sat back down, leaving her alone.

CIA agent, Katie Brooks, lay broken in too many pieces to count but was not dead yet. With little time left but desperate to have her say. "My baby Belle, I'm so sorry. You are my greatest *'gift'* and I love you more than the beyond."

She drew in a ragged breath and confessed aloud to no one. "Bill dearest, I love you so. Take care of our darling daughter and please forgive me for leaving you both."

With only a few shallow gasps left, Katie's final words were for her treasured husband. "I will always be, forever yours." Out of words, she lay sprawled on a busy London street. When looking up, found herself staring at the mysterious shadow that had been tailing her.

The stalker stood silently, scrutinizing Katie's dying body.

At long last, the man who had been following her mother came into view. In the present, the sight caused both Belle's heart and breath to come to a halt.

Although the face was younger, there was no mistaking it.

Ever since touching the article in Florida, etched into her brain was a picture of the stranger. It was the one face she would never forget. Shocked beyond belief because the image belonged to the man who had been in the back of the limousine with Sam.

Belle roared back to the present, surprised to find Remy sitting beside her on the couch, with his arms wrapped around her.

Delighted with the sensations his touch erupted inside her. Another experience she had never had when coming back from her gift. Although spent, was not depleted because of whatever he was doing, which is what always happened after such an emotional experience. The remarkable deed left her with euphoric-like essence and Belle found herself staring up at him with those big saucer eyes asking in a husky tone. "How'd ya do that?"

After hearing those four little words, he knew right then, he would jump off a building if she asked. That fact scared him to death. Remy settled the dilemma of his out-of-control feelings, by playing it cool and turning on his special kind of charm. "Do what, sugah?" That Prince Charming smile shining down at her.

When first meeting this blue-eyed devil in Palm Beach, the man had nearly knocked her over and the unusual impressions he wielded truly scared her. She was experiencing those feelings again, almost like being shot out of a cannon but in a good way, if that were even possible. Right now, those same sensations Belle had experienced at Lennox House were roaring back to life.

Frightened by both the man she had recognized from Sam's trip and her budding feelings for Remy, she scrambled out of his embrace.

Practically leaping off the couch and knocking over both coffees.

The horrible memory of seeing that man's wicked face had scared her badly. "It was him, Remy. It was him. I know it's him. Damn it, he was younger, but I'd recognize him anywhere." Babbling, Belle paced back and forth across the hardwood floor. "You were right, my mom was a spy. Holy crap this thing just gets crazier every minute." She could not stop the rush of adrenalin coursing through her body.

By this point, he knew the hyped-up clairvoyant needed to let off steam. So, Remy just ignored her while picking up the fallen mugs, then walked back into the kitchen for some towels to wipe up the mess. After cleaning up the spill, gently took her hand and slowly led her back to the couch, sitting the tense girl down next to him. "Belle, please, honey, let's just start from the beginning."

He continued holding her hand and sent the pretty princess, his own type of tranquility. *Sitting here with her, looking so small and pale, that's what she reminds me of. One of those Disney princesses. Hell, she even has the name, and I don't have to guess who her Beast is because she married him.* Remy returned from his mini daydream, recognizing that nowadays they always seemed to end with unpleasant thoughts of Sam.

Worried his magic might not do much good, not with the state she had worked herself into. He tried anyway to bring peace to her. "Sweetheart, what exactly did you see?" Steady soothing words were what would be best right now.

Still in agitated disarray but at least calmer, Belle swallowed her swirling emotions before putting her fears into words. "The man from the back of the limousine, the one Sam was talking to." Concentrated on Remy's comforting touch and not the monster involved with killing members of her family. "He followed my mom and stood over top of her while she died."

Goosebumps broke out on her arms, prompting Remy to rub his hands up and down on them. The kind act made Belle feel safe. "She had a meeting with a Russian at Harrods. Holiday shopping was her cover and noticing on the way, someone following her. My mom tried to see who tailed her in the glass reflections, but she wasn't able to make them out." By this time, that strong-willed head hung low.

As she sat staring into her lap, he looked on warmly, and hoped his magic was helping. Remy continued to rub her arm, sending her all the power possible while he waited patiently. This was her dilemma to work through and needed to do this in her own time, in her on way.

Finally, Belle started again. "When the bomb blew, she…um…I mean, she…no…my mom. Oh, crap Remy, it was horrible." Tears steadily fell from those beautiful eyes. "I mean, my mom didn't die right away." Straightened her shoulders and lifted her head up, staring ahead at nothing. "I heard her Remy. She spoke to me and my dad."

After a bit, Belle was still having difficulties with her experience but did not appear to be as despondent as before. "Oh, my Lord, it was so hard to see her there on the ground, but I know she died loving both of us."

Unsure of what else to do, just wrapped his arms around her tightly. More than anything, Remy wished he could give some much-needed relief to her.

After a long while, she drew a deep breath to gather her strength because it was time to move forward. Once Belle found the men responsible for all of this, there would be plenty of time to collapse.

Until then, she would go on fighting right up to the bitter end.

CHAPTER 17

Charm of Protection

Apparently, these people kept showing up in her life and that thought flustered her considerably when contemplating the man had also been following her mother. This forced Belle to leave the comfort of Remy's arms and she went back to pacing, the habit helped her think. *I'm sure that man is connected to Sam's secret society.* She could feel it in her gut.

The other man, the one who killed her grandmother, well, she did not need a crime report to reach a logical deduction. Her *'feelers'* were telling her; he was one very bad dude. Buzzing instincts screamed at Belle to stay far away from him. This discovery made her curious about what else these men had influenced or controlled.

Suddenly remembering something else her mother said, Belle grabbed the locket around her neck. "It's called a Warrior's Shield." Brought the necklace up so Remy could see it clearly. "On it are the classic knots and other Celtic symbols. The number three stands for the Holy Trinity. The number four, represents the four elements of the Earth." Pointed out each of the features to him and used the actual pendant to make her point. "This charm, she purchased for me on that London trip." Recalling the conversation Katie had in her head. "It incorporates both Christianity and Celtic beliefs." Trusted him enough to reveal it now. "She bought this with the hopes it would always protect me."

Tears once again ran down her attractive face. "I wear this charm every day and never take it off because it was a present from my mom."

A picture of her beautiful mother's face was all she could think about as she spoke regarding the pendant. "Maybe because I have only a rare few." Automatically reaching for her crystal, the one Belle always carried in her pocket. The unusual stone was another heirloom from her stunning momma.

It was time to tell him the opinion she had had since returning from her supernatural travels. "Call me crazy but I was wearing this the other night when those bombs exploded at Granny's. I think this charm did its job." Tentatively, Belle glanced at his shocked expression. Hopeful, he would believe her, but she knew it would be difficult to convince him. "Because I wasn't really hurt."

The memories of that horrible night came flooding back, which caused something to dawn on her. "Oh my God, Remy neither were you." Her hand went flying toward her mouth. "How is that even possible?" Panic was starting to build again. "You were right outside the door when those blasts went off, but they didn't hurt you." Accusingly she pointed a finger at him. "Why weren't you hurt?" Whipping around towards him, as an idea light bulb flashed inside her head. "Were you touching my car?"

Up on her knees now, turning all the way around to face him. "That's it, isn't it? You were touching my car, weren't you?" Punched him in the arm. "Come on, Remy, tell me I'm wrong." Grabbed hold, looking at him with those huge round eyes and appearing like she had seen a ghost and won the lottery but both at the same time. "Com' on Remy, tell me I'm crazy. Oh my God. This charm saved us. Didn't it?" Scared and giddy but convinced she was right. Belle seemed to move in triple time as she paced once more. "My momma saved us from those blasts."

He tried to calm her down, by gently going over and putting his arms around her shoulders. Steering her back to the sofa, Remy sent his soothing magnetism deep into her being. But Belle did not seem to notice in her current state. "Yes, you're right, but please, let's sit down first. *Mo ghra* you have to calm down. Please, sweetheart, come sit next to me."

Once he got her seated on the couch, he continued explaining what happened that night, ignoring his sudden peculiar need to use the Gaelic words for my love. "As I was walking over to meet you, I stumbled. To steady myself, placed my hand on your car about the same time as the first blast." Accepting Remy's gifts and the unusual that occurred around them was like a normal everyday thing for this fascinating woman and shook his head in amazement.

The charm around her neck had saved them both and she did not even blink an eye. All the while, expecting him to believe her in a leap of faith, with no evidence to back it up. Insane as it seemed, Remy knew what Belle was saying rang true because for the life of him, could not figure out any other reason they were both still alive.

Ever since those bombs had gone off, he had been trying to justify how they had survived. So far, Remy could not come up with any logical explanation. Although they had only suffered minor injuries, those blasts should have killed them both. Any sane person knew this and the cop in him suspected there had to be more to the story.

The problem was wild emotions had affected him since the shootout in Palm Beach and he had little time to process. In addition, they both had also survived the attack at her grandmother's place. Her insane explanation of their most recent brush with death was sinking in, but around her, his mind simply did not function properly. An experience Remy had never found himself in before. The crazy confession had left him utterly breathless. "Good God."

Not caring what she or anyone else thought, he quickly gathered Belle up in his arms and squeezed her tight. Right then, realized he could have lost her in the blast and found he would not have survived, which was an unexpected feeling. Also, Remy was not willing to take a chance to do anything to lose her nor willing to let her out of his sight anytime soon.

At long last, acknowledged his true soul mate was in his arms but Remy doubted she would be happy about his declaration. Promptly clearing that last thought of eternal bliss from his mind. He realized this was not the time nor the place for such things, but looked forward to when there would be an occasion and the clash that was sure to erupt.

Turning back toward Belle, he attempted to find the strength to release her. After several minutes passed, he finally did so. Slowly and reluctantly.

"She saved us Remy. My mom saved us." The pleasant memory of his heavenly hug was pushed away for the moment. His touch had calmed the anxiety storming inside her and she walked the perimeter of the room but in a more reasonable fashion.

She knew they needed answers, so Belle went back over everything. "The Seachd Righrean were following my mother. Why?" Asking no one in particular. "Why blow-up Granny's?" Turned back to Remy, who by now was returning from the kitchen with freshly filled coffee cups, making Belle smile. Thinking, she could get used to all this service from a man and not just the hired help.

Remy sat the steaming mugs down and turned his charming grin toward her. "Let's start at the beginning. What else did you see when you touched the election article?"

Only two days ago, she did not want to deal with Sam's lies but they seemed trivial now. She took a deep breath because Belle decided to begin with the truth and knew the FBI guy was going to love this humdinger. "Sam married me for business, not because he loved me. I don't know what kind of business but the last two years of living with him are finally making sense." Embarrassed by the confession, she shamefully added. "I'm going to go reheat my coffee."

Before he could respond, Belle rapidly made her way back into the kitchen. The shaken lady needed some space to think and catch her breath. After divulging Sam's cruel confession, it surprised her to find the pain barely registering. What should have been a terribly hurtful and very private thing was not, but it still hurt some, finding herself surprised she had told Remy. Although there were more important things going on than her loveless marriage.

The wounded woman knew there was a lot of work left to do. *Maybe this man sitting in my front room was the reason I'm handling this in such a nonchalant manner, but I doubt it. He may have helped but maybe I feel like this because I will not allow Sam to harm me any longer.*

All the standard phases dealing with hurtful situations she had learned in grad school were springing to mind. *Too much has happened that he caused. Too many things, which couldn't be explained away.* The late Mr. Randall had done a great deal of damage to many people. Belle was determined to survive this chapter and eventually move past him. Hoped the pep talk would work because she would have to face Remy again. While she said it did not matter about Sam, in many ways it still did.

She spent a few minutes gathering her strength like Granny had taught her. *That part of my life is over and I'm moving on.* Concentrated on taking big deep breaths. *First, I'm focusing on finding the people responsible for killing my grandmother.* Her determination was returning and after some time, Belle found the nerve to rejoin Remy.

When entering the room, she did not immediately see the handsome agent. It took her a minute because the designer drapes hid him. Tall and sexy, he stood at her large picture window looking out toward the Capitol and she decided to kid with Remy to lighten up the mood. "What are you doing? Playing hide and seek in the curtains?"

Immediately he rushed over, surprising Belle by wrapping his arms around her. "Sam was a bigger fool than I originally thought."

Confused by his statement, but appreciating the tenderness, she looked up with an odd expression on her face. His proclamation and show of affection had caught her by surprise because Belle had already put their conversation about her horrible husband behind her. *I don't know what's up but...Hell Yeah...These are some mighty fine cuddles.* His warm embrace was quite nice.

"If he considered you a business deal, Sam must have been deaf, dumb, and blind." Lush lips gently brushed against hers but not like he so desperately wanted to do. Just enough to let her know he was interested. Though not too much for her to think of him overstepping any boundaries.

Speechless, Belle never had anyone cast such wonderful strong feelings toward her. Also, she loved the titillating sensations he was causing inside.

His forehead leaned against hers. "I probably shouldn't have kissed you either, Doctor. I wanted you to know, something doesn't seem right with all this, but it's not you." Butterfly wings seemed to whisper against her lips. "It's not you and don't you dare think it is."

Blinked and snapped back to the present because it felt like she had been in a trance. To cover her blunder, Belle laughed and shot back. "Well, thanks for the special support, Mr. G Man. I'll keep your encouragement in mind." Reluctant to admit it, she was enjoying the light-hearted banter they were sharing and surprised to find Sam's business arrangement did not hurt nearly as much. It felt good to laugh and be in Remy's arms. That unhappy chapter of Belle's life was over and a new one was beginning.

But first things first, they needed to find the persons responsible for causing all these recent misfortunes.

Now that he was holding her again, releasing her was not something Remy wanted to do. His internal struggle made Belle laugh a little more because it showed on his handsome face, again. Nevertheless, there was much to do and eventually, she moved toward her treasured pad of paper. "Let's not talk about my marriage right now, although I think this society killed Sam."

"What makes you think they did?" His brow was wrinkled with confusion because Remy thought the same.

By this point, Belle had gone down the hallway to fetch the election newspaper article. Her voice ricocheted from the dining room. "Because one thing Sam said from my session was, he had to lose the election but not by much. Remy, the Dochloite Laoch lost by a landslide." Jogged back into the living room, carrying the piece. "I think those electronic voting machines didn't work, as expected. I'm pretty sure someone made a huge mistake."

On a roll now and Remy was not about to stop her, so he just encouraged her. "Go on."

She handed him the article. "Although the Seachd Righrean got what they wanted, you mentioned there were formal charges being filed soon. Whoever is behind this group will not be happy about any kind of investigation. It's tough to stay a secret society, with those types of actions taking place." Finished with her thought, Belle stood waiting for his response.

Flabbergasted because in four days, this woman had figured out what had taken him almost two months. *Well, she did have an unfair advantage.* Still, Remy could not believe how quickly her mind worked, and he loved that about her. "Okay, let's say you're right. What's next?" She was in a groove and Remy did not want to mess with her train of thought. He had figured correctly because Belle had already considered their next move.

"This." Belle held up what looked like a safe deposit box key, but Remy could not be sure, although it looked like one from where he was sitting. She brought it over, and after he examined it, even knew what bank it belonged to. "That key is for a box at the Scotland Royal Bank."

"How do you know it belongs to SRB?" Fascinated by Remy's abilities, even if she refused to tell him.

"Because, I keep a box for business at the one in New York City." He countered back while pulling out his key. "I opened it when I was with my father's firm."

As soon as Remy spoke, she remembered the stupid sentence Sam was always spouting. The foolish ditty made her believe the box could be at the bank in New York. Belle explained her husband's constant silly remark and recited it from memory, exactly the way Sam had repeated the words since their wedding night. "If you ever find yourself in trouble, there are plenty of lads and lassies with chests of wealth in New York. The city will always have the answers for you."

Back up and pacing again. "Sam must have said that stupid saying to me a thousand times. I enjoy New York but I'm a psychiatrist and capable of getting my own answers. I thought he was being ridiculous." Belle came to a dead stop, her face becoming paler. "Maybe, he was trying to leave me a clue." Suddenly, she looked at Remy's key, realizing it seemed to be exactly like hers, which was kind of spooky.

The big grandfather clock in the hallway loudly struck one in the morning, shocking him because the evening had flown by. Amazed at the late hour but thinking Belle must be exhausted because he sure was. This evening's difficult discoveries were on top of her being in a coma, plus all the other craziness they had been through in the last couple of days. They should wrap this up because another huge adventure was imminent. Come tomorrow morning, it looked like a road trip to the Big Apple was on the schedule. He nodded his head toward the other room and their collective paperwork, while looking down at her. "Do you think I could leave my things here for tonight?"

"You're going?" She squeaked, as panic at the idea of him leaving filled her voice, while the anxiety built inside her again. "I mean, I thought with it being so late, you could just stay in the guest room."

With his head turned toward the big window, he quietly answered. "If you want me to stay, I will." Although, Remy could not look at Belle, unable to trust himself. Afraid she might see the desire, which was suddenly flaring up again.

They stood side by side while lost in their own individual minds. Close, without touching, while both were thinking the same thoughts, until they could not stand the tension any longer. The awkwardness forced them to quickly fly apart from one another.

Returned to the kitchen with their bundled emotions firmly under wraps and dealt with the few dishes they had used. When done, they quietly climbed the stairs together with their sparking desires firmly under control. The two of them were relieved because everything seemed to be back to the way it had been, earlier in the evening. Comfy and enjoying their camaraderie like they had been living in this house together for years.

At the top of the staircase, each went to their own room, to spend the night alone, because not enough time had passed since Sam's death. Plus, there were too many other factors currently in their way.

However, those circumstances did not stop each of them from tossing and turning all night, both dreaming the same thoughts about the other, with neither of them getting much sleep.

Eagerly waiting to see one another again when dawn broke early the next morning.

CHAPTER 18

What Happens on Prom Night

For most folks, visiting New York City at the last minute on St. Patrick's Day was an unrealistic objective. Early the next morning, Remy found nothing was impossible for the powerful Buchanan Industries Corporation. With BI's resources and Belle's tenacious determination, she was able to secure them a two-room suite at the Waldorf Astoria in record time. The hotel reservation was a backup plan in case the key did not belong to the Scotland Royal Bank, and they needed to check others in the city.

Remy considered himself a frequent world traveler, but this woman's resourcefulness was amazing. He was shocked, they were booked and underway by eight thirty a.m. to Washington's Union Station. Upon arrival, it was still crowded with late morning commuters, but luck was on their side, and they made it through the ticket line in record time. Quickly securing passage on the *Amtrak Express* and bound for the Big Apple by ten a.m. The two first-class accommodations offered an expected arrival time into New York's Penn Station just shy of one o'clock.

Instead of flying, they opted to take the train because the upgraded seating permitted them privacy. It also gave them three uninterrupted hours to review their individual notes. The added time necessary to try and absorb the massive amounts of information each had collected, since most of the data had yet to even be discussed.

Neither of them talked about anything important during the ride to the station, nor during the shuffle of getting their luggage secured on board the train. When purchasing the tickets, Remy flashed his FBI badge to the attendant, who glowed with a spiritual purple aura. The extra federal muscle ensured their privacy, by listing them under assumed names. Fate was still on their side because only five additional ticket holders were making the first-class trip, instead of the normal forty passengers. The almost empty compartment had granted them the private seating they were seeking, far from the other train riders.

Belle's odd statement, that Randall had married her strictly for business, badly disturbed Remy. During his restless night, deciding to confess his nightmare of prom, what happened with Jennifer Randolph, as well as what Sam's role had been in it all. This morning, his internal gifts were zinging about what occurred all those years ago, somehow fit in with the events taking place today. Unsure how or why, but he was convinced the quick-witted Belle could help figure out this complicated mess.

Once the train was New York bound, both settled into big comfortable chairs, while a porter with a light blue aura, took their coffee order. Once the carafe of java was poured, it was time to begin. "Belle, ah…there's something I need to tell you about Sam and me. Um…something…ah well…that happened when we were kids."

Remy's awkward tone made her glance up with a look of surprise. She was unprepared for something from his past, but then Belle remembered his stumbling statement back in Florida. With a nod of her head, waited for him to proceed.

"As I told you when we first met, Sam and I were inseparable during most of our childhood. Classmates in prep school, from kindergarten through twelfth grade; we did everything together." His fingers twitched faster with each sentence. "Sat next to one another from our first day at school. Played baseball, football, and basketball together. We first raced bikes, then cars, up and down the streets of our neighborhood chasing each other. Then of course, beautiful girls."

Unlike when he spoke about his wife, Remy was extremely tense when talking about Sam. "We did almost everything you could imagine together and were really more like brothers because both of us were only children with no siblings." Very much on edge, every part of his being was on high alert. Out of habit, wiped his hand down his face and struggled to keep his emotions under control. "The older we got, the stronger our rivalry grew until it became almost unhealthy, but our parents were business associates. My father's business partner is Sam's parents' personal attorney, and they encouraged our friendship."

To brace himself for what was to come, took a sip of coffee. "Again, because we were only children and had no one else to watch our backs, so to speak."

After taking another breather, found the courage to continue. "Most of the things we got into fights over were harmless. Normal stuff brothers would fight about, that is, until girls entered the picture. Then the bastard really changed."

Unable to keep the anger in check, he stopped for a moment to quell his temper, not wanting to risk harming her in any way. Instead, wished Sam was here to unleash his fury on. Remy looked down at his clenched hands, as instincts kicked in and activated the finger drills, immediately causing a wave of calm to wash over him.

She noted his increased stress, along with his interesting finger fix but out of respect, Belle continued to keep silent.

After he was able to get himself under control, Remy went ahead with the tale. "I was the only one, who saw the transformation because I saw his changing aura. It went from a light bluish gray to a dark black-like gray almost overnight and was never blue again."

Belle continued to stay quiet because could tell how much this confession affected him and it made her heart ache. She wished something could be done to help but these were Remy's internal demons and his alone, to grapple with.

"No one knew about my gift; it was not something I could share with anyone, except my mom. She told me to be careful, but to accept Sam for who he was and hope for the best." A bright smile appeared,

just then, on Remy's face as he turned more toward her. "You need
to understand my mom; she literally oozes joy and happiness. I'm not
sure my momma can think bad thoughts about anyone. I was young,
so when she told me to accept Sam, I did."

"Big mistake because he seemed to be on a mission to always do one
better than me." The stress showed painfully on both Remy's face and
in his voice. "I don't know why but he set his sights on Jennifer. The
poor girl had done nothing to him, other than the unfortunate luck of
being my girlfriend."

The retelling of his childhood memories with Sam were taking a toll.
"I'm sorry but this is difficult for me." His beautiful features reflected
the deep pain resounding in his voice.

To help him cope, Belle reached over and grabbed his hand for
support.

Uninterested, he pushed her away. Remy desperately needed a
break. "I'll be right back."

He stood up and sprinted toward the bathroom for some much-
needed air.

Even the water he splashed onto his face did no good because this
was a very dark part of his past. Primarily, it stayed in the far corners of
his mind, where he had forced it. The fact he had to relive this painful
memory was sheer torment.

Ten minutes later, Remy returned to his seat, drawn and pale.

In an attempt to cheer him up, Belle had ordered the server to refill
the pot, with fresh coffee. As soon as Remy got comfortable across from
her, she poured him a new cup. The stress was still apparent on his
face, happy to see improvement from the devastating expression earlier.

He quietly thanked her for the kind gesture. "The senior prom
was held downtown at the Mayflower Hotel in the beautiful Grand
Ballroom. It's the one with the balconies overlooking it. Everyone had
rented rooms but of course, Randall had to reserve the one-of-a-kind
Presidential Suite where he threw a huge pre-prom party. No money
was spared on the over-the-top soiree and Sam's extravagance even
impressed the wealthiest of kids."

The memories were getting to him, causing Remy to fidget in his chair but he went on after clearing his throat. "Jennifer's father was a diplomat for a small country in central Europe. I forget which one but was of noble birth and fairly well off. We had dated for almost six months. It was Senior Prom and I thought at a point, we um, should, you know, um."

All of a sudden, his face turned beet red, and she was curious about what was making him so uncomfortable. Up to this point, had kept quiet to let Remy tell his story, in his own way without interruption. But his discomfort was growing, and Belle did not understand why.

Suddenly, she figured out his distress. "You wanted to sleep with her, and she was having a problem with it. Is that it?"

"Yeah." Hung his head, too ashamed to see her reaction to the embarrassing confession. "Do you think I'm awful?" Looked up at Belle and prayed she did not think too poorly of him. "I hope not because I was eighteen and really randy." No sooner had he spoken, Remy's surprised face turned an even brighter red, embarrassed by his vulgar outburst.

With a kind smile, she answered him honestly. "No silly, you were a teenage boy, and I would think something was actually wrong, if you weren't looking to get laid during prom." Laughed in disbelief over this incredible guy, who was worried she would think him dreadful because he had wanted to have sex on prom night. To help make him feel better, Belle pressed him on. "Sooooo, Sam had a great suite filled with everything imaginable...Remy, what happened next?" Gently squeezed his hand to let him know everything would be okay.

Relief slowly spread across his face, allowing him to continue, because this unusual woman understood him on a whole other level. "We arrived later after everyone else because our mothers took a thousand pictures. I asked the limousine driver to take the long way there and he drove us down the GW Parkway, past the Jefferson, Lincoln, and Washington monuments."

He described it with such vivid details, Belle could see the ride in her head. "We finished the enchanted drive with a tour around the Capitol and White House. The night was magical, and we were having the time of our lives." As the train rolled on, she envisioned in her mind the city ablaze with all the beautiful nighttime colors that illuminated the decorated streets and monuments. "I thought this was it. I would finally get with Jen. We pulled up to the hotel, which was lit up like a Christmas tree and I thought nothing could ever be that perfect." Smiled a little as he spoke about their drive to the dance, even though the happiness did not reach Remy's stunning eyes.

That chiseled face of his, becoming more strained as he spoke again. "I didn't mention to Jen that I had a suite. Hoping to save it as a surprise for later in the evening but I didn't expect it to be much of one, since almost everyone else had at least reserved a room. I thought she would have known but I was wrong."

Shook his head and whispered. "Boy was I wrong."

At this point, he needed another break and stood up while running his hands through his beautiful black hair. Belle deduced; this was another habit of Remy's when he became nervous.

After a few minutes, sat back down and eventually took a drink from his coffee. "Somehow, Sam knew she was clueless. How he knew, I never figured out."

Strangely, his emotions were actually spilling out of his person, because literally, oozing into the atmosphere from his tortured soul, was anger and bitterness. "During the party, Sam took Jennifer aside. Afterwards, she became furious with me." Belle was doubtful, he even knew it was happening when he was this agitated. "I just assumed it was about the suite and my plans to get into her panties later. Honestly, I don't know what Sam said to make her so angry."

The next words, he barely uttered. "Because we never spoke to each other again."

After another extremely long pause, Remy struggled on. "Anyway, she stormed over, then slapped me across the face, in front of everyone in the class. Sam stood off to the side with a stupid malicious smirk and Jennifer ran into his waiting arms."

She was quite aware of the expression Remy was referring to because it had recently scared Belle. At the time, relieved it had not been directed at her but one of Sam's business associates.

"Sam had accomplished what he set out to do, which I assumed was to ruin prom for me. Wrapped his arms around Jennifer and escorted her into the dance." Looking defeated, he stopped and took another sip of his coffee. "Unfortunately leaving his own date all by herself. I was mad and confused but felt bad for Sam's ditched date. I don't recall her name but remember her being a nice girl. Anyway, I ushered the poor thing into the ballroom because didn't want her to have to walk in all by herself."

Charmed by his action, she admired Remy's kindness. It was a trait seldom seen in a rebuffed teenage boy.

He drew in an extra deep breath because the hardest part of the story was next. "Prom ruined and my girl on the arm of the biggest jerk in the world. I got drunk with a group of guys who were not happy with their dates either. Most of our lives, we played ball together and were all good chums."

Even after all these years, he was going to need every bit of his inner strength to get through this.

"All night long we went back and forth from my suite, drinking the booze we snuck into the hotel. Ran back and forth between the upper balconies and watched everyone else below having fun." He dreaded having to finish the story. Remy would be forced to recall all the ugly details, requiring him to deliver another nasty unknown fact about her recently deceased husband. "After the prom ended, I hosted a large party of my own, where many of my classmates danced and drank until almost morning.

Hung his head back down, unable to bear looking at the pain he was about to inflict. "Four of them spent the night, thank God because they provided my alibi when the police came the next day."

When he finally had the courage to look up, shock registered all over Belle's face.

"Police? Good Lord Remy, what did Sam do?" Concluding she did not know the man she had married at all. Anxiously, waited for his answer but her innards were saying it would not be something good.

Still speaking rather softly but determined to get through this. "When Jennifer never came home the next morning, her parents contacted the police. They spent much of the night calling everyone else's parents in the class." The instincts inside him buzzed, suggesting this somehow fit in with the trouble Belle was experiencing today. "Around eleven a.m. the police came knocking on the hotel door. Of course, the five of us were still sleeping. I'm the son of an attorney, so the first thing I did was call my dad, who came down to the hotel right away."

That fateful morning still sent chills up Remy's spine. Without his friends staying the night, it could have easily gone the other way.

"Needless to say, my father was not a happy man. Unaware of my overnight plans, when Jennifer's parents contacted him hours before, he could not help them. Angry at my recklessness but my dad still came to help as soon as I called. Immediately, he contacted the other boy's parents who met us down at the station." The overwhelming scrutiny of the police and press was constant during the days following Jennifer's disappearance.

With no solid alibi for an angry missing girlfriend, Remy would have been forced to face the nightmare alone, if those four men had not stayed with him. *Putrid green.* The color of the room the police held him in during his long interrogation popped into his head. He shook it off, focusing instead on his narrative. "Someone questioned each of us separately, but our stories were all the same. Not sure why but Jennifer had gotten angry with me at Sam's party, and I hadn't seen her since she went off with him."

A sad grin crossed his face at the memory of those school pals who stuck by him and told the truth. "Those gentlemen backed up my claim and all vouched for me." Remy chuckled at the memory from that long-forgotten party. "A night, which included lots of drinking, dancing, and Olympic mattress-diving from anything close like the dresser, table, or chairs. Charlie even figured out how to jump off the

TV." The memory of Dooley's spectacular dive, off the new forty-inch high-definition Trinitron was one of his favorites. "You should have seen him." By now, a wide smile appeared on his face when recalling the good part of that night. "It was the winning entry for the money pot we'd taken up for the challenge." An amazing feat, which included a twisting backflip kind of thing. "It's nice to have a good memory from that horrible night." The pleasant thought allowed him to push on, but he was unable to maintain the boost to his confidence for long.

Prominently on display in those beautiful Caribbean blue eyes was stress and sadness. "All over Washington, days of intense searching for Jen occurred, with hundreds of volunteers taking part. Because of her father's position, the international press covered the story from everywhere — in front of the school, the hotel, and the houses of everyone involved."

To steady himself against the onslaught of repressed images that were streaming across his vision, Remy gripped the coffee cup with superhuman strength. "It was a media circus, and someone was always sticking a camera in our faces." Gulped down the remaining steaming liquid but afterwards, just sat there staring at the empty cup.

"Finally, three days later." Tears formed on the bottom lids of his ocean-blue eyes. "They found her upstream in a remote section of Rock Creek Park."

Remy swallowed the lump in his throat, whispering the final horrifying detail. "Raped and savagely beaten to death."

Wished there was more she was able to do but Belle could only grab his hand, offering as much sympathy and magic as possible. "Oh Remy, I am so sorry. It must have been horrible for you, especially at such a young age and the world's spotlight shining on you too." She continued patting his hand but wished more could be done. "You poor thing. I'm so very sorry." All her years of schooling were failing the successful doctor but knew books could never fix pain this deep.

Just with her touch, Belle helped ease the stress of reliving that horrendous period. Grateful for the thoughtfulness and boosted by her kindness, Remy proceeded with his tale. "The coroner put her death between three and six a.m., the morning after prom. Although questioned extensively for days, Sam had an air-tight alibi, I think it was provided by his housekeeper. She claimed he came home around one a.m. shortly after the dance and hours before Jennifer died. With his alibi in hand, Sam never wavered from his story, and he got away with it."

After all these years, Remy still got choked up and angry by the tragedy, but he needed to finish explaining all the details of the cold-blooded murder. "Since Jennifer was found in the water and exposed to the elements for many days, they discovered little evidence with the body." Ran his hand through his hair, then down his face, taking another long pause. "No one was ever charged with her murder, and it is still unsolved to this day."

The next part would be the most difficult. It was imperative she understand how deadly Sam had been and looked directly at Belle when delivering his next sentence. "I know he killed her. Because he would stare at me, smiling that evil way and his aura would turn completely black. Belle, I'm sorry to tell you this but after seeing his evil-tainted aura, I think Sam also enjoyed it."

At his shocking statement, she gasped out loud. "Oh my God." This man, just told her the person she married, had killed a girl when he was only a teenager, and left her outside in a park. Just like a piece of trash. Not wanting to believe it, but she suspected Remy was right about Sam and his vile crime. Because Belle knew who had covered for him.

Back to being ashen faced when grasping her husband's many sins, she softly choked. "It wasn't the housekeeper, it was Cook."

"What did you say?" Leaned in and grabbed her hand because Remy could see her face had turned pale again. "I'm sorry Belle, I couldn't hear you." Somehow, he could feel the anxiety building inside her and it had returned with a vengeance.

"I said it was Cook. Oh my God, I can't believe it but it's true. Cook would have been the one who said Sam was home that night because she would do anything for him." Disbelief was pouring from Belle at the chef's deception. "Even lie for him to cover something up like this."

"You mean the large woman I met at Lennox House?" Unable to answer him right then, Belle simply nodded her head. "Well, that explains the confusing woman's brown aura. It's an unsettling trait and you don't find it in many people unless they have deep-rooted issues of turmoil. Interesting, because her other color was pink which is love." He had found the combination very strange. "It seems odd, the prom night incident still haunted her." With everything that occurred, Remy had not thought about the unusual aura since returning from Palm Beach, mentally kicking himself for the mistake.

The false alibi the servant had provided for Sam was ages ago. It should not be in such an uproar fifteen years later. For a moment, he just sat quietly, desperate to figure out how all these pieces somehow fit into what was happening today because Remy knew it did. *None of this makes any sense. The deeper this goes, the more confusing it becomes.* After contemplating the matter for a bit more, he looked over at Belle with a new determination on his drained face. "How about we go over all the evidence we've each accumulated."

"Maybe we can figure out what's really going on."

CHAPTER 19

Sam's Will

"That's an excellent idea, but first I need to tell you about my meeting with the Buchanan family attorney." Ducked down and pulled out a pad of paper from the briefcase at her feet. "It took place the afternoon I arrived at Granny's cabin in Virginia." Reappearing quickly, settling on using humor to diffuse the extremely upsetting subject. "If you're confused now, just wait until I tell you about Sam's last will and testament."

Belle kept her head down, as she reluctantly went on about her strange appointment. "The prenuptial agreement we signed before our marriage was fairly standard." Still unable to look at him. "A contract, which covered the two of us equally because each of us had extensive holdings and property prior to marrying."

With each word spoken, Belle became more distant and based on her body language, Remy braced himself for another bombshell.

Since Sam and I are only children, our parent's estates will belong to us exclusively." With little emotion, quickly went on. "I'd already received my inheritance, whereas Sam had not."

The way she dealt with stressful situations was fascinating and he watched as she doodled intricate Celtic symbols on a pad of paper. "All of this was addressed in the document we both signed. As I said, it was a very fair arrangement." As he admired her work, was mesmerized as she wrote out an old Scottish prayer in perfectly formed calligraphy.

"If we dissolved the marriage, I would retain my holdings while Sam would keep his."

A beautiful illustrator, Belle had surprised Remy again with her many talents. "As I said before, the agreement contained all the standard percentages and other terms usually included. As a lawyer, I'm sure you're familiar with what I'm referring." To confirm he understood, she looked up for his acknowledgement.

After nodding, he became curious as to what could have made her look so upset. "Yes, I understand the type of contract you are implying." Clearly Belle was not herself, setting Remy on edge.

"After arriving at the office, I was introduced to a Mr. Hamish Howe. After a few minutes of niceties, the attorney read Sam's will." She stared out the window, attempting to draw some much-needed strength from Mother Nature. "It seems Sam left me a rather large sum of money." Hesitated because was still adjusting to the unexpected terms. In her embarrassment, she fumbled. "Uh...the um numbers... well they're way above our agreed upon figures."

Still unsure of what was troubling her, Remy had heard nothing that should put such a look on that lovely face. It sounded like she was getting more money. *So why the troubled expression?* She still would not look at him directly.

"When he went over the details, the sully looking attorney explained that Sam had made the changes right after the holidays. Apparently, my late husband had been very specific about what he wanted amended for the biggest beneficiary."

She was still not over the outrageous amount. "Me."

Pointing to her rapidly beating heart.

"Well, I was completely surprised by his generosity because Sam did not love me." She did glance up at that shocking declaration but only for a brief second. "After touching the article, I knew he had only married me as a business deal, so why leave me anything extra in his will? We both signed the agreement and that should have been it. All that was required and all I should have received."

Still shocked at Sam's unusual gift, her voice suddenly dropping to a whisper. "When he died, we were barely speaking, and I told the lawyer that very thing." Sad about this unfortunate fact and their failed marriage. However, the discussion made it easy to recall how impossible it had been to conform to Sam's ridiculous demands.

Remy reached for her shaking hand, gently rubbing it. "Did the attorney give you any sign of why Randall made the recent changes?" He was aware the anxiety was building inside her once more.

"No, but the attorney asked several rather peculiar questions." This added burden had been unexpected, making Belle tremble from the memory. "Ones, I don't think he should have been asking. Like what was Sam working on, as well as where his files were located."

"Of course, I informed him I had no idea about such things because Sam never discussed business with me. With his questions, I played the dumb grieving wife." Belle demonstrated her impersonation with hands flipping around like a senseless nit wit. "He even asked if Sam brought any unusual objects home in the last days before his death. I found this question the oddest of all because he was clearly looking for something."

Swallowed her growing anxiety and went on with the details of that awful afternoon. "I maintained my disguise and told him that whatever files were in the guest house, I'd packed up myself and shipped everything back to Buchanan Industries." Head still bowed but her voice was becoming stronger. "Also, offhandedly I told him I knew nothing about any objects of Sam's that were unusual or otherwise. Everything else had been returned to his parents and he should check with them because I had kept nothing from our marriage."

Clearly, the appointment had been trying, but Remy had seen her like this before. The sensible doctor would work this out, and merely sat holding her trembling hand. "I mentioned the missing laptop, which seemed to make him happy, but his reaction instantly put my gifts on high alert." Uncomfortable with the entire experience, Belle was still unclear how the lawyer played into this situation. "Remy, I don't know why but I didn't tell him about your visit." However, he was confident she would figure it out.

"Odd but the old man was rather knowledgeable about the shootout." The enticing devil's magic touch helped to soothe her mental state, enabling her to continue with her bizarre tale. "Keeping up the pretense, I told him my interaction with the authorities had been minimal. My only contact had been in connection to the commotion next door, but I sort of left you out of my story." At the mention of her deception, a brief genuine smile brushed across Belle's face. "My statement seemed to make him even happier. It almost relaxed him some."

While speaking, she had been attempting to hold her sentiments together, but Remy could tell the ugly truth was about to be revealed. "Moving him effortlessly away from the shootout and onto the will. His next sentence shocked me senseless because never in a thousand years could I have guessed the topic."

Remy watched as her facial features changed completely, prior to uttering her next words. "It seems, Sam added a rather interesting addendum to his will."

Not liking the sound of this, Remy's face took on a look of sternness. "What was included in the addition?" He kept her small hand tightly covered and sent as much of his soothing magic as possible.

With each passing minute, Belle's skin was becoming translucent.

"Apparently, Sam was a planner, something I would have never predicted." She stopped because her hands were shaking so hard. Pulled them away from Remy, quickly slipping them into her lap.

Suddenly, unable to go on. Belle twisted her face away because could tell it was becoming flush with embarrassment. "It appears he wanted his name to be carried on."

Grabbed the cup, to cover up her mortification and practically gulped the coffee down. "To ensure there was a Randall slash Buchanan heir to their empire."

Kept her eyes glued to the inside of the mug because Belle was uncomfortable talking about this subject. "Evidently, he went to one of those, um clinics."

It was imperative Remy understood Sam's last wishes. "And, um...I don't know. Oh, I'm not sure what he did but I guess he had his sperm frozen."

Rushed her words, finishing as quickly as possible. "He supposedly arranged all of this, I guess around the time we married."

Impossible to keep the embarrassment out of her voice or off her face, finally went on but she still talked into her empty cup. "If I agree to be impregnated artificially and give birth to a healthy child, I'll inherit the rest of his vast estate."

When Belle looked up, just stared into Remy's completely shocked face.

It was difficult to find some humor in this travesty but could not help herself. "Bet ya didn't see that one coming, huh? Remy, it just keeps getting more outrageous by the minute, doesn't it?" A nervous giggle slipped out before Belle could stop it.

It was a good thing her husband was dead because there were no words to describe how much Remy wanted to kill Sam Randall right then.

"Do you mean to tell me?" To calm his raging anger, took a slow deep breath. "He wrote out a legal document, asking? No wait a minute, Sam isn't really asking, is he?"

The octaves in his voice rose with each new sentence.

"Demanding you get pregnant with his child?" His volume continued to grow louder with each comment. "Completely alone? All by your damn self? In exchange, the stuck-up bastard will leave you the rest of his large pile of money?"

Only able to nod at his rapid-fire questions but already feeling better because Remy was also angry at Sam about this. Not only was Belle's disgust about his request overshadowing her judgment but there was this incredible fury burning inside her as well.

The start of a smile appeared on her face because Remy was still carrying on about Sam and he was definitely having a hard time, accepting his rival's peculiar ultimatum. "Unbelievable but typical of the selfish, spoiled brat." Mumbling under his breath. "Thinking only of what he wanted and believing everything is about money. That anyone could be bought with it."

Just sharing her husband's bizarre request, with someone who thought like her, seemed to lighten the burden Belle had been lugging around since the reading.

At last, Remy seemed to be over his personal tirade but was still angry. "Did he even make decent provisions for the child?" He wondered how a man could be so cavalier about the miracle of producing another human being.

"Remy. It's a lot of money." Murmuring into her coffee cup, too embarrassed to look at him.

"You're not even considering this, are you?" Practically shouting his anger at Belle.

Mad by his outrageous question but also, furious about this whole ridiculous situation. Her anger at Sam for putting her in this bizarre position made Belle answer him more sharply than intended. "Of course not, Remy. I can't believe you'd even ask such a question."

Sheepishly, he sought her forgiveness when realizing his mistake too late. "I'm sorry Belle, I should not have reacted that way." Ashamed of his jealousy. "Please forgive me." Prayed, she would grant it and peered around, to make sure none of the other passengers noticed their outbursts, but no heads were lifted.

"You're forgiven but you should know." Finally, Belle looked up into Remy's beautiful but sad eyes. "We're talking about billions of dollars."

Remy whistled low at the huge sum.

"I suppose many women would have a child for such an extravagant amount of money but I'm not one of them."

A look of misunderstanding was now etched across his face, making Belle exasperated at his petty resentment. "Good lord, I have all the money I could ever want or need. I never have to work again if I don't care to. Daddy left me well off and I own several pieces of property including both my house in the city and at the beach in Dewey."

Irritation echoed throughout her voice at the distasteful description of her vast wealth. Although, the anger was making the new widow feel a bit better, so she continued to list her assets. "After my mother's death, I inherited her family's trust. It's a rather large yearly stipend. I also keep a fairly successful medical practice and I haven't even started to disclose my portfolio yet. So, you see, I don't need Sam's damn money. The most important point, I don't want a child by a man who didn't love me and cheated on me the entire time we were together."

Hands up in the air as he mockingly surrendered. "Okay, okay, I think I get the picture. I'm sorry, just got caught off guard. Please forgive me, again." He smiled that wicked grin of his, as a look of relief blossomed over Remy's face. "Well, I'm glad to hear you're not considering this bizarre mandate because it's kind of creepy." Quickly adding, afraid he might have offended her. "That is, if you ask me."

At a loss for what to say but to make this easier for her, Remy decided honesty would work best. "More than anything, my momma wants grandbabies, but I don't think Momma Montgomery would require my widow to go through a pregnancy and childbirth by herself. Just to inherit my money."

"Wow, that's something." He looked tenderly towards her. "His parents never mentioned anything?" She shook her head as he shuddered at the absurdity of it all. "Belle, you know this just got really weird."

Feeling better, she laughed out loud at his silly statement. "Yes, I do but weird was about three days ago. Officially, we are now in the *Twilight Zone* but what I want to know is, why." Disgusted with Sam's request, Belle could not figure out his bizarre motives. "Why would he make such a peculiar demand, then think I would even consider such a thing?"

She stared off into the distance for quite some time, finally admitting. "We talked about having children because he brought it up all the time, but I refused because of his infidelity. The fights were legendary, but they were always strange conversations because Sam didn't really like kids. In fact, it got to a point where I wouldn't even discuss this issue until we fixed our problems." Red faced with shame, Belle could not get past Sam's disloyalty and the foolish belief, one day he would settle down with only her.

"Maybe he didn't want to be forgotten and Sam thought this was a way to ensure the family name continued on." Digging for anything that would help make this easier, Remy was at a loss for words at her husband's bizarre request.

Determined to figure this insanity out, Belle was perfectly honest. "This is just too weird, even for Sam. Something isn't sitting right with all of this but I don't know exactly what it is. Too much has happened, too quickly and in such a short period of time." All her mystic *'feelers'* were vibrating with intuitions, which signaled there were pieces missing from this picture, making her desperate to find them. "It's hindering my ability to think this through. So, let's go back to the beginning."

Before going on, she turned toward him making sure he took her seriously. "Remy, we still have over two hours before we reach New York. Let's go over all the facts, again." Excited, by this train of thought. "Maybe we can discover a new piece of information or connect something together. One, which we hadn't noticed before."

She knew this was the correct direction because they needed to figure out how these parts all fit together. "Or maybe something might make sense now, which didn't earlier because we both know more about each other and Sam." Belle used her hands to stress her points. "Sound like a plan?"

Again, he was struck by how amazing this woman was in both beauty and brains.

Calmly, she sat informing him Sam was trying to bribe her into manufacturing a test tube heir, while trying to pretend this was just a normal request. It was not. The fact Randall was forcing her to endure such a thing was making him even madder. Like typical Belle, she instantly moved past it, diving right back into whatever needed to be done.

Besides figuring out all the details, she wanted to concentrate on who the bad guys were and how to stop them. If he allowed himself, Remy just might fall in love with her, but that was impossible. He pushed those ridiculous thoughts out of his head and put his FBI face back on. "Sounds perfect. Let's start from the beginning." Switched gears to shield his emotions. "I'll go first and Belle, you jump in whenever you have something to add. Like you, I feel there are several events which have occurred." Reached down into his briefcase and pulled out another file filled with more evidence about Sam. "Actually, I think, maybe both of our lives might be linked to this society."

"Can you do me a favor, start a list that includes any details we agree could be connected?" He needed to concentrate on the difficult problems facing them and the country, but not before stealing one last glance at the beauty across from him.

Then, Remy went back to work.

CHAPTER 20

A Thoroughly Long List

"I would be happy to." Reaching under the table, she pulled out one of her multi-colored notepads, from her briefcase below. "Actually, I already have one started and it has, one...two..." Belle counted all the events she had attributed to the bad guys. "I've come up with eleven items."

"Here, take a look at my list and let me know what you think." She showed Remy the one she had made the evening before, after their awkward moment in the dining room. She had written it deep in the night, when sleep simply would not come.

After reviewing it, he found the following in her interesting handwriting.

- *Society is Seachd Righrean. Translation—Seven Kings.*
  - *— Who are these guys?*
- *Sam married me for business, not love.*
  - *— What possible reason?*
- *Society had Sam fix the recent Irish election.*
  - *— What did they gain from it?*
- *The upcoming US presidential election???? Holy Crap!!!!!*
- *Sam's laptop is missing. Who took it?? Why???*
  - *— What's on it??????*
- *200+ newspaper articles hidden in a drawer. Why???*

- *Secret safe deposit box key.*
  - *Where's the bank? NYC????*
- *Man with Sam in Ireland*
  - *Same person following my mom, 30-year link???*
- *Society killed Granny.*
  - *What did she do? What kind of threat did she pose?*
- *Shoot out-Lennox House — How does it tie in?*
  - *Not a drug deal gone bad!!!!!*
- *Crazy addendum to Sam's will & baby. But why?*
  - *Who wanted this?*

After looking it over, Remy acknowledged her itemization was thorough, but thought the following should be added. "Sam was laundering money for the cartels, which should be number twelve."

With downcast eyes, he desperately hoped Belle believed his next premonition. "For some reason, my instincts are telling me Jennifer's death is also somehow involved. I can't explain why but I believe it should be number thirteen." It was another important step for Belle to take toward Remy and he was anxious about her response. "That is, if you agree."

She did but Belle was nervous, convinced the list should also include one more item.

"Yes, of course. Please, add both to the list." Unaware, she passed his test because was too worried about his reaction. Her instincts were screaming, because total focus would be necessary to approach her own unpleasant list addition. "Please don't take this the wrong way, because I'm not trying to hurt you and have no proof to back this up."

Left her seat on the opposite side of the table and came over to Remy. Placed her hand on his shoulder, to provide comfort during the telling of her off the wall notion. "I believe we should consider another item for our incredibly long list."

She waited for his full attention before going on.

He took a few minutes before giving it because wanted to brace himself for another one of her bombshells. Remy could tell by her behavior, that whatever Belle wanted added to the list, was not something he would like.

Reluctantly, raised his head to give his full consideration.

She spoke softly to ease his pain, yet, pleaded with him. "Will you at least consider what I have to say carefully?" Pausing for quite some time. "Before disregarding it as nonsense?" Those beautiful emerald-green eyes implored Remy with that famous earnest glare. "Please?"

Eventually, he acknowledged and agreed to her conditions, with a small nod of his head.

She stared directly into his sinfully gorgeous eyes, while leaning down. Grabbed his hand to let him know she understood how much this would hurt him, but conceded it needed to be said. "I don't know why, but I believe Amanda's death might be connected to this society as well." With determination, Belle pointed at the pad of paper, in front of Remy. "I think, it should be added to this list."

Astounded at her declaration, for a few minutes, he was unable to speak. Hesitant on what to say or think, because at first, Remy thought Belle was crazy.

Finally, settling on the obvious. "Wow, I wasn't expecting that one. I don't know how you could connect Amanda to this group." Shocked by her statement because other than growing up with Randall, Remy hadn't seen or spoken to him since high school and his life with Amanda had nothing to do with Sam or his family.

After contemplating her outrageous scenario, for quite a while, that tiny something way deep down inside him was pointing out, maybe the little list maker might be correct.

But he still wanted to debate the issue. "Even after almost six years, I have found no real clues to who killed her." With great effort, Remy kept his emotions under wraps, but his gut said only honesty would get them any real answers. "Yet, my instincts tell me you might be right about this one."

He surprised himself with his quick consensus. "The murder of Amanda Edwards' will be listed as item number fourteen." Tipped his head toward her then plunged right into their exercise.

They agreed to take each item individually, consider what both knew about each point and see how it fit into the overall picture.

Hastily, he began with number one. "When translated, Seachd Righrean means Seven Kings. You're convinced, it really means seven clan leaders, correct?" Remy moved swiftly away from Amanda and her tragic murder.

Relieved, he had put his wife's death on the list, but she was doubtful Remy had accepted the idea. It was a start. Belle answered him honestly and sat in the seat beside him. "Yes, it's the only translation that makes sense. I think seven clan leaders are the men who control this society." Their two heads were close together looking over the lengthy list. "We need to quickly figure out which clans are connected, but with Sam's deep involvement, you can bet one of the *'Seven Kings'* is a Buchanan." She whispered, even though there was no one nearby.

"They are one of the most powerful families in the world, and their corporation is the largest privately held company in existence. My guess, Sam would not make a move without the backing of his family. That makes the Buchanan's our first name associated with the Seven Kings." Dr. Campbell Brooks stated this, with a look of total confidence.

Even on this sparsely populated train, Remy was nervous accusing the influential family of belonging to this farfetched tale of international intrigue and murder. "Okay, we'll go with your theory and list the Buchanan's under number one." Scribbled the powerful clan's name on their list. "Who are the other six or how do we find them?" Quietly questioning, because had spent his entire life around politics and he knew the two of them had to tread lightly.

"I'm not sure about the other six, but something must connect them together." Frustrated, Belle could not find any clues or links to this mysterious group of people. "We'll need to discover what that is, before we can figure out the other families involved. But, at least, does this seem to make sense to you?" Watching as his head moved up and down and decided to let him in just a bit more, Belle confessed shyly. "I'm not sure why but somehow, I think my grandmother might have known these individuals. Maybe, even how they're all tied together."

Internally, his first reaction to her startling statement was one word. *Astonishing!*

Remy only managed to choke out. "What gives you that idea?" Suspected her grandmother was somehow involved but did not think it was with the actual society. Apparently, Belle thought differently.

"My instincts are telling me Granny knew a lot more than she's been sharing. Even though she's gone, if there was information about Sam, she'd have left it for me to find." Tears formed in the corners of Belle's eyes. "If we cannot figure everything out in New York, we might need to return to whatever remains of the compound in Virginia." She fought off a bout of crying because there was still much work to be done before Belle could mourn for her beloved grandmother.

"Could that be why the Seachd Righrean targeted your Granny?" Remy was enjoying trading questions and answers with the intelligent lady but acknowledged, they shared the pain of grief as well. "Because there were little, or no clues left at the site."

What Remy had to say next, would not go over well and braced himself for her reaction. "The FBI lab could find no conclusive evidence for the two explosions at your Granny's place — not man-made or natural. Whoever did this was very good." Back to using his official voice again. "Only about three people in the world have the skills to do such a job and the cost would have been astronomical, meaning your theory about the involvement of the Buchanan's still holds."

This time, he tipped his hand to her as a sign of respect because Remy was starting to buy into her crazy notions.

"I have to believe Granny knew something, the information is at the cabin, but somewhere safe." The tears were stationary at the edge of Belle's eyes. Her resolve continued to amaze the special agent.

Before he went on, Remy wiped away her tears. "Number two, we discussed back at your house, but at the time we were both exhausted." Still having a tough time believing Sam had married this goddess strictly for business. "Do you have any new theories to add?" He wanted to verify her statement again because if that were the case, he thought Randall should have had his head examined.

"No, none. What kind of business deal could I have possibly been for Sam?" Belle was at a loss. "It just doesn't make any sense." Could not figure out what Sam would get out of marrying her for professional reasons. "What's your take on this?" Her face searched his for some answers.

"Well, when you told me back at your place, I figured it was kinda twisted. Even thought, maybe you heard him wrong." He was striving to find the right words, to help ease the blow. "Then you told me about Sam's will."

Suddenly, her husband's weird request made perfect sense. It was like something clicked into place inside her head. "You think, Sam married me to have a child and to produce an heir?" Belle's tone was a harsh one because she was very uncomfortable with this topic of conversation.

Unable to look at her, Remy just nodded. "Yeah, I think he chose you or maybe his parents chose you. Damn, I'm sorry to say this but I think to...uh...I guess, breed with you to carry on the family name, is about the only way to say it. If we found his laptop, I think there would be searches about you. I bet, long before you met."

He felt like a heel but was trying to do this, as tenderly as possible. "I'm really sorry, Belle, and I know this has to be very difficult for you, but can you think of any other reason?"

"No." Came her soft reply. Suddenly, Belle thought this is what championship horses and prize-winning dogs must feel like.

He moved quickly forward to help get past her discomfort. "Three, fixed the Irish election." Speaking to himself, while sorting through his piles of papers. "Why did they vote the other party in?" Finally, found the copy of the election clipping from the Palm Beach house. "What did Sam actually say when you touched this article?" Politely asking, while passing the newspaper clipping to her.

Held her hands up. "Give me a minute to gather myself."

To prepare for his question, jumped up and walked down the aisle to help her clear a mental path. Belle was definitely not planning on using her gift on the train.

Instead, sat down on her side of the conference table and quietly informing Remy. "Please, place the article down in front of me."

Once it was there, she spent a few minutes concentrating on the piece of paper, focusing on the various conversations of her criminal husband. "Sam said they needed to lose the Irish election but not by too much. This society actually likes the Dochloite Laoch, which had won almost every election for the last one hundred years."

Turning toward Remy again. "Mostly, he was having a problem with himself." Adding sadly. "I really didn't know Sam was filled with so much self-loathing and so little self-esteem." Distracted by his infidelities, forcing herself to concentrate on the difficult memory again. "The Shannon O'Malley woman, from the electronic voting machine company, appeared to be in on it. Although, Sam never actually said anything to indicate that. It's just a feeling I got because I never heard him speak to her."

Belle's face turned beet red at another one of Sam's numerous indiscretions. "Only felt his…um…yearnings for her."

Rapidly, moved on to the next subject. "He seemed to be plotting something big against the society itself. Sleight of hand is what he called it. Said they would never suspect it, so what was he really up to?" Although trying to keep contempt out of her voice, Belle was losing and forged on with the recollection. "Whatever it was, he's been planning it for over two years." The red returned, brightly to her cheeks. "Meaning, he's been planning this since before we even met, and it involved getting rid of the society's top people. The old guard. His words, not mine." She turned back toward Remy. "Also, this new regime was coming into power soon and Sam had high hopes of running it."

Stopping for a moment to draw a deep breath, hoping for calm. "It reminded me of the newsreels I've seen of Adolf Hitler. They scared me because he truly believed his own lunacy and Sam was the same way." Even though she had not actually used her gift, it still took a toll. Simply reviewing the difficult conversation had left her drained. *The long-forgotten Nazi memories had been vivid which I'm sure isn't healthy for my recovery but I'm glad to be finished with such things for now.*

To combat the weariness, Belle focused on childhood summers spent with Granny and eventually went on. "Which means we need to discover why the Seachd Righrean would want the Dochloite Laoch out of the way."

Already deep in thought regarding her answers, he was unaware of her rising discomfort. "What did the society oppose, need or desire from the winning party?" Remy was talking aloud to no one but himself, trying to figure out the international dilemma. "Because there is no other reason to replace them after such a long time in power." Right then, thought of something that could give them a hint and turned his full attention toward Belle. "Let me make a phone call. I'll get my buddy working on a list of legislation that's been tied up in Parliament or the courts. Everything that's been opposed by the previous party but will now pass because they're out of power."

Pulled out his phone and speed dialed Dooley to run the necessary programs, knowing he was going to get cussed out if he woke his new baby. After dodging an Irish lashing, hung up with his best friend, happy to discover it should be ready by dinner time, later that same evening.

"Remy, why do you think they want to control the US election?" After working with her these last few days, he was not surprised by Belle's question.

Due to the sensitive nature of the topic, he was back to whispering. "Because of the email messages I intercepted. They were encoded but after deciphering them, they appear to be referring to the upcoming election but found nothing to back up those claims. I've spent the last two months trying to uncover something, anything, and so has my friend in Europe. He, too, is coming up empty." Looking a little defeated but he pressed on.

Frustrated, Remy pulled the list over to study it. "For right now, it's a dead end because there is not enough evidence to even pursue it, so let's set this one aside." Quickening his finger exercises because they always seemed to bring calm back into his essence.

She moved forward with number five when realizing a few moments were needed for the tense man to compose himself. "Sam's laptop is missing. The only reason I can think of, there was something on it which could be incriminating. Whoever killed him, took the laptop so the police or maybe me, would not find out whatever he had stored on it."

It was still difficult to talk about Sam, yet Belle was desperate to get past the embarrassment and move on with her life. "I doubt we will ever find it again." Wanting to be hopeful, she went on. "Whatever was on it, it's probably gone for good but maybe, just maybe, Sam saved everything he had on the laptop." A brief twinkle appeared in her eye. "Maybe, it's in the safe deposit box." Finished the rest of the statement a bit more quietly. "Or at least I hope it is."

Then Belle attempted a truly optimistic smile toward Remy. One, he halfheartedly returned.

With his irritation under control, reached into his briefcase, pulled out the folder filled with all the newspaper articles and placed it between the two of them. "What are your thoughts about these?"

After looking at the folder, Belle knew what they were. Thanks to her increased 'feelers', she was fairly certain Remy would not like her answer. "Those are all the events this society has had a hand in shaping."

"What do you mean?" Growled at Belle, while taking another sip of his coffee. Remy required the familiar taste of caffeine to bring his reactions back into the proper line of reason.

She ignored his hostile mood. "In other words, I think the society decides who and what they want. Then they find the people to make it happen. I know it sounds crazy but it's the only explanation." Grabbed the file and pointed to the articles inside. "Look what's in this folder Remy. The most profound historical events are in here." Virtually shaking it in his face. "These guys strike me as seeing themselves as gods."

While speaking, Belle continued to pull out several articles. "They name their secret society Seven Kings. If they consider themselves kings, considering themselves gods is not a big stretch."

She laid each one carefully out on the table. "If they have the financial means like the Buchanan's, it would be quite simple to steer the course of history to your liking." The determined woman placed the articles, one on top of another for his review. "With no one being the wiser."

Astonishment continued to spread across Remy's features, as her statements began to sink in. Bewilderment coursed through his answer. "If you're right, this would be incredible. Imagine a group of people, shaping history, and doing it for this long." Clutched the folder tighter in his hand. "With no one knowing about it." He blew out another soft whistle and ran his hands through that thick hair again.

At long last, at a loss for words, Remy called the porter over and ordered a fresh carafe of coffee. Both spent time in silence, merely staring at the spring scenery outside the train windows but pondering the sticky predicament they currently found themselves in.

Belle knew they needed to finish the list before reaching New York. Eventually, she looked at him and whispered. "The man in the back of the limousine with Sam was the same gentleman following my mother, but I don't know why or even who he is."

Belle needed Remy to focus, so she pressed on. "I think we covered number nine already which is why they killed Granny. "What are your thoughts about the shootout at Lennox House?"

Instincts began kicking in and he did not want to scare her. But he remembered Belle had already held up under the most intense pressure. Braced himself for the sparks, then, told her what he really thought. "I think they were there to kill either you, me or both of us."

"That's what I thought too but hoped you had a better idea." Letting out the little laugh, Belle made whenever nerves got the better of her. "Whew, that sure wasn't fun hearing. Especially when you realize it could be true and someone is really trying to kill you."

He hated telling her such shocking news, as Remy grabbed her hand to send his magical soothing sensations to offset any anxiety she must be feeling. "Well, it's no guarantee they were trying to kill you by blowing up your grandmother's house. Unfortunately, between what happened at the cabin and Palm Beach, it's most likely you're a target."

"Thank you for being so kind. I would rather know the truth and be prepared than be lied to and dead." Happy to see the stubborn streak in the doctor was showing up again, because Belle was going to need it to get through this with her life.

Although, he did not want to ask this next delicate question, Remy needed to hear her response. "We spoke about Sam's will." It could make a substantial difference in which direction they went for answers. "Do you believe Sam was the one who wanted you to have the child, or do you think someone else put him up to it?"

For quite a while, Belle contemplated the question and answered it the best way she could. "If I had to make an honest guess, I'd say someone else because Sam really didn't like children. Yes, he was always asking me to have one but whenever we were around them, it was almost like he hated kids." As Belle continued to talk, Remy frantically wrote notes next to each of the items. "I'd say someone put him up to it. Again, my guess would be his parents, Lloyd and Jo. I can't think of anyone else who would benefit from an heir except, maybe them."

Carefully, he reviewed the list, then moved on. "Okay, the only items left on the list are the money laundering." Counting the last ones off on his fingers to combat the frustration which was creeping back into Remy's demeanor. "What I cannot tie my case to, is Buchanan Industries and I can't figure out why."

Excited now because Belle knew her instincts were stronger than before, and she was on the right track. "Could it be about the takeover of the society Sam was talking about?" She pulled the Irish article out of the pile and pointed at it enthusiastically. "Remember when I told you Sam said he would not have to put up with the old man in the limo for much longer?"

Nodded in agreement because Remy clearly remembered her detailed description of Sam's conversations.

"Everything was finally falling into place. It was only a matter of time until they would sweep away the old guard and a new regime would come into power." She stopped to consider her husband's motives. "Maybe he was laundering the money to put those new people in place."

Her idea gave him an alternative clue and Remy bent down, withdrawing another folder from his briefcase.

He spent the next few minutes reviewing the contents, then looked up from his inquiry, and loudly exclaimed. "Well, I'll be damned. It makes sense, especially if you are planning some type of coup of an organization, which has the power and money this one seems to have."

All at once, he was pulling on multiple pieces of paper and typing on his laptop while sending texts to unknown sources. "Sam would need incredible resources to overthrow them and washing drug money is the fastest way to millions of undocumented dollars."

Almost totally ignoring Belle, but she had grown accustomed to his unusual work habits, when suddenly he surprised her by lifting his head. "Good call on this one. You could be right. A much clearer picture of what was going on is forming in my head." Smiling, Remy immediately went back to disregarding her.

Aware of his commitment, Belle understood the dedicated agent was processing the latest information, with the evidence he had already gathered. She had no problem waiting until he came back.

After about ten minutes, looked up from his work, ready to deal with the next item. One, Remy was quite insistent about, so he dived right in. "Sam killed Jennifer Randolph; I know he did. More important, I feel somehow her death is tied into this society and what's happening with us, today." He shook his head at those crazy intuitions. "Don't ask me how I know that. I just do."

Her response was to laugh out loud at his unusual statement. "You really don't need to explain yourself to me." After getting a hold of herself, went on. "Remember, I'm the woman who can touch something and go back to wherever it's been. Not to mention, it seems I can now go several days beforehand as well."

Her outburst seemed to make Remy relax just a little. "Let's just agree strange and weird are our new normal, okay?"

That left only the last item on the list to discuss, and Belle took the lead because knew this would be difficult for him. "Remy, you grew up with Sam your whole life and said you thought Jennifer's murder somehow ties into what's happening today." Gently placed her hand on his arm. "I think Amanda's death is part of this too. My instincts tell me the way her calendar was staged, along with leaving no clues was all faked to look like a suicide, just like the newspaper articles and shaping history."

She was worked up because Belle knew both his wife's and Sam's deaths were almost identical and were too much of a coincidence for her. "I know this is hard for you, but it's exactly the type of death the society is known for. Look how Sam died. Made to look like a drug overdose too, but if I had to guess, I'd tell you Sam didn't do drugs." Picked up the pen. "I think his death should be number fifteen on the list."

Reaching over, she slid the list in front of her and quickly added Sam's drug overdose to the bottom of the piece of paper. Hoped she was getting through to him and continued with her similar circumstance's theory. "The doctor's appointments, the pills and the notes with the dates when she was supposed to be having an affair." Using her own form of finger counting to make her point. "All manufactured to look like Amanda was a strung-out drug addict, who killed herself. People would shake their heads and quickly move on with their lives." Pointed her finger at Remy. "Only, you didn't believe it." Shaking it at him. "Everyone else bought her suicide but not you."

"All because of one night." Tried to be as delicate as possible but this was too important, so she gently pressed him. "Let me ask you a question. One, I'm sorry to have to ask but I must. If you hadn't gone to dinner that night and found out you were going to be a father." Uncomfortable pushing, Belle paused because she hated hurting him. "Would you believe the evidence they had put together?" This challenged him to the limits, but it was imperative she get him to review the overwhelming facts.

The look on Remy's face cracked her heart, even more.

Barely above a whisper, he replied. "I probably would have because it was significant and convincing. The only reason I didn't believe was because of the baby. It hurt too much to tell anyone else, so, I kept it to myself. Everyone thinks she killed herself and I'm wasting my time looking for a murderer who's a ghost."

Even though Belle's speculations were plausible, Remy was still having a difficult time believing. He could not wrap his head around the real-life cloak and dagger madness of it all and he did this shit for a living.

"Just consider the possibility and think how Amanda might have crossed paths with Sam." Gently taking Remy's hands in hers, to let him know she was there and understood his pain.

"Thank you for your kindness. I appreciate it, but right now, I need some air." With that, Remy hastily stood up and walked toward the restroom again.

Sam Randall is damn lucky he's dead. Damn lucky.

CHAPTER 21

What's in the Box?

With Remy gone, she decided to close her eyes to help shut all the nonsense out and clear her head. When the silence descended, Belle slowly went over the items on the list because it was quite a farfetched set of circumstances. If all of this were true and not some dream or movie, then this society has been controlling both of their lives for a very long time. A fact, which was almost too large in scope to comprehend. But she still doubted everything.

"How could I have not known about these people?" She stopped and looked down at the folder, with all the newspaper articles in it. Her reasonable thinking took over and wondered if anyone for the last sixty years, including Congress and all the presidents who had served had even suspected this society existed. "Dear Lord between Sam, Granny and now the items on the list."

Belle inhaled a huge breath and slowly let out a big sigh. "I'd say, this is an awful lot to take in." Understood, it was imperative to figure out what this society was up to, plus discover what Sam had been planning because these guys needed stopping. Absolutely no one should hold that kind of power.

Both she and Remy needed to spend time alone to gather their inner strength. The answers were right there in front of them but because of the current upheaval, they could not think. Too much information and too many events were flying around in her head. They were blocking her gifts with intense overload which kept her from getting to the truth and the people who killed Granny.

Determined to find them as quickly as possible, she shut out all the outside stimuli and focused on the details they had just discussed.

The next thing Belle knew, Remy was lightly shaking her.

Already at Penn Station and the train stopped, the interior lighting caused her to blink. "Oh my, I was trying to figure out some things and must have dozed off." She looked up through partially closed lids at the mighty fine-looking agent.

Quickly shuddering off the weariness, Belle sat for a minute and studied him. "Remy, how are you?" Sympathetic eyes conveyed her sorrow about hurting him earlier, when she suggested the society was responsible for Amanda's death. Desperate for him to know she would be there if he needed her.

Remy smiled down at her, just not as brightly as he had done in her kitchen, although better than earlier. "While you were sleeping, I spent the time thinking about everything. The more I go over it, the more your outrageous theory makes sense." Shook his head at her insane notion. "Even though I cannot think of any time when Sam might have met Amanda." Vibes filled with anger and frustration poured out of him, but Belle knew they were not directed at her. "I have gone over every part of the last couple of months of Mandy's life which leaves only one other possibility."

Staring straight ahead, not at her because Remy knew this theory was a doozy. "The man in the back of the limousine."

His unexpected idea made Belle gasp because she had not thought about that scenario, but it made sense.

It took a minute, but she shook off the painful memory because he was onto something. "Somehow we have to figure out who he is, and find him, because he's been a part of this from the very beginning."

After pulling herself together, continued with his theory. "Thirty years ago, he followed my mother, and you think he's the link to Amanda's murder and this group. Interesting. I think you could be right, which means we need to find him soon."

Still hounded by the demons of his wife's death but determined to face them finally, Remy stood up. Helped her from the seat and grabbed both of their overnight bags, leading the way out of the compartment and into the busy station.

After about one hundred yards, spotted a man holding a printed sign with Belle's name on it. Suspicious, he instantly went on alert and turned. "Did you call for a car?"

Startled by his intensity but she could not resist a quick peek into his calming eyes. "Yes, I'm sorry, I forgot to tell you, but I thought it would be easier than trying to get a taxi on St. Patty's Day." Thankful for his company during this difficult task. "Especially, because of today's parade and the huge crowds expected to turn out." For the first time since they boarded the train, Belle broke out in a genuine smile. Chuckled, when a picture popped into her head of the FBI guy trying to flag down a cab while fighting off the drunken mob that would walk the streets today.

With no real danger in sight, Remy relaxed. "Good call."

Placing his hand on the small of her back. "Do you want to go to the hotel first and change or go straight to the bank?" Out of the corner of his eye, watched her wistfully as she kept pace beside him.

She walked out the glass revolving door and into the bright sunshine, answering him while searching for sunglasses in her large designer bag. "The bank first, please. I'd like to have as much time as possible to review whatever Sam might have left. Since it's already after one and with the parade, we'll be lucky to make it there before it closes."

Suddenly, felt defeated and slipped on her glasses. "If this is even the correct bank." Waited while the chauffeur opened the back door for her and climbed in first with Remy following close behind.

They placed their overnight bags in the trunk, but their briefcases went into the backseat with them. Her anxiety was back, and he wanted to do anything to help. Gently took her hand, laid it on top of his other and held it softly. For the duration of the ride, Remy tried to supply as much soothing comfort as possible. The city was packed with partiers because everyone was Irish on this day. The mood was as bright as the warm spring sun, plus today's parade was special, marking the two hundred fiftieth anniversary of the celebration.

He was pleased with Belle's careful planning of hiring a car, because the parade crowds were expected to be even larger than years past. People would be packing every street along the designated route in observance of the half-quincentennial, with the expected attendance numbers to be the biggest ever. Not only was she beautiful and smart but the doctor had also been right.

Shortly after they were underway, Remy discovered the crowds were huge and like their helicopter ride from the hospital, spent the trip commenting on other things. Today, it was the people reveling in the festivities. He delivered funny stories and commentary to amuse Belle out of the gloominess she seemed to have slipped into.

After a while, she could no longer resist his charm and giggled along with his enchanting stories, as they worked their way through lower Manhattan. The enjoyable ride took almost two hours to complete. They spent the last half of the journey talking about their past visits and favorite places each had in the city. They found several places in common with many favorites, being off the beaten path and their light banter seemed to relieve some of the stress from Belle's face.

At long last, their stretch limousine pulled up to the front door at the main branch of the Scotland Royal Bank, where Remy believed Sam had his hidden box. Before getting out, Belle admitted out loud. "I'm a little nervous now that we're here." To boost her spirits, Remy grabbed hold of her hand and squeezed it tenderly.

As they entered the large marble columned lobby, he transferred back to the intense FBI agent and was instantly on alert. His growing anxiety made Belle even more nervous, but she was determined to see this through to the end. Pulling herself together, straightened her back, then walked toward the bank manager's office with Granny's encouragements whispering inside her head.

She approached his administrative assistant, who resided outside his door. "Could you please help me?" Placing the safe deposit key on the blotter for her review.

After spending a few minutes examining it, the girl returned it to Belle. Looking back and forth between the two of them, she appeared more nervous with each turn of her head. Whirled towards her computer and from memory, typed the series of numbers embedded on the front of Sam's key. The secretary's face changed dramatically as the confirmation of her request came up on the monitor.

She stood up, knocking the chair over. "Could you please excuse me for a moment?"

Closely, he scrutinized the rose-colored woman's aura, then swore. Remy watched as it became a murky gray during her walk to the nearby office. Puzzled by the fact, he had literally just witnessed her aura instantly change color. Remy cursed, because the phenomenon was something he had never seen before. *That can't be good.*

The girl hastily ducked through the doorway and Remy turned toward Belle to whisper his observations.

A few minutes later, the two of them were quietly speaking when they heard someone say. "How may I assist you folks this afternoon?" Both turned swiftly toward the sounds made by the nervous man emerging from the bank manager's office.

Again, found herself back in her new role as a widow. "Hello, I'm Campbell Randall and I believe my late husband Sam Randall kept a deposit box here at your bank." Held the key up for the manager to see. "Does this belong to a box here in your vault?" The key was shaking so hard, Remy reached over and gently folded her hand back inside his. This sent a shot of soothing magic into Belle to help settle her nerves.

Loudly gulping, the banker was unable to answer her right away.

Although wanted to let Belle handle this, after observing the manager's strange behavior, Remy thought it was time to move this show along. Thrust his right hand out to the little guy, deducing the man's name from the sign on the office door. With his left hand, whipping out his ID badge while shaking the manager's hand. Then, he proceeded in his most cheerful voice. "Good afternoon, Mr. Gordon." Continued to pump the sweaty executive's hand. "I am FBI Special Agent Remington

Montgomery. I'm here with Mrs. Randall this afternoon, as just a friend, helping her finish up with her husband's estate."

Placed his arm around the pint-size guy continuing in his most soothing voice. "I would imagine the Scotland Royal Bank would love to assist in any way they can, the widow of such a prominent client as Mr. Samuel Randall." Steering him toward the stairwell that led down to the vault. "I bet you'll be personally escorting us to the box today won't you sir?" His Prince Charming smile was shining bright.

Remy's antics left the bank manager with his head bobbing up and down, while falling all over himself to please the two of them.

Still amazed by his abilities, Belle loved watching Remy use them. Unable to get over the influence he wielded, she grabbed his arm and leaned in, while placing a quick kiss on his cheek. A treat for getting the little twit to swiftly lead them to Sam's hidden box. Silently, she wondered how much power he really held over others and to what extent could manipulate people.

Although on figuring Remy out, she sided with Scarlett again. *That thought was for another day.*

Once they were downstairs, Mr. Gordon turned toward Belle. "Unfortunately, I cannot open this box without the proper password."

After hearing this newest twist, hastily swung her head toward Remy but was not worried. Convinced they could handle whatever obstacle Sam had placed in their path and motioned the manager to carry on.

Upon entering the actual vault, Belle was struck at how large it was and how many boxes were lined up from floor to ceiling. The one they were interested in was toward the back by the far corner, down toward the bottom. She noted it was one of the largest boxes available.

The manager stood there looking like he had never been more afraid in his life, waiting for Belle to produce the secret password. A devil-like twinkle sparkled in her eyes because she knew what it was, thanks to her increased powers and informed the jittery man. "Seachd Righrean."

Immediately, the frightened man's shoulders relaxed, becoming a different person, once she produced the secret words.

With a nod of his head, the manager quickly inserted his key into the front at the same time as hers. Once the door was opened, slid the large box out and he placed it on the conference table in the middle of the room. "I'll leave you in private for now. When you're ready to leave, please press the button here." He indicated the blue one on the panel by the door. "Someone will come down to escort you out. The bank closes at four p.m., which is in about an hour." Out of politeness, stopped at the door. "Is there anything else I can do for you, Mrs. Randall?"

"No, but thank you, Mr. Gordon for all your help." Belle waited until he was completely gone before turning toward Remy and the mysterious box. "What color was he?" Took off her coat and made herself comfortable while waiting for his answer.

"A dark, dark brown, which is not good at all because it means he's very unsettled. That man has either been paid to watch this box or knows something that's going on with it." Remy's eyes darted around, because the nervous man's aura had bothered him and wanted to leave immediately. "I think we should spend as little time here as possible. Clear everything out and take it back to the hotel. We can go over it there, but not here, where that man or his cameras can watch us."

Remy was right, and she yanked open the lid. Surprised to find the box was almost full. "Good God, there are all kinds of things inside here. Look at this." Picked up a folder filled with newspaper articles. "Looks familiar, huh?"

The agent was extremely curious about what was inside and reached in, first pulling out several UBS drives. Next came a photo of the undersecretary of Health and Human Services. When lifting the picture, he discovered what looked like a weed of some sort under it. "Hey, do you have any idea what this could be?" Remy noticed nothing amiss until she did not answer.

After a few minutes of rummaging through all the evidence, he looked over and found her a ghostly white.

"Yes, I do, but why would it be in here?" Staring straight ahead, she appeared to be in a trance. "What would Sam want with that?"

"What is it?" Remy was curious but noticed Belle had stopped moving and stood strangely staring at the plant he held in his hand.

"It's dried spring sage but why would Sam have any of it? Granny would never give it to him." Again, Belle was standing dead still. "She didn't even like him."

Back to looking like she was going to pass out, he finished moving all the items out of the box, shoving everything into their briefcases. Completely filling both of them and putting the rest in her handbag.

Afterwards, he rushed over and pushed the blue button by the door several times. Quickly, grabbing Belle's coat and helping her into it, then closed both cases. Remy set them on top of the table and after collecting everything else, he forced her to sit down and wait for their escort.

By this time, the administrative assistant had arrived and not wanting to alarm her, Remy explained away Belle's odd condition. "Mrs. Randall has been through an enormous tragedy and thought she was up for this task today. But as you can see, was unprepared and not ready. So, we'd like to have the box put back into place and we'll retrieve the contents on another day. Can you do that for us, please?"

"Yes, of course." The still shaken secretary answered, as he helped Belle back to her feet and they made their way to the exit. The young girl immediately went over and reinserted the box into the proper vault slot.

While walking back up the stairs to the lobby, the kind assistant could not hold back her sympathy. "Mrs. Randall, I'm so sorry for your loss. I knew your husband and he was a fine man. If there is anything I can do to help you, please don't hesitate to contact me."

The young woman's heartfelt condolences made her wonder if Sam had slept with the girl. Right away, she felt guilty, but the lovely thing was probably just trying to be nice. Because of Sam's antics, Belle now automatically thought the worst of everyone, and was sad since she had never been like that before.

The administrative assistant ushered them swiftly toward the front door and the limousine waiting out front. Apparently, the girl could not get them out of the bank fast enough, and the observant agent noted her interesting mannerisms. Suddenly curious about the employee's peculiar behavior but he could not spend the time finding the reason, too worried about the shaken widow's condition. Instead, Remy thanked the young lady, while promptly loading an unresponsive Belle into the car.

They were underway within minutes. At first, just let her sit there. She had not uttered a word since leaving the bank. Dazed, she was back to looking like she had on the drive home from the hospital. Unfortunately, Remy needed answers. Pushing her for some, he finally asked. "Belle honey, what is spring sage?"

"It's the name of my grandmother's farm"

Well, that was not at all, what he had expected to hear and tried another approach. "What else is it, sugah?"

She spoke like in a trance. "An herb, my Granny uses all the time. For a lot of different things. It's her best one and has super-secret healing powers." Barely speaking above a whisper. "It's imperative that it be handled properly and with care or it can seriously hurt or even kill you." Leaned over, and placed her head on his shoulder, because Belle was done with talking.

Finally, letting the tears she had been holding back for days fall for her much-loved grandmother.

Remy decided they could go over everything from the box, once they reached the hotel, because Belle needed time to recover. Wrapped his arms around her and leaned back against the seat, while she spent the rest of the ride grieving for her cherished Granny.

When arriving at the Waldorf Astoria, the manager of the famed five-star establishment met the car. Amazed by the power of Buchanan Industries, they were whisked upstairs to their adjoining suites, accompanied by four bellmen. Once their bags were unpacked and both assured the staff there was nothing more for them to do, they were left alone.

Still worried about Belle, he gently suggested. "This stuff's not going anywhere." Waved his hand over their briefcases. "Why don't we both change? I'll order some food and coffee, we can meet back here, in say an hour. How does that sound?"

She looked better than at the bank, but still not over the shock of finding the sage and could only nod her head. Turning, she made her way to the master bedroom without a backward glance.

He watched longingly until the door closed shut, then reluctantly made his way toward the other suite on the opposite side of the living room.

When returning forty-five minutes later, Remy was surprised to find Belle already there and sitting on one of the designer couches, with a cup of coffee in her hand. "It just arrived. Would you like one?" Tilting it up at him.

Relieved to see her almost back to normal. "Please, I'd love one." Remy came over and sat down, taking the freshly poured coffee from her. "When I ordered this, I told them to send up the food around seven thirty but there should be snacks to tie us over until then." The minute she saw his bright smiling face, Belle could not help feeling better.

After she suggested where they were, he grabbed the tray from the cart and brought it over with that brilliant smile because he enjoyed just being around her. Man, did he appreciate the view before him, noting that Belle was in a suite, which probably cost five thousand dollars a night but seemed content just being barefoot and makeup free. She appeared perfectly comfortable picking finger food off a platter balanced between their legs. Few of the women Remy had dated would be in that category, including his lovely Amanda.

The more time he spent in her company, the more he was falling for her. Somewhere deep, hoped she was feeling the same way too. There had been a few instances over the last several days, when he thought Belle might be. Then caught himself. Immediately stopping that train of thought. A relationship with her or anyone else was not in the cards right now. Until they figured this whole mess out, there was no way any of those strange feelings could ever go anywhere. *It's impossible.*

Time to move on like Remy always did when it came to matters of the heart. Back to reality and responsibility, he decided it was time to peruse all the information from Sam's box. "Okay, let's look at these items, one at a time." After digging into his briefcase, Remy came up holding the picture they had found earlier. "Do you know who this is?"

She had seen him at functions, but Belle did not. "No, not really." Her head shaking from side to side. "Who is he? I mean I've seen him at different events, but I really don't know him or even his name."

He placed the photo on the coffee table for her review. "This is the undersecretary of Health and Human Services, Malcom Calhoun but why would Sam have a photo of him?" Again, Remy appeared to be talking to himself. "While we were freshening up, I had an associate run a few inquiries on Mr. Calhoun. It seems the rumors are that if the GOP wins the next election, Malcolm will make the move to the secretary seat at HHS. He is well liked by both parties, but other than that, there is nothing out of the ordinary about him." Remy used his fingers to make his points. "Calhoun has no scandals, no active affairs, and seems to lead a fairly normal life." The picture perplexed him, why would Randall have it in his possession? "Therefore, it makes no sense for Sam to keep it in his box."

"Okay, but let's back up a minute." To stop him, she threw both hands out in front of herself. "Wouldn't he be the ideal person for the society to use?" The question was a rhetorical one. "Think about what you just said." Utilizing her own finger move, for every detail. "Nothing out of the ordinary. No scandals. No affairs." Emphasizing each item. "Nothing, which would draw attention to him, and he would be the perfect pawn to implement whatever it is they are trying to do. Keep in mind, this society despises attention, therefore a person like Malcom Calhoun is perfect because you would never suspect him."

He became excited because she was on to something.

Once again, she had pointed out the obvious. *Belle was absolutely right.* No one would think anything was amiss if Calhoun was named to the cabinet position. In fact, Washington was expecting it to happen. "But why him? What do they need the secretary of HHS for?" Put his hands on his head while basically talking to himself. "What will pass or be approved that wouldn't be if he were not in charge?" This puzzle piece bothered him badly, but he did not know why.

With no answers forthcoming, Remy set Mr. Calhoun aside for the time being.

Gently, he approached the next subject because it was a part of this somehow. His insightful instincts kept telling him it could be the key to this whole mystery but was worried how it was tied to Belle. "Are you ready to talk about the sage yet, sugah?" He felt so bad and did not want to hurt her, but Remy knew this was an important piece of the puzzle.

"Yes, I think so, but I'm still all mixed up about it. How could Sam have gotten a sprig of Granny's famous remedy?" Shocked, he even knew about it because he had shown no interest in her own herbs.

"What about if he didn't get it from your grandmother?" Remy's response was unexpected, and his question triggered a look of surprise that took her completely.

"WHAT??? Where else would he have gotten it?" Belle was utterly confused. "It doesn't grow anywhere else, that I know of, except on her farm."

Positive his instincts were correct, Remy decided to follow his intuitions. "How do you know that?"

Convinced he was wrong, certain about her grandmother's never-ending lessons. "Because Granny told me when I was small. Said it took her a long time, but she finally found a way to make it grow over here, and it was almost impossible. The rare herb would grow nowhere else, except on Sinclair Mountain."

Remy reached into his briefcase, pulling out the original folder Belle had found hidden in Sam's desk drawer. After rummaging through it, removed a small article about a patent, which recently had been preliminarily approved for fighting Alzheimer's disease. The article boasted about the almost overnight new drug's bonus side effects, which make the patient look five years younger. It quoted numerous studies completed, with additional research on order, but the initial findings were remarkable.

He placed the article in front of her and pointed at it to emphasize his position. "Could this be your Granny's wonder drug?" Now that he had Belle's attention, Remy asked more gently. "Because if so, this definitely would be something to kill over."

Still confused but she understood what he was getting at and replied honestly. "Yes, it sure could be, but how would they have gotten their hands on it?" Unconvinced, anyone affiliated with the farm was involved. "No one on the mountain would have shared it with any outsider. In fact, I'm not sure Granny shared the knowledge about her sage, with many people except maybe me."

"Let me do some research on it." He needed to concentrate and knew he could figure this out with enough time. Once more, Remy almost disappeared before her eyes but this time, she was prepared for his intense working mode. "We're assuming they got it from your grandmother but what if they got it from somewhere else?" Snapping his fingers. "Then, learned your grandmother had it. They could have wanted her out of the way to protect their patent."

With that, he started typing with one hand and dialing the phone with the other. Belle spent the time allowing Remy's theories to sink in, while combing through the rest of the mysterious box.

Once completing his emails and phone calls, the agent's essence came back into the room and turned his attention back to Belle. It was also when the knock came.

Instantly on alert, he reached for his gun and quickly made his way to the door. He checked through the peephole, then, under all the covered plates, tablecloths, and cart before allowing the server to bring the food in. Belle suspected Remy to be a little paranoid but was grateful.

All the unusual items in Sam's secret box confused her but the events at the house in Palm Beach and at Granny's were no coincidence, nor were they accidents. Meaning, someone had been at least trying to kill her grandmother and maybe her too. They had been successful with Granny but so far not Belle, causing body shivers again.

Those nasty thoughts vanished when over his shoulder Remy called her name while pulling out her chair. "Ready to eat? I'm starving." He decided it was best to put the box away for a while and wanted the opportunity to unwind. To just take pleasure in this woman's presence and forget the insanity which had overtaken their lives. Surprised to find themselves famished, the two of them spent the next hour getting to know one another. For a brief interlude, they left the world behind and delighted in one another's company.

After finishing the enchanting meal, it was time to get to work and he grabbed the numerous USB sticks Sam had left in his off-the-record box. Nervous, because Remy's instincts were telling him the clock was ticking. Their time was running short to find out what was actually happening with this whole international mess, and to put an end to this secret society's diabolical plots. *Whatever the hell that could end up being.*

Over the next four hours, the two of them spent the time reviewing the massive amounts of information Randall had compiled. There were hundreds of files which contained large amounts of materials. Each stick was comprised of many subjects such as the recent Irish election, untold future international elections and the upcoming one in the US.

While shocked by the numbers in front of him, Remy could not believe his good fortune.

Also included in the files were enormous volumes of data on the numerous different projects, like the many shell companies Sam had set up. Apparently, these were the corporate fronts, involved in the money he was laundering for the drug cartels. It also included the information on where Sam was funneling it, along with where the arms he bought with it went. After reviewing each one, he began sending the evidence to Dooley for further analysis. The preliminary reports would be available by morning because it was Charlie's turn to feed his newborn son. Instead of going back to sleep, the tired Interpol agent went right to work.

The initial findings were staggering, and Remy spent most of the evening just trying to get a handle on all the data Sam had stashed away. It appeared some of those same companies were also affiliated with *EVE*, the *Electronic Voting of Eire Corporation*. According to these documents, they had set up several firms of the Irish company to secure contracts in key US electoral states to become the supplier of their new electronic voting machines. The ploy was to position themselves with a way to fix the approaching presidential election. This was solid proof of a way to tamper with both the Irish and the American election. Remy was blown away with their plans but for the first time since discovering Sam was up to no good the perplexed federal cop felt like he was making real progress.

Once again, he looked up at Belle excitedly. "At last, some real hard evidence on how this group could attempt to fix the election. I need to make a few calls and get some people going on researching these companies right away. Can you excuse me for a while?"

With the phone already pressed to his ear, he slipped away again.

CHAPTER 22

One Letter Changes Everything

"If you don't mind, I think I'll retire for the evening." She got up and started toward her bedroom because Belle knew his mind was elsewhere. "It's been a long day, actually it's been a very long couple of days." Not waiting for his answer and without him noticing, quickly slipped something into her pants pocket. A sealed envelope, she had found amongst the many items in her husband's hidden box.

Ashamed to be concealing her actions from Remy but unable to do otherwise.

Belle had kept it to herself because it was addressed to her and been written in Sam's own handwriting. Plus, Granny's spring sage being in the bank box had shaken her badly and she hoped to find out why, in Sam's letter. "I would really like to just go to bed and start fresh in the morning." Her speech was pleasant, but she was faking it.

When Remy responded, she got caught off guard, thinking he hadn't been paying her any mind. "Sure, of course. Go right ahead, there's at least another hour or two of work before I can hit the hay. If you need anything at all, I'll be right out here. You just let me know, okay?" Those gorgeous blue eyes hinted Remy truly meant the words he was speaking, and Belle appreciated his kindness.

"Thank you and good night." Swiftly spinning, she quietly shut the door behind her. The clicking noise made by the lock when the door closed was so loud it froze Belle in place. She was terrified by what the contents of the note would reveal and clutched it in her pocket.

For a moment, Belle found herself just standing with the wood against her back which was helping to hold her up. *Why had I not shared the message with Remy?* Irritated but switching her tactics and snapping back to no one. *Because it was for me.* Attempting to give herself more confidence, but not wanting to read Sam's words.

Eventually, she got enough nerve to drag the folded note out of her lounging pants. The outside was simply addressed.

To My Belle

Clearly, Sam intended the letter to be read just by her. She owed her husband nothing, but still felt an obligation to read his last correspondence in private. After getting the courage to leave the safety of the doorway, Belle crawled into the big California king-size bed.

With trembling fingers, sliced open the final message from her complicated husband.

My Dearest Belle,

If you're reading this, then I am gone and cannot apologize in person for all the pain I've caused you over the years. You're a wonderful woman and didn't deserve what I've put you through. He dragged you into this, not me…but I didn't have a choice in the matter. It happened a long time ago and I hope someday you'll find it in your heart to forgive me.

Seachd Righrean — Iarr air t' athair

Sam

PS Please be careful and steer clear of him…he's a very dangerous man.

She sat staring at the handwritten note for a long spell because the letter was not what Belle had been expecting.

For a while, she stayed propped up on the headboard of the bed trying to make sense of the cryptic note. Confused by Sam's mysterious message, read it several more times, then grabbed her phone because was unsure about the last sentence in the letter.

Pulling up the Internet, searched for the translation site from several nights before. After a few unsuccessful attempts, found Sam's words were in Scottish Gaelic. Baffled by the translation because it meant: *Seven Kings — Ask thy father.*

When she glimpsed down next, noticed he had written the note on some kind of company letterhead. After peering closer, Belle was shocked the stationery belonged to the Law Offices of Montgomery & MacAlister. The same law firm, which is owned by Remy's father. She covered her mouth just in time to stifle the scream that was desperate to get out and looked around in confusion.

After the shock had settled in, she quickly scrambled off the big bed. *Oh My God. No, it can't be.* Rapidly, Belle threw a few things into her overnight bag, because Sam had warned her from the grave that the man in the other room was dangerous.

Stopping a second to catch her breath, because it devastated her to find the person who she might be having real feelings for, could actually be responsible for all the horrible things occurring in her life. Stunned, to find out the bad guy was sitting right outside her door while providing support throughout each event, but the entire time had been trying to kill her.

In total shock and struggling with simple tasks, Belle was having a tough time believing his deception, counting them off, one by one. *Arriving at the house in Palm Beach, shortly before the bullets began to fly.* Reviewing all the times, he had been present during the chaos that had become her life. *Leaving her grandmother's house, right before it blows up and even spinning a story about Sam and their sordid childhood together.*

Each time Remy had been there, comforting her while making her feel safe and secure. All, so she would trust him. *How could I have been so stupid?* She retreated to the bathroom and Belle collected her toiletries, trying desperately to keep panic at bay but unable to stop the movie reel from playing the events of the past few days. *Always there to rescue me, making it easy to believe the attractive agent's story.*

Mad, hurt, and scared, as she hurried with her packing. *It's those devil good looks that did it.*

Belle could not believe she had handed him exactly what he had been searching for this entire time. *The information from her criminal husband's laptop.* In her heart, she knew Sam had undoubtedly double-crossed Remy, which is what had probably gotten him killed. Still distressed by his deception, then, remembering Sam's secret warning. Aware it was critical; she be discreet and careful.

With tears streaming down her face, quietly finished gathering her things. Not wanting to alert him of her pending departure, the frightened woman could not help wondering, if he was even a real FBI agent.

Afraid but determined to stay alive, she calmly picked up the phone and Belle informed the concierge she would be leaving right away. "No, Mr. Montgomery will stay on and be returning in the morning."

Belle requested he immediately arrange a car to take her to the airport as well as a jet to fly her back to Washington. "Yes, everything was fine with the accommodations, but I need to return to the city right away. Please tell the pilot, I want to take off as soon as I arrive and will be down on the next elevator."

After only a few moments, she cut off the employees' endless questions. "No. No, of course not." Belle became impatient with the manager's attempts to determine if the staff's services had caused her abrupt checkout, but she seemed unable to get rid of the insistent man without a plausible explanation and gave him one, to get him off the phone. "An emergency has arisen, and I need to return directly." Curtly whispering into the phone. "Yes, I appreciate it but don't need any assistance. Just have someone meet me in the lobby. Thank you and I'll see you in a few moments."

Abruptly, she hung up the bedside telephone, then picked up her bag.

Opening the hallway entry, quietly exited the room by the outer entrance and softly shut the door, so Remy would not hear her leave. Prayed her departure would not be discovered until the next morning. While in the car, Belle contacted the Buchanan helicopter pilot and informed him of her estimated arrival time into DC, along with her determination to take off as soon as the jet touched down.

Once her plans were finalized, she settled down into the back of the car. At long last, Belle could relax because she was going home, even if her homecoming was several days late. She let out a big sigh of relief at finally achieving this accomplishment.

A few hours later, arrived at what was left of the cabin and found the sun just coming up above the horizon. The destruction threw her bearings off, and she politely asked the pilot to circle over the property several times. This maneuver allowed Belle to see how much damage had been done and to get a bird's-eye view of what was left of the compound.

It took all her strength to put the grief and pain aside, while drawing additional power from the beauty of the sunrise. Fondly recalling one of her grandmother's teachings which made her sit a little straighter.

She concentrated her aerial search on locations that had survived the blast and Belle was looking for any places Granny might have logically hidden information for her to find. After several trips up and down the mountain, she instructed the pilot to land as close to the house as safety allowed.

After climbing out of the chopper, she apprised him she would call when ready to return to the city. Something that would not happen until Belle finished her business here, but that could take days because the farm covered the entire eastern side of the mountain.

For a long while, after being dropped off, Belle just stood in the front yard. Memories and heartache bombarded her as she tried to deal with the devastation that had once been her beloved home. Nevertheless, there was quite a bit of smoke smell surrounding the area. The first hour was spent searching the outside buildings and barns due to the overpowering fumes.

Desperate to find anything to be positive about before proceeding into the remains of the cabin but Belle did not have much luck. She stepped over pieces of the charred front porch, thankfully finding the first floor and basement still standing. A large portion of both had been built into the side of the mountain but the blaze had consumed many of the actual interior walls.

Also, there was not much of a second floor either. The same could be said for the back porch along with the roof but she was trying to be optimistic. Noted with happiness, the stone shell of the house was still intact, and Belle surmised with a lot of hard work, the house could be livable again rather quickly. Even the water wheel continued to turn but was missing many of its paddles.

The winter greenhouse had received the most damage and had been completely leveled. Although, almost all the other outside buildings had survived the explosion. Meaning, much of the livestock was probably around, as well. The mountain folk would collect and care for the animals until Granny returned, as was the way in these parts.

While walking around in the rubble, memories came flooding back to Belle from every year of her life. Recalling the time during mating season, when she had been about seven and a randy bull had not been too happy with Billy Ray McGregor. Mad at the farmhand's intrusion, while repairing the far fence, the big bovine had charged the cowboy unexpectedly. The animal's anger nearly cost him his hand. Granny had sewed the dangling appendage back on, almost as good as new. She recalled the scar it had left, which was wrapped all the way around his right arm. One, even Frankenstein himself would be proud of.

There was also the year she turned twelve, when an outbreak of convulsions and high fever had swept across the valley, overflowing the house with patients. Everyone infected had been treated with a special elixir of crushed yarrow flower mixed with valerian root. Belle had spent that entire summer collecting the wild herbs that grew along the Sinclair River. Hundreds of people were alive today, because of her Granny's special remedy.

Just then, the memory conjured up the sweet smell of that fragrant medicine mixture, causing Belle to stop and enjoy a piece of her childhood.

Struggling, tears formed when thinking her grandmother was really gone. Which made her wonder what would become of the Appalachian people in this area, without her Granny to care for them.

She made a mental note, to work out plans to put the money her late husband had left her to good use. With Sam's extra inheritance, Belle could create a first-class medical facility for this rural area in Mavis's name. Thank God, none of the dollars would be associated with his disturbing billions-for-a-baby scheme.

With honoring her grandmother taken care of, she took the stairs to the basement and when reaching the bottom, noticed the blast had shifted a few things. The inconvenience forced her to move around a couple of pieces of furniture, which had been stored down here for years.

Along a back wall, noted most of the canned jars of fruits and vegetables her grandmother put up every year had not been destroyed. *Well at least something survived this horrible ordeal.* Soon, Belle would go through them and make sure they were distributed to local families who needed the food. It was the reason Granny canned them in the first place.

She stared at the shelving for a while because Belle thought something seemed different. Previously, she did not remember there being a gap in between them and immediately walked over to investigate.

In between the two shelves, there appeared to be a space. "But how could this be?"

Upon further review, noticed there was indeed a small opening. "Well, I'll be…where did you come from?" Carefully placing her hand against the shelf, Belle gave it a push.

It easily relented.

Shocked, because before her lay a dark passageway leading away from the secret opening. Something she never expected to unearth. "Oh my God." Nervous, she talked into the emptiness. "How is this possible? How could this get here?"

"Me had it put in, when me built the house." A familiar, loving voice declared from beyond the shadows.

For the third time in as many days, Belle's world went completely black. She simply shut down and hit the hard floor. Out cold.

Sometime later, she woke up in a strange room and discovered herself in an unfamiliar bed. None of that mattered because just like when she was a little girl, Granny was holding a cool cloth to her head. Her eyes blinked; convinced she was dreaming. *This is impossible.* Belle could not believe her grandmother was alive and thought she must have hit her head.

She struggled to rise off the bed, but Granny just held her down. "Don't push ye' self lass. Ye' had quite a shock to ye' system. Give ye' self some time to get ye' bearings together. Didn't me teach ye' better than that?" A broad grin spread across her grandmother's face, as she fussed over Belle.

Even now, Granny still could not help but scold her impatience. A virtue she had been lacking her entire life, but Belle was in no mood for lessons. Instead, she sat up, threw her arms around her grandmother, and hugged her with all her might. "Are you real? I thought I lost you Granny." That was all she could manage before bursting into sobs, which racked her entire body for quite some time.

"There, there, child, everything is going to be fine." Granny patted her back and rubbed her precious granddaughter's arm. "Me is right as rain, as ye' can plainly see with ye' own two eyes. Now dry'em and tell me's what's ye's doing here snooping around in me cellar."

It took another ten minutes before Belle could calm down enough to explain what had happened since they had last talked. "Oh Granny, I can't believe you are here. I love you so much."

Tenderly touching Belle's face, Mavis did her best to comfort her, but needed to hear all that had happened since they last spoke. "Me knows ye' do lass and me loves ye' too. Now stop all ye' gushin' and tell Granny what's goin' on." The old woman needed to figure out what had turned their world upside down. "Ye' look a sight and me don't think it's me back from the grave that be puttin' that look in ye' eyes. Now, is it?"

Belle shook her head. "No, no, it isn't." She elected to start at the beginning, on the day Remy showed up on her doorstep since she had not mentioned him over the phone. Described in detail, the handsome FBI agent, along with his crazy accusations about Sam's involvement with numerous bad guys. She explained his amazing ability to see people's auras, along with how Belle had shared her gift with him by touching the election article.

While raising her eyebrows at the surprising confession, Mavis kept silent, allowing her granddaughter to continue with her account of these unbelievable adventures without her usual interruptions. The shootout was difficult because Belle remembered little about it but then recalled how her gift had changed. She sat up, clutching the covers with a timid tone, asking Granny about it and what the difference meant.

"Ye' remember when ye' father passed away? How ye' powers changed then?" Nodded her head at the memory. "It's the same as before. Like another door opened up or another eye. One which allows ye' to see more because ye' experienced more."

Once she heard the description, Granny's wisdom made perfect sense.

Satisfied with getting her answer, now, she wanted to uncover the many lies regarding her life, along with discovering who were the members of the very scary Seachd Righrean. Reluctantly, she told Mavis about Sam's confession, regarding their marriage. Belle was curious and sat back awaiting her grandmother's comments.

Strangely, Granny remained quiet, expecting her to move forward while giving no wisdom. She found this behavior very odd but knew that look, so went on.

Hesitantly, Belle informed her grandmother about Sam's bizarre addendum to his will, cringing when revealing all the unusual details. Still shocked by the position her husband had placed her in, as well as being embarrassed to discuss it with her beloved Granny.

It was at that point she noticed how pale her grandmother had turned. "Are you all right? By the way, where are we?" She tried to figure out where they were, but it did not look familiar. It appeared to be some type of gigantic cave, with a ceiling stretching to almost ten feet tall, and the room itself being at least a thousand square feet. The safe room included a full kitchen, along with a small bath nestled off to the side.

"When me built the house into the mountain, me had this room constructed, in case of an emergency. Good thing 'cause it saved me life the other night. Also, me used it a time or two when the house be full of patients and me needed a little peace." A grin broke out on her grandmother's face, but it was still too pasty for Belle's comfort.

"Granny, are you sure you're alright?" Thrilled to have her treasured grandmother back, but Belle was gravely concerned by her colorless appearance.

"Yes, yes, gracious sakes, me is just fine, but please go on with ye' story lassie." Shooing her away with her hands because Granny was back to looking like herself, making Belle smile at her grandmother's gumption.

"After I left the lawyer's office, I drove straight here, but when I arrived, Remy was coming out of the house. Before I could get my car door opened, the explosions occurred." Turned toward her grandmother and Belle delivered that famous stare. "Granny, Remy told me he came here to talk to you about my mother's death. What did you tell him?"

Ashamed of her many secrets, Mavis needed to turn away from her granddaughter. "Me never really got to speakin' with him, other than he be sayin' howdy." She was not up to discussing Katie's death right now because it was imperative Belle finish her account first. "Told me who he 'twas and why he be here, then went out to that fancy car of his." Granny fussed with something in the little kitchen to help distract her. "Me hardly spoke with him."

Suddenly, realization hit Belle that stopped her questions in their tracks, and she stood staring at her grandmother, who smiled from across the room. "How is it you're alive?"

To help settle down her darling granddaughter, the elder Dr. Brooks shared a little of what had happened that night and walked back over, sitting down on the bed beside her little lass. "When that government guy went outside, the air started to smell funny. Ye' know to use all six of ye' senses, not just one or two. Well, anywho, me knew something 'twasn't right. It 'twas comin' from o'er by the water mill and the foul smell twas o'er by the back wall too."

"Must say, me never smelled nothin' like that before 'cause whatever came callin' the other night, well it surely 'twas not of this world. Of that, me is certain." She needed Belle to comprehend her interesting statement. Although, at this time, Mavis did not want to dwell on it, quickly going forward with her account, hoping her granddaughter would draw her own conclusions.

"Been plannin' me entire life for just this. Me knew, so me shot down to this here room." Mavis brushed a stray hair out of her baby girl's eyes. "Please don't cry child, I swear I'm good." Leaned down, gently placing a kiss on Belle's forehead. "This here ole woman knows how to handle trouble, and as ye' can see, me is perfectly fine."

"Well, I didn't know that and what do you mean, it's not of this world?" Belle spoke through the tears which were slowing down some. "I thought you were dead and so does everyone else."

"For right now, maybe that's a good thing lass." She wiped away her granddaughter's tears and avoided talk of the terror stalking them. "Clearly someone wants me dead, so me thinks me will stay that way, for the time being." Mavis gave her treasured jewel an encouraging hug.

Deliberately ignoring the question about the demon that had come calling. Relieved Belle had not pushed it because that thing would take all her powers to go up against. Right now, Mavis' focus needed to be on her granddaughter's troubles, not something Satan had sent.

With Granny's handkerchief, she finished cleaning her face, then continued with her story. "Anyway, the blast flipped my truck over, destroying it and I ended up in a coma. Remy stayed with me in the hospital. I thought, well I really thought he was a good man. Even had me believing his crazy theory, the one about his dead wife." Angry now, Belle did not notice her grandmother's wrinkled brow. "Anyway, when I got out of the hospital, Remy was supposed to drive me back to the city, but only a few miles into it, I asked about my mother's death."

The unnatural look on Granny's face was back, but joining it were grief and pain. "Me is truly sorry about not telling ye' Belle but there didn't seem to be any need. Ye' father insisted ye' not know, unless it be absolutely necessary. He thought it be best and 'twould keep ye' safe. The Lord knows how many times me wanted to say something but ye' rarely ever spoke about her. Sweetie, me thought it best to leave sleeping dogs lie." Grabbed Belle's hand, her eyes pleading with her granddaughter's. "Please grant me forgiveness."

A loving smile broke out on Belle's face, directed at her cherished Granny. "I don't blame you but as you can imagine, it came as quite a shock to me. Especially when Remy told me there was an FBI file on it. I didn't take it well, made him pull over to a rest stop, jumped out and threw up all over the ground." Remembering what a gentleman Remy had been, helped make Belle smile. *I was so embarrassed, but he was a doll.*

Immediately, she wiped the grin off her face, which left her grandmother wondering what was going on between the two of them. Belle continued, when her swirling emotions were once more under control. "We ended up taking the helicopter back to the city. After arriving at my place, I used my gift to touch an article about the bombing at Harrods."

Again, the tears slowly fell down Belle's lovely cheeks. "Granny, I heard her voice, saw her walking and talking. My momma was so beautiful. Right before she died, Mom spoke to both Daddy and me." Snatched up Granny's hand, squeezing it lovingly. "Talked about how much she loved us and how sad she was about not being here." A warm smile appeared on Belle's face, but Mavis knew how hard the experience must have been. Tightly holding her hand and sending special magic towards her baby girl to convey how much she loved her.

Boosted by her grandmother's warm love, went on about meeting her mother. "It was one of the hardest things I have ever done. When I came back, Remy was holding me, and it wasn't so bad like it usually is when using my gift." At the mention of the FBI guy again, Mavis found herself curious about this government gentleman.

"You know how it normally is for me and this one…well it sure was a doozy." Belle's nervous laugh slipped out before she could continue. "Anyway, I shouldn't have been able to move for days but cradled in Remy's arms, I was fine when I returned." Again, she remembered the strength he had provided her. "Tired but fine." It made his betrayal all that much harder and she looked away for an instant to gather herself.

After catching her breath, eventually went on. "Afterwards, I showed him a key I found on Sam's hidden keychain. Of course, Remy told me it belonged to a safe deposit box at the Scotland Royal Bank in New York City. We took the train yesterday morning and emptied the box out in the afternoon. Granny, it was filled with all sorts of things. Files, photos, newspaper articles, even a copy of Sam's laptop, which strangely went missing after he died."

"But the weirdest thing, was discovering a piece of your spring sage, inside the box." Stared at her grandmother directly, finally expecting the truth about Sam. "Did you give him some of your special cure?"

Glaring down at her granddaughter, Mavis Brooks looked rather cross. "Now child, ye' should know better than to be askin' me such a question. Couldn't stand to be in the same room with that boy. What makes you think me be givin' him one of me best remedies?"

"Well then, how did he get it?" The question came out sharply.

"Finish ye' story, then me'll tell ye' mine." Shooed her on, because the elder Dr. Brooks knew they were finally getting to the part she needed to hear. This information was essential to understand exactly what was taking place in their lives.

This time, it was Belle's eyebrows that shot up at her Granny's statement. "Okay, well it seems Sam fixed the recent election in Ireland and somehow was working on fixing the upcoming presidential election here in the United States. Also, he was laundering millions of dollars for several drug cartels and apparently wants Malcolm Calhoun to be Secretary of Health and Human Services."

"Dear lord, that boy's been mighty busy. Do ye' know why he wanted this Malcolm to be in charge, child?" The old woman asked innocently.

"I think, this society has a new drug to treat Alzheimer's and it needs FDA approval. There must be problems with it, but they're only promoting the bonus side effects, while hiding the downside ones. Overnight, it makes people look five years younger."

Then, she turned back toward her grandmother again. "I think it has something to do with your spring sage." Because Belle just knew Granny was not telling her everything.

"Me knows it does, lass. Is that all ye' have to tell?" Granny asked in her most innocent voice.

Her grandmother's matter-of-fact statement had surprised her the most regarding the sage. Belle knew that look of determination and understood no answer would be given until Granny had heard all the particulars.

"No. The last thing is this note Sam left me." Pulled the folded letter out of her pocket and handed it to her grandmother. After Mavis had read it, Belle looked affectionately into her grandmother's violet eyes and quietly confessed. "I thought I might have real feelings for this FBI guy, but he was playing me the whole time. I was such a fool."

"How could I have been so stupid and naïve?"

CHAPTER 23

A Tale of Two People

"Granny, what's the matter with you?" Mavis was again, a ghastly shade of white. "Please, tell me what's wrong because I've never seen you look so poorly." Real apprehension was building inside Belle, due to her grandmother's deteriorating appearance.

"Heavens to Betsy, why do ye' think the FBI agent is the bad guy?" Whispered the ashen faced senior Dr. Brooks.

Still angry at herself for these foolish feelings, which caused her to momentarily forget about her declining Granny. "Because Remy's father is Quintin Montgomery and Sam wrote the letter on his law firm's Montgomery & MacAlister letterhead." Her annoyance at the entire situation was apparent in her irate tone. "Sam grew up with Remy and was warning me to be careful about him, right here with his P.S." Pointed sharply at the paper still clutched in her hand. "They must have been in business together and my husband double-crossed him or something."

"Granny, what else could it be?" With frustration coursing through her, Belle waited anxiously for her grandmother's answer. She turned suddenly, terror striking her frightened eyes when hearing the shouting coming from above.

Remy had finally found her, as a blanket of dread seemed to engulf her.

When she looked in the hollering's direction, Mavis was already making her way up to the ground level. Fear forgotten; Belle jumped up, yelling at the retreating tiny sprite. "Come back!! Please Granny don't tell him I'm here!"

Her grandmother swiftly continued up the steps without a backwards glance, all the while completely ignoring her pleas. As the shouts upstairs grew louder, Granny's footsteps continued to climb.

"Belle, where are you? Belle, I know you're here. Please, tell me why you left? Belle, pleeeeasssse." Horse from his sleepless night, Remy's desperate pleas echoed across the quiet mountain morning. Frantic to find Belle because he was at his wit's end. When stepping across what was left of the front door, he was struck frozen by the sight before him.

In the rubble of what was once her beautiful cabin, stood as big as you please, Mavis Brooks, back from the grave.

"Mornin' Mr. Montgomery. If ye' will stop shouting, me'll take ye' to Belle." Stood smiling up at him, like nothing was amiss. The senior Dr. Brooks just appeared out of nowhere, startling Remy but he quickly recognized who was standing before him.

Completely shocked by the impossibility of it, he slowly slid down to sit on the charred steps.

At first, he could only whisper to the dead woman. "How is this even possible?" At that point, his Quantico training kicked in and Remy attempted to gather his composure while practically shouting at her. "What the hell is going on???"

Granny reached down, grabbing his arm, and encouraging the exhausted man to stand. Then, led him downstairs toward the hidden room and Belle.

Remy followed like a lost puppy.

Once seated at the table, stayed silent while Mavis brewed him a cup of her famous ginger root tea. This gave him time to calm down and take in the newest developments. "Now that I'm thinking clearer, the other night, you escaped into this room?"

She nodded. "Yes, Mr. Montgomery, me did. And for right now, me will continue to stay here. Dead. Until me figures out exactly what's goin' on." With a flick of her wrist towards the outside world. "Out there."

Emotions back under control again, he turned his attention to the real reason for this visit. "Belle, are you alright?" Troubled because looked quite frightened. "I've been worried sick about you since I knocked on your door to ask a question and found you gone." There was no mistaking the extreme hurt resonating in his voice. "Why did you leave without telling me?"

The grief-stricken woman cowered on the bed and was tucked up in the corner between the headboard and the wall. In a small voice, Belle softly murmured. "Remy, I found out some things about you and thought it best I put some distance between the two of us."

"What things?" His painful reply because he had dropped everything and come running. Never once did he consider she thought badly about him. Clueless about what he could have done to make her look as if her entire world had crashed, but Remy was also confused because Belle should be elated about her Granny being alive.

Unfortunately, this meant he must have been the cause of her ugly mood. Frustrated by his unknown transgression, found it difficult to hide the pain her rejection was inflicting. The distress was written across his face and carelessly oozed out of him.

"ENOUGH!" Came the bark from the doorway. Both looked up in shock to witness Granny Brooks breathing hard and fast, staring at the two of them intensely. "Stop it both of ye'…lickety-split." A bright glow was shining intensely all-around Mavis. Her unusual aura was so brilliant it was almost burning. Another paranormal experience Remy had never witnessed before.

Finally reigning in her anger, the elder Dr. Brooks turned and pointed at him. "Sam wrote Belle a letter, which she found inside him's secret box."

Then pointed toward Belle, who was again being subjected to her Granny Brook's famous stare. "A letter, the lass obviously didn't tell ye' about." Another beneficial trait she inherited from her grandmother.

"And baby, the man in the letter is not Remy. Trust me on this but if ye'll both calm down," Mavis stopped and took a deep breath to quiet her nerves. "Me'll tell the twos of ye' who it be."

Mouth hanging open, Belle just sat there in shock staring back at her grandmother because she could not believe her ears. *Her Granny knew the man Sam was referring to in his letter. Confused because how was that even possible? How could she know who it was?*

Terribly perplexed now, Remy looked over at Belle, trying to figure out what the hell was going on. Quietly mouthing to her. "What letter?"

The question prompted her to pull it out and hand it over.

Quickly unfolding it, he read it several times before looking up at her puzzled. "Why would Sam write a note to you on Montgomery & MacAlister letterhead?" Confusion was written all over Remy's face.

"Cause the man Sam's talkin' 'bout in him's note is Reid MacAlister." Granny's whispered response shocked them both.

Belle could have sworn, in the last few minutes, the old woman had aged several decades.

"What?" Remy whipped his stunned face back toward Mavis and barely choked out. "My dad's business partner is the man Sam is talking about? But why? And how?" Baffled once again, his nervous habit of running his hand through his hair, then down his face emerged. "Wait! Wait just a damn minute." He was virtually shouting now because none of this was making any sense.

To get her bearings under control, Mavis took no notice of the two of them. Slowly, poured herself a cup of tea which always seemed to calm her nerves. With a favorite prayer, she took a minute to acknowledge the Lord's displeasure because, at long last, it looked like it was finally showing up on her doorstep. Surprised it had taken this long, and very sorry it involved her little lass.

Carefully, she walked back toward them, moving gently so as to not spill any of her favorite drink. Softly whistling, while strolling across the mountain room, she spent the additional time examining the two of them, long and hard.

Eventually sitting down, joining Remy at the large table. She devoted a few extra minutes making herself comfortable, while the two of them continued to holler questions at her. Granny maintained her disregard, praying all her planning had been enough and took another big sip from her cup.

Noticing Mavis's aura was back to its normal unusual color and with a head nod, Remy pointed to Belle about his observation, but it did not stop him shouting questions about Reid.

After drawing a deep breath, Mavis sat her teacup down and raised her hands waiting until they were quiet. "What me is about to say, hasn't crossed me lips in a very long time. So, be kind if it takes a bit to get through."

Took another sip and began her tale. "Me real name is Morna Bruce, not Mavis Brooks. Me 'twas born the only daughter of Rutherford Bruce, the Earl of Sinclair."

At her first words both Remy and Belle were rendered speechless, but Granny just ignored their shocked faces, distracted by the internal struggle of having to divulge her ugly human past. "In May of nineteen forty-four, me lived on the outskirts of a town called Kirkwall in the Orkney Islands of Scotland. Me family's beautiful manor house is the famous Sinclair Castle."

"Twas springtime and the beginning of the end of the war but at the time, we did not know it." Unable to keep the melancholy smile off her face. "One fateful day, a Royal Naval battleship come into port, on it 'twas a rather dashing lieutenant commander named Lord Reid MacAlister."

She remembered vividly the first time encountering him. "Twas so long ago and so hard to explain. Them times, they be difficult; the war 'twas bad for everyone, and we be forced to live off rations. Me family endured, but others did poorly. We looked after all, including the ones who lived on the surrounding islands. Me 'twas just a young lass, and in town for supplies." Paused briefly because was having trouble swallowing. "Barely sixteen, me had led a very sheltered life, 'cause of 'me father's position and the war had put a stop to everything. Me met him in the market in the spring of nineteen forty-four and fell head over heels in love." Mavis was becoming choked up by the forgotten memories of that life so long ago.

Eventually, pulled herself together. "After receiving permission from me father to marry, we proceeded to embark on a whirlwind romance. Lord, those were some wonderful times, and it was during these adventures, me was foolish enough to share me spring sage with him." She glanced up at both of them with such sorrow and incredible longing. But from their expressions, they understood how difficult this was for her. After taking a short break, Mavis went on about her most secret of remedies. "The magical herb grows only in a few parts of Scotland, Northern Ireland and of course, here on me farm. But me ne'r told a soul about me ability to grow it here." Lovingly gazing up into her granddaughter's face. "Except of course, me Belle."

"The only thing me can gander is Sam was smarter than me figured. Maybe, he tested one of them jars me sent home with you." Affectionately nodded at her baby girl, but shame quickly engulfed her, over such carelessness and Mavis dropped her head in disgust. "Me pride was also irresponsible with me secret by naming this place Spring Sage Farm."

The next part of her life was the hardest to explain because her upcoming admission would shock Belle and leave her feeling ashamed. The strong-willed woman was having a difficult time confessing the ugly past to her precious gem. A rare occurrence.

She was in luck because Remy suddenly jumped up and blurted out. "I'm sorry Dr. Brooks, I don't mean to interrupt you, but this is important. Can you hold that thought for just a moment, while I run upstairs and get my laptop?" Raised his index finger to make his point. "I'd really like to check something out." He gave Mavis a half bow of respect. "That is, if I have your permission." Awaited Granny's nod of approval before proceeding up her steps.

Mavis gave it because she was silently relieved by the request. It meant she would have more time before having to reveal the worst part of the story.

"Good lord, Granny, I had no idea." Stunned by her grandmother's confession, Belle did not know what else to say.

"No one did, lass. Since leavin' Scotland, me only spoke that evil name once." Swallowed another sip of tea to help calm her nerves.

"Been almost seventy years since that night and fifty since me told ye' father what happened." Still anxious her granddaughter would think badly about her before this was all over.

Her concerns, interrupted by men's feet running down the stairs, as Remy came back in carrying his briefcase and laptop.

Quickly, he powered it up and opened an Excel spreadsheet. "This is a report, I asked a friend to compile on all the projects, ordinances, and laws. Well, pretty much everything in Ireland that would either now be passed or not passed, because the Dochloite Laoch are no longer in power. Remember Belle when I requested it the other day from Dooley?" He was striving to keep his mind on the subject, but silently wished she would look at him the way she had yesterday.

Nodding at his question, while he continued to scroll through the file. "Well, one item on this report is a parcel of land." He pointed to line number thirty-two on the screen. "It had been slated to become a national park in the northern part of Ireland, but because there's a new regime, instead, it sold three days ago to a company for pennies on the dollar."

"A company." Pulled up another file and pointed to a different line. "Which just so happens to be one of the shell companies Sam had listed on one of his UBS drives and ties back to *EVE*. It's the reason I flagged it in the first place." Remy was excited, because finally the bits of evidence he'd been gathering for months were falling into place. "I think the Seachd Righrean wanted the Dochloite Laoch out of the way to obtain this piece of land."

Directed their attention to a place on a map he had pulled up on his screen. "To corner the market on spring sage. Because if it were a national park then the country of Ireland would own the rights to it, not a corporation." He frowned directly at Granny. "If I had to guess, there are millions of dollars at stake, correct?" Patiently waited for Mavis to respond.

Her head nodded in agreement. "Yes'um at least that much, but what they's ain't tellin' nobody is them long-term effects, well them things can be very deadly." Frustration seeped out of Mavis because of her careless youthful mistake. Now, millions of people could be in harm's way.

"Me guess is they know, oh thems know alright but they be hidin' it from the public 'cause thems short-term results are amazing. Which, is why they be needin' Mr. Calhoun." As a healer, the fears she had lived with her entire life were coming true. "Him's probably be gettin' that fancy position to fix any problems. Make sure them's miracle drug sails through real smooth and lickety-split quick." This was all that horrible man's fault, who was still haunting her after all these years.

"Wait a minute, Granny. Are you telling me your spring sage is going to kill you?" Concern spread across Belle's face.

"No lass, but in the hands of others, ye' darn tootin. Ye' know it must be handled precisely, measured perfectly, and can't be misused. Me beat that into ye' head since ye' 'twas in diapers. It's like magic, so ye' knows thems folks can't help it." After taking another long sip, Mavis set the delicate teacup down. "Theys overdo it and takes too much, wishing to be young in a jiffy, but alas, it will only kill'em slowly."

With an effort, she went on because all of this stemmed from that fateful night so long ago. "Years from now when their scandal breaks, thems big shots of that corporation will all go to jail. Thems members of this society, well…they'd be long skedaddled before then."

Shook her head at the insanity of it all. "Walkin' away billions richer and nobody wiser. Only thems greedy men will knows the truth. They be laughing alls the way to the bank and the people wills be clueless. Thems folks will still perish from this group's lies." The celestial being could not stomach the numbers who would die and dropped her head in shame.

Remy just shook his head in amazement. Quietly, absorbing all that Mavis Brooks had revealed. Eventually, acknowledged her no BS statement with a military-style salute because she had hit the nail on the head. Once again, it all boiled down to money.

A low soft whistle escaped his lips at this group's solid brass balls, along with their total disregard for human life. They had no problem conspiring and killing, all for the sake of wealth and power, something

Remy could not tolerate. "Okay, so let's see if I get this straight. You think Reid MacAlister is also involved in the Seachd Righrean?"

Quick to respond, Granny was adamant about her answer. "Me knows he be involved, 'cause Reid be consumed with only two things for pert near seventy years. That be making fists full of money." Counted each detail off on the digits of her left hand. "And findings me."

The tired man noted happily, Mavis was genuinely smiling for the first time since meeting her. "Luckily hims only been successful at one."

The sight of Granny's delight painted a picture for him of what the lovely vision from the spotlight would look like years from now. Unable to keep the wonder from his eyes, when beholding Belle's future enchanting self. These women were definitely not quite human, wishing there was more time to figure out exactly what they could be.

Instead, spun back to his keyboard because he needed to focus on work and not the girl. Jiggled his head to clear it, while pulling up multiple files onto his computer until Remy was back to himself.

"Would you mind coming over here to look at this please?" Kindly, making the request to the younger Dr. Brooks.

Since the handsome devil was being nice, she did so without objecting. Secretly, Belle was thrilled to find out he had not lied, although still hesitant about trusting him. Crawled off the bed and made her way over to the monitor to see what was causing Remy to look so grim.

When first glancing at the picture, she gasped and jumped back. "Oh, my goodness that's him." On the screen was a website featuring a standard head shot picture and short bio. Terrified, a trembling hand clutched the front of her blouse. "That's the man with Sam, who was following my mom." Even though he was not in the room, just looking at his photo scared her.

"That's Reid MacAlister, my father's law partner and the second person we can connect to the Seachd Righrean." To stop her from shaking, Remy wrapped his arms around her, something Belle did not even know was happening until he made it cease.

In the background, the elderly woman's breath caught when first viewing this older version of the monster. After all these years, the only picture Mavis had of him had been in her head. It featured the diabolically handsome rake she had met, almost seventy years ago, on that far away cobblestoned street. A frown suddenly appeared on her wrinkled face, when remembering how he had ruined those beautiful memories.

Sadly, convinced that life was behind her, but she should have remembered, her liege would eventually make her pay. However, Mavis was having trouble believing he would sink low enough to use Reid to plague her family.

No matter who was the cause, her burning determination would prevent that animal from ever hurting her granddaughter because this time around, the elder Dr. Brooks would do everything, including unleashing her powers, to stop him.

After Belle was safe, she would attempt to settle her misunderstanding with the Creator and this time around, hoped he would listen to reason.

Fueled by that focused purpose, Mavis asked a bit too sternly of Remy. "What do ye' intend to do now?"

After a minute of thought, confessed honestly. "I'm still working with all the information Sam left behind. Once we have enough to secure warrants I'll go after all the companies and people involved."

Dropped his head because was reluctant to make his next statement. "But we currently have nothing on Reid. Not one shred of evidence, except Sam's coded letter. Evidence, which doesn't even name him, so it cannot be used for anything at this point." Wincing in defeat, at the many dead ends he had found during this investigation. "To the best of my knowledge, nowhere in these files is he even mentioned."

Waved his hand over the briefcase in frustration. "No evidence, nothing at all to follow up on." For the first time he appeared beaten. "Right now, that's it." At a loss for ideas, Remy prayed she had some. "Why? Do you have any suggestions, Mavis?" Hoped like hell she did because it baffled him on what to do next.

Out of the blue, Belle darted toward the stairs. "Wait a minute, I might have one." Without waiting, she dashed up the steps, two at a time, racing after the mysterious key stashed inside her briefcase. "Be right back." The muffled response drifted down the staircase in her wake.

"That child hasn't changed one bit in all these years. Could never sit still, not fer more than a minute." Chuckling tenderly, Mavis just shook her head, but he could tell the old woman adored her. "Patience is not something me lass is capable of."

A few minutes later, the younger doctor returned to the hidden room carrying a small black velvet bag. "I probably should've shared this days ago but didn't know you well enough." Shyly held up the satchel but looking guilty at Remy. "I wasn't sure I could trust you yet and my instincts told me not to do so."

Unsure why, it felt like a knife had just been thrust into his heart. While the pain showed on his face, Belle attempted to describe her reasoning. "Don't ask me why because my gift doesn't always explain."

But it was important, he understood. Belle lifted his head up with her finger and smiled broadly. "I feel differently now." The act caused a giggle to slip out and he marveled at her special laugh. The tinkling sound helped melt away the wall of ice that had been surrounding Remy for the last six years.

With her aura once again glowing bright, she continued to explain. "Anyway, wrapped it back up and put it away. Forgetting all about it until now." Suddenly a sense of calm overpowered Remy, when realizing how lucky he was to have this astonishing creature come into his life.

Next, Belle turned to the woman who raised her and professed her elevated abilities. "It's evil Granny, evil like I've never felt before. It's also a key. Again, I don't know how I know it's one. I just do." Carefully, opened the bag and took out the extraordinary metal disc. Admiring its demonic beauty, she placed the round key on the table, in front of the agent and her grandmother.

"I've seen that symbol before." Shouted Remy but still surprised it's been in plain sight for his entire life. "It's on the back wall in Reid's office." Thought what a fool she had been to doubt him and without hesitation, Belle knew she could trust him now.

"Ye' gift has changed much, hasn't it lass?" Mavis picked up the object and thoroughly inspected the unusual item. "Cause, this here is indeed a key and a very evil key at that. Me thinks, only a very exceptional telepath could be tellin' that from just a touch." Twirling it around in her hands. "What do it say to ye'?"

Written all over Belle's face was confusion because she did not understand. "What do you mean?"

"Ye' heard me. What's it be saying to ye'?" Granny asked, a bit too sharply. "Open ye' self-up and listen." It dawned on Mavis that her baby had recently been to hell and back, so said it softer this time to encourage her along. "Let it tell ye' it's tale."

With her eyes closed, cleared her mind's path, and instructed herself to hear the evil key. Instantly a door appeared in Belle's mind. "This key belongs to a room behind a hidden wall." She eyed Remy hopefully. "Could it be in Reid's office at the law firm?"

Intently nodding his head. "Yes, it sure could." Determined, there was not enough time to explain his dad's obsession with secret passageways and hidden panels, therefore Remy just shared the basics. "The office occupies the entire upper floor of the firm and except for some wonderful pieces of artwork, there is nothing else but that symbol on Reid's back wall. It's been there since I was a child." Indicated toward the key, Belle held in her hand. "There could be a room behind it, and no one would ever know." Suddenly, Remy looked disheartened and sat down hard, placing his head in his hands.

Disturbed by his unexpected mood change, Belle rushed over. "What's wrong Remy?" Draped her arms around him for comfort.

"Worried about ye' father, aye?" Came the question from across the table. When opening his eyes, Remy found Mavis Brooks' violet gaze staring straight into his turquoise blue one.

Softly, answered her candidly. "I'm afraid he's somehow mixed up in this and would hate for that to be the case because it would kill my mother."

Mavis was not about to let him off so easily because the Brooks' were a non-fibbing type of family. "What about ye'? Wouldn't it kill ye' as well, laddie?"

Granny Brooks' tone forced Remy to answer honestly. "Yeah, it would kill me too."

Still staring directly into his eyes, Granny informed the worried son. "Ye' father not be a part of this. He don't know nothing of Reid's actions and woulda stopped him, had he known."

Stunned by her statement, Remy was incapable of grasping Granny's many talents. "How can you know such a thing?" However, his instincts indicated she was right, despite the impossible, she somehow knew his father's true actions. Her shocking declaration caused him to just sit there staring into space. Desperate for the unbelievable abilities of Dr. Mavis Brooks to sink in.

"Because my Granny just does." A proud, smiling Belle declared loudly. "Remy, I told you before, some things you have to take on a leap of faith. My grandmother would never say such a thing if it were not true." By this point, Belle had completely gathered him up in her arms and was holding on tight.

The old woman looked upon the two of them approvingly, while patiently waiting for him to accept her announcement. After a long time, Remy finally did.

Eventually, unwrapped himself from the pretty because there was still so much to do. Suddenly, Remy recalled where he had seen Belle's grandmother previously and decided to share the vivid memory because by doing so, would reveal his '*gift*' to her, as well. "You know, Dr. Brooks, I saw you many years ago in Georgetown when I was still in college. Tried my darnedest to get to you but lost you in the crowd." Blushed a bit, embarrassed by his enthusiasm and nervous about her response to his revelation. "Your aura fascinates me. It's the most beautiful one I've ever seen and is absolutely amazing. Similar to a kaleidoscope and it's exactly like Belle's, all multi-colored and iridescent. Honestly, I've never encountered another one like it." He chuckled at his blunder.

"Except hers, of course." Remy felt comfortable in this old woman's company and enjoyed her awareness of his gift. A fact only a handful of people knew existed. Mavis Brooks was truly a one-of-a-kind woman and it thrilled him to meet the person who had shaped the lady he was falling for.

"Please Remy, do call me Granny." Spreading her hands wide. "If ye' goin' be fallin' in love with me granddaughter, then, ye' might as well be gettin' used to being a part of this here family." Granted the honest man a sly but friendly grin, and if Remy didn't know better, imagined Mavis could almost read his thoughts. "Because as ye' can see, we are not like other people."

Her incredible gifts forgotten because her revelation made Remy ecstatic. Flashed Granny his brightest and most charming smile because Mavis had just announced his growing affections for Belle. Something the hard-hearted man himself had only recently figured out but he was liking the sound of it.

For the time being, he needed to ignore her love announcement, because common sense prevailed. "Okay Granny but I need to get back to Washington and see if I can get into that hidden room." Positive, now was not the time to act on his feelings. Although secretly, he sure enjoyed hearing them said aloud.

"NO!" Shouted Belle, which made both Remy and Granny jump. "You will not go after that man by yourself. He is dangerous, and I can't lose you." Grabbed hold of him and Belle squeezed him tight. "Not when I just found you." Surprised that last announcement did not terrify her.

Hoping to make light of the situation, a playful laugh erupted from him while gently pulling away. "You forget, *mo ghra* that I am a federal agent of the FBI and it's my father's law firm we're talking about." Held her apart from him so Remy could look directly into her beautiful green eyes. "It won't be difficult to figure out a way into Reid's office." Still not divulging his father's love of convenience and intrigue. "Please Belle, don't worry about me. I promise not to do anything stupid to get myself killed."

He continued to stare affectionately while trying to provide her with reassurance. "Because for the first time in a long time, I have something to live for." Gathered up the delicate beauty and lightly kissed her. It was almost like the kiss Remy had wanted to give her since feasting his eyes on the gorgeous vision bathed in that spotlight.

Almost.

CHAPTER 24

Faded Photograph

Spring was almost here, but not quite. The spattering of raindrops falling this early evening made Sir Reid MacAlister's old bones ache something fierce. He sat quietly, while trying to ignore the pain, watching as water slowly dripped down the glass windows of his top floor DC office building. Like the methodical rain, gradually building inside him was steel determination. *I will never give in to the pain.*

He had withstood numerous obstacles, along with surviving a duel to obtain the prize. *And by God, I will prevail.* Eighty-seven years old, but he was too close to fail. Reid had waited his entire life to acquire it. Because of those failures Eden had been denied. *To him. He still couldn't believe It had denied him that right.* The only one who knew what Its capabilities were.

At the end of the war, he spearheaded the retrieval of It from those ungodly men, right before meeting Morna. Now, after more than a half century, the reward was so close. The patient man could almost touch it. Stretched his hand out, before catching himself because the prize was within his grasp, meaning Reid would never stop. Not ever.

If only that idiot nephew of mine hadn't screwed up the society's carefully laid plans so badly, he might still be alive. Bittersweet sentiment brushed across his thoughts, but he quickly dismissed all sympathy for the lad. The end goal might have been achieved, but now, there were inquiries occurring in Ireland, which were simply unacceptable.

Over and over, Reid had lectured the boy about failing, but apparently, Sam had not been listening. Too busy sticking it to that Irish girl, instead of accomplishing the individual objectives for the society. It was that stupidity, which had gotten him killed, along with his childish plans to overthrow the prime council members. *Such a waste of talent but it could not be helped. Too bad.* All his life Reid had a soft spot for the boy because in many ways, Sam was like a younger version of him. *Again, it's too bad.* Because Sam would have played an important part in the next step of the council's complicated plans.

It doesn't matter, what's done is done. The backup plan is solid, I'll need to move swiftly to implement it. In his mind, the cold but honest thoughts were as good as Sam Randall deserved. Lord MacAlister elected to move on, just as he had always done in the past, every time death had come calling. Yet tonight, Reid could not seem to proceed. The boy had gotten under his skin, and it appeared he was getting soft in his senior years.

A bit melancholy, the old man decided to allow himself a couple of minutes to grieve. It was a small luxury and decided to indulge in a few extra moments reminiscing about the only person he had ever truly loved. After removing it from its secret desk compartment, Reid lovingly caressed the old, faded photograph held softly in his hand. He stared intently at the small black and white snapshot as he lovingly touched it, like he had at least a thousand times before because it was the only one, he possessed.

The treasured memento permitted him to travel back to that blissful era from long ago.

After almost seventy years, he could still remember every sight, sound, and smell of that favorite time. Those weeks in Scotland, the cold-hearted sinner considered the happiest of his life. *Funny, how you remember the little things.* Once again, blinked and found himself not at war, but at his desk, atop the glass structure that was Montgomery & MacAlister. The discovery brought a smile to Reid's face, relieved he was not in danger of dying tonight. He glanced down at the picture, remembering these were just memories and the war was not happening outside his window.

At ease again because death was not looming, the photo memories took him back to the first night he met Sir Rutherford Bruce. The Earl of Sinclair had grilled him for hours about the MacAlister family tree, along with his future intentions regarding his daughter. Unlike his nature now, Reid had been completely honest and poured his heart out since he had fallen foolishly head-over-heels in love with Morna. Hours later, he finally won the old man over with his enthusiasm and charm.

Truth be told, even after all these years, he was still in love with her. An admission that brought another sad smile to the old swindler's face and was reflected in the large glass windows before him. The weather, along with Sam's elimination was making him downhearted.

Not ready to return to the present yet, Reid allowed himself a few more turns down memory lane, recalling Rutherford had plenty of sons but only one beautiful daughter. The Earl had named her his Beloved and she was his most precious possession. Therefore, her father had been extra careful not to allow anyone near Morna, but of course, that had not deterred Reid.

In fact, it had just fueled him even more.

The backdrop of war had provided the perfect cover for his rage against everything, which was at its height during that period. A sinister smile appeared upon his face when remembering that time, so long ago. *Her father's caution was nothing more than an additional incentive for me.* His face was reflected on the windowpane, but the ugliness was back to the more conducive one Reid wore every day.

God, how I miss Morna. But she was gone. Vanished into thin air like the wind. The love of his life had disappeared completely after that fateful night. Reid had spent hundreds of thousands of dollars, along with searching for decades, attempting to find her.

Waving away the unpleasantness of the failed past, he decided to put it aside, dismissing it because it was a waste of time to dwell. "What's done is done. She's dead and gone. Something I accepted a long time ago."

Still, just sitting here thinking about the beauty hurt like hell. Reid needed to move forward, like the chameleon he had always become in the past. Wanting only to concentrate on the future and Morna's replacement because it was all that mattered.

The Spear had passed over the old fox, locking him out of the Seachd Righrean inner circle until he fulfilled its long-standing quest. After seven decades, Its wishes continued to burn bright inside him, making Reid feel desperate. He waited his entire life to feel complete and Reid could feel salvation was within his grasp.

The prize would soon be his. Very soon.

Acknowledged another sad truth to himself, as rain continued to streak down the windows. The beautiful goddess, spotted in that faraway street market, still stirred incredibly strong feelings inside. It would have killed him to sacrifice her to the Kings. Nonetheless, to survive another day, Reid must find a way to put this sentiment aside and focus on the work at hand.

There was much to be done since the boy had screwed up the election in Ireland and the complications had taken days, but Reid had fixed almost everything. With most of the problems solved, it appeared their plans were back on track. They had obtained the land at a bargain price, destroyed the reckless idiot's laptop, along with the evidence the fool had stored on it and the box in New York had been secured with an impossible password. They had been unable to retrieve its contents, because after an extensive search, Sallos had been incapable of finding the key. The hired mercenary had watched Belle for days and assured Reid the vault box was secure.

Also concluding, the girl knew nothing of the whereabouts of the Spear, which was most unfortunate.

Although, this discovery had allowed the Vrykolakas vampire to move on to the odd farm in Virginia. Supposedly, the lone inhabitant had been taken care of several days ago, along with any crops she might have possessed. All the same, Reid's patience was running thin with the death dealer.

The last of the loose ends was being handled by his other demon, Leonard. This afternoon, an unfortunate car wreck involving the Irish girl had taken care of that last problem. This enabled the society, to remain in the shadows, continuing to control world events, while making billions for the Kings, along with its society members. He picked up the receiver because Reid was finished with nostalgia for now. A menacing smile firmly in place, he dialed the phone and went back to work.

With each punch of the numbers, Reid plotted to move the pieces of the world's history board around to his liking.

After hanging up his cell, Remy turned back toward the two women, but Belle intuitively knew something was terribly wrong. "What is it?"

"In Dublin this afternoon, a car crash killed Shannon O'Malley, the woman from the Irish voting machine company. It appears to be a coincidence, but I know the society had her murdered, although there's no way to prove it." Frustration and weariness vibrated off him as Remy's down-turned head shook. "It seems just when we get a break they swiftly move in and eliminate any evidence of this group's existence." Even Mavis noted the defeat conveying outward from all parts of the unhappy man. "Always two steps ahead of us."

Could feel the bitterness pouring out of him, but her intuitions were buzzing inside. Certain they would beat them eventually, Belle softly whispered into his ear. "Don't give up, just yet." Engulfed her arms around Remy while running her hands over his back for comfort. "They might have been at this for a long time, but we know about them now. I will not rest until we take them all down."

Surprised by her determination and bolstered by her fortitude, the lack of sleep from the last few days had finally caught up and Remy had let this setback get to him. Reminding himself that he was an FBI Special Agent who never gives up, just like he has never given up on finding Amanda's killer.

Feeling his confidence return and acknowledging Belle was correct. It was possible to beat these Seven Kings, but to do so, he would need to get into Reid's office. A bit of a twinkle was returning to his gorgeous eyes, as Remy tilted his head toward hers until touching. "Once again,

I'm going to say it. I'm sorry for temporarily losing hope, please forgive me." Lifted his forehead up, stepped away and raised his right hand. "I promise it will not happen again." Directing his most brilliant smile at her and even Granny was impressed by his talented grin.

"We need to return to the city, make a substantial plan, then execute it quickly before more witnesses disappear or turn up dead." He took a second to decide on the best course of action. "I don't think we should return by the Buchanan helicopter. It's too dangerous. I'm going up to call Parker Anderson." His attention went back to Mavis to explain. "Parker is the director of the FBI and I need to fill him in. If you're comfortable with me doing so, Granny." Stood waiting for her approval because Remy knew in his heart, if her grandmother did not agree, then neither would Belle.

"Do ye' trust this Mr. Anderson?" Although, the old woman appeared tired, Granny easily conveyed her lingering suspicions with that legendary stare.

"With my life." Quickly, Remy countered but took notice of where Belle had gotten her notorious glare.

"Then do what ye' think best." The resilient lady responded, and he rushed up the steps.

After hanging up with the director, he returned downstairs to the cleverly hidden room and ordered the women to gather their bags. Their government ride would be here shortly, but Granny was just glaring at Remy, like he was crazy, and declared forcefully. "Young lad, me is not goin' anywhere."

"I'm sorry Mavis, I'm not leaving you here, all alone." Remy proclaimed to the hardheaded lady, while looking every bit like the FBI agent he was. "Besides, you know Reid better than anyone. Therefore, I'll need you close at hand, in case I have questions or require additional information."

Waited patiently for Granny's response but Remy was determined. "Director Anderson is sending a helicopter for us; it will be here shortly." Ready to stand his ground because would not take no for an answer. Again, unleashing his bright smile on the women. "So, I will wait upstairs." Bowing an acknowledgement, then closed his briefcase. "For the both of you."

With that, he picked up his attaché and made his way out of the concealed room. Glancing back one last time, to admire the old woman's ingenious planning which had saved her life.

Mavis ignored Remy's departure, but Belle knew a 'row' was coming, quite familiar with the look on Granny's face. If need be, she was ready to exercise force on the stubborn old mule. "Granny I'm not leaving you here by yourself." The younger Dr. Brooks used the stare inherited from her grandmother. "Remy is right, you know this man better than either of us. We must try to stop him because he killed Sam. I know you didn't like him, but he was my husband. You know darn well you can help."

Dropped her head in frustration, yet she was determined to convince her grandmother to return to DC. "This guy tried to kill both of us, not to mention he was there at the bomb blast that killed my mom. I don't think he's going to stop unless we put an end to all of this." Pleading her case. "Please, just for once, don't be pigheaded. Granny, just do what Remy says and come with us." In order to get this inflexible old mountain goat to do as she asked, Belle would say just about anything.

Mavis tilted her head towards the back of the room, replying reluctantly. "Me bag is already packed and be over by that cabinet." Pointing near the far corner of the room. "Be a dear, go fetch it, then go join Remy upstairs." This time pointing in the stairway's direction. "Me needs to retrieve something out of the trunk, at the foot of the bed." Mavis felt old. "Then, me be right there." Older than she had ever felt in her life. "Promise, lass." Patted Belle's hand before watching her baby girl retrieve the satchel, then proceed up the steps.

Still unwilling to expose Belle to this part of her past, she waited until her granddaughter was gone, then opened the hand carved chest. It only took a moment to dig around until finding the beautiful box, which had continued to hold them securely for all these years. She withdrew one of the matching pair, silently slipping it into the large pocket of her full-length skirt. No one would know what was hidden inside until it was necessary. This time, Mavis was going to be prepared and would not allow Reid MacAlister to hurt another living soul.

Especially her beloved Belle.

Unlike previously, the FBI chopper ride was done mostly in silence, with Remy spending all of it online or on the phone, with various people at the Bureau. Once they landed, an unmarked car took them to a safe house.

After reaching their destination, sleep was needed by all because hardly anyone could keep their eyes open. Remy ordered everyone to rest for the next three hours, and no one objected. Other than a few stolen snatches here and there, Belle could not remember the last time she had gotten any real rest. Apparently, the past few days were finally catching up with her.

After taking a quick shower, she went fast asleep, long before her head hit the pillow. When Remy peeked in, he was relieved to see how peaceful the doctor looked. Shortly thereafter, he too went off to bed.

At long last, the safe house was completely quiet, leaving Granny all by herself, with just her thoughts of Reid and their tortured past. How she hoped and prayed this madman would get nowhere near her baby girl. She knew deep inside her heart, when it came to him, every time Mavis had been wrong. Especially after learning he was behind several devastating heartaches for Belle. The elder Dr. Brooks was sick with worry, over what else the lieutenant commander had up his sleeve, while she tried to sort out how much the Kingdom was playing a part in all of this.

Transported to America in her precious hope chest, it was difficult not to constantly rub the antique in her pocket, because touching it had always given her strength. For the first time in many years, Mavis was very thankful, she had never disposed of them. She had kept his clan's treasure, as a constant reminder of what would happen if you allowed a monster into your life. In the beginning she had even brought them out a time or two, when considering letting someone else into her little family. All the young mother had to do was open the hand carved centuries old box. Instantly, the memories from that horrendous night came flooding back and forced the broken woman to slam the lid shut. Quickly locking the box away, along with whoever was attempting to make their way into her shattered heart.

After spending decades shrouded in secret, it was fitting both Morna and this vintage gift to her father were finally being unveiled. She hoped it would be unnecessary to use it, but knowing Reid, understood it was only a matter of time. Mind made up, Mavis finally took Remy's advice and crawled into the big bed. Appreciating, they would all need as much rest as possible to take on her long-time enemy. Before slipping off she sent up special prayers that no one discovered the real secret she had kept hidden from everyone on Earth.

Several hours later Belle was angry to discover the bastard had gone to the law firm without her. Remy had left nothing more than a note, notifying them he would be returning shortly to report on his findings. Furious at his deception even though he confessed his love at the bottom of the letter, she burst into her grandmother's room. "I cannot believe Remy would do this without me!" Fuming mad, she was waving his crumbled note around in the air. "He knew I wanted to go."

Granny sat up and wiped the sleep from her eyes. "Maybe that's exactly why he went when ye' were asleep child." Secretly glad about Remy's actions but in her current state, Mavis doubted her granddaughter would be happy to hear that opinion. She decided instead, to use reason. "Ye' not an easy person, especially once ye' git somethin' in ye' head. Me guess he opted to do his job." Captured Belle's shaking hand, hoping to calm her down. "Somethin' that's probably a fancy bit easier for him to do without having to worry about ye'."

The old woman's logic was sound, but it did not make her any less angry. "Yes, but there are lots of things inside Reid's office I could've helped with." She hopped onto the mattress. "Items Remy will never be able to get a reading from. That man can be so stubborn sometimes." Crossed her arms and stewed about Remy's ruse. "Well, I will not let him do this by himself."

Jumped off the bed and she started toward the door. "I'm going over there to help him."

"Wait, just a darn minute child." Grabbed Belle by the arm. "Ye' can't go stormin' into that building all by ye' self. Ye' could git killed and me won't allow that to happen." Twisting her granddaughter about and forcing Belle to look directly into Mavis' eyes. "Do ye' understand lass?" Anguish surged out of the elder doctor. "Me's lost everyone but ye." *Me vow to die before that occurs.* "Me will not lose ye' too."

Understood Granny's anger but she was not interested. "Well, I will not stay here and wait to see if he comes back. I'm done sitting on the sidelines, waiting for someone else to take care of everything." Using her arms to make the statement flourish with an air of boldness and brass. "All of that ends tonight. Granny, I'm going to Remy and don't you dare try to stop me." Defiant, she stood there challenging her grandmother.

Breaking out in laughter, Granny gathered her beautiful granddaughter into her arms and began patting her on the back. "Come on lass, let's go help ye' man."

The old woman continued to laugh at Belle's utterly shocked face, as she led her down the small hallway.

CHAPTER 25

Full Circle

To get past the guard was easy because Remy had known the old timer since he was a child. After a few moments catching up with Arthur, he rode the elevator to the tenth floor, not the top. He had spent countless hours on these many floors, and it was those memories that worried him about being detected. Those concerns also forced him to exit onto the floor below. The one that housed his father's vast office suite. The detour was necessary because the eleventh-floor elevator opened directly into Reid's outer atrium and was positive he would be discovered if the partner was still working.

Silently, he stepped onto the concourse of his dad's inner domain, Quickly, passing through a series of security checkpoints, the passwords Remy had memorized in elementary school.

After entering the office, he went directly to the far wall and pushed on the concealed door, disguised as a panel. The hidden entrance popped open, revealing the staircase both partners used frequently throughout the day.

Soundlessly, he walked up the secret stairway, climbing each step slowly, in case MacAlister was working late. Once reaching the top floor, he cracked the small door. Frustrated to discover Reid at his desk, apparently just staring at a photograph. After assessing the situation, it surprised him Reid's aura was a mixture of intense pink and dark gray, a very odd combination of great love and malevolence.

For the moment, while concealed in the stairwell, Remy decided to wait until the senior partner left for the evening. Opted to settle down and get comfortable because he did not know how long the old man was going to be working tonight.

After waiting about fifteen minutes, thought he heard some possible exit sounds. "Remy, I've waited long enough. You can come out now." A familiar Scottish tinted voice came from beyond the doorway. "I would have thought, you'd have discerned that I'd surround myself with the most sophisticated surveillance equipment in the world."

Of course, he should have known better but Remy was inside his father's firm and had made certain assumptions. *Stupid mistake.* He heard the gunshot, just as he pushed open the door because was still operating under the false pretense that the family firm was safe. It was not until the bullet penetrated his shoulder, rendering his shooting arm useless, that he fully comprehended just how much trouble the special agent was really in.

Standing tall, Reid continued to aim the firearm at him. "Put the gun on the floor in front of you, then slide it over here and for God's sakes place this over the wound." Tossed a piece of material at Remy to cover his bleeding injury. "I don't want to have to explain why there is blood all over my office floor. By the way, what are you doing here?"

Astonished, the wounded man looked up while holding the rag in place. "Do you mean to tell me you shot me first, then are asking why I'm here?" Incensed because he could not believe this man. *He point-blank shot me, a man I've known my entire life.* He had no clue about Remy's motives, but without blinking an eye, MacAlister had put a bullet into his own partner's son using the shoot first, ask questions later method of interrogation.

Un...frigging believable.

As the taxi pulled up to the building, she decided to walk up to the guard and just ask for Remy. Belle was at a loss for what else to do.

Nerves frayed and still boiling mad, she opened the heavy glass door, playing the part she had dressed for. "Hell….Low cutie." Literally, batting her mesmerizing eyes at the old guy. "My name is Candi Brooks and I'm supposed to meet a tall dark and handsome Mr. Remy Montgomery here tonight." Trying to act sexy and coy, reached over the counter and gently caressed the guard's hand. "So, sweetie pie, I was wonderin' if he's arrived yet."

From behind the desk, the old goat smiled up at her and responded breathlessly. "He's been here for about twenty minutes and is up in his dad's office. Mr. Montgomery's space is on the tenth floor, give me a minute." Arthur picked up the phone and dialed, continuing to get distracted by the beauty standing in front of him. "I'll call up there to let him know you're here." His smile expanded, indicating Belle had correctly deduced the old guy had a soft spot for Remy.

Gently placing her finger on the hang-up button, sent him her best wink. With her pretend racy face and pouty red lips, whispered. "Aren't you just so helpful. If it's okay with you, I'd like to go up and surprise him." Twirled around for his enjoyment, strutting a bit in Remy's borrowed oversized Burberry raincoat, all the while trying to stay upright in her four-inch blood red pumps.

By the huge grin on his face, the guard plainly understood what Belle was trying to convey and cleared her through with a wave of his hand. As she walked away, Arthur noted the enjoyment her back view caused him was almost as much as the pretty's front.

Once inside the elevator, Belle almost collapsed from all the stress. Quickly, pulling herself together because her 'feelers' were zinging away. Her instincts said the state of the situation was terrible, but she could not focus enough on the trouble to see what might actually be coming.

Stepping out of the elevator, she swiftly removed the big raincoat and high heels, replacing them with the comfortable loafers tucked away in the inside pocket. Silently, following the open doors Remy had left unlocked, until she arrived in a large but empty office. Belle wondered where the sneaky rascal could be because there was no place for him to hide.

Frantically, she searched until seeing the impossible. No way could it happen twice, but just like at Granny's, there was a small crack in the wall. This time, it was easy to find the hidden stairwell since Remy had left the wall panel slightly ajar.

Scared by what could face her ahead, Belle tried to put those fears aside and clear her mind. Drew strength from the missing man and her growing feelings for him, a detail she was starting to figure out. Tried to brace herself for what might be waiting upstairs, considering they were dealing with very dangerous people.

Suddenly, a sense of calm overwhelmed her which meant bad trouble was about to come callin'. The gifted psychic wanted to find Remy soon, then get the hell out of here and explore these growing abilities. It was like her gifts were continuing to get stronger. Also, she hoped the missing agent was safe because as Belle slowly traveled up the steps, those instincts increased the higher she climbed and screamed at her to run. But it was those same enhanced feelings that would not allow her to leave the blue-eyed devil alone to face whatever atrocities this society had hidden upstairs.

She stopped briefly to analyze her growing feelings for Remy. Once pausing, realizing it was that possible promise of love that continued to drive her up those spiral steps. She pressed on, yet, ignored those emotions. When reaching the top, Belle heard two voices. Recognized the special agent's deep tone but could not make out the other. Also, she was unable to figure out what either of them were saying.

Her instincts were pulsing away and vibrating her entire insides. It was at that instant when it hit her. The man who was slowly stealing her heart could be in real trouble.

From the other side of the door, Belle leaned closer and made out a muffled accented voice. It sounded like an invitation to come in. "My dear, what a pleasant surprise this evening has turned out to be." Instantly, understood that the beast who had haunted her for days had spoken. Terrified of what to do but she would not leave Remy.

Slowly, Belle pushed the panel open.

As soon as she stepped into the brightly lit office, discovered Remy was bloody and tied to a chair. He had been shot and Reid was still pointing the gun at him.

"We finally meet face to face." The old man stated. "I had truly hoped it would have been under more pleasant circumstances." Unable to understand the armed man's cultured statement, Belle rushed through the doorway toward Remy's bleeding side. Quickly dropping to her knees and tried to ascertain what could be done about his wound. "You must know I have been waiting years for this moment."

After examining Remy thoroughly, she placed the cloth back over the wound and deduced the bullet was still inside. Rewrapping the bloody hole as best she could, turned her attention to the baffling guy pointing a gun at them. Not knowing what this man could be talking about, but Belle knew it was important to play along.

Directing one of her legendary stares toward the madman; she stood furious and scared. A lethal combination in the gifted. "I'm afraid you have me at a disadvantage Mr. MacAlister because until a few hours ago, I was unaware of your existence."

Her only concern was for Remy and continued to examine his wound. Although, noticed the bleeding had slowed down enough, which meant he would not die from the blood loss just yet.

Satisfied with the situation, Reid settled back down in his large leather chair. With a wave of his hand, indicated Belle to sit in the other. Reluctantly, she accepted his invitation after patching Remy up as best she could. Cooperation was the only way to secure their survival.

"I planned that as well. You see, I forced Sam to marry you." She listened intently, with a caring face because Belle wanted to ensure both of them would get out of here alive. "My dear, Destiny has always wanted you since It first laid eyes on you. I'm intelligent and knew you would never agree to marry an old man such as me, so I had to compromise." An evil grin appeared on the absurd man's face.

Angry at his outrageous announcements, along with his treatment of Remy, she lost her cool because had no idea who or what It was. Just as Belle was about to scream how insane his statements were, chimes began tinkling inside her head. They reminded her of Sam's business deal conversation and thought maybe she was about to get some answers. "What do you mean you forced Sam to marry me?" She reigned her anger in and for the time being, decided to let the strange It statement go.

The crazy coot looked over toward her blue-eyed devil, confessing his long-awaited plans. "Remy, you should remember this." Gleefully, Reid turned back to her, boasting in a too cheerful tone for Belle's taste. "My darling, unfortunately, you were married to a murderer. Your husband killed a girl when he was in high school, and I covered it up for him. Got Cook to give him an alibi for it." She sat shocked at his disregard of Sam's heinous crimes, along with the old man's role in the manipulation of her life.

Watched in fascination as the mask the insane geezer constantly wore momentarily slipped. "Belle, I waited patiently until you were finished with your residency." Captivated, she watched as Reid's regular sinister face fell firmly back into place. "Advised him, to figure out a way to marry you or I'd turn the evidence I possessed over to the authorities. You see my dear girl, there is no statute of limitation on murder. Sam was required to do as I deemed necessary because the proof, I held was overwhelming." The ominous grin which accompanied his statement made Belle cringe all over.

His plans still made no sense and filled her with confusion. "Wait a minute." Bewilderment was winning over fear. "What do you mean you waited until I finished my residency?"

Reid seemed to almost be in a trance. "My sweet, I've been waiting for you, well for almost a lifetime. You remind me of someone I lost a long, long time ago. When you were only ten years old, I saw you at a party and It picked you. Ever since, I've been doing everything in my power to possess you."

During their conversation, Remy figured out what was happening. Without drawing the lawyer's awareness, attempted to capture Belle's attention to make her understand not to tell this mad man that her grandmother was alive.

Confused by Reid's complicated scheme but she could not figure out who he was talking about that had picked her as a child. Also, turned toward her wounded warrior because understood the signals he was sending, but they were unnecessary. Belle had no intention of disclosing any information about her Granny to this lunatic. Although, she still could not fathom what he actually wanted from her because that answer seemed a critical piece to this insane puzzle. "Why would you want Sam to marry me? And who the hell is doing the picking?"

His wicked laugh roared when revealing his clever plan. "Why??? So, you would produce a child, of course." Delighted to finally be divulging the grand plan to his obsession. "Don't you understand? Sam wasn't allowed to have a child with you naturally. If he was foolish enough to do so, I'd have released the evidence to the police." The crazy moron seemed to be enjoying every minute of this and continued to leer at her in an evil yet affectionate manner. "That way, you would be forced to use a fertility clinic that would impregnate you with my sperm, not Sam's. Of course, I have made provisions for the child, as well as for you, with both mine and Sam's estate."

After hearing his diabolical plan, she burst into a state of total shock at the utter madness, but the peculiar request in Sam's will, now came into a whole new light. Not knowing what to do or say about this crazy man's declaration, Belle realized Sam's infidelity also made perfect sense. For their entire marriage, he had been forbidden to sleep with her, for fear of ending up in jail for the rest of his life.

"Oh my God, how could you have done such a horrible thing?" On the other hand, Belle recognized there was no feeling sorry for Sam. The fiend had killed a girl in cold blood, which had landed them both in this ridiculous predicament. Since Sam's death, the confusion and heartache she had been experiencing seemed to be diminishing. Although, a small part of her felt bad about the position it had placed Sam in because of this man's fixation.

His evilness was helping Belle find her bravery. "You do realize I will not have your child, don't you?" In a strong voice, dared him to think she could be controlled like her selfish husband.

"Oh, I disagree." Stood and stretched to his full six-foot one-inch height and although Reid was old, he was still an imposing man. "In fact, I know you'll have my child because if you don't agree." Without emitting another word, pointed the gun directly at the bound agent tied to the chair and fired. "The next one, I'm placing in the center of his heart." This time, the shot pierced Remy's left thigh. "Don't let the old age fool you, my dear. I'm still an excellent marksman." He continued to smile with that creepy Joker-type grin.

Unable to believe the gall of this man, as she tore a piece of her designer blouse to make another bandage and dropped down to stop the new blood flow.

Pain consumed Remy but when he looked into those large emerald eyes it made him bolder. The alpha male knew she was going to agree to this madman's demand and that was something his heart could not allow. To get Reid's attention off Belle, he changed the subject. "Did you kill Amanda?" In considerable pain, grunted through clenched teeth because he had to know. After all this time, imperative he find her murderer, plus it kept the insane guy from focusing on the beauty kneeling beside him. He did not like the sick way MacAlister had manipulated her for years.

The unexpected question had snapped the ancient relic's attention back to the present. "Of course, I had her killed. The little bitch found out about the society, while working on a project for me and she was going to expose a very lucrative business deal. A deal, which netted us truckloads of dollars in only a few months' time." Reid sat back down and got comfortable. "I couldn't allow your wife to live, and since you're the only one who thinks she was murdered, it worked out splendidly." The wickedly evil sneer was back. "We made millions and silenced a problem. Although, I must admit, it was very difficult disposing of her because Amanda was one hell of an attorney."

Momentarily forgetting his bleeding wounds, he was furious his lifelong mentor's account of Mandy's assassination was so nonchalant and struggled frantically to break out of his binds, but the plastic ties were too tight. As he continued to fight the bonds, an eerie presence washed over him and knew that could not be a good thing. As the phone rang, the captured man looked up and found Reid flashing that disturbing smile.

In the meantime, the pretty doctor was still kneeling on the floor. Her hands busy assisting Remy, but her mind was wrestling with the craziness Reid had accomplished. Astonished at the depth of his malevolent actions, this man had basically been stalking her since she was a child. Manipulated Sam, into marrying her to give himself an heir, and also killed Remy's wife in order to make a buck. There was nothing this insane man was not capable of doing and she was petrified something awful, when imagining what his next actions could be.

After hearing his list of dirty deeds, Belle was glad to have talked Granny out of coming. Just as that thought crossed her mind, a strange sensation engulfed her as the elevator doors opened in the atrium. Watched as the phone slipped out of Reid's hand and she gawked oddly at the strange look on the evil man's pale face.

Only a few minutes ago, thought nothing could touch his wicked self but stood gaping as Reid's entire face turned completely white. Belle wondered what had transpired to cause such a reaction from this evil man.

Quickly, she turned toward Remy who was still struggling against his restraints and Belle motioned him to pay attention. Both watched in astonishment, as the monster rose from his chair, stumbling abnormally against the desk. Even though she did not think it possible, the lunatic was becoming even paler.

Slowly, the glass doors of the office opened, and the old goat turned three shades whiter. Belle gazed in amazement as her grandmother came strolling in while pushing one of the building's cleaning carts, pointing what appeared to be an incredibly old pistol at Reid's head.

"Git away from me grandbaby." Slightly, Mavis turned her head toward Belle. "Lassie, untie Remy. Then help'm out of here and don't argue." Expecting obedience and sharply glared at the bleeding young man in the chair. "Either of ye."

An extremely pale Reid did not appear to see anyone else but Mavis. "I thought you were dead. How can you be here?" Unable to swallow the lump in his throat at the sight of his long-lost love. "I've looked for you all over the world. Where have you been hiding?"

Mavis ignored his questions and decided to ask one of her own. "Do ye' remember this gun, Reid?" Still pointing the steady pistol directly between his eyes.

Enthralled by her presence, but desperate to act unafraid, the mesmerized man answered her fondly. "That's one of the Flintlock dueling pistols Mr. Haugh of Dumfries Scotland made for my family almost two centuries ago. I see you've taken good care of it, since that night." Trying to sound charming. "Thank you." Reid nodded toward Mavis affectionately. "That fact means a lot." But his face and demeanor were the exact opposite, because clearly Granny's presence, along with the gun, had spooked him.

"Its twin is still at me cabin ye' blew up the other day. Fortunately, me had these in a safe room." The old woman stood her ground, while waiting for Belle to finish untying Remy. "Me built it, just in case ye' ever came callin' again." The old gun began shaking slightly, but this time determined to defeat him. "Because one day." Paused for a half a second, then she went on. "Me knew ye' would."

The sickly-looking gentleman appeared mighty distraught by Mavis's words, and Belle realized Reid had forgotten all about the two of them. To him, the only person in the room was her grandmother.

"That was your place we destroyed?" It filled his face with anguish, as well as remorse. "I swear, I had no idea." Reid rushed around the big desk to stand before the tiny lady. "When the society did a search, we discovered a farm in Virginia named Spring Sage. We couldn't find an actual owner of the property or anything about it, so to cover up any loose ends, we decided to just destroy it." Tenderly he reached for Mavis. "I'm so sorry Morna, I didn't know. I would do nothing to hurt you. Ever."

At last, something she said penetrated his brain. "Wait a minute, did you say grandchild?" Instantly, Reid's expression became a mixture of confusion and fury.

Mavis waved the gun to show she meant business. "Stay back!" Angry at all the things he had done, plus all the years on Earth he had stolen from her, and she screamed her pent-up anger at him. "Me name is Mavis Brooks, ye' bastard!!" The gun was still pointed steadily at him. Years of suppressed tears were streaming down her cheeks as she continued shouting. "Ye' killed Morna Bruce sixty-seven years ago, on that night when ye' brutally ravaged her."

Now untied, the badly wounded Remy was being supported under his left arm by Belle but neither of them were moving a muscle. She would wait all night for her grandmother to end this confrontation. No way was she leaving Mavis with this insane maniac.

With his head down and ashamed to look at her, quietly tried to explain. "I'm so sorry about that night Morna, truly sorry. First that awful mess with Randall and afterwards I simply got carried away but would have made it up to you. I love you and didn't mean to hurt you. I was insanely jealous of my brother, but all that happened ages ago. Can't we just move on from that unpleasant business? I've waited so long for you." The demented man was starry-eyed over her grandmother, who was madder than a wet hen.

Red faced and yelling but her hand clasped the dueling pistol, rock steady. "Carried away Reid? Is that what ye' call what ye' did, after using this gun?" This was not the way she wanted Belle to find out about the past, but there was no choice. "After the stupid duel, ye' repeatedly raped me, then went strollin' away like nothin' happened. Ye' left me and the guns there. All alone. Broken and bleeding because of ye' jealousy over Randall's intentions. Those 'tweren't mine Reid but ye' wouldn't listen. Then ye' had the nerve to come callin' the next day like nothin' happened."

Mavis needed this to be over, once and for all. "How could me love someone who murdered ye' brother, then afterwards treated me no better than an animal? Ye' left me on the ground, like me was a piece of rubbish. Congratulations, ye' successfully killed two folks that night."

Reid's need for answers burned bright inside him, while completely ignoring her questions. "She's your granddaughter?" He had waited a lifetime to find her and was trying hard not to get angry, but the reason was killing him. "Why did you leave?" His anger came through in his voice. "Who did you marry?"

Reid reached out; still in disbelief over finding her alive. The sudden resentment dissipating because his heart knew, she would not shoot him. Even as Mavis reminded him, the opposite was true, with a flick of her wrist holding the loaded pistol. Alas, Reid continued to believe the fairy tale scenario, he was imagining inside his head. *After all these years, here she was. Once more, right in front of me.* He felt like a young man again, experiencing the same feelings he had gotten after stepping off that warship.

"Morna, I never married. I lost everything, including immortality because of that night." Telling the truth, for the first time in a long while. "All these years, there was never anyone but you." Tenderly, Reid asked what he most wanted answered. "Who finally captured your heart?" Even with love bursting in his, knew he would have the man killed at once if he were still alive.

Belle had been dying to know the answer to this question her entire life. Somehow, she propped the wounded agent up against the wall and was not moving until Mavis replied.

With the pistol still pointed directly at his head, the weary woman calmly drew in a deep breath because it helped to bring peace. "Me married no one." Mavis needed the extra calm when finally having to explain the ugly past to her granddaughter. "Disgraced because of what ye' did that night, me was compelled to leave Scotland and run away to America."

Paused, before dropping her last bomb. "After ye' raped me, me knew that night. Me be pregnant." Quickly wanting to finish her story, Granny moved away from that ugly part of her life. "Me brothers set up a company, one where ye' could never find me and lived happily here on me mountain in Virginia ever since." Belle's grandmother's smile was not one she ever wanted to see again. "Without ye."

Unable to think it was possible, but when Belle looked over at Reid, he had become even paler.

The broken man slowly began sinking into his seat. "No, no, no, that cannot be because Destiny would have foretold about him." Fighting to keep his balance and find the chair behind him. "He could not have been my son. The Spear would have revealed such an important detail to me." Thrashed his head back and forth. "How could this be possible? Morna, please tell me he was not my son." Muttering to himself. "Please, tell me he was not my son." It was all the old man kept repeating over and over as he sunk into the large revolving chair.

By this time, Mavis noticed something was terribly wrong with Reid and took advantage of his distress. "If ye' are referring to me boy William, then yes, of course he was ye' son. Why ye' be asking? Did ye' be killin' him too?" Practically shouting, as the old woman continued to share more family secrets. "We suspected ye' killed Katie. After her passing, me rarely left me mountaintop for fear me somehow give away William's identity." Pride came through in her tone. "Me boy, he always knew who ye' were and what ye' had done. Me never hid it from him because me thought he should know."

Mavis' screams loudly echoed throughout the dark corners of the large office, but her gun hand never wavered. "'Twas why he worked for the CIA, to stop ye'. Me darlin' lad spent his entire adult life trying to thwart anything ye' was involved in." When glancing at his stunned face, Mavis knew she was correct about his role in William's death.

With the truth finally revealed, the sorceress's aura was burning brilliantly again. "Reid, ye' really killed him, didn't ye'?"

Astounded by each shocking confession, Belle listened in shock, as her grandmother and technically, the man who was her grandfather, discuss killing their son, who had been her father. The Jerry Springer episode that had become her life, was just too much and she thought her head was about to explode.

At last, the meaning of his statement computed in her brain, causing her to shriek loudly. "Why would you kill Daddy???"

All her bottled-up torment was shouted at Reid's bowed head. "What did he ever do to you????" Belle poured all the years of built-up anger into her loud question.

"It's not what me William did but what ye' wanted." Her grandmother glared at Reid with such malice. "Don't that be right, Reid?"

The gun was still aimed at the demon, but Granny looked at her so lovingly that it almost broke Belle's heart. Mavis also looked rather guilty. "Ye' see sweetheart, he wanted ye' and me boy was in the way. Ye' father would have never allowed Reid anywhere near ye' knowing how dangerous a man he was."

Turned her attention back toward Reid. "So ye' got rid of him, didn't ye'?"

Back to looking at her precious lass, Granny continued to explain with a pained expression. "Me tried the best me could to protect ye' but didn't know Sam was involved with Reid. Otherwise, me would have never allowed ye' to go anywhere near him." Mavis placed her hand on her granddaughter's cheek, to let her know how much she was loved. "Me gift failed me child, and for that, me truly sorry."

Belle kissed her grandmother and turn to face Remy's kidnapper, who was still mumbling to himself and no longer paying attention to anyone in the room. "No, it cannot be." Reid continued to babble variations of those sentiments to no one. "The boy couldn't have possibly been my son." Constantly babbling, head in hands. "Destiny would have enlightened me. It would never have hidden something like this. The Spear should have known, because the boy was exactly who It had desired for all these years."

Granny did not understand Reid's strange statements, nor did she care he was inconsolable. She just wanted this nightmare to end, tonight. No longer would Mavis allow him to haunt her dreams or hurt Belle. "So ye' see Reid, me cannot allow ye' anywhere near me granddaughter." Staring at his bowed head. "Ye' done enough damage to me family to last a lifetime."

That was when the younger Dr. Brooks heard a very distinct noise, one that shocked Belle silly. "Me will not tolerate ye' destroying another generation." It was the sound made when you pulled the hammer back on an old pistol.

Belle rushed to her grandmother's side while keeping an eye on Remy, making sure he was okay, and out of harm's way. This clearly was between her grandparents and unless it was necessary, she would not interfere.

Belle reached her Granny's side as the old man looked up at his long-lost love and appeared even more defeated. All three watched, as Reid slowly opened the desk drawer. "That will not be necessary, my love."

The gun he had used on Remy earlier appeared back in his hand. "Remember what I have spoken here today, Morna. The Spear is to blame, not me. It's the one who demanded you."

"I meant every word I said." Reid's eyes begged Mavis to grant him forgiveness. "I never cared what the Spear wanted." Effortlessly, he placed the barrel directly against his temple.

"For me, there was never anyone but you." With his next breath he fired the gun, instantly killing himself before any of them understood what he was planning.

At last, Mavis lowered the eighteen hundred Celtic dueling pistol, because it was finally over. Sad it had to end this way, but she had known there was no other acceptable outcome. Puzzled by his odd Spear statements but right now, Granny was too grateful to bother with figuring them out. She turned around and ended up in a group hug.

Thankfully, all three of them had survived but they were anxious to be free of this horrible scene. Granny took Remy's other arm to help carry the injured man; between the two Dr. Brooks' they were able to get him into the elevator. On the way down, they worked out a plan to avoid the guard discovering their involvement in the messy situation upstairs.

Ten minutes later, the old woman opened a service closet on the ground floor and wheeled the cleaning cart into it. She spent the next few minutes informing Arthur about the man on the top floor who had been behaving rather strangely. The fellow upstairs had not looked well, and Mavis recommended he check on him soon.

Up next were the two lovers, who several minutes later emerged from the elevator disguised enough to play their parts. While Granny was distracting the guard with her report, the special agent pretended to be intoxicated, as the two of them hobbled through the lobby. The injured man was slung around the pretty doctor's neck. The coat and pumps Belle had worn into the building were back on and all of Remy's spilled blood hidden from view.

Several times they faltered before walking out the door to the taxi Granny had called from Quintin Montgomery's office. The two of them appeared to be having the time of their lives. On the way out, they received an approving grin from Arthur and Remy gave him a little salute before turning back toward the woman of his dreams. The prodigal son would have some explaining to do to his dad before the guard told a tall tale on him.

Arthur had been employed by the firm for more than thirty years, therefore, decided to ignore the substitute cleaning woman's suggestion because Mr. MacAlister was the only person on the top floor. The guard knew he often worked late. Plus, he had frightened numerous nighttime employees, leaving the old timer feeling no urgency to check up on him.

Thirty minutes later during his routine rounds discovered the body of Lord Reid MacAlister slumped over his desk. The firearm used to kill himself was found tightly wrapped in his hand. The District of Columbia's Police Department investigated and ruled his death a suicide.

An open and shut case.

Epilogue

Unbelievable. The only word circling around inside her brain.

The monster, who had harmed the man she might be falling in love with, had really been her grandfather. This shocking piece of DNA news was one Belle still could not wrap her head around, setting it aside for now.

At this time, there were too many other critical issues to deal with, including the potential love thing because that scared her most of all. After retrieving the bullets out of Remy and stitching him back up at the safe house, the two of them filled in both the FBI director, as well as Remy's father, Quintin Montgomery, on all that had occurred.

They were afraid to include too many people, until they could discover more about this society. After many long and loud discussions, it was determined they would keep all this shocking information to themselves. For now.

After studying all the materials from Sam's secret box, they agreed this group was too powerful and dangerous to not take every safeguard.

As a precaution, he would request a leave of absence on paper, but Director Anderson had given Remy his real orders. Find out who these people were and put a stop to their intentions of manipulating the upcoming election. By working quote, unquote, off the books, he would not have to follow the extensive FBI protocols. Remy knew before this was over, it might be necessary to violate a few constitutional rights. A couple of biblical commandments would probably be broken too, before this was all over.

Secrecy was key to catching this society, and it was critical to keep their knowledge of the Seachd Righrean quiet, for as long as possible. This strategy was vital to capturing them. Their plentiful resources were worrying Remy. Once the members knew they were being hunted, the experienced investigator believed the extremely wealthy participants would simply disappear with their plots and plans. They would be gone like the wind; never giving him or Belle the opportunity to catch these maniacs or gain control over their lives.

To pull this off, they would need to put together a small elite team of people, who they could trust beyond a shadow of doubt.

First, both needed time to heal and they waited a few days before entering the secret room of the Seachd Righrean. It was right where Remy thought it would be, behind the unusual wall symbol in Reid's office.

The large meeting room contained vast amounts of materials and artifacts, but Belle was beyond frustrated because everything seemed to be encrypted with a complicated code. A cypher, that so far, she could not crack nor could anyone else.

For the first time in her life, when touching anything they had retrieved from the society's secret facility, Belle could not *'travel'* using her gift. Nor was she able to *'feel'* any of the contents. The only impression coming through was a sense of blockage, almost like there was a barrier of some sort impeding her abilities. Frustrated by this unusual circumstance, she spent hours handling hundreds of papers or the many relics on display inside the unusual room. After days, Belle's persistence paid off and she could get a slight sensation from a few of the items.

At first, reluctant to put into words her growing perceptions.

Daily, she struggled with the irrational thoughts that continued to surface with every item she touched, until remembering the sound logic that was used by Sir Arthur Conan Doyle's famous detective. *"When you have eliminated the impossible, whatever remains, however improbable, must be the truth."* Hoped the fictional Sherlock Holmes was indeed correct because otherwise, she was certifiably insane.

As crazy as it seemed and as best she could tell, every note, file, object and even the office supplies seem affected. Absolutely everything they had found hidden inside their secret room had encountered the impossible because the only thing Belle could determine blocking her gift was some sort of intricate magical enchantment. Almost like what she imagined a charmed cloaking-type spell would feel like because nothing else made sense.

If that was not enough, when handling a few of those same files, an ominous presence came crashing through. Stronger and stronger each time she touched them.

She was convinced it was the same *'thing'* that had been outside her houses in Palm Beach, at Granny's and maybe, even at her home in DC. A perception that sent chills up Belle's spine because she could swear the manifestations written on quite a few pages were referring to a legend.

A myth, publicized heavily by Hollywood.

As impossible as it seemed, her gift said the information was about a real vampire.

Not completely positive, yet, Belle's impulses were telling her the writings were about a mercenary slash bounty hunting bloodsucker.

One big and very bad dude, meaning there were others out there like her and Remy. Special. Gifted. Entities different from humans and this society was using them to fill their pockets full of gold.

While she spent the long hours reviewing the society's endless materials, Belle found her mind sometimes wandered. *How many of her patients had secretly been sent by the Seachd Righrean?* This question made her feel even more manipulated. Another one that plagued her. *What had Reid been talking about when he kept going on about a spear?* Belle kept this uneasiness to herself, opting not to share these feelings with Remy because she still had concerns about his recovery.

Combined with all the things found in the secret room, the ramifications of having to fight a powerful witch and an immortal vampire troubled her. Not to mention how to deal with the Seven Kings and what kind of future they represented. It was a feat Belle did not think she was ready to master but recognized there was time enough for those secrets to come out. Once she figured out how to break through the magical barricade that was currently blocking her gift, then she could move on to figuring out a way to deal with these supernatural monsters. *I'm going with Scarlett again on this one. Another day.*

A few days after everything was out of the hidden room, Mavis decided it was time for her to go home. No longer willing to contribute much else, the doctor was eager to get back to her mountain. She had faith Belle would figure out what was occurring with the spells and the journey would be good for Remy too. Although, she did not think he fully understood what he was yet. The two of them needed to discover this complicated puzzle for themselves because their gifts were strong and growing each day just by being together.

Legend had whispered of such mated people, along with the amazing things they would accomplish for this world. Mavis had never actually witnessed it in person but was looking forward to the future fireworks that were sure to erupt between these two.

Wished it was possible to change her grandmother's mind, but Belle knew she would be unsuccessful at convincing Granny to remain any longer. Although, she was surprised because the old girl had stayed with them for almost three weeks. Mavis was opting to return to her farm this morning to begin rebuilding the cabin. Besides, both of them needed some time alone to come to terms with the extraordinary developments that had happened these past few weeks.

Unfortunately, before returning to the Appalachians, her grandmother had refused to talk to anyone, including the FBI director. The old sorceress had remained silent about her earlier life and declined all attempts to discuss Reid, Morna Bruce or anything else that had happened prior to her arriving in America.

Begrudgingly, Granny acknowledged her beloved granddaughter was due a more detailed explanation. For one final time, the old woman sat down and laid out all the unpleasant events of that awful night, which had changed the young girl so long ago. Mavis gave Belle permission to disclose the information to Remy after she'd departed for her Virginia compound. It seemed her grandmother had put that part of her life behind her and just wanted to be done with that horrible night.

When finally completing her heartbreaking tale, and at long last finished with Reid, Mavis declared wholeheartedly. "The most important thing me wanted to tell ye' is this." Her trembling hands were holding Belle's face on either side. "Me is truly sorry for causin' all this ruckus." Tears streamed down her slightly wrinkled cheeks. "Me knew Reid was obsessed, but me had no idea it would transfer to ye'. Again, me is so sorry lass."

Looking lovingly at her grandmother and insisting. "Granny, please, stop blaming yourself for his crazy fanatical infatuation. You couldn't have known he would see me when I was a child and become fixated. How could you know he would manipulate Sam into marrying me, because he killed that poor schoolgirl." Wrapping her arms around Mavis, pleading with her grandmother. "Please stop condemning yourself. None of those things are your fault. I love you and need you to be my rock."

Belle's nervous little laugh popped out like it always did at these times. Grabbing Granny's hands in hers and looking directly into her eyes. "You are everything to me. I need you to help me find the rest of the people, who are part of this society." A serious expression was etched across Belle's beautiful face. "These are terrible people who have to be stopped and I need your help to do that." Becoming intense and whispering sternly. "Please, Granny, let's forget all about that horrible man and the things he did to both of us. Let's put our lives back together by rebuilding the cabin and hunting down the bastards who are the rest of the Seven Kings." Smiling widely, she added. "With Remy's help along with our magic, strength, and love, I know we can beat them."

Grabbed Mavis's hands again and held them tight. "Deal?"

Looking older than ever, Mavis stared tenderly at her granddaughter. "Me don't know, child. That's a mighty tall order, and me's a very old woman."

Determination setting in, Belle would not take no for an answer and stared Granny down with her own glare.

"Oh, all right." Chuckling, Mavis finally relented. "If ye' think me can help, me will do whatever ye' need. Just give me a shout and me'll come running."

Jumping up, the young Dr. Brooks threw her arms around her grandmother, hugging her with all her might because with the old woman's help, she was confident they would not fail.

The handsome agent was unaware Belle watched him work, while he reviewed the over one thousand facial recognition photos captured during Sir Reid MacAlister's funeral. She marveled at how quickly Remy was recovering from his wounds and enjoyed watching him sit at her big dining room table, his head bowed down, silently working out the pieces to this complicated case.

Thankful he had survived, but Belle was still having a challenging time accepting the fact she had almost lost him to a madman that night. All the while, attempting to also deal with the disturbing details the young doctor had learned on the top floor of the Montgomery and MacAlister building. Not to mention everything that evil man and this society had done to control her life, along with the lives of her loved ones.

The house was empty without the old woman.

She was already missing Granny, *something awful.* A smile appeared on her face as one of her grandmother's many famous sayings slipped into Belle's thoughts.

Their heart-to-heart talk had taken place three nights ago. Grinning wider, at the warmth which had instantly surrounded her when thinking about the wonderful lady. Already eager to see her again this weekend but understood her dedicated grandmother's place was in the Appalachian Mountains taking care of the people who lived in that rugged area.

Looked over at Remy in amazement because could still not believe such a man had come into her life. Excited to discover if this thing called love was what the lonely widow was feeling towards this hunky guy. Got up and stood behind him, glancing over his shoulder at the array of pictures he was perusing from the funeral. Both believed the remaining members of *The Celtic Seven Kings Society*, as they had taken to calling them, had been in attendance that day.

Instinctively, Remy grabbed her hand as she snuggled at his shoulder. The kind gesture made Belle feel like no matter how bad the past few days had been, the future was looking brighter and brighter.

A man sat reflecting in the dark, smoking a hand rolled Cuban cigar and sipping hundred-year-old brandy out of a cut crystal glass. He surmised congratulations would soon be in order because it was only a matter of time before the lovely lady would be his.

With Reid out of the way, the last hurdle had been overcome and soon she would belong to him. The Spear had promised him everything, if he delivered the girl. He could do that, unlike his hotheaded outcast brother. The fool had been obsessed with having a child by her. *Why? When he could have spent eternity with her.*

The thought also reminded him of the last time he had run his hand over the sacred blade. Destiny's edge, stained with the blood of Christ had still been sharp, even over two thousand years later. Thinking about the lost relic made him furious because once again, the youngster had bested him, even if it was just for the moment.

Quickly shaking off the anger because he did not want to spoil the evening.

Every available resource was looking for the Spear and although Sam had been a genius, he had only acquired it less than forty-eight hours before dying. That limited the places he could have hidden the priceless artifact. Smiled slyly because the *Spear of Destiny* would soon be back in his possession and the sword would definitely help him bring beauty to the beast.

Raising the glass, he toasted the moment, after waiting for what amounted to two lifetimes, for a prize like Campbell Brooks. The King knew it would only be a short while before he would finally possess her. Body and soul.

A sinister smile spread across his face, as the thoughts of his long-sought desire warmed his cold hard heart.

Granny Brooks' Famous Cinnamon Rolls Recipe

Dough

1 package active dry yeast
½ cup warm water
½ cup scalded (then cooled) milk
1/3 cup sugar
1/3 cup butter or shortening, softened
1 teaspoon salt
1 egg
3 ½ to 4 cups of all-purpose flour

Filling

4 tablespoons butter, softened
1/2 cup sugar
1/2 cup brown sugar
1 tablespoon ground cinnamon

Glaze

1 cup powdered sugar
1 tablespoon milk
½ teaspoon of vanilla
Mix until glaze is smooth

In a large bowl, dissolve yeast in warm water. Mix milk, sugar, butter, salt & egg into yeast. Add 2 cups of flour and beat until smooth. Continue to mix in remaining flour until dough is easy to work. Turn dough onto lightly floured surface; kneading for at least 5 minutes until smooth and elastic. Return to greased bowl and cover. Let rise in warm place and double in size, approximately 1 ½ hours. Punch dough down and return to lightly floured surface. Roll dough into rectangle approximately 15x9 inches. Cover the entire area with softened butter. Mix sugar, brown sugar & cinnamon together and sprinkle mixture over buttered dough. Roll up tightly on the 15-inch side and pinch edge of dough to seal. Cut dough roll approximately 1 ½ inches thick and place in a greased glass dish. Let rise again until double, about 40 minutes. Heat oven to 375 degrees and bake 25 to 30 minutes until golden brown. Spread glaze on rolls while warm.

COMING SOON

GREEN EYED MONSTER

BOOK 2

THE CELTIC SEVEN KINGS SERIES

The heat was overwhelming, as were the insects, but Belle was determined to follow the demon, no matter where he traveled or how. Over the last few months, she had seen many unusual things, and it demanded her to become a forceful wielder of witchcraft. If what she was observing on this hot July night here on the Bayou was real, then this was definitely a sight to behold.

The evil presence, that had been tracking her across several states since Sam's death, was now the one being hunted. At almost seven feet tall, the mountain of a man was unafraid much of the time, which also made him careless. This was one of those times because he was clueless about being followed to his lair. In their favor, Belle had become a powerful medium with the help of her magical grandmother and months of training. Conjuring up a potion that cloaked both her and Remy as they trailed behind the beast in a canoe.

But their time was running out.

Their motley crew had been successful in discovering a number of critical things about the Seachd Righrean, but they still needed to figure out how this creature fit into the society's overall plans. It was important they captured him during the early hours of sunrise, when he would be at his weakest, in order to administer the serum and have enough time to question him.

The Hollywood motion picture people had gotten it all wrong. Another little item their team had uncovered. Vampires could appear in the sunlight. It did not kill them, and they did not sparkle like diamonds, unlike their silly stories wanted you to believe. The sun just made them normal and turned them human, with regular human weaknesses. Which meant it was the only time that a mortal had a fighting chance at killing one, but Remy didn't want to kill this beast. He wanted important information and was desperate for the critical pieces needed to this perplexing labyrinth and he would go to hell itself to get those answers.

Watching this monster, atop the large swamp animal was pushing his nerves to the limit tonight, stopping the paddle in the muddy water to calm down. Since the shooting at the firm, Remy had not been himself and knew he needed to keep it together in order for Belle not to suspect anything was amiss.

As soon as they came to a complete stop, the marsh animals awoke, and he turned to watch the sun as it began peaking over the horizon.

Belle saw the fatigue that was settling in him and was worried for both of them. They had been on the run for weeks chasing this demon and were hopeful he held the answers they needed. Confident he could lead them to the Spear's hiding place.

Belle was still in awe of its existence.

Imagine actually holding it. The lance that had touched the Lord. It was too much to fathom and Sam had not only held it in his hand but stolen it from the Seven Kings. She chuckled softly at his cleverness, but it was fleeting because it also made Belle angry. Mad, because her own grandfather, who she had no idea about until four months ago had dragged her into this whole insane mess.

Too late to feel sorry for herself, she smiled at Remy because the insanity had become the norm around the two of them. Although, she should be afraid of this hellish fiend, she simply was not.

Wonder was all Belle could feel, the entire time they had been following the Vrykolakas. Joy and awe were shooting through her aura, as they both watched in astonishment, while Sallos rode the waterways of the Bayou for hours, laughing and singing the night away. The vampire was riding atop a fifteen-foot alligator and appeared to be having the time of his life.

I wonder how old he is. It surprised Belle to find she did not have an ounce of fear for this unusual King of the Underworld and was excited to be meeting him soon.

Acknowledgements

As a career marketing and broadcasting executive, I never had any aspirations to write a novel. In fact, other than headlines and advertising blurbs, I had not written anything substantial, other than commercials or board of director reports, since college. But that did not stop the people who reside inside my head.

They have been telling me their story for quite some time.

In fact, had gotten so used to their story, I made a joke about them and the book they wanted me to write, at a dinner party thrown by my best friend in 2011.

After losing my husband to cancer in late 2009, a couple years later, I developed several disabilities that forced me into an early retirement. At the party, I joked, I finally had time to write the novel the people in my head would not shut up about and laughed it off. My bestie didn't think it was so funny and wanted to know why I wasn't taking this more seriously. Through laughter, I explained I was a marketing whiz, not a novelist and had no desire to write a book.

Susan Hinkle Arnsteen would not take no for an answer and launched a campaign to get me to change my mind. The woman is persistent, as well as one of the finest ladies, I know…and I do mean lady. She texted, emailed, and called me for three weeks until I went online and found a website that listed 8 Steps to Writing a Novel. I sat down and wrote the book in about 3 weeks…then spent another year learning how to get all the details out of my head and onto the pages.

It was the perfect therapy for my grief and in 2013 I registered my first draft with the Library of Congress. Unfortunately, I had several health setbacks and by the time I was ready to publish my book...the most far-fetched scenario I had dreamed up for my plot...was actually starting to play out on my television set every night. After much debate, I decided to put it in a drawer until the world settled down. Well, it's been ten years and since the world doesn't look like it's ever going to settle down, I decided to move forward with my cast of crazy characters and hope you enjoy them as much as I do.

Thank you, Susan...for everything you, Michael, and Nola do to make my life better, including saving me after Hurricane Ian. I can never repay y'all's kindness.

My family has also been a huge supporter of me and this book. Like Belle, my Daddy, **Raymond Howard McDuffie** was a single father, raising me in a huge house filled with family, music, and love. Although the dreaded cancer spell got Daddy too...he is still a big part of my life and am proud of the woman I am today because of him. My grandfather, **William Gregory Howard** is the other man who shaped me into me. I cannot thank him enough for making me believe..."I could always be better than any boy." Getting that advice as a little girl in the 1960s made the woman in the 1980s a powerful broadcasting executive. *Thank you from the bottom of my heart.*

Both my grandmothers, **Lorraine Brooks McDuffie** aka Nanny, and **Pauline Lambert Howard** aka Ma, were inspirations for Granny Brooks. In fact, the cinnamon roll recipe on the previous pages, actually is my Ma's. Although, I was forced to use Betty Crocker to fill in some blanks. I laughed when my mom sent me the picture of Ma's handwritten recipe that was tucked into her cookbook. It's written on a brown paper bag and simply says: Put in bowl; let double in size; roll out flat long; add cinnamon, sugar, butter, brown sugar; roll & cut this thick (dough), with a hash mark that's 1 ½ inches high and an arrow pointing to it. Put in glass dish 425 degrees is crossed out and 375 is written under it. 20 – 25 mins. Frost. I can assure you these are the best things you have ever tasted, and you'll be glad I asked Betty for assistance. Enjoy!

I don't want to leave my momma out. Even though her momma taught me how to cook, **Pamela Miller McDuffie** taught me how to love. She married my daddy when I was 5, treating me as her own daughter ever since. She is kind, funny and a joy to have around, plus her charity work has made a huge impact on the panhandle communities of West Viriginia. I'm so proud of my mom and the good she does. Grammy Pammy is an inspiration to all. *I love you, Momma.*

I also want to thank **Michele Krueger**, my amazing editor for her unbelievable guidance and support. You opened my thinking and my writing improved tenfold. I can't wait to work with you on the remaining books in the Celtic Seven Kings Series. The other folks who helped me through this difficult first launch were the wizards at **Palmetto Publishing**. I can't thank y'all enough for always answering my endless questions and look forward to working with y'all again on the upcoming books in the series.

I cannot fail to mention my friends at the Manatee Island Bar and Grill. Although it goes by another name, it will always be the "Tiki" and I cherish the many wonderful memories from those crazy times. I learned how to return to life after Dale's death from laughing and enjoying every moment of life with the special members of the **Lemon Drop Gang**. I miss those times and can't thank y'all enough for the healing you provided. A special shout out to **Barbara Corliss Hanrahan, Sheila Sander Jones,** and **Denise Trempe Trusley** for their unconditional support throughout the years. Without you ladies, I'm not sure I would have made it some days. *Thank you from the bottom of my heart.*

Like Remy, I was married to my best friend for almost 25 years. We grew up 3 blocks apart, but the Lord had other plans for my love, **Dale Robert McMannis** and there are no words to describe losing him or having to live every day without him. So, I'll simply leave my promise I made to him all those years ago. *I will always be…Forever Yours.*

Also, like Remy, after a decade of widowhood, I was convinced my heart had died, along with my husband. So, imagine my surprise when shortly after Covid hit, to find it beating again. Just like the brokenhearted FBI agent, someone out of left field kicked it back to life. He didn't get to keep it but I'm eternally grateful for the jump-start spark because like Belle, it reminded me I was still alive. *Thank you to one of PG County's finest — #1047.*

My final thank you is a very special one and goes out to my son, **M. Stephen Kinder**. In addition to gifting me three of the most adorable grandbabies, he is a dedicated father and husband, of whom I could not be prouder. Thank you, Lord for blessing me such a wonderful man as a son. *I love you more than words could ever describe, Boy.*

If I've left anyone out, I deeply apologize because there are many folks who had a hand in helping me achieve this goal. From reading those first horrible drafts, to giving your opinion on cover art, as well as lending a hand to help me stand on two feet again. *I am eternally grateful, and this finished novel is, as well.*

I hope you enjoyed this book. Please visit my website www.mjmcduffie.com and let me know your thoughts, as well as information on upcoming books in the Celtic Seven Kings Series.

Thank you again for taking the time to read my debut book. I hope you enjoyed it. Please visit my website www.mjmcduffie.com and let me know your thoughts, as well as information on upcoming books in the Celtic Seven Kings Series.

Wishing you warm tropical breezes to soothe your soul

In writing this book, I was influenced by hundreds of artists, authors, and musicians whose works have inspired and enriched both my research and this manuscript. You will find many, many references to those works of art throughout my novel. Thank you for all the joy and comfort you have brought to me, especially in my darkest hours.

These two deserve special recognition for practically carrying me.

- Stevie Ray Vaugh — *"Life without You"*
- Eric Clapton — *"Tears in Heaven"*

Reference Materials used:

www.Wikipedia.com

www.DeliriumsRealm.com

www.translate.com

Naval Life and Customs by Lieutenant Commander John Irving, Royal Navy, Published by Sherratt & Hughes, Altrincham, UK c1944

Celtic Lore & Legend by Dr. Bob Curran, Published by Career Press, Franklin Lakes, NJ c2004

Betty Crocker's COOKBOOK, Published by Golden Press/New York, c1978, 1969

Partial List of Grief Groups

Please check your local yellow pages, online resources, and county mental health facilities for participating groups near you.

www.griefsjourney.com

www.griefshare.com

www.healgrief.org

www.goodtherapy.org

Facebook and other social media outlets also have numerous support groups who can help with grief's journey.

MJ McDuffie

BLUE-EYED DEVIL is MJ McDuffie's debut book in the *Celtic Seven Kings* series.

When tragedy struck more than a decade ago, she never dreamed the movie inside her head would help cope with the overwhelming grief life had dealt her. The therapy of writing blossomed into this thought provoking and action-packed mystery thriller. Also, adding to the unique captivating plot twists - a dash of paranormal.

It's impossible for the Nana of 3 to be far from the sea. Although MJ is a native Washingtonian; she has lived in the sunshine state of Florida for almost twenty-five years and now considers it home. This novel happened because one beautiful woman believed in her enough to convince an old marketing and broadcasting executive to give book writing a try.

The former DC swamp rat and die-hard University of Maryland fan is currently working on her second book in the series, *GREEN EYED MONSTER*, which will debut in early 2024. An electrifying international tale of deceit and intrigue that MJ will weave into another suspenseful and action-packed novel.